STORMS OF TYRANNY

C. J. CLARK

outskirts press

Storms of Tyranny
All Rights Reserved.
Copyright © 2019 C. J. Clark
v5.0

This is a work of fiction. The events and characters described herein are imaginary and are not intended to refer to specific places or living persons. The opinions expressed in this manuscript are solely the opinions of the author and do not represent the opinions or thoughts of the publisher. The author has represented and warranted full ownership and/or legal right to publish all the materials in this book.

This book may not be reproduced, transmitted, or stored in whole or in part by any means, including graphic, electronic, or mechanical without the express written consent of the publisher except in the case of brief quotations embodied in critical articles and reviews.

Outskirts Press, Inc.
http://www.outskirtspress.com

ISBN: 978-1-9772-0390-8

Cover Photo © 2019 www.gettyimages.com. All rights reserved - used with permission.

Outskirts Press and the "OP" logo are trademarks belonging to Outskirts Press, Inc.

PRINTED IN THE UNITED STATES OF AMERICA

CHAPTER 1

Monday, January 3, 2056

Captain Meyers ducked as he entered the lecture hall doorway and removed his wool coat. Distinguished theologians, whose portraits lined the walls, kept a vigilant watch over the budding biblical scholars. Among them, Augustine, Luther, Spurgeon, Henry, Gill, Wesley, and Graham.

God whispered in his ear to ready himself for an answer to a prayer. A blonde female collegiate nudged another student; she smiled at him and tilted her head backward and licked her bright-purple lips. Her darkened eyebrows lifted as she sucked on her middle finger up to her knuckle and winked at him. A stylish gold-plated chicken bone necklace hung on her porcelain neck, drawing attention to an unbuttoned red leather vest and her well-developed breasts. *Christian schools differ from years ago*, he thought. *Lord, she cannot be the one.*

"Hi, gorgeous. How about you and me—?" Her mouth fell open as he held his hand up to reject her spicy offer. "Fine. Plenty of hungry men on this campus."

The smell of Sweet Cannelle cologne drifted in his direction. A woman with a golden-honey complexion peered over her tablet. *At last.* The female turned her head away. Again, she peeked over her reader, eyes sparkled as she twisted her hair around her fingers.

Be patient. He stood next to her and prayed to make eye contact again. The color in her face deepened, eyebrows raised. Her eyes lifted; a sudden smile dazzled him. *Ask her.* His heart pounded; a dry, pasty tongue stuck to the roof of his mouth.

"Are you saving this seat…for anyone?"

"Well, yes…saved…for you." She slid her long delicate hands down her cheeks. "Uh, you must be the most handsome man God put on this…um…planet. Those dark-brown eyes and black hair."

"Thank you. Your name is?"

"Do you sing? Deep bass voices sound so sex…sexy…Didn't mean to blurt out that…"

"At least I made a favorable first impression. Tell me your name preference. Unless you prefer Blurty." He took a peek at her ringless left hand as he sat next to her. A hopeful sign, although fashionable women may not wear a ring. Doubt filled his mind with imagination. *Already married to three husbands, with five obnoxious children who could dismantle a Navy destroyer in under two minutes. Did her master's thesis in the nineteenth-century tea trade between Bavaria and China and how the industry transformed the course of the Civil War. Owns a Great Dane named Poco.*

"Dakota Elizabeth Brown. Introduce yourself. Otherwise, I will identify you by your rank, Captain."

"Horace Wexler Meyers, United States Marines, your humble fellow student, ma'am."

"A term of politeness for little—old—ladies."

"Little old ladies? Certain officers, I am acquainted with might… disagree with you."

"Correct, they would. I'm not a military officer. Therefore, I am not—"

Humored and fascinated by her comebacks, he gazed into her deep amber eyes. "Yes, you are not a little old lady."

"What degree are you working on?" She held a pen between her fingers.

Two female students lingered nearby; the redhead flipped

her hair in his face. The taller teenager fanned herself as though overheated in the cold room. *One way to get rid of the overstimulated pair. A wink should do the trick.* They rushed off to find seats near the back. Dakota turned her lips downward, for the briefest of moments—however, long enough. *Yes, she is interested.*

"Biblical languages and military chaplaincy, for now. What about you?"

"Public safety; my minor is in theological studies. An odd combination."

"Our common pursuit is fascinating. My duty assignment is at Quantico in security while earning a theology degree."

"Long drive to the base?"

"Captain." Suspicion ran through him as a dark-haired male paused by their seats and bowed. Sirens vibrated inside Horace; by instinct, he touched his holster.

The man moved up the incline and selected a seat on the rear-row next to a bald Japanese student with a tattoo of a peacock. Tail feathers crossed her eyelids, cascaded down the sides of her face and along the back of her neck. Without a word, she thrust an oversized tote between them and gave him a hard glare. She reached into the bag and snatched out a ball of mustard-yellow yarn and a set of chopsticks.

"Name is Kyoko. Don't bother me."

She glanced behind at the man, who tipped his leather cap. "Do you recognize him? Why did you go on a full-alert as soon as he passed this row?"

"The SpeedTube cuts the transportation time by half. The professor is here. Go with me for a cup of coffee afterward?"

"Changed the subject on me." *Click, click, click,* she pressed the button of her pen hard several times; the ink cartridge shot straight up into the air and fell to the floor like a missile failure.

"Lucky for you, I transported extra rocket launchers in case of emergency."

Students sat at cluttered counters and bistro tables as the Java Hut filled. First-years engaged in games and text-talked until their next lecture. Music played from tiny glasslike balls on their necks; colors changed as the tempo varied. They chatted over the weather or current politics with coded nicknames for the supreme commander such as Rattlesnake and Goofy Soup, for his son, the Legatee.

Stacks of solar-power personal transport boards, warm coats, and jackets scattered beside plastic chairs cluttered the aisles. They stepped over piles of laptop tubes and hunted a table. Discarded drink wrappers, half-eaten carrot-kelp bars, asparagus pizza, and assortments of well-used hand wipes made an empty seat hard to pinpoint. A busser drone with an absent tub knocked the trash on the floor and darted off to unclutter another section.

"Do you always accept offers to coffee with a man right after meeting him?"

She traced her finger along the list of beverages on the menu; her brows lifted as indecision reflected on her face. "Chocolate peanut butter espresso with cream. Whom should I trust if I can't count on a Marine?"

"Armed forces personnel don't always conduct themselves with honor. A few bring dishonor." *Dark roast black.* He made his selection and set the tablet back into the stand.

"My father teaches Greek and Hebrew; he told me about a tall military person enrolled in his classes."

"What keeps you busy when you're not studying?"

"Spent many Saturdays riding in equestrian events; the university won the championship four times in the conference and twice in the nationals." Dakota's complexion deepened as she coughed. "Anyone significant in your life?"

He interlaced his fingers together and rested his chin on top of his hands. "Why don't you blurt out and ask me if I am single? Yes, I am." *Good, she is interested.*

Her face flushed as she strained to stifle a cough. "Didn't want to keep you from a wife or girlfriend."

He moved the condiment stand from one side of the table and stacked the creamers into a pyramid. "Travel around much?"

"No. Born here in Virginia, lived in the same house my entire life. Attended Christian schools. What about you? Any hobbies?"

"No matter how much I dig into the Bible, I crave more."

"You and my dad would work together."

"Wasn't planning on proposing marriage to your—" *Why did I reveal my plans too soon?*

She remained silent, gaze intensified; her mouth twisted back and forth. A server drone set two plastic mugs of coffee in front of them. "Wait! A marriage proposal to whom?"

Feisty—Dakota stands up for herself. Not a fragile, cowering flower. At least she didn't jump up and run out the hatches screaming. Encouraged, he decided to explain himself.

"The Lord laid upon my heart to ask if I might sit next to you."

She rubbed her hands over the sides of the hot mug. "Uncertain how...to reply."

"Did God ever urge you to interact with someone?"

She poured creamer in the beverage and shrugged.

"Is he speaking now?"

"Yes, he is telling me you are...way past crazy."

"Do you believe your words? Come on—what is he saying?"

She caressed the gold cross on her necklace. "On occasion, my imagination runs away. First, what did God say to you? Afterward, I will let you know what he told me about you."

"An obstinate personality. Fine. Stubborn-people management is my specialty." He ran his finger across one of his ribbons. "This ribbon shows I am a recalcitrant tactical expert dealing with tenacious people. A dare? Good, I will. Though, you must answer my question. The instant I stepped into the room, you gave me a magnificent smile. God said, 'The woman who sits before you is your spouse.'"

"Your...pickup line is unique. Why didn't he say it to you in the King James Version? 'The woman thou hast casteth thine eyes upon is thy wife.' Israeli Defense Medal, not dealing with stubborn people."

"Sounds as if I'm lusting after you. God didn't speak in KJV since no one speaketh like this any moreth. Familiar with military ribbons?"

"My grandmother is a career Marine, so yes. Now I will answer your question. Thus, saith the Lord unto me, the man who speaks to thee is thine husband."

"Are you ridiculing me?"

She spun the empty coffee mug around. "No sarcasm intended. Perhaps I wanted to shock you. Find out who you are and why this outrageous marriage talk. Who bothers with legal contractual stuff nowadays? Other than my parents, and I only assume yours did. Do you believe in biblical marriages?"

"Without hesitation. What would your father say?" Horace took a sip of coffee.

"Declare us harebrained for discussing getting married on the day we met. Take time.

Get acquainted. My dad will want to become familiar with you before we date."

"After taking every one of Dr. Julian Brown's courses, your father should know me by now."

"He hasn't seen you around his daughter."

"Not a problem...to rectify."

"Should we discuss our differences, before meeting my dad? Ask me a question; in turn, I will ask you one."

"Are you one of those women"—he made circular motions with his fingers around his face— "who sleep with an inch-thick layer of green facial goop on every night?"

"Do you ever forget to put...the toilet seat down?"

"Is making liver casseroles an area of expertise of yours?"

"Will lack of experience make a difference?"

"No."

She gnawed on a fingernail and snorted out a laugh. Three short snorts came from the back of her throat. "Leave dirty underwear on the floor?"

"Depends on which room."

"Where does a man dump undershorts other than the living room?"

"Why? Are we expecting relatives over to visit?"

"The doorbell is ringing."

"Go see who is at the hatch."

"Why don't you answer the door?"

"Busy in the bathroom, putting the toilet seat down."

"Try removing an inch-thick green goop off your face. Oh, bother. Let me sneak a spy drone out the window, so I don't scare anyone. Hey, three police officers are here."

His mouth dropped open in feigned shock. "For what?"

"Um, detectives are doing a neighborhood search."

"How come?"

"A treacherous underwear thief is stealing from solar air dryers in the community."

"Dangerous? Apt a man with a fetish. Men's or women's underclothing?"

"Uh—women."

"Guess the police will hunt elsewhere. Bad luck here, regulation undershorts only. Stockings? Leave them hanging in the bathroom?"

"No, over the fireplace mantel."

"To dry?"

"No, on Christmas Eve. What woman still wears nylons?"

The dark-haired man from class sat in a booth. He sipped on a cup of tea and stared at them. To keep the man in his sight, Horace moved closer to Dakota. *No visible signs of tattoos or scars; nothing unusual with his hairstyle, a military haircut in need of a barber.* The man lingered and continued to watch. He clasped his coat and leather cap and rushed to the student lot exit.

"Did you listen to one word I said?"

He clutched his vehicle security fob. "Do you take the bus to go home or drive?"

"Is this a marital compatibility question?"

"No, to make sure you arrive home safe."

"Walk—my home is next to the church."

"May I take you home? Much too cold to trudge through the snow to your house."

"My dad is strict with me meeting young men. Be careful; he might embarrass you by interrogation. Challenge you to a snowball fight before we go inside."

"For a moment I thought you meant your father. Devoted dads protect their family." He held the car door for her to step in.

"Different questions."

"Oh, meaning, how I will treat you?"

"Of course."

"Am I scheming to carry you off in a horse-drawn golden carriage fit for a queen with a Happiness to the Bride and Groom sign hanging on the back?"

"Funny man. My home is straight across from the entrance."

Reminiscent of being a part of an old Christmas card snow-covered lawn, evergreen trees lined the driveway to the Federalist-style two-story red brick house. A frigid breeze blew flurries of snowflakes across the yard as the two braced themselves from the cold bite of air. A patch of hidden ice caused him to slip on the double-driveway. He steadied himself as Dakota climbed out.

"Got out without your help."

He scooped up an armload of snow and dumped the mound on Dakota's woolen cap. "Bet you thought I forgot."

She knelt and packed the frozen mixture into a solid icy sphere and hit him in the chest. "No, I didn't."

"Caution; I seek revenge. Hey, you can't hide from me, I am an expert snow tracker."

She peeked out at him from behind a tree and giggled. "Catch me."

"Now I'll get you hiding back...Oh—" He fell sprawled on the lawn, lay motionless, and kept his eyes shut.

Dakota knelt beside him and patted his cheek. "Are you hurt?"

He opened his eyes and pulled her close to him. "Gotcha. Lively too." *Spirited gal, she can handle challenges.*

"The creepy guy who's in our course—he's standing over there stalking us."

"Better go inside—too cold out here."

The facial-identification scanner unlocked the door as Horace hurried to catch up. He searched the street as a man propped himself against a light pole to read a three-dimensional news tablet. Images of events around the world rotated as the man scanned through the afternoon briefings. The wind blew snowflakes into small swirls as the man walked away.

Warm air enveloped them as they went in the living room and stood next to the fireplace. "Put your coat on the rack, ready and toasty when you leave. What do you think?"

"Beautiful home."

"Mom, Dad. Company."

A middle-aged woman came into the room. "Please introduce your friend. Professor Brown is finishing his last lecture; he should be home soon." Her bronze complexion and short, curly, black hair with golden highlights drew attention to her smoky topaz eyes.

"Dakota didn't inform me about her dazzling younger sister."

"Mom, this is Captain Horace Wexler Meyers of the United States Marine Corps. May I introduce my *mother*, Gwen."

"My, you are the flatterer. Make yourself comfortable; my husband should be in soon."

"Most appreciative, ma'am."

"How did the two of you meet?"

"In class together almost three hours ago…Allow me to ask Dakota out."

"Young men still ask approval from a parent to go out with someone's daughter? No one asked permission to date me."

"Now I can breathe easier; I thought you planned to ask something else."

A burst of cold air penetrated the room as the door opened. Julian hung his coat in the closet and entered the living room. A paunchy redheaded man standing five-six grasped his hand. His smile created lines around his green eyes as he leaned his head back.

"Captain Meyers, my daughter found you."

"Yes, sir. For clarification, the Lord led me to her." He took a glance back at Dakota. "With your permission, I would like to marry—"

"Oh my. Dad, he is joking."

"No, I am serious."

"Son, decelerate."

Dakota flushed as she slapped the sides of her face to regain her composure. "Father, if you knew what...thought he was teasing."

"My honor as a Marine. Our discussion centered on compatibility. For instance, where we leave our dirty underwear and nylons."

Julian's eyes twinkled; his lips curved upward. "This means?"

"Sir, we equally dump them in the living room."

Julian tapped his fingers on his chin. "All righty, throwing stockings and undies on the floor, a true match for compatibility. Both of you talked in-depth about a future together. Why would anyone leave their underwear lying around, so a person might see?"

"Ask Horace."

"No, I said, if the police came searching for stolen women's underthings, mine are military-issue. Nobody would steal those things."

"So, therefore, you throw your nylons on the floor?"

"Wrong again. We discussed Christmas stockings, remember."

Gwen rubbed Dakota's shoulder. "For a marriage to work, it takes more than a well-honed sense of humor. Though a good nature will help. Captain Meyers, dinner will be ready in ten minutes. Join us."

"Mother is fixing one of her specialties. Hígado stew."

"Excellent."

"Dear, I never prepare liver. Her poor cat became the victim of what our daughter didn't like to eat."

"Mom!"

"Fed Libby brussels sprouts, who hid them in our bed."

"Oh. A valuable piece of information. Now, who is...?"

"My parents gave me a kitten as a birthday present years ago.

She didn't like baby cabbages any more than I did." She threw a rubber ball against the wall. "Used to come running when I bounced this on the floor."

"Did you discuss," Julian asked, "who will make the coffee in the morning?"

"At home?"

"Where else?"

"My employees prepare the meals, clean the house, and tend any task necessary. Which includes picking up my dirty underwear wherever I leave them. My aunt Maddie might give me a harsh scolding if I took up the habit of depositing them in the living room."

"A captain in the Marines employs a staff?"

"He is kidding, Dad."

"Yes I...am joking."

"Ever meet any high-ranking officials?" Julian asked, transferring his weight from left to right.

"Yes, both are evil. Christianity may become illegal the moment Gifford assumes the throne."

"What do you think he will do?"

"Sir, his last name is perfect for him. Anyone who does not worship him will face severe persecution."

"Are you making plans?"

"Whatever I can do to protect people from him. Sapros is shutting down Quantico and the remaining military bases now under control of New Liberty. Which forces me to go back to the US."

"Does my daughter fit into your plan?"

"Sir, I requested our Lord show me the right woman to be my wife. For her to say a phrase, like Abraham's servant, inquired God while he sought Rebekah. Each occasion, wherever I found a young woman, I asked a simple question; every time none gave the right response. Today, Dakota responded with what I expected my future bride to say." *Hope I didn't sound too ridiculous.*

"At least I got to see my potential husband beforehand. Can you imagine poor Rebekah lamenting?" She spread out her hands. "No wonder Abraham ordered his servant to a far-off country to find a wife for Isaac. Way too far to run back home."

"Not so long ago, people dated before they joined in matrimony. Let me clarify if they bothered."

"This is my final semester. After graduation, I will deploy out. Only a brief time to allow ourselves to know one another before we marry."

Dakota raised her eyebrows. "Do you mean in the biblical sense?"

"Let me reword myself. The quicker we become husband and wife, the better we can know each other...biblically."

"Oh...You are embarrassing me."

"What do you say, daughter?"

"How can you approve of this craziness?"

"Tell me when you sought our permission to do anything."

"The thought of marrying a stranger frightens me. Figured the Lord would point out my husband and bring us together. Instead, God directed someone who is hunting for Rebekah—When should the wedding take place?" Dakota took a sip of water and rubbed off the condensation along the sides of the glass.

"Honey, I'm assuming you prefer a Christian ceremony?"

"Of course, Dad. Wait, what am I saying. Check to see what is open. The church is always busy. Should an available Saturday come up soon proves God desires us to marry."

Julian swiped through the calendar, rubbed his nose, and shook his head. "Special events fill each weekend for the next two years."

She tossed a napkin on her plate. "Guess God did not intend us to be husband and wife. You misunderstood what he told you."

"The ladies luncheon canceled, making this Saturday open."

Dakota put her hand on her stomach. "Ten pounds of rocks tumble inside me. Now what do I do?"

"We can wait until later to set a date. Find another site. Right after class on Monday, in the student center, the gym, men's locker room, dissection laboratory, your choice."

"The dean must authorize any ceremonies on campus.

Regardless of where the ceremony takes place. The lab?" Julian asked.

"Mere technicalities. The clerk's office?"

"Find a place more romantic. Government agencies are too gender-neutral, religion-neutral, or species-neutral." Dakota shook her head in protest. "Prefer they did not pronounce us bound as a creature and a creature, shaggy beasts creeping out of a swampy lagoon somewhere in Florida or Louisiana."

"Name the time and place. How about an official military ceremony? At least I should be in my dress blues, not this Bravo uniform.

"Now."

"Tomorrow more than quick enough."

"No, I mean here and now."

"For somebody who claimed she swallowed a rock, you changed your mind in a hurry."

"A test on your sincerity."

"Did I pass? My honor."

"Are the forms in your den?"

He pushed himself from the thick-cushioned chair. "Cyber documents are always available. Not as young as I used to be, or the seat is deteriorating."

"This is one crazy fantasy I am having. In the morning, I will wake up from this ridiculous dream laughing. My old senior cotillion gown will do."

Snow covered the trunk of Horace's sedan; he shoved off the pile and removed his black leather briefcase. "Dakota is a gift from God." He took the Marine yellow-and-white-gold rings in his hand and put them in his pocket.

"Captain?"

"Who are you? Why do you keep following me? What do you want?"

"Your time."

"Now? I'm busy."

"Ah, soon. No matter where you are, I will find you. A topic of

13

concern the both of us share." The cold breeze blew open his coat, exposing what Horace thought might be a tallit. Determined to talk to the man, he ran after him on the quiet street, puffing out small clouds of breath.

"How did he escape from me so fast? Does he live in one of these houses?"

Snowplows cleared the streets earlier, left the sidewalks covered with no sign of foot traffic since the snow stopped. *How can someone not cause footprints unless he walked on the road?* Branches in an evergreen swayed as a cat lept from the spruce and ran under the stone steps of a Victorian-style house. Still, something unusual appeared to sit in the tree. He unsnapped one of his holsters, removed an object, and aimed the search analyzer. A blue beam outlined the shape of where a man had been sitting on a branch. No life signs. He found a man's tattered coat and a cap on a limb, abandoned by someone months ago.

White lace curtains parted in a Cape Cod–style home as he trudged through the snow back to the house. Goose bumps raised on the back of his neck; his stomach churned as he imagined someone tracked him. A short-haired calico cat jumped to the window; her yellow eyes followed him as he walked next to the curb. Everywhere he found humor. *An infiltrator up every tree, cats spying on him out of every porthole and doorstep. Like some conspiracy kooks claiming Randall Sapros came from an alien planet.*

Warm air thawed him as he paced the room. Sounds of footsteps upstairs as someone hurried from one place to another. He took a seat and pushed his cuticles back with his thumbnail.

"Mom, I can't find my hoops. Where are they?"

"In the attic, last I saw of them. How is the yellow dress?"

"Fine for spring, besides a stain—on the back. Remember, Patrick came up behind me and smashed a blueberry pie on my—"

"Oh, rhubarb. I'll go find the hooped slip."

"After dealing with my cousin, they should make fourteen-year-old boys illegal."

"Seems you were fourteen once."

"Yes, sensible and not a boy."

"Who pretended to be twenty-one."

"Perhaps a...little difficult."

The sound of Gwen's movements echoed downstairs.

"Found your hoops."

"Mom. A giant rip in the side seam of the purple one. The blue one will work aside from the matching wrap is missing. May I borrow your white fur?"

Chimes from the tower clock announced half past the hour. *Thirty minutes since Dakota went upstairs—all worthwhile.*

"Let me zip you up. You did a nice job on your hair. The cape is perfect for your dress."

She reached the hall closet, took out a garment bag, and stood at the top step. "She'll be ready soon. Julian, phone your parents to come over here—we need witnesses. Your mother will nag me forever if you don't call for them to attend. Both of us know the reaction if they miss their only granddaughter's wedding."

Fifteen minutes later, William and Kami Brown arrived. A petite, plump woman around sixty-eight shook her finger at Gwen. "Why didn't you tell us sooner? You gave us no time to shop for a gift."

"Captain Meyers met Dakota this morning in class; she brought him home to introduce him, and he begged permission to marry her."

"Sir, please do me the honor to be my best man?" The rings slipped from his hand and fell to the tile floor. He retrieved the set and handed them to William. "A bit edgy this afternoon."

"Nervous, eh? Describe me as proud to take part, if this marriage is what my granddaughter wishes. These are exquisite; you carry wedding bands in the event someone is willing to marry at a moment's notice?"

"A long story, although, yes, I suppose so."

"Computer forms are ready; we need the bride."

He admired her charm as she hesitated on the top stairs. The sapphire floor-length velvet gown with a white fur cape set off her beauty. Tiny white baby's breath flowers tucked into her swept-up hair that flowed into ringlets on her shoulders. Her color deepened as she took her first step down the oak stairway. How graceful—light as a bubble she descended the staircase. Dakota gasped; her shoe caught the hem of her dress. She fell on her backside and bounced down three steps. Her black satin petticoat flew above her head and exposed her red lace panties.

Horace ran to Dakota's side and pulled the hoops down. "Are you injured? Were you trying to do something romantic? Dive into my arms? Scare three lifetimes out of me? Let me check your ankle. Any pain?"

She leaned over, buried her face and snorted. "No, I'm not hurt except for my pride. Sorry you found out this way, I'm a klutz. You would find out after I tripped over something ridiculous like the size of an Army tank. Dub me the awkward ballerina in a hooped dress. Rather than the always poised and elegant Princess of Wales, whom I imagined myself as, instead of concentrating going down the steps."

"Now, shall we continue, or should your father perform the ritual while Her Royal Highness sits on the stairs in an un-princess-like manner?" He held out his hand to help her up and guided her to the white brick fireplace.

Julian chuckled as Gwen tugged on Dakota's skirt. "Are we ready?"

"Horace?"

"Yes."

"Scared."

"Of me? Are you worried because you consider yourself a klutz?"

"Yes—I mean no."

"Delay the wedding for a few weeks?"

"May I ask you a question?" She sank into the plush cushions on the sofa and waved her hand for privacy. "An important one."

"Go ahead—whatever you desire to ask."

"How did you fall in love with me so fast? We don't know each other?"

"The moment I came into the room, the smile, those glistening eyes. You blurted out I was the most handsome man on this earth. Why didn't God speak in the King James Version? The princess tripping on her dress."

"My worry is tomorrow or next week after I wake up from this fantasy, I fear I will find the whole thing...an illusion. And I will... not—"

"Do you want in on a secret? I'm scared too."

"A Marine, one who runs to danger, yet marched up to a woman he met hours before expecting her to marry him, now you decide you are frightened?"

"Funny thing: placing faith in God ahead of fear causes one to do courageous things. Yes, I charged forward at the considerable peril of getting hurt by rejection. Took the risk of ridicule telling you the Lord spoke to me."

"A feeling is urging me to marry you now."

"Can you grow to love me? Will our marriage be a dream world? Doubtful. A promise I can pledge, I will forever be faithful to you." He knelt on his right knee, took her hand. "Royal Highness Gaucherie, Princess Dakota Blurty Elizabeth Brown of Lynchburg, please do me the privilege and be my wife."

She wrapped her arms around his muscular neck and closed her eyes. "This is insane; yes, I will marry you. First, I must stop laughing long enough."

Tuesday, January 4, 2056

Dakota sipped a cup of cocoa as the mid-day sun gave a warm glow to the kitchen. "Mom, Horace treated me like royalty last night. He contacted the base, and his commander gave him a two-week leave, but we can't take one from classes. This morning we told everyone we got married last night; the professor's jaw dropped open, spluttering his best wishes."

"Conferences from relatives asking why we didn't tell them of the sudden nuptials. One questioned if...People still become concerned? Where is your husband?"

"In his advanced Greek class, with Dad."

"Aunt Emily demanded to know if you intend on a celebration?"

"My sister focuses on extravagance. Are you serving pheasant or lobster? She is a self-proclaimed expert on modern reception etiquette. Ha! Poor dearest sister can't distinguish the difference between rotisserie Cornish game hen with oyster dressing from roasted possum with dandelion stuffing."

"Kami, please. What are you planning on doing?"

"Amazed how he thought of everything. Aside from ordering stuffed possum—At least I...no, he wouldn't...Well, he is from Alabama. Saturday next week at the Grand Cortez. He asked how formal I wanted the reception. Astonish me with as much pageantry as possible; he snapped his fingers. His dad is flying his aunt Maddie, the grandparents, plus other relatives up here. Notify anyone who can come on short warning. One thing he requested: no gifts, as we won't need anything."

"On his salary? In a new home?"

"We didn't need anything; since he can give me whatever I desire. Mentioned he staffs individuals for cooking and cleaning. His aunt Maddie administers the team. He claims the house is more than one person can keep clean."

Kami set her cup on a saucer. "Yes, he employs a staff of over one hundred people. We checked out the captain. He is from old money; credits are running out of their ears. Anderson Meyers is a former US senator; their home is in Alabama. To describe the house as massive is an understatement—closer to enormous. The whole clan can live in one section and never meet, wandering lost for days. He is an up-and-coming star. My sister, Emily, will arrive with her extra-large tote to shovel up the leftovers."

"Why are you ringing the doorbell?" Gwen asked as she opened the door. "You are family now. Come on in out of the frosty air."

"Facial recognition denied my access."

"Julian ought to update the identification pad."

"Captain?"

"Yes, my Alpha Unit. The term means the spouse of a Marine."

"My grandmother says you are well-off?"

"Does the fact I am wealthy affect your feelings for me? A wedding planner is handling the complete reception. My holdings account contains enough credits to satisfy the utmost demanding party guest."

"My sister, Emily, is one of those people."

"How many people may we invite?" Dakota asked.

"Not counting the Marine orchestra, the buffets, the servers, armed personnel in their ceremonial dress blues, the room holds six hundred guests; do you need more space? No, you can't peek at how the planner is decorating the ballroom ahead of time. A surprise for you."

"Emily will love this shindig."

"Why are the honor guards carrying weapons at the reception?"

"My father invited several senators to attend. Randall and Gifford imposed themselves on the banquet. Social standards among the military consider not requesting them an insult. Repugnant as they are, keeping them close is important, so they will continue to inform me of their plans. Goofy Soup's hatred for people will surpass his father's. For us to keep others safe, we must remain in his leniencies."

Saturday, January 15, 2056

Dakota's mouth dropped open as she took in the lavishness of the banquet room. With an air of glamour from another era, the antique Baccarat crystal chandelier shimmered like diamonds. Floral arrangements of wisteria, mauve, and ivory roses stood at the entrance. Blue lighted holograms of swans, doves, and rearing horses rotated around the buffet tables. In the center of the table stood a six-foot cake with a winding staircase lit with tiny white lights. Pieces of oranges, cherries, pineapple, strawberries, and lemons floated in a crystal fountain punchbowl that stood nine tiers high. White linen tablecloths and draped chairs with floral accents in bows adorned eighty-five round tables with centerpieces of cherry blossoms and white roses.

A jittery little man approached with lemon-yellow hair, a peacock-blue silk suit, knee boots, apple-red bow tie, and glittery teal pince-nez glasses. "Hurry—we must form the receiving line. Randall Sapros and the Legatee arrive straight away. Your father, your aunt, Mrs. Meyers, parents, grandparents. Let me place you. Come on, everyone; over here so I may arrange you."

Horace squinted his eyes and scratched his right ear. "Sorry; didn't catch your name."

"Chandler Fuller. Sir, the line."

He took her by the hand and followed the organizer to the reception line. "Come, my wife. Time to introduce ourselves to the dear leader."

"What do I say to them?"

"Tell them how privileged you are they chose our celebration. How dizzy with delight for your opportunity to meet them. You can never use too much fawning on those two. Be charming; smother them with compliments. Faint if Randal kisses your hand; he loves women to swoon over him. Act like a melodramatic teenager."

She put the back of her hand to her forehead, her knees buckled, and she fluttered her eyes. "Similar to acting this way? Randall Sapros. How grateful we are you came to our ever-so-informal reception. How I do worship you so. You are much more handsome in person. Afterward, I will collapse in your arms from a fainting spell."

"Don't you dare make me laugh. Those two are too full of narcissism to realize your feigned admiration."

Sirens wailed in the distance as the Sapros motorcade approached the hotel. The honor guard exited the door to receive the leader. News reporters shoved and pushed each other for the best camera spots to record the event. Newscasters reported on live broadcasts; the supreme commander takes an interest in the lives of the military. Chandler bobbed and pulled him to the reception line. Bodyguards charged forward to drag the planner away.

"Security, my great presence is overwhelming the man. Allow him to introduce me to the wedding party."

"My contribution for Captain Meyers and his enchanting wife, Arizona."

Chandler's hands trembled as he guided people through the line. "Excuse me, sir, her name is Dakota."

"An insignificant detail—so I got my states mixed up. Why should I care?"

Elevated shoes made Randall appear taller. Each person was greeted in haste until he grabbed a microphone away from a reporter. "An announcement to the happy couple: I will promote Meyers to the rank of colonel. Best dreams for your marriage."

"Thank you, sir. I am honored to be of service to you today."

"May I assume your complete loyalty? To disappoint me would be most unfortunate."

"I know whom I serve. Neither do I intend becoming a disappointment."

"So, I will receive your support. Fine." Randall held out a limp and clammy hand for a gentlemen's handshake.

"No need for me to repeat my pledge."

"Soon I will become supreme commander. I expect the same allegiance." Gifford stood to wait for his father to present himself to other dignitaries.

"Sir, you will obtain the same honor from me as I give your father."

"My supporters are rewarded beyond their dreams for their devoted loyalty. My male parent is not healthy; the title of supreme commander will soon be mine. How much authority will you need?"

"Legatee, my advice, sir: wait until you are in power. People might make assumptions you are hastening the demise of your father."

"Agreed."

Dakota leaned to her left, keeping her voice at a whisper. "The sight of him makes the hair on my neck stand."

"Your intuition serves you well. A most intimidating man."

"Congratulations to the newlyweds," a Marine said, "and his promotion. The chow line is now open. To my port side is the salad buffet; to my starboard side is the hot food. Behind me is the dessert bar. Servers will come to your table for your drink request. Sorry, Colonel and Mrs. Meyers requested we not serve alcoholic beverages."

Randall took a seat and held his palms upward, making an offer. "May I propose a grand opportunity to you? General Brinkman is transferring to Philadelphia. Upon your return from deployment and training, you will assume the title as security chief of the Southeast Quadrant."

"A promotion?" Horace asked and thought, *What is Randall planning?*

"For national defense reasons, Brinky always delivered what I ask, although, he tolerated unfavorable press coverage concerning how I manage the United States."

"Sir. Will my responsibility include censoring the media outlets?"

"Not at all. News agencies must file their articles with me first for my authorization."

"May I ask, what am I supposed to do in these matters?"

"Most obvious, Colonel. What do you think I should do?"

"Your solution is improving the character of the security chiefs. Should their integrity improve and you amend yours, this might resolve any difficulty with media coverage. Sir."

"A brilliant idea. Any other ways to better my reputation among the people?"

"What do the people say? Examine those pointers to find your solution."

"Many people say I am bloodthirsty. Others say I am a despot. We can't leave out the few crazies, who believe I am the Antichrist."

"Work on these points to show people this belief is untrue."

"Colonel, are you agreeing with these accusations against me?"

"What I meant: put effort into changing the citizens' viewpoint. Heed my advice; this does not mean reinforcing those beliefs by the intensifying heavy-handed actions."

"Are you suggesting my executions are excessive?"

"May I be candid? Without retribution?"

"Speak on."

"Sir, small groups give their full support no matter what you do. Still, many people do not understand why you persecute those with religious beliefs. Most of them are harmless; they bother nobody. Many perceive you torment them without cause, orchestrating their execution. Countless believe you ignore heinous crimes of murder, kidnapping, sexual abuse, the list goes on."

"I'll consider your suggestions. The people must recognize me as their provider, not an unspecified god."

"Worship Sapros statues?"

He directed his eyes past the bride and groom. He kicked morsels under the table as food dropped to the floor. Gifford's head bobbled like a toy as his father talked and waved his hands. "Is this a fine dining buffet?"

The mysterious man shuffled through the line and muttered to himself. He placed baked chicken, green beans, carrots, and bread on his plate, passing the cheese delicacies. *Jewish? Why is he here at the reception?*

"Dakota, do you recognize the man in the gray suit going through the buffet?"

"The guy from our class? You didn't invite him?"

He wiped his mouth with a napkin. "No, but somehow he has an invitation. Did Sapros work something out, persuading him in here? Time for me to find out the identity of this person."

"Be careful."

"No need to worry."

The man shifted his eyes between the commander and Gifford. "Why are you contacting me?"

"Why are you tracking me?"

"You are not whom I follow; we share an interest in the same end game."

"What do you mean?"

"You understand my intentions. Congratulations, Colonel and Mrs. Meyers."

"Why are you following me, or are you talking about my wife?"

"Enemies are everywhere. Do not count me as one of them. 'Stay with me; do not be afraid, for he who seeks my life seeks your life. With me, you shall be in safekeeping.'"

"You quoted First Samuel 22:23. Who is seeking both of our lives? Why should I trust you?"

"Ah. Familiar with the Tanakh."

"Jewish? You are taking a risk coming here should Randall spot you."

"Messianic."

"Sapros cares nothing what religion one is, Christians alike."

"We share mutual interests. Excuse me. Expect communication, much to discuss." The man strode to the double doors with two sentries opening and closing them behind him.

"Did you find out anything?"

"He didn't give me his name. Got a plate of food and departed without eating."

"Here or gone, they scare me. Fearful of not knowing what those two are doing makes me too tense to eat."

"Both covet luxurious one-of-a-kind gifts with butt-kissing groveling. An elegant contribution thanking them for my promotion and for attending our reception should work well for our goal. The gift will make them soon forget. What I give them will engross them more than what I am doing."

"Bribery is immoral."

"My sweet wife. Persons of my rank and higher prefer the term *survival*. These donations are essential concerning Sapros. God will use me to protect people from those two."

"Where do I enlist?"

"You enlisted when you surrendered to the Lord, and he assigned you to my unit."

The announcer said, "Listen up, everyone. A few moments ago, I received word about a tradition in the Meyers family for the bride and groom to dance to 'Endless Love.'"

The lights dimmed, a spotlight shone on the couple as the song began. The crowd chuckled as Horace picked Dakota up, holding her close as he danced to the music. Tears ran down her cheeks as he sang. *"Two hearts that beat as one. Our lives have just begun."*

"You made me so happy." She laid her head on his shoulder and closed her eyes, allowing the sound of his voice to float through her.

"Happiness is where I intend to keep you."

She wrapped her arms around his neck. "Call me crazy for almost saying no to you."

Chandler held out goblets of sparkling grape juice, stumbled, and dumped the beverage on the formal dress uniform. "Sorry, let me clean…"

"The holographer can make the stains disappear. Where is Uri?"

"With the supreme commander taking holographs surrounded by young women."

"Considerate of me to pay for—"

"Sir should humble anyone to give holos of their wedding day to Randall Sapros. How many people can say the great leader attended the happiest day of their life?"

CHAPTER 2

Friday, August 18, 2056

Oppressive heat and dense black smoke from burning fuel choked Horace and an injured Marine. Sounds of crackling electric blasts and automatic weapon fire grew louder from advancing forces. He pulled bandages from a field pack and ripped the trouser to the hip, examining the African American's leg.

"We need to stop your bleeding."

Blood pulsed a warm sticky ooze through the bulky gauze as he added another layer on the wound. He removed his belt and wrapped the band around the shattered limb. A silent prayer followed as he thought about the possibility of amputation. Red stains seeped through the layers as he laid compresses on the injury.

"This should help until the medics arrive." He took off his helmet and mopped the sweat from his forehead. The *chak chak chak* of an approaching helicopter grew closer. Horace stretched out his arms, signaling for assistance. The pilot acknowledged and circled.

"Will you wake me up as soon as they land?"

"Stay with me. Come on. Talk. What is your name?"

"Michael Billings, sir. Why are you guys so darn bossy?"

"Bossiness is part of our calling."

"What made you decide to go into the chaplaincy?"

"After enlisting, I spent two years in combat duty. The corps requires their chaplains to understand the hardships of those who served in warfare by having the experience themselves.

After I submitted a request to be a specialized combative chaplain, General Dunlap revised the Marine Corps Order—must be the hand of God. A transfer to Quantico for instruction in security followed. Concurrently, I attended a university in Lynchburg for the rest of my military, religious education."

"Please pray for me. Are you a Baptist?"

"A pastor for two years before I joined."

Horace froze for a moment as male voices shouted in an unfamiliar language. He held out his hand, releasing a housefly-sized drone, which translated the conversation:

"Two American devils are hiding behind the burned concrete barricade."

They laughed as he planned how to make the two Americans suffer. "A wounded Marine and the other is unarmed."

The display showed eight men in tattered army frog skin camouflage uniforms two hundred yards to the southwest. They pointed M4 Carbines, preparing to fire.

"Quiet. Stay still. May I borrow your weapon?"

He reached back and pulled the laser gun in front of him and eased himself over the barrier. Sounds came from the advancing troops; he peered over the four-foot-high concrete barricade, leveling the rifle at the enemy. The scope analyzer focused on the men; target-distance range ratio for an optimal kill decreased. His finger pressed on the trigger as he took his time to fire. "Come on... nearer. Closer. One...more...step. Bye-bye. Enjoy your existence in your next life."

Swoosh. Thud. Silence, except for the distant sound of helicopters approaching. He reached into his pack again and released an armed video drone. Visuals of dead combatants appeared on the screen.

The camera scanned the narrow rut-filled dirt road for movement. "Assailants won't be bothering us now. Where is our support?"

We are humbly grateful, Father, for protecting Lance Corporal Billings and me. We owe our lives to you this day. Please heal Michael, Lord. I pray for his full recovery, in Jesus's name.

"Got a wife?"

"No, I got a girl back home; she proposed. A simple wedding ceremony as soon as I go on leave. What about you?"

"A few months ago, I married a beautiful woman who works as a law enforcement officer at the university we attended. She is staying at her parents' home until I am stationed again at Quantico."

Voices of military personnel grew louder. A lieutenant knelt beside Michael. "Medics are on the way. We are moving you and the chaplain out of here."

Two corpsmen examined Mike's leg, approving the first-aid job while laying more gauze bandages on the wound. "Yer gonna be ready for the field again. Once the helo lands, we'll load you up. How did ya fight off those combatants, me lad? Ya couldn't position yarself."

Michael winced as the medics moved him on a stretcher. "Where are you from? You are not from where I live."

"Haggs, Scotland. Our tiny town is famous for the little haggis running in the fields. Do ya know what a haggis looks like?"

"Something like a hedgehog, I guess. Why are you snickering?"

"Haggis is not an animal but a joke we tell on the name of the village. Haggis is a Scottish dish people either love or hate."

"Know anyone who makes haggis? Sounds like something to try."

"Proper service requires a bagpipe player."

The lieutenant stood and tilted his cover back to scratch his head. "Now, how did you fight off those attackers?"

"Those rebels wanted to kill both of us; we took defensive action by my taking the lance corporal's weapon to fire upon the insurgents. What is your name?"

"Spencer Harris, sir. Proud you are one of us."

"God comes first, and he will oversee the rest."

"After witnessing so much horror back home, I doubt he cares. A loving God who permits the meaningless slaughter of little children. People unable to protect themselves rounded up and shot for no reason. Can't describe what happens here."

"The Lord is in control; otherwise, I might lose my stability. My faith in him gives me the courage to continue his work. He will place me to bring him glory."

Fifty yards away, a medical helicopter landed. A dusty red cloud enveloped the craft. From the haze, a crew of medics ran toward Mike, picked up the stretcher, and carried him to the medivac. The rest of the group climbed on, took their places as the aircraft lifted into the air, and headed for a trauma facility.

A female medic touched him on the shoulder. "We gave you something for the pain. You should feel better soon. The medication side effects might make you loquacious."

"Chaplin, after my surgery, notify my folks. They don't need to worry while expecting a callback."

"More than pleased to; we will arrange for a holo-conference for you to talk to them."

Mike twisted his identification band around his wrist. "Prepare yourself for my mother to go into a frenzy. My mom's baby, the youngest of eight children. Twenty-two years old and she still refers to me as her little man."

"My dad claims I will understand after I become a father. He still considers me his boy. No one to shift the responsibility to if something broke, being an only child."

"Blame the dog. My sole line of defense being the youngest."

"My dad's number one rule: no pets in the house. To accuse a pet, a cat, or a goldfish sounds foolish. Did blaming the mutt work?"

"At five, I realized my dad would never believe a ridiculous story of a fish causing any of the catastrophes I produced. I'd be way past desperate. Glad I had something to blame. A few words of advice: never say a cocker spaniel wrote vulgarity on the sidewalk. He did not appreciate the humor telling him of Rufus's deed. Mom wailed up a storm thinking her little boy uttered such vile language. Now, if she became aware of the vocabulary I learned since enlisting..."

He mimicked his mother's voice: "Oh, my baby, where did you learn those expressions? What can I do? Better be glad your grandmother isn't around to hear you talk like a lost heathen. Chaplain let me tell you about my granny."

Spence nudged him with his elbow. "You got to listen to the lance corporal's story, Chaplin. The meds are taking effect."

"My mee-maw out-swore any drill instructor. Teach them words they'd never dare to consider, much less utter. Yes, one foul-mouthed, whiskey-drinking, poker-playing, cigar-smoking, tobacco-spitting, go-to-church-on-Sunday-morning, Hallelujah-shouting, King-James-Version-Bible-toting woman. A deaconess, an elder of the congregation, sang in the choir, fire-and-brimstone preacher like you never heard. Now, she never swore or smoked in a house of worship. Come Monday morning, look out, Methuselah, she's ready to take on the vice squad."

"Your grandmother sounds like an amazing woman."

"She'd be here today if she hadn't wrestled a twelve-foot Florida alligator, nicknamed La Boca Grande, on her sixty-fifth birthday. People claim the gator weighed over a thousand pounds. Mee-Maw almost won too. Clenched a Churchill between her toothless gums. She is no bigger than an AK-47 and as dangerous. Waded out into the infested lake to her waist, snatched one by the tail with both hands. Hoisted the old snapper over her shoulder, dragged the reptile to the shore. She marched up the sandy beach like a Marine going into battle. Boca Grande made a smart-alecky fuss. Mee-Maw whirled around, whacking her old wooden boat paddle on the head five or six times. *Whop, whop, whop,* until the gator's beady eyes spun around like a hypnotic spinner. She clutched the tail again and dragged the snapping, snarling creature farther up the shore. Got within a cow's breath of the finish line and Mee-Maw dropped like a pigeon. Dead of a heart attack. Poor alligator limped back to the lake on three legs, never to be seen again. Doc swore women her age ain't designed to be wrestling gators, no how. No, sir."

"A sixty-something-year-old woman somewhere might disagree

with the doctor in the strongest use of the term."

Spence squeezed his eyes shut. "One time she fought a grizzly bear in Alaska, a mountain lion in Montana or maybe Wyoming. A boa constrictor in the Everglades. The Adventures of Mee-Maw—what will she do next? We need women like her; she would make one heck of a Marine."

The female medic checked Mike's vitals and patted him on the shoulder. "The medication made you a tad talkative. How are you doing?"

"Don't need doctors at all. Loquacious shots are miracle drugs. Let me up to show you."

"No, buddy. Landed at the hospital; medics are taking you to surgery. You will see me when you wake up." Horace held Mike's hand to say a prayer before the health team wheeled him to preop.

He ambled around the chapel and studied the brightly colored stained-glass windows with no apparent religious belief. The glass decorated with palm trees, an underwater scene with seahorses and tropical fish of teal, yellow, green, and orange. Another displayed a brown bowl of apples, purple grapes, and bananas. The other side of the room exhibited a blue lake, a red sailboat with yellow sails, and fluffy white clouds above.

A layer of dust covered the beige plastic altar with a floral arrangement of silk carnations, mums, and ivy. On the rear of the pews hung favored novels from a century ago. He swiped through selections: *Jonathan Livingston Seagull*, *Love Story*, *The Joy of Sex*, besides many others. The readers contained thousands of works of fiction but not one version of the Bible. Those who wanted spiritual guidance must request counsel elsewhere. *No wonder the world is in this shape. The reading selection is from nothing to too explicit. One only finds the mention of God's name, in the hyphenated form.* He thrust the tablet back into the holder and attempted to find a cleaner place to sit.

Early-century soft jazz played too loudly for prayerful meditation. Coffee stains were on the pews, and padding poked through small holes in the upholstery. A half-eaten meal sat on the carpet, with evidence rodents had sampled the remnants. Tiny pieces of wrapper strewn across the floor trailed to a hole.

Groups of people came and went. One came in with his lunch to eat in quiet. Another came in playing a gamepad, with annoying bangs, thuds, and screams each time the player scored points. A doctor with an intern entered and whispered meeting later for dinner at her apartment. The other plotted how to make an excuse to her wife with a sudden emergency. He sighed at the flagrant indiscretion, retaking a seat to pray again. Quietness settled in after the couple departed the chapel as someone sat behind him.

"Colonel Meyers?"

"Yes."

"Time for us to discuss a few things. Lance Corporal Billings is still in recovery."

"What? How did you find my location? Why are you trailing me?"

"Ah. You think I am stalking you? We possess similar interests in spirit. Israeli government dispatched me here to assist you." The man slid into the pew beside him.

"In what way? Also, how much will all this help cost me?"

"Nothing more than your friendship."

"Friendships start out by introducing oneself to another."

"Regulations require a member of an organization to combat anti-Semitism to protect identifications, Colonel. Procedures prohibit me from telling you more." He reached into his jacket and pulled out a box the size of his thumb. "Here is an address. The T-35 is a fine military weapon. Simple to carry and hide."

"This location is in Birmingham, Alabama."

"Near the construction site of your base."

"What facility?"

"Satellites tell us many things, Colonel."

"Six to seven months before I go home."

"Time is on our side, my friend. At least for now." The man walked halfway to the doors of the chapel turning. "Until Birmingham. Shalom."

Horace opened the case with a note. *Colonel, this is a prototype of a weapon valuable to the military personnel you trust. This tool is capable of both lethal and nonlethal settings. The device will follow telepathic commands if necessary. We also can supply personal protection devices for nonmilitary persons offering the stun option. Until we see each other again in Birmingham.* He massaged his temples with his fingers. *All this and he is a salesman. Why the covert behavior?*

"Sir, Lance Corporal Billings is out of surgery. The doctors amputated his leg above his knee and expect him to make a full recovery with the new prosthesis. You may visit him in about an hour."

"What? Did I doze off? How long since you came in?"

"Not long. Lost back at home?"

The device is small enough, easy to transport and conceal. Horace reached his hand in his pocket, stroking the soft leather box the man gave him. *Now the question remains: will this weapon do the job the man claims?*

"Colonel?"

"Don't worry—I will make contact with his parents."

Horace dragged a padded chair next to the bed as Michael opened his eyes and reached for his leg. "What happened?"

"The doctors tried to save your limb; too much damage to the femur and tibia bones to expect recovery. Amputation became the one alternative. Contacted your parents and spoke to your father; he wanted me to tell you they love you and are looking forward to you arriving home."

"Goodbye to my career."

"Prosthesis is nothing like the ones twenty years ago. Those who received a new one swears the leg feels the same as their own or better. Painful to bang your foot on the bed. You can do whatever you want."

"Yes, the first thing for me is to test out my toe to see if I'm getting one as you claim. Sir."

"Lance Corporal are you threatening to injure yourself on purpose?"

"Sir?"

"You kept mumbling about wanting to punt a colonel's biblical donkey while under the influence of anesthesia."

"No, sir, I would never boot a poor defenseless animal. Kick your sorry butt first. Sir excuse my comment...The little fellow might repay the favor."

"You misunderstood me. The donkey wouldn't be able to kick while unconscious. Michael, I apologize—I am having fun at your expense. Your sense of humor is refreshing. After the new base is operational, I will require topnotch people running the security squad. Are you interested?"

"Yes, sir, honored to be a part of your unit. Mike, if you are using my first name."

"Lieutenant Harris. You possess news."

"Sir. A change of orders. Report to Quantico after the doctors clear you for duty."

"Security?"

"Yes. My orders as well."

"Men. Time line for full-operation by the end of your schooling. Lance Corporal, you will go through officer training class.

"Thank you, sir."

Criminal-activity statements, piled on his desk, waited for his review. His thoughts drifted to the strange little man who would not yet tell him anything. *Is this man trustworthy? Every time he makes contact, he leaves in a greater mystery.*

His wrist holophone rang. "Colonel Meyers."

"My sweet colonel."

"Blurty. My gentle Alpha Unit, what brings this pleasure?"

"Need to ask you something?"

"Ask me anything; your deepest desire will come true."

"Too late you did what I desired before leaving for deployment. You don't realize what I plan to ask?"

"Sounds ominous. By the tone of your voice, whatever I did, made you cheerful. So, what do you want to ask me?"

"Need to send you a live holograph and ask a question."

"Transmit; I am ready."

A tiny baby appeared on the screen. Eyes open, thumb in mouth, she moved her little feet. The caption read, *Hello, Daddy, I am your new daughter.*

His voice broke as he reached out to the image. "Honey. This is the—best news. Is this live?"

"In the doctor's office now, watching her. Five minutes ago, she punched me."

"How soon will our little one be here?"

"The doctor estimated mid-February. Will you be home in time?"

"Central Command did not set an exact date. Let's have dozens of children."

"Uh, how many? Easy for you. I'm not a rabbit."

"We will work on the final number later. My dream is lots of kids around me."

"Biological?"

"Ours, of course, but if not, we can adopt. What about your job?"

"Administration reassigned me as a minor crimes detective. Not as hazardous as patrol, although more action than dispatch, Cyberbots handle the communications center. Did you see the news about Gifford's baby boy? Named him after Alexander the Great."

"You are not considering the name of Alexandra?"

"Repulsive idea. How about Kassidy? Our daughter will not associate with Sapros."

"Yes, I like the name. How about we name her Horacia?"

"She might run away if we called her—"

"Named after my great-great-great-grandmother Horacia Gertrude Stowe."

"Oh, quit. Not a Horacia or a Horace in your genealogy."

"Too smart—can't sneak anything by you."
"Somebody ought to keep you in line."
"My dear, you are the perfect person to do so."

Mike sat on the side of his bed, sipping water, waving to Horace to enter his room. "Come on in, Chaplin. Doc informed me my physical therapy begins soon. My progress is a blessing for sure. What got you so giddy-humored this morning? Must be winter holiday morning and Santa left you a new pony. What's got you excited?"

"My wife holo-conferenced me last night; we are about to become parents."

Mike reached into a drawer of the bed stand and lifted out an oak wooden box carved with teddy bears and a brass latch. "A celebration. A cigar?"

"Uh, I don't smoke."

"They made them from high-quality chocolate. So many of my buds are becoming dads; need to keep a supply on me by reordering the variety pack from Switzerland."

"How thoughtful. The one wrapped in pink foil. What do the other colors mean? Green, orange, yellow, purple?"

"Those are for the non-multi-gender specifics."

"Um."

Mike pressed two fingers to the side of his head, closing his eyes. "Hmmm, my keen sense of psychic ability reveals your wife is expecting…a girl. Am I right?"

"You possess observation skills, yet your paranormal ability—your humor—is stronger of the two. My, this is excellent. Where did you find these?"

"While on active duty in Germany for two years, I went on liberty to a village in Switzerland and found them in a specialty shop…A bit pricey, though worth the cost."

"Extra laps around the course should work this off."

Spence tapped on the door. "Sir, I came to visit—Excuse me, sir, are you eating a cigar?"

"Why? Are you insinuating I am not to snack on one?"

"No, sir...most people smoke them."

"So, munching on a stogie is healthier than smoking one in a hospital?"

"Uh, sir. Who am I to judge you if you eat tobacco?"

"Lance Corporal, what is the key ingredient?"

Mike opened the box and handed the wrapped treat to the lieutenant. "Chocolate, sir. Chaplin Meyers and his wife are about to become parents."

"Yes, thanks, congratulations, sir."

A ranking female officer in an Alpha uniform came into the room. Both men jumped from their seats, coming to attention, saluting with the cigars protruding from their mouths. "Mum."

"As you were. Major General Jasmine Wetherington. Pleased to meet you, Colonel Meyers. One of my duties is to come to the medical center to visit the injured as often as I can."

"How are you, Michael?" she asked, taking his hand. "Your mother called me this morning. So, I came to call on my beloved grandson."

"Do you expect me to refer to you as Major General, ma'am?"

"Until the doctor releases you back to duty, Mee-Maw is fine. Can you tell me as to why I am finding tobacco products in this room?"

"Hey, the colonel found out his wife is pregnant. Here is a cigar to help celebrate."

She unwrapped the chocolate and placed one end in her mouth. "Not my normal preference—still, this blend surpasses all the others. Let me explain, gentlemen: my grandson called me Mee-Maw after I became commander of the Marine Air Wing. Blessings, Chaplin, and a new great-grandchild for me. Colonel, I am so sorry I missed the reception; my grandson Patrick graduated from flight school the same day."

Spence pulled a chair across the room for Jasmine to take a seat next to Mike's bed. "Ma'am."

"Blurty told me her grandmother is a career Marine. She did not tell me her name."

"My daughter Gwen told me she found a nice young one. Cherish my granddaughter."

"Aye, ma'am."

"Hey, Chaplain, this means we are cousins. Dakota and I are close; my brother Patrick tormented her…Surprised she allowed him to live."

"Heard her mention his name."

"Uh, Mike, is this the grandmother who—?" Spence hid his mouth with his hand, dashing out of the room. Laughter echoed in the corridor until the sound of the elevator door shut.

Jasmine caressed Michael's shoulder, turning to face Horace. "So, my grandson must be entertaining you with his Mee-Maw, the monster-killer, stories. A hunch tells me he told you about my travels in Kenya on safari riding a wild rhino and rounding up a herd of fierce aurochs."

"No, ma'am. This story of Mike's centered on you wrestling with an alligator in Florida."

"Amazed at the free time the Pentagon allows for accomplishing such feats. This grandson of mine is a talented storyteller. He joined with my urging. Now he entertains those who are unsuspecting of the identity of his grandmother."

"Your mortality status is amazing, after the gator incident."

"Colonel, I possess more lives than a hundred cats after each encounter with a ferocious beast. My favorite tale is about the time I took part in a security detail, in the jungles of Venezuela, saving the life of Aston Sapros from a Goliath Birdeater. We trudged through a swamp full of insects buzzing like dentist drills and slithering venomous snakes able to kill a human in fifteen minutes. We heard strange clicking sounds and investigated, making a bad choice. This monster spider sank long fangs into Aston's leg with excessive force; he screamed like a girl. Flashlights flew in all directions. With unsurpassed bravery, I got out my trusty boat paddle, walloping the beast until the noises stopped. With no moonlight, unable to tell what I beat on. Daylight came—we discovered I killed the spider by mistake. A massive hairy thing too, the size of a Shetland pony."

"You need to write a book about your adventures sometime."

"My grandson is far more aware of my escapades than I am. Now, Michael, about this alligator in Florida."

Monday, August 21, 2056

Ian Knupp straddled a chair, placing a bouquet of white roses and pink carnations on her desk. He brushed back a lock of blond hair; blue eyes twinkled; dimples formed in his cheeks. "Detective Meyers, a florist delivered them for you."

"My husband is so sweet."

He handed her an emerald-green bag from an upscale store. "Go ahead—I want to see your expression."

Dakota grinned and tossed him a sour-apple gumball. "Your favorite flavor."

She unwrapped the gift and lifted out a little dress blue uniform. "Horace will love this. You took the time to think about this. Daddy will want her wearing this in her first official holograph."

"Comes with matching booties. Respect for the military and their spouses. Hard job dealing with everything while they are away."

Ian glanced at a pile of paperwork on her desk. "Healthy stack of follow-up requests."

"Not too bad. Most are petty with no leads. They misplaced these items."

"Get a lot of those. Girls lose something, and they're adamant someone stole their whatever. Hey, could you show my sister around campus? She and Mom plan to visit for a week. I'm working the day shift—no time to take them to my place."

"What time will she arrive?"

"This afternoon. Arrival time is the same as emergency-drill training. Can you meet my sister, Millicent, and my mom, Tennille? Please take them to my apartment? You've been by where I live on Leviticus Drive. Give this to my mother, so they can go inside." His hands trembled while he tugged on the gold collar brass.

"Sure. Nervous about your family coming to visit?"

"Haven't seen them in a couple of years and...Milli dreams of acting all grown up and becoming important with lots of power. Randall doesn't grant women authority. Not a real influence in any case. Otherwise they...caution her about getting involved with...?"

Dakota leaned her head on her left hand. "You can't talk her out of such a dangerous plan?"

"Another woman closer to her age might get through. Mom tried; Milli rejected her efforts. Young women are asking for trouble sometimes."

"Detective Meyers, these petit thefts require follow-up. What is going on with so many larcenies? Statistics show a few incidents occur a month; what we once did in a semester now comes in one day. The major is not happy with the crime stats. Odd belongings, like memory drives, markers, pens, earbuds, packets of coffee, nail clippers, perfume, hair brushes, to stuff like ladies' undergarments."

"Strange; people don't bother reporting those items. I'll do a supplement and see what I can come up with."

"What did your husband say about your news?"

"So happy, he wept; he can't wait to be a dad."

A 3-D mockup of the campus indicated each incident with a color code. She massaged the center of her forehead. *Majority of the crimes took place between ten in the morning and noon on various days. Thefts occurred in the first-year-student parking lot in the flagpole area.*

Security videos observed students in the lot. First-years hopped into their vehicles, leaving while others came on campus. A patrol vehicle unit, number 5123, stopped next to the pole for forty minutes. Three female undergraduates paused, speaking to the officer before dashing off, heading for the graphic arts building. Dakota surmised the young women, enamored by the youthful single officers, desired a relationship.

A young woman crossed over the parking area with her head bowed. With slow, cautious steps, she moved to the right side of the car, peeking around before sliding into the seat. They talked for several minutes before leaving for another location. Dakota noted the time as ten thirty-eight hours. Upon their return, the student exited, clutching her tote against her body, hair disheveled, clothing in disarray, and hurried away until out of view.

The next day, number 16942 pulled up, time ten thirty-nine hours. "What is going on? Who is driving my unit?" Once again, groups came and went.

Dakota directed a security drone to hover over the area to gain an angle for surveillance of the activity. Two females approached the vehicle; soon, a third ambled her way to the driver's side. One woman took a quick glance around before she got into the car. She altered the view of the tactical device to a lower level, obtaining the identity of the officer inside as he sped away.

Major Radenbaugh placed a chair beside the desk. "What is wrong?"

"Why is Knupp using my unit?"

"The sergeant's is at Fleet getting upgrades; you won't be driving during light duty. Until finished, yours is available. Does this bother you?"

"Uh, no. The officer drove off several times a week with a female in the front. Until I review all the videos—"

"Male officers are not to transport women alone."

"Leaves with a woman; an hour later, he submits a report

involving a theft. Video gives a time frame for these incidents."

"I'll call down to Fleet and request them to check Knupp's trunk and do a complete inventory if any of those items are in his vehicle..."

Major Radenbaugh rapped on Dakota's desk and left the office. "Bras and panties will place him in a predicament."

Tuesday, August 22, 2056

"Detective Meyers."

"Yes."

"Fleet found numerous articles in Knupp's trunk; by an odd coincidence, they match the reported stolen objects. Call those students; ask them to come in for a sworn statement."

Dakota submitted the reference data to the computer. "Major, Knupp talked with this student twice, without filing a follow-up."

"Ask for her to come in for a supplement report."

An hour later, an officer escorted a young woman with long brown hair into the office. "This is Ms. Xavier; you requested her to come to the station."

"Thanks. Have a seat; you are not facing disciplinary action. I am doing a supplement on the incident you filed a couple of months ago. Can you give me any further knowledge involving the theft?"

"No."

"Sergeant Knupp called you three times concerning this minor larceny. Did he say if he made any progress with his investigation?"

The woman twisted her silver rope ring on her right hand. "He calls to find out how I am doing."

"You reported the theft of your panties. Why? People don't bother with a single item of clothing. Any way possible you misplaced them?"

"I—I am positive."

"What makes you say stolen?"

The woman glimpsed over her shoulder. "I am certain."

"Who took your panties? Provided if we figure out who committed the thefts, proving is another matter."

Ms. Xavier nibbled on a thumbnail and remained silent.

"Talk to me. Why are you so apprehensive?"

She peeled away a broken fingernail. "The university will throw me out if I say anything,"

"Why do you think the school would expel you?"

"Sergeant Knupp claimed the dean would. He is protecting me."

"From what?"

"For parking in a restricted area. So, Sergeant Knupp is helping to keep me from getting ejected."

"In a wrong section? On the floral emblem at the entrance?"

"My first class is next to the senior lot, and I didn't want to be late."

"How many times did you do this?

"Once. One time too many."

"Sergeant Knupp told you this?"

"Yes, my first year in college. We are not to park anywhere except in the approved area."

"The worst penalty is a fine, or suspension of privileges for a brief period. Expulsion is a trifle extreme."

"He terrified me; he intimidated me."

"Why did you affirm someone stole your panties?"

"Ian forced me to give him my underwear and file a theft claim. He threatened to charge me with filing a false police incident if I reported him. The university will expel me."

"Did Sergeant Knupp ever request you enter his vehicle?"

"Yes, he coerced me to take off my...Afterward he—I might be pregnant."

"Let me set an appointment for you at the clinic for an examination. We'll find out if you are...and who fathered your child. Knupp won't be a worry; you are safe. Hold up your right hand. Do you affirm everything you stated is true?"

"Yes."

Tuesday, September 5, 2056

"Major Radenbaugh, the investigation is complete. Two will testify; DNA evidence proves Knupp impregnated five women who reported to the health section. Two births, one miscarriage, two terminated off campus. Child Support is deducting payments from his pay voucher."

"Notification to the dean; the administration will decide on disciplinary action. Splendid job, Detective Meyers."

"Ian's sister gave me some information on him regarding his behavior while they grew up."

CHAPTER 3

Monday, January 22, 2057

"Sir."

Horace returned the salute as he scanned the daily briefing. "Yes, Spence? Warm for this time of the year, approaching middle seventies by noon today...What's wrong?"

"An Israeli representative is here to discuss urgent business with you."

"The State Department didn't inform me of any sanctioned visits."

"He didn't ask for one, for reasons he will explain."

"You verified his credentials?"

"Yes, sir. He is whom he claims to be. A high-ranking officer with Israeli Defense."

"Show him in."

The mysterious man strode into the office, extending his hand. "Shalom, my friend. Hope I did not give you too many sleepless nights."

"Take a chair. You never introduced yourself. Tell me who you are before I demand a palm and iris scan. What do you want? The strained relations between the United States and Israel is over thirty years old. I pray for improvement."

"I am Deputy Ambassador Eliyahu Stein, a Messianic Jew. The supreme commander praises your abilities on national security. We share the same feelings concerning the dynasty. Your devotion to Yeshua is a common sentiment."

"What do you want from me?"

"Your aid in fighting Sapros."

"We are discussing treason."

"Colonel Meyers, I must keep our people safe. Prime Minster Roshal admires your integrity."

"How can I help Israel?"

"Please deed properties to us in your quadrant to construct shelters for those in need, both Jews and Christians."

"You are familiar with Gifford's plan once he takes his father's title?"

"Not a secret by any means, we station our people everywhere, including the palace itself. Randall's health is failing. How long will he live? Adonai holds the answer."

"Which properties interest you?"

"Allow us to purchase abandoned houses to enable us to protect people from henchmen."

"How long before Sapros figures out what is going on?"

"Give these people time, a place to hide until we can transfer them to New Liberty. Otherwise, their situation may be permanent. At least until the regime crashes down."

"Aston came to power before my birth. The country New Liberty now divides the Northeast Quadrant and the rest of the States. Virginia, West Virginia, Maryland, Delaware, New Jersey, Ohio, Michigan, Indiana, Illinois, Wisconsin, Missouri, Iowa, and Minnesota. Guam and Puerto Rico joined them a year later. At some point, Gifford takes control, and Alexander is his heir."

"President Adeline Forrester allows your squad to fly over their airspace; to your advantage, she does not permit Randall the same courtesy. At this time, you can count her as an ally, should the need arise."

"A colonel in the Marines. The commander of Camp Sumiton lead a military coup? We are discussing treason. Lowest ranked in charge of a quadrant." *No listening mechanism on him.* "How can I trust you? Sapros pays informers in gold. Prove you are not one of them."

"Colonel Meyers, I am aware you scanned me for transmitters and know I am not. You keep your office clear of mechanisms, making you free to speak as you want."

"You are knowledgeable of this how?"

Eliyahu leaned forward. "My little gift to you. The weapon will detect surveillance implements, including hidden explosives. Did you not examine my little gadget? Colonel, I am surprised at you. Ah, but you did. Yes, I see the subtle way your eyebrow lifted upward. Your body language says you want to believe me, but you can't make yourself."

"Out of necessity to gain an advantage, not out of fear."

"Wait too long; Adonai may give you enough reasons to go after Sapros. Persist in prayer, and he will deliver him into your hands. Remember the Canaanites, delivered into the hand of Joshua."

"Are you a prophet? An angel of the Lord?"

"No, I am a man, the same as you. You help Israel; we will supply the technology to defeat Sapros. Adonai will guide people to you who will make your mission possible. Not talking about a takeover tomorrow, he will deal with him in his own time. He will give him a chance to repent."

Thursday, February 15, 2057

Horace paced the nursery, showing Kassidy the walls painted with trees, grass, pink flowers, and baby forest animals. "Jesus loves you, this I know, for the Bible tells me so." He reclined in a mint-green cushioned rocker, kissing the top of the baby's head.

"Please stop crying. You're not hungry; you belched like your mother after a meal. A bad habit I hope you don't continue. Your diaper is dry. Mommy and Daddy are sleepy. Little marines need their sleep. An order from Colonel Daddy."

"Need help, son? Maybe she wants me to get her to settle

down. Hold her against your chest, so she can hear your heart beating. Something I learned from my father when you refused to stop crying."

"I never cried."

"Correct—you screamed. Which is why I'm deaf in my left ear." Andy took Kassidy in his arms and sang to her.

"You aren't hard of hearing in either one. Grandpa and Grandma Wexler are begging to see their great-granddaughter. We haven't seen them since the reception."

"Don't let Lyell and Autumn spoil her. On weekend visits with Nana and Pop Pop, they made you into one rotten little...We can put her back in her bed. Dakota and Gwen did a beautiful job decorating your old bed. Now, while you can, get to sleep. No trainees until ten hundred hours."

"Thanks, Dad. Rotten...me?"

Andy laid Kassidy in her crib. "Took us a week before you would eat a proper meal, instead of crying for frozen cream cakes. Maddie will make sure the crew is quiet in the morning. So, you rest."

"No break for me. Introductions to recruits at zero six hundred hours."

"Suggest you go to bed. Time is now zero three thirty."

"Go to bed; time for me to feed her." Dakota sat in the rocking chair, wrapping herself with a blanket to nurse.

"We gave her a bottle about an hour ago. Is she hungry again?" Horace reached down, stroking Kassidy's cheek with his finger.

"She wanted a snack. Now she's asleep. I'd get to feed you if Daddy and Grandpa Andy stopped spoiling you.

Appreciate all the help you give me, but I want to experience being a mommy. In the morning and need to nurse, I find out you took her to work."

"Baby-bootie Marine training. Her first words: 'Aye, Dada.'"

"Give her an order, and she will more than likely give you a loud no."

Horace clapped his hands and winked at his father. "She might. Like her mother needing a—"

Dakota waved her hands above her head. "Horse potatoes. You are so full of heated self-importance, I can prick you with a pin. We would watch you fly all over the room, deflating."

"Come on, you two. Off to bed with both of you."

"Might as well stay up Dad; must be at the induction center in two hours. Guess I'll surprise the recruits by having breakfast with them."

Wednesday, April 18, 2057

"I'm sorry, Blurty—orders. This mission is short. Colonels have little input."

"Why can't we go with you?"

He wrapped his arms around Dakota, embracing her. "Provided the tour lasted a year, no question my family would travel with me. This deployment will last three or four months at the most. Honey don't cry. I must force myself to leave you and the baby here and not hold you. Birmingham Police will keep you busy in your new job next week."

She sniffed and nodded.

He lifted her face to him. "Hey, look at me. Now, smile. Much better." Horace took Kassidy, cuddling her. "Behave for Mommy while I am gone."

"Dada."

"She said dada. Yes, sweetheart. Dada will miss you. Daddy promises to be home soon."

Backpack in place, he slung the duffel bag over his shoulder. "Dad and Maddie will keep you company. Should you become bored, ask for the blue box. Once we get squared away, I will call you. Crazy about you."

A Jeep pulled up; the driver saluted as he climbed into the back seat. Dakota stood at the door as her husband held up his thumb, index and little fingers, sign language for "I love you." She waved as the vehicle exited the driveway and headed for the main gate of the compound.

Andy put his arm around her shoulder. "Never gets easy, watching a loved one go off on maneuvers, including a short one. You agonize every day until they are back safe. Like my wife cried as I left on deployment, the way my parents worried. Yes, I worry too."

"Why on my birthday? They are so unfair."

"A fair day does not exist. Another day would be someone else's or an anniversary. Postpone a wedding until the service person is home."

"Given they come back—"

"Don't think negative thoughts, Dakota."

She sank into the sofa and hugged a pillow. "Last time deployed, my husband involved himself in a battle and saved my cousin's life. How can I not think about...?"

Andy patted her hand. "He worries about you being out on the streets of Birmingham and wonders which is more dangerous, his job or yours. Both are difficult occupations. He agonizes...you might enjoy yourself too much—"

"No, he doesn't. What concerns him is the police chaplain showing up here, telling him I'm not coming home. Kassidy is teething. The baby book suggested feeding her unsweetened yogurt. She spits the stuff out all over me."

"Don't blame her. Try mixing in mashed bananas," Maddie said. "Andy likes to tell stories about how your husband spat everything out. How he got so tall on so little food."

He stroked the top of Kassidy's head. "Sometimes I wasn't sure who wore more chow. Horace or his mother. Ate like a starving dog in his teens and needed longer pants every two weeks."

Dakota smiled as Kassidy cooed. "Not a mental picture I want to keep. You are not picking up Daddy's bad habits. No, you are not, my sweet girl."

Friday, June 22, 2057

Andy handed a package to Dakota. "Came priority delivery. I'll be in flight instruction. Maddie is shopping, back in an hour or two.

Any plans next week for Horace's coming home? Every day he calls to speak to you. Kassidy crawling, saying dada made him one proud father."

"Special plans. Thanks, I will be fine."

Dakota unsealed the box and lifted out a holograph photo album. *Horace mailed something romantic.* She replayed the video as her throat ached; her eyes burned as a knot formed in her stomach. Memories of her reception flooded her mind. The song "Endless Love" played in her thoughts like a cruel joke. "This can't be happening."

With slow, careful steps, she wandered into their bedroom. She slung open the closet doors and stuffed clothing into her suitcases, desperate to leave the house. "Come up to the colonel's sleeping quarters and bring down my luggage? I'm leaving to visit family."

She crammed Kassidy's clothes, toys, and diapers in the baby bag. "Got everything she will need until I am home."

"Dakota. You need help?" Mike stood in the doorway of the nursery.

"Didn't mean for you to do this, Mike. Would you take these bags to my vehicle…? I'm leaving soon."

"Isn't Horace back next week? Why are you taking off to visit your parents now?"

"Oh, Mike—I'm dumping him."

"By the stars in heaven, why? He loves you so much. Nadine and I are looking forward to a family reunion of sorts."

"Ask him." Dakota threw her ring on the bed. "Provided he can muster the nerve to tell you. He will not treat me like I am nothing."

"Cousin tell me what is going on. Mee-Maw can come and talk to the both of you."

"Grandma thinks Horace is perfect. Tell her he is not."

"Aunt Gwen and Uncle Julian would tell you no man is flawless. Why don't you work this out?"

"Help me to my vehicle. Mike, I must leave—now."

"Okay, okay. Wish you would tell me what in the blazes is going on between you two."

Monday, July 2, 2057

"Son, before I left to teach flight, everything appeared fine. Dakota talked about you returning. After I came home, Maddie showed me the note and ring lying here." Andy sat beside Horace, rubbing his back. "Two days later, a courier collected the rest of their things."

He thumped his fist on his right leg. "I don't understand. Mike knows something. Questioned him why she left; he saluted and walked away without saying a word. Called her parents' home; no one answers the holophone—semper fidelis. Why didn't she wait and give me an explanation?"

"Excuse me, sir," a Marine said, saluting. "This came for you."

"Thank you, Corporal."

Horace opened the packet and pulled out papers. He read them and covered his eyes with his hand. "Dakota filed for divorce, requesting full custody of Kassidy. The restraining order says I am not to see her...ever."

"Did she say why?"

"No, nothing in the documents says why. I am driving to Lynchburg to talk to Dakota to find out why she is doing this. Pray I am not too late to save my marriage. Dad, I love her. Feels someone yanked my life out from under me."

"Let me fly you to Virginia in the morning. You should not drive yourself."

Tuesday, July 3, 2057

Horace rang the doorbell and waited. "Access denied?"

Julian's voice came on the intercom. "She does not want to see you, Colonel Meyers. Now, go."

"What is with the formality? Why did Dakota file for divorce? Please let me speak to her."

"My advice is to let her alone and go on with the life you chose."

"What are you talking about, Julian?"

"Address me as Dr. Brown. Don't pretend with me."

He laid his forehead against the door. "You've known me for a long time. Dakota shutting me out is killing me. What happened?"

"Does a certain wedding remind you of anything?"

"Ours?"

"One more recent."

"Major Harris and Colette's? Mike and Nadine's? Why the guessing game?"

The door swung open, Dakota's eyes red from crying. "Quit playing innocent. Come in here so I can embarrass you to your father. With proof."

"Evidence of what? You packed all your belongings. You told Mike but too much trouble to wait to discuss anything with me. Cut off all communication. You think I am supposed to know the reason for your behavior."

Dakota held her hand up to stop them at the front door. "Take one more step, and I will call the police for violation of a restraining order. You betrayed me."

"How? What are you talking about?"

"Read the wedding ring. You lied. Fed me the always-faithful crap. Yeah, right." Dakota stepped back for them to enter the house.

"Play this, so Andy can watch your betrayal. My mother is tending Kassidy; you cannot see my daughter. Sign the divorce papers and disappear."

He turned on the player. "I am not signing anything. I promised only in death will we part."

A woman dressed in white chiffon and French lace walked down an aisle.

"Colette?"

"So, at least you admit you know her."

"By being a member of the groom's party. Yes."

"Object to the role you played."

"Are you balking because I served as Spence's best man?"

She beat his chest with her fists. "Best man? Try again, jerk. Why did you scam me into marrying you?"

Horace took her wrists, holding them against him. "Hey. Calm down. We can figure out what happened. If. You. Stop." He bent down to rub his shin. "What is the matter with you? Is this how your parents settle disputes?"

Julian took his daughter by the hand and led her to the sofa. "Colonel, I assure you. We did not raise Dakota in this atmosphere. She claims you mistreat her."

Andy held his palms up before him. "My son never raised his hand. He loves her. We are confused by the sudden and unexplained behavior. The day she left, everything appeared fine, at least, until Maddie got home and found her note and her wedding ring on the kitchen table."

Dakota pointed at the player. "Play the holograph. Witness the truth about your perfect son."

A beaming bride walked down a rose-strewn path to two Marines standing next to an altar. She smiled, taking the hand of the groom. The mouths moved without a sound; music played in the background.

"Why am I in the groom's place, and why is Spence wearing my uniform? What the—? Dakota, I never kissed Collette, nor did I marry her. Where did you obtain this?"

"By messenger, the who and why don't matter."

"You are a trained security specialist and failed to detect this is a poor computer hack job? Did you notice I am wearing a captain's uniform?"

"I understand what I am looking at, Colonel. You committed bigamy without telling me."

"Another spouse? While marrying multiple partners is legal, Blurty, I did not. How can I prove to you this is bogus?"

Julian traced his finger on his Bible. "May I interject something? Professor Smyth teaches holographic cinematography. He can tell us if this video is genuine or not."

"Will you return with me if he says someone altered this?"

"Promise me. Never get in touch with my daughter or me again if he says this is legitimate."

"I am confident this is a fake—but agreed, I will not communicate with either you or *our* daughter again. You broke my heart."

Wednesday, July 4, 2057

Gwen poured Dakota a glass of lemonade and took a seat at the kitchen table. "Dear, you need to talk with your husband. He is innocent."

"What if he never trusts me again? Ran off and left him, taking Kassidy with me. He is right; I didn't see the fakery."

"Tell Horace you are sorry and ask if the two of you can mend your lives. Your father and I worked long and hard on trust."

"You and Dad? What happened?"

"Let's say we put this behind us. By placing our reliance on the Lord, our marriage...Don't want to think about the alternative. You were too little to remember, like Kassidy won't recall."

Dakota gripped the player, remaining silent. "What I saw shocked me to the point I felt so betrayed and hurt. Ian Knupp. He promised he would get revenge...He found a way. My ring finger feels naked."

"Horace will place the wedding band back on your hand soon, I am sure. Your husband and Andy are here. Dear, you need to discuss this with him."

"You ran out the moment Professor Smyth told us Knupp made the video as an assignment. May we talk now?"

Her hands shook as she shoved the player away from her. "The edited-out sound kept me from hearing everyone spoke French except you."

"We both suffered, Dakota. Someone broke our hearts but not beyond repair."

"This is difficult to say."

"We need to put our lives back together. I brought something with me." Horace held out his hand with Dakota's ring resting on his palm.

"I don't know."

"Wait. After counseling couples this close to ending a marriage, I insist they repeat their vows to each other. After you two talk things out, I urge you to renew your pledges. Take two or three days to discuss your struggles. Grandpa and Grandma will tend to her until you come back."

"Wait a minute," Dakota said.

"Dada."

"Yes, sweetheart. Daddy is home. You and Mommy will come back with me." He took Dakota's hand. "You are coming home, aren't you?"

"We should talk. Let's go to the hotel for privacy? Remember our honeymoon?"

"Does this mean I won't be sleeping on the sofa?"

CHAPTER 4

Tuesday, April 10, 2074

The sun began to set as darkening clouds sailed over a crowd of sixty thousand people squeezed into Sapros Stadium to celebrate Gifford's fifty-second birthday. Thunder rumbled in the distance as Army bands and choirs performed "Ode to Gifford" in the tune of "Old Kentucky Home." Children, with cheerful faces, sang "We Love You, Gifford," as thousands of red and yellow balloons floated into the air.

Personnel representing each branch of the military pushed a silver cart supporting a six-foot-by-ten-foot rectangular cake decorated with a rotating, holographic, flaming Chimera, a Greek mythological giant lion with a goat's head on the back and a snake bearing fangs for a tail. The creature flexed dragon-like wings, stretching them out and resting them again.

"All are privileged to be in my presence today, to celebrate the ultimate date in history. April the 10th, 2022, the day Randall and Fallon Sapros honored the world by my birth." Gifford stood with his hands to his chest. "I admire your kind support, loyal people of this beautiful country, of mine."

Forty teenagers in red-and-yellow translucent bodysuits danced on Gifford's platform, motioning the crowd to chant with a deafening roar.

"Your honor is so glorious to love me more than any other ruler. Not everybody loves your sovereign in the same way as you here worship me. Can you believe these individuals disagree with your leader? These people are obstructing progress for everyone."

The performers again led the people in hoots and hisses, churning the passions of the crowd. Like a mass of frenzied sharks in bloody water, the mob wrapped their arm around the person next to them, swaying from side to side. People chanted, "Bring them out."

Silence filled the stadium as he lifted his hands. "Be patient, my beloved people; they will soon meet their end to satisfy your craving for bloodshed. First, this was the most successful roundup of dissidents in the history of my reign. Your pleasure will more than compensate for the cost of the credits you spent for this event. Tonight, my precious people, over five hundred rebels are awaiting their deaths. Treasured people do not believe I am compassionless; I am not. I gave them enough opportunities to commit themselves. Unbelievably, those Christians chose their god over me. Foolish, senseless people, where is their god? Am I not worthy of them? No, they shouted. So, they will die."

Cheers erupted from the stadium as fireworks lit up the evening sky. The band played "Ode to Gifford" once again. Uniformed personnel shoved people wearing black burlap sacks to obscure their sight as the trembling group trudged to the center of the arena. Several of the shackled stumbled, falling on the person in front, causing others to tumble forward. The heavy-booted guards kicked prisoners and jabbed them with sharp sticks, forcing them to continue to the middle of the field.

Horace took his garrison from the hat tree and opened the door, waiting for Spence to exit the office. "In two years, Gifford will celebrate his birthday with us. Each celebration demands to be greater than the last. I will not disappoint. A double lobotomy excites me more than hosting this event. Noncompliance is not an option if we are to protect the compound and the quadrant."

"Sir, Sapros suspects your allegiance lies somewhere other than with him. Use caution."

"Monday morning make sure the senior staff is ready at zero nine hundred hours for a security briefing."

"Aye, sir."

Monday, April 16, 2074

The conference room filled with officers wearing their Alpha uniforms. A buffet contained coffee, water, doughnuts, fresh fruit, and bagels with cream cheese arranged for a light breakfast. Horace set a folder at the head of the table; he read the roster and acknowledged their salute. "Morning. I trust you enjoyed your day off yesterday."

"Yes, sir."

"Take your seats. Wonderful. Shall we start? What difficulties are occurring in the Southeast Quadrant requiring our immediate action? Lieutenant Colonel Yon."

The woman pointed a laser light on a map where the worst criminal activity occurred. "Sir, stats show a continual difficulty of cluster crimes in many areas. Majority of them homicides, burglaries…robberies. Hot spots around Atlanta, Tampa, Miami, Birmingham, Memphis, and Louisville are becoming war zones."

"Are the local authorities requesting our aid?"

"Sir, Sapros's demands overtax the small municipalities, which do possess the number of cyborg officers to manage the crimes committed. Androids can process the data faster; however, like their human counterparts, they can only be in one place at a time."

"How many?"

"Two hundred or more."

"Sir, agencies are overwhelmed investigating illegal worship services—"

"Effective now. You are not to investigate church functions. Robberies, along with other quality-of-life issues, take precedence. General Brinkman thought otherwise. I am in charge now. We will treat those as intelligence only. Do you understand?"

Officers persisted in their silence. He tapped a pen on the podium to accent each word.

"Do any of you comprehend my order?"

"Yes, sir."

"Now, Lieutenant Colonel. How many are investigating worship services?"

"Over four hundred, sir."

"Instead of scrutinizing civilians attending church, free personnel to spend their time assisting the local law enforcement agencies to solve real crimes."

"Sir, if I may."

"Go ahead."

"One of my men is on a prominent case, with people of notability. The agent gathered enough evidence to offer enough malcontents to Sapros for his next birthday."

"Denied. I order everyone's efforts located elsewhere. Not harassing people who bother no one. Whatever you hold, seal the file as concluded."

"Aye, sir."

"Personnel unhappy with how I run this quadrant, you are free to request a transfer. Though your new assignment will not treat you as fairly as I will. You do your job with honor; I will back you all the way. You make a mistake, inform me. I expect honesty plus integrity from my Marines. I will give you mine regardless of how you conduct yourself. Any other activities require our attention?"

Horace sat at his desk with his forehead resting on his right hand. He recognized the sound of Spence's footsteps in the room. "Sit for a moment, will you?"

"Aye, sir."

"Do you suspect any of the officers will cause me any difficulty? Will any of my people report me to Sapros?"

"Marines understand new commanders. Everyone served under multiple commands. To them, you are one of many. A leader demands the best from his people. Once they adjust to you, they will give you their loyalty."

A telemonitor lit up. "Kassidy, how is my much-loved daughter?"

"Dad, I'll be going for my college project soon. I love you. My professor assigned me to a reeducation camp."

"Honey remember our sign if you need my help. Would you wait until you are older? Sixteen is too young to take this class. Later, if you enlist, it will provide invaluable experience. Won't be able to talk you out of going. Be careful; if you encounter difficulties, contact me at once."

"Dad, the Lord will let nothing bad happen. You read the Scripture about God sending an army of angels around me. I will write to you to tell you what is going on at camp. With any luck, the staff will permit me to phone you if trouble comes up. My ride is here; I got to go. Love you, Dad."

"I love you, honey."

She blew him a kiss as the call disconnected.

"Seems like a year ago. Justin turned six months old. Dakota took Kassidy shopping to purchase a birthday gift. Dressed in my blues preparing to speak to shoppers about the Toys for Tots Program at the Plaza. She handed me her doll, using her best Daddy-can't-say-no-to-me voice, 'Hold Babs, so Mommy and I can buy you a present.' Like a dope, I stood around with this squalling doll, unable to turn off the darn thing. I tried everything. She always got the doll to quit crying. Specific techniques aren't reliable on a toy or a real baby.

An elderly woman about as tall as a peanut comes up. She mistook me for the collection barrel."

He imitated how the woman loaded toys into his arms. "I didn't want to hurt her feelings, so I took them to the drop-off site. The pile stacked up so high, I couldn't see my way."

Spence tilted his head and found a moth caught in a web. "You should do something about the spiders in here. Don't want Dakota to run screaming."

Horace removed his T-35, aimed at the spider, and pressed the trigger. "Pity the eight-legged critters; she laser-zaps them."

"How did you find the drop-off point?"

"A blind guy with a cyborg service dog helped me find the toy collection spot. I got to the place where these two clown Marines tending the barrel jumped up, saluted, and remained like statues. With what now felt like a hundred pounds, my arms aching, fingers frozen, unable to move, I shouted, 'Cut the procedures and help unload my arms.' After removing the tonnage from my now numb arms, I made sure Kassidy's doll, now screaming at 125 decibels, did not go into the barrel. Dakota and Kassidy found me, and I asked her how she got Babs to stop crying. With hands on her hips, in a most exasperated voice, she said, 'Daddy, if you want Babs not to cry, press the button on her back.' By this time, a crowd of about the size of two platoons had formed. Entertained themselves watching me try to make this toy stop howling. She took the toy from me and lifted its skirt and pressed a touchpad, and the doll quit. Everyone howled at this giant Marine unable to shut off a toy doll."

"This is too funny. How did I miss this? Are you trying to top Captain Billings' great yarn stories?"

"I told those two lieutenants if either of them breathed one word about what happened, they would scrub the chow hall decks for a month."

"Are those two still with us?"

"Captains Billings and Rios. You so much peep, expect to scour the chow hall deck for two months."

"So, a high-tech gadget like a doll outsmarted you? Besides, Dakota would never allow you to treat her cousin—"

"Blurty would be scrubbing the deck right along with them."

Spence tossed a balled-up paper at Horace. "She would be using you for the mop. All over the deck."

"Someday, Spence. Exasperate me one time too many. Poof, I will bust you back to the bantam cadet program."

"You mean, if one existed."

"After what Babs put me through, she belonged in the trash barrel."

"No, you wouldn't. Break Kassidy's heart?"

"You won't let me worm my way out of anything, will you?"

"No, sir."

CHAPTER 5

Thursday, July 20, 2079

Rex Jenkins, along with his wife, Marley, glanced at the clock in their modern Greek family living room, waiting for their son to come home to the gated community in Greystone. Both worked as corporate attorneys for international business.

Silas entered the house and placed his gear bag next to a red leather recliner. "Didn't expect you to wait up. What are you doing here, Lauren? Is something wrong?"

He settled his lanky frame into a chair, running his hand through his shaggy blond hair. His blue eyes moved from his parents to Lauren. The exchange of silent communication between the three caused concern.

Lauren nodded to Rex. "Say something."

"Rumors are circulating about you. We hope you can relieve our apprehensions. Several of our clients allege you are frequenting an area where secret religious gatherings are taking place. Do you associate with these dissidents?"

Silas scratched his right cheekbone. "How many? One, two. Why are your patrons jamming their beaks in my business?"

"Calvin Gaskins told us he hired someone to follow you; he informed us you're attending church."

"Why did your father place surveillance on me, Lauren?"

"To make sure you're right for me. You joining an outlawed religion is cause for concern about your stability."

"So, what you are telling me is hacking into a university computer system to modify your grades is acceptable. Though attending church, which bothers no one, is not?"

"My father conducts a significant amount of business with Gifford Sapros."

Rex folded his arms. "Is this true, son? Are you attending... Sunday services?"

"Suppose I am, what?"

"I am compelled to tell you, leave our home."

"What are your thoughts...?"

"My father doesn't approve; I can't marry you."

"You are an adult. Think for yourself."

She flung her two-carat pink heart-shaped diamond back to Silas. "A Christian, you are pathetic."

He squeezed the ring in his palm. "Yes, I am a believer. Glad this happened. God showed me how shallow you are, Lauren. Foolish me, believing you loved me, begging me to alter your test results. Played innocent, denying any knowledge of my actions to the dean. Despite your forgiveness after your father came to your rescue, you still graduated with high honors. A bunch of baloney served with a bitter whine."

She pushed him out of her way. "Grow a backbone."

"True. It would benefit me a great deal to build some fortitude. Our relationship ended long ago. My biggest regret is meeting you, let alone asking you to marry me." He threw his gear bag across the room, turning his back on her.

Lauren slung her purse over her shoulder, stomped out, and slammed the door. The sound of her vehicle engine and squalling tires broke the quiet of the night as she sped down the driveway.

"We insist...you move out first thing in the...morning. Until you come to...your senses, you are not to communicate with us. You are no longer welcome...under our roof."

"I will pack my things and leave before daylight."

"We will make up a story, to cover our embarrassment of you becoming a Christian. We'll tell our friends we cannot tolerate your gambling, your drugs, and your alcoholic binges." Marley rushed to the stairs, stopped, and gazed back at her son as a tear fell on her cheek.

"Please, Mom, try to understand."

"We want you gone...by morning." Rex kept his back to Silas. "To repeat your mother's words, we will cover...for you."

"Whatever reason makes you comfortable. You made up the lie, not me."

After he tossed his duffel bag into the passenger seat, he slid in his Aston Ranger. A light came on in his parents' bedroom; his mother stood on the balcony and waved as she eased the drapery back into place. He sighed and pressed the identification starter to exit the neighborhood.

Darkness made driving down the winding two-lane road treacherous, as a deer might dart into the roadway, causing a collision. A red light flashed below a broken guardrail leading down into a deep ditch. The side of the road provided room to park and get out to survey the crash. *Someone's car went down the embankment.* Branches caught on his blue jeans as Silas crawled down the incline.

He pressed the emergency number on his wrist phone. "Assistance to Hugh Daniel Drive. A vehicle in a ditch, trapped driver with injuries. No, no. Lauren."

Amber crash warning light flashed on the dashboard as Silas forced the door open. He placed his fingers on the side of her cold neck in search of a pulse. Lauren's pale bluish face stared, her lips parted, about to speak to a mysterious object. An empty bottle of scotch lay in the back seat. "No—No—No—Please, Lord, not Lauren."

Sirens grew louder as voices of cyborg police officers approached.

"Down here!" Silas's voice broke. "The driver is dead—Possible intoxication."

"Are you acquainted with this woman?"

"Lauren Gaskins. Last night she came to my home to break off our engagement."

"Where do you live?"

"Until ten minutes ago, in the mansion at the top of the hill.

"Where did Ms. Gaskins live?"

"Mountain Brook. Her father is Calvin Gaskins."

"Did you witness the crash?"

"Lauren might still be alive if I had. I still love—her."

"We need for you to come to the station for an interview and find out what happened before the time of the incident, for classification."

"Whatever I can say or do to help in your inquiry."

"May we call someone to drive you downtown?"

He scratched his throat. "My parents kicked me out."

"Why?"

"Their decision. To spare Mom and Dad further grief, I agreed to move out."

"Did this happen at the time Ms. Gaskins broke off your engagement?"

"Yes."

"Place your right thumb here."

The cyborg held out the identification wand and laughed. "Silas Eugene Jenkins convicted of cyber espionage. You altered somebody's grades at college."

"Your central control databank requires checking; I observed signs of...system failure." He placed the palms of his hands on his leg as additional officers climbed down the embankment.

"I am functioning at the optimal level."

"Why did you laugh?" Silas asked.

"I do not laugh."

"You mean, you're not designed to if you're at an optimal level. Ugh. No sense in arguing with a cyborg."

"Be at the station by eight this morning. Our traffic homicide detective will talk to you. His designation identification is Investigator Fifty-Two."

"Your designator?"

"Officer Nineteen-Nineteen."

Additional investigators climbed down into the ditch. He returned to his vehicle and leaned his head on the steering wheel, hiding his face. "Lauren. Why did you do this?"

Someone knocked on the car window. "Excuse me, do you need help?"

"You're human."

"Yes, sir."

"My fiancée until about eleven thirty last night. She gave back her engagement ring and broke off the commitment."

"Ms. Gaskins show any signs of being distressed?"

"Lauren expressed her feelings. Got her purse and slammed the door. She screeched her tires pulling out of the driveway. So, yeah, Lauren left the house upset."

"Did she drink any alcoholic beverages while at your parents' residence?"

"Returned home from a late class and she did not appear intoxicated. Otherwise, I'd have driven her home or called her father."

"Distraught enough to kill herself?"

"Perhaps. Lauren is—She liked getting her way."

"Did the two of you argue?"

"No, she ended our relationship."

A dark-colored vehicle drove up and parked on the side of the road. A Marine in a Charlie uniform exited and stood silent for a moment.

"Chief Meyers, sir. Why are you responding to a traffic fatality?"

"The incident went up the chain of command involving a suspicious death and an identified criminal."

"Why report to your office at this hour in the morning? The cause is undetermined, sir."

A cyborg officer climbed out of the ditch; mud clung to his tactical boots as he tramped to the human police officer. "We found a dead deer nearby. Front-end damage to the victim's vehicle shows blood and deer hair embedded in the grill. The toxicology scan confirms alcohol is a factor. We took a bottle containing 7.5 milliliters of scotch into evidence."

Horace leaned down to Silas's window. "One of my staff will drive your vehicle; I will take you to the police station."

"Sir?"

"Silas Jenkins."

"Sir?"

"No need for alarm; I promise not to stun-bop you."

"Uh."

"In my vehicle, so we can talk. Front. I am not your chauffeur."

"Sir?"

"Your vocabulary is larger than the word *sir*?"

"Yes, sir."

"How long were you on familiar terms with..."

"Began in the first grade, a typical grade-school crush. I chased Lauren with bugs. She screamed. The principal sent letters. Until we got into high school." His voice broke as two cyborgs lowered a body bag stretcher into the gulley.

"What did they think of her?"

"They preferred her. At least my dad. I am a disillusion to them."

"Why are they disappointed in you?"

"Drugs, gambling, drinking."

"Your father is an attorney, correct?"

"Yes, much of his work is in corporate law. My mother too."

"You are at the university in Birmingham?"

"Yes, sir."

"Your major?"

"Data security and cyborg technology."

"Remarkable. We are at your destination; your vehicle is behind us, parked in the visitors parking lot."

"You are most kind, sir."

"I will keep a watch on you."

"Sir?"

He smiled, rolled up the passenger window, and drove to the

other side of the parking lot to enter a private entrance. Military personnel saluted as he walked to his office.

He dropped his satchel on his desk, poured a cup of expresso, and glanced over the briefings waiting for him.

"Spence."

"Sir."

"What is this?"

"A message from Sapros, for you to call him back as soon as possible."

"Did he indicate what he wanted?"

"Other than to brighten your day? He didn't give much of one."

He spoke to his holophone. "Call Supreme Commander."

CHAPTER 6

Wednesday, September 27, 2079

The neon signs of Ollie's Little Norway brightened the deserted strip mall in the old theater district, one of the few lingering restaurants in Birmingham. Grass and Quaker Lady flowers sprouted through the cracks in the parking lot. A warm gust of twirling wind scattered trash on the property. Faded and torn placards of Randall Sapros flopped against the walls and promised a better tomorrow. Spray-painted boarded-up windows with rival-gang graffiti warned others they did not tolerate trespassing on their territory.

Coydogs roamed the area, rib bones protruding from their sides. The hair stood straight on the backs of the hybrid animals. They hissed as they stalked diners to their vehicles. Security personnel in a black van stopped and aimed weapons at the canines. Red beams of light struck the coydogs as they yipped in pain and collapsed to the pavement. Agents wearing protective clothing collected the dead creatures and dumped them in biohazard plastic bags. They tossed them into the bed of a pickup truck and drove off in pursuit of more stray animals.

Inside the café, the primary source of illumination came from the north and the east windows. The only other supply of light flickered from a small solar-powered candle in the center of each table. Crammed into a narrow corner chair, Horace kept his back to the chipped Tuscan-ceramic-paneled wall; his tall stature gave little room for him in the busy café. He stared straight ahead with a slight shifting of his dark eyes, observing people entering and exiting the establishment. Muffled conversations drifted around him. Someone's sister lived in Nebraska, suffering from a terminal illness. A woman's daughter intended to enroll in a college in Texas; a man stated he requested clearance from Meyers for passage to Iowa for his family; another complained about his home under surveillance around the clock. Diners sitting nearby tried to quiet the man. He glared, saying it did not bother him if the chief heard him or not.

The required display of the portrait of Gifford Sapros and the new United States flag, a cadet gray with a yellow horizontal stripe and a red Chimera set inside a gold oval ring in the center, stood against the wall. A cartoon-like poster displayed people standing at attention with the national motto, "Let Every Person Be Subject to the Governing Authorities," hung near the restrooms. Sapros permitted the owner to add a touch of ambiance, provided nothing was defamatory against Gifford or violated the antireligious laws. Old family digital photographs of the proprietor depicted happier times and were positioned on a river-rock electric fireplace.

The well-worn wooden floor dulled from neglect. Twenty square tables with chipped paint of red, blue, green, and yellow crowded the dining area. Black-and-white plaid tablecloths hid the years of harsh use. Time-worn brown wicker chairs were arranged at the sides of the table. Each cushion matched the color of the table and, though threadbare and stained, gave a slight hint to the better days of the declining café. A generous person might call the eatery shabby-chic, while others denounced the place as dilapidated and hazardous to one's health.

Next to the café entrance, a bulletin board displayed photographs from parents who sought their missing children. People stopped for a moment and examined the pictures. Horace sighed and hoped someone recognized his daughter Kassidy to negate the unconfirmed reports of her death.

He tucked his cover over his belt and read the small card mended with yellowed adhesive tape. The prices marked out and rewritten showed steep price increases over the past couple of years. A cup of chicory and a tuna salad on toast appeared appetizing as he shoved the menu back into the empty condiment stand.

The color drained from a server's face, and he fumbled for his order tablet as he recognized the security chief; his electronic pen made a loud snap as the implement fell to the floor. "Thank you for the privilege to serve you today."

Horace handed the broken device to the server. "Your pen's recorder appears damaged."

He made a mental note of Brad's brown left eye, a hazel right eye, and a small scar on his chin. "The chamber cracked. Uh, what may I bring you?"

"Tuna salad on whole-wheat toast and a cup of chicory, black."

"We are out; I can offer a toasted hotdog bun. The bread might be stale."

"Been served worse in the chow hall."

"Anything else?"

"I'd like to talk with the proprietor if he or she is available."

"Uh, uh, maybe he is. Let me check. My name is Brad if you need me."

Brad carried a pot of chicory and poured the brew into a red ceramic mug. "The owner will be with you soon."

Several people wandered into the café and glanced over their shoulders. A group of teenagers covered their mouths to prevent him from reading their lips. An older couple came in, recognized the chief, and hastened their steps to exit the eatery.

Minutes dragged by before a pudgy man around sixty shuffled his way to the table. Despite his Norwegian name, an unusual mix of accents made determining his origin difficult. "You wanted to speak to me. I hope you find everythin' to your likin'."

"Mr. Johansen. Please join me for a moment."

Ollie straddled a wooden chair and faced Horace. "How may I help you?"

"Someone gave me reliable information; you are serving particular...clientele in your place of business, those whom Sapros banned." He took a sip of the black brew, set the mug down, and coughed. "Curious flavor. Cayenne?"

He tilted his head to the left and licked his lips. "I'm unaware of any illegal people. Comin' into my café."

"Do all your employees"—he stood next to Ollie, "check customer IDs before taking orders?"

He craned his neck back. "Possible new workers or one or two may forget once the crowd comes in."

Dangerous to eat here, he thought as the sandwich skidded across the table. The server hurried off and whispered to the others before he dashed into the kitchen. Dirty dishes clattered as waitpersons gathered plates and refilled empty cups with chicory to appear busy. Two females peeked out, gawking at him; Horace's wink sent the teenagers away, giggling.

"I'm sorry for the behavior of my worker. Let me fix you another sandwich."

"Don't bother yourself. No sense wasting more of what you are deficient in."

He reached into his pocket and took out a small, black, leather business case. He handed a beige card to Ollie. "After my arrival here, one couple came in. The instant they saw me, they left. Did the café burst into flames? Can you explain why they reacted this way?"

Ollie dabbed his face with his apron. "Perhaps they remembered somethin' crucial to do."

"Hmm."

His eyes shifted from side to side, searching the room. "People 'round here get intimidated seein' you. Everyone recognizes your power. Only Sapros holds more authority than you."

"I prefer people be honest with me, rather than fawning at me with flatteries, hoping for a small trinket of favor."

"I gotta start cookin'. Customers are hungry."

Horace remained silent, placing his fingers next to the handle, turning the mug around.

Ollie stopped and turned the card over to examine the message on the back, taking a quick glance back at the chief before he pushed the doors and went into the kitchen.

He took a bite of the sandwich and grasped a paper towel, covering his mouth. "This is bad. The merciful thing to do is call Hazardous Waste Management for disposal."

A little silver bell jingled on the door as a tall, slim, younger version of Horace arrived. He maneuvered around customers and plopped into a seat. "Dad, why did you need to see me here? Not for lunch, as you already started eating."

"Intelligence indicates the toxicity concentrations of the food exceeds legal levels. The chicory exhibits an unusual flavor, which I suspect is a lethal dose of cayenne."

"No place in here with more leg room? I'm six-six; you are bent up like a paperclip."

"A squeeze. Easier to stay on guard sitting facing everyone, a safety precaution. Didn't you learn anything from me? I am placing you on an assignment."

"Well. Are you ready to order?" Brad asked, bumping Justin's chair with his hip.

"Don't ask for the tuna salad on toast, or chicory."

"A glass of water, a bowl of tomato soup, with a grilled cheese sandwich." He slipped off his backpack. "Dad, why did you want me to come here?"

"Ask Mr. Johansen for a position."

"In this place? Why? My second job with the university pays higher."

"Your assignment is to work here as an investigative Marine. Intelligence briefs show Ollie's Little Norway is a place where banned people meet, and Goofy Soup is pressuring me to find out what is going on. Shut the site down. Make captures, brutalize people, whatever pacifies. Now, if you're employed, I can tell him I assigned you to the job, keeping him appeased."

"Dad, they won't believe us, nor do we trust them."

"I realize the implications as Gifford is getting impatient. Furthermore, he will announce new restrictions soon."

"What now?"

Three different shades of lipstick smudged the rim of the glass of water. A half-pint-sized bowl of lukewarm tomato soup, and a well-blackened grilled cheese sandwich tittered on a repaired broken plate.

"Anything else you might like?"

Justin cringed; smoke curled around the black square, resembling a burned sacrifice. "No, thanks."

Horace pressed his thumb on the wand. "Lunch is on me."

Brad snatched the payment rod, knocking over the glass. "Sorry, I'll get another."

"Clean one this time."

"They expect people to pay to eat their garbage? Best not complain; no describing what will come out next. Now, how will my employment be of any help? People will start rumors your son works here; resistors will find another place."

"So, you can say you saw no unusual activity taking place in the establishment. No clandestine meetings or anything risking Gifford's ire."

Brad placed another tumbler in front of Justin. "Here."

He picked up a towel and wiped off the rim of the glass with one shade of lipstick; took a sip of room-temperature water. "I asked for a clean one. Onion juice."

Justin flicked a dead housefly to land on the plate of an older woman in the next table. "What if I find something?"

"I apologize. May I pay for your meal? My son does not always use his...best judgment."

Horace resumed his attention on his red-faced son. "Notify me."

"What about Gifford's new limitations?"

"Sapros will outlaw humanitarian services to people in poverty, including provisions provided by private individuals."

Justin forced himself to keep his voice at a whisper. "Can he make those restrictions?" He took a bite of the sandwich and spat out the contents. "What did they put in this?"

"Waste-dump material. To answer your first question, one person possesses the power to stop him. So far, God allows Sapros to continue in his station. One thing Gifford is proficient at, he becomes careless leaving ambiguities in his edicts, which I use to my advantage."

Brad popped a wad of bubble gum. "Would you like anything else?"

"Ask Mr. Johansen to come to my table again."

"Right away."

He placed his hands around his throat and pretended to choke. "Please complain about Brad trying to poison me. What, not impressed?"

The server rushed to the counter; moments later, Ollie came over to the table, using his apron, now stained with chicory, to dry his hands. "What may I do for you?"

"My son is seeking a job. Your sign outside says, Help Needed."

"For a dishwasher."

Horace extended his right hand with his palm facing up to Ollie. "Hmmm, the title of a server or a maître d' might be better, to take off the pressure. What do you say?"

"Another waitperson, I suppose. Many places own cyborg servers, which are less expensive overall. I can't afford the models, which can do the job as efficient as a human."

"Wonderful. I appreciate those who cooperate with me. I overheard Brad telling one of your diners you are out of your mustard allotment until spring."

"Yes, the rationin' is challengin'. Two small bottles don't last a month, except the supreme commander says we must sacrifice for our country. Put the least amount of condiments on the sandwiches as I can an' only if requested. Still doesn't last long enough."

The table tipped forward as Horace stood, scattering the contents on the floor. He lifted the table back to collect the debris.

"A server will clean up the mess."

"At what time do you want my son to start? Justin, what time is your last class?"

"My classes end at twelve hundred hours. I can be here at thirteen thirty."

"Fine. Tomorrow is one of our slow days."

"Excellent. I will forward you a case of mustard, salt, pepper, sugar, cheese, plus other food items not in the process of decomposing. Expect them here in the morning. The supplies should last you until spring."

"Thank yar, father."

"He is pleased to do so. My dad is not an evil man."

The blue double saloon doors swung back and forth as Ollie called from the kitchen. "I'll meet you tomorrow."

Repurposed oak flooring restored to former beauty, recovered from a demolished church, served as a table for Dakota to study her Bible. She jotted down notes into a spiral-bound notebook. "Odd I never noticed this. Romans 13:1: 'Let every person be subject to the governing authorities.' The phrase is in all public buildings I go into; those same words are here. I am sure the Grand Poohbah does not intend the same inflection as the Word of God."

The garage door opening caught her attention. She rose from the chestnut-colored leather bench and lifted the lid to hide her Bible and notebook, unsure if Horace invited home a guest. He came into the butler's pantry and kissed her on the cheek.

"How did work go today?"

"Same old thing. College kids are angry because of the cutback of meal vouchers. They claim Sapros is starving them by rationing lunch to four ounces of navy beans and a one-inch square piece of cornbread. Female students want to organize an illegal demonstration with signs, demanding his resignation from office. They believe if they all picket, we won't be able to arrest the entire campus."

"The number of protestors is of little concern; cyborg police will exterminate them by his order."

"Too many undergrads gathered about for a lock on their identification chips. The drones did identify our son."

Horace nodded.

"What are you planning to do? Stop pacing."

"Student unhappiness falls under your duties."

"Justin can keep track of the activities. I realize how you hate Gifford's unexpected appearance when people act restless."

"Correction, I loathe his visits, period. Anyway, Justin's new job at Ollie's Little Norway will keep him busy.

"Ollie's old dive? The dishes might be clean half of the time."

"Don't criticize them...Food served on soiled plates is a different matter. Gifford made life almost impossible for establishments to offer a decent menu. The café is out of mustard, salt, pepper, sugar, and other staples people expect a restaurant to provide. He stocks moldy cheese, and the best description I can give is cheap, rotting cat food."

"Are you a connoisseur of cat cuisine now? Is Ollie on his adversary list? Which means he is now on your watchlist."

"He cannot afford the kickback demands to ignore his feeding the poor. Provided he had enough credits, I'm not sure he would. The guy appears to be a man of character."

"Why did he hire him?"

"I talked him into hiring Justin as a server; he wanted a dishwasher. Ollie agreed. For a goodwill gesture, I am sending him a generous supply to last him until his next allotment."

"To bargain with people with payoffs is disgusting. Will you quit pacing."

"Don't consider them as bribes. My way to spread the blessings the Lord gave us over all these years. To hand out provisions by someone with my rank arouses suspicion. Fixes and rewards for a favor. Gifford and his butt-kissing sycophants will not question my motives—a way of life for this evil world."

The years of pain from a back injury took a heavy toll and made her appear ten years older. She shoved back a lock of gray hair from her face. "Still, doesn't mean I prefer this way of helping people. I rather assist those in impoverishment, without the impression of being an incentive, bribe, or buying someone's support. This is wrong."

"Sun-Tzu once taught, 'If you know the enemy…' The reason I make Gifford my business is to be familiar with Sapros and understand him well."

"I still hate this."

The muscles in Horace's jaw tightened. "What do you want me to do?"

"I didn't mean to annoy you. Monday let's go for a drive, however, not in the formal limo or your security vehicle; you need to see something for yourself."

"I'm not annoyed. Where are Maddie and the crew?"

Dakota reached out and caressed his cheek. "Quit tensing your jaw. Five-Star, I learned to recognize your expressions long ago. She and Andy drove to Birmingham to visit Great-grandma Jean; I forgot about them going before I gave the employees the night off."

"Her one hundredth birthday. Terrible of me not remembering. She never forgets a special date. We will see her soon."

Thursday, September 28, 2079

Dressed in his crisp new server's uniform, Justin beckoned to workers as they scurried about filling bowls of hot soup and dumping food on fading Norwegian design plates. He scowled as he viewed piles of rancid dinner scraps everywhere. Hordes of German roaches nibbled on fresh sandwiches. In the back corner lay a dead rat ready to burst next to a garbage bin overflowing with trash. A female server dropped a sandwich on the floor. She brushed off the dirt and served the unsuspecting customer.

"Excuse me. Where is Mr. Johansen?"

"In the storage room."

"Am I permitted to go back to where he is at?"

He gestured to the back room and hurried out into the dining area. "You work here now, from what Ollie told us."

Justin wandered into a small back room lit with a laser diode light bulb. The near-empty dusty shelves contained a one-gallon jar of mayonnaise, a small bottle of ketchup, five one-gallon cans of white beans, three bags of chicory, and a loaf of moldy bread. A commercial refrigerator displayed foods nearing expiration dates with a list of reorders on the doors. Inside the fridge sat ten transparent cartons of stew-like meat of an unknown variety. Other items included nondairy products of chicory, imitation cheese, aging vegetables, celery, carrots, and three potatoes. The stainless-steel sink piled with dirty dishes waited for someone to place them in the old conveyor dishwasher. Thirty cardboard boxes with *Spring Tree Industries Incorporated* stamped on the sides in blue block lettering sat on a wobbly jade-green metal table. Ollie waved his hand at the containers. "They arrived this morning."

"My father keeps his word."

"I shouldn't take them...He might expect me to...Your father is the security chief."

"My dad is not an unfeeling man."

"I didn't mean—He is wonderful. So is Gifford. My loyalties will always be with Sapros."

"Why don't you open them?"

"To be indebted your father and unable to repay?"

A door ajar across the room caught Justin's attention. Above an old desk hung a painting of Jesus knocking on a door. "We owe someone a tremendous debt we cannot pay. He paid our penalty for us on the cross, over two millennia ago."

"I—don't understand what you're talkin' about."

He took Ollie's right hand into his. "Yes, you do. Now, where do I start?"

"I guess you can help me unpack these boxes."

"With relish." He cut open the first box and pulled out a printout. "Your invoice with a list of all items."

"Not since Christmas mornin' did I feel like this. In the past, before the holiday became illegal."

Ollie reached into a box and pulled out a jar; he wiped away a tear. "Here's a container of relish for your sandwich, my boy. Mustard, salt, pepper, malt vinegar, horseradish, pickles, real sugar, flour, and pure chocolate. Do you realize how long since I served anythin' with chocolate, not somethin' of an odd mix of whatever?"

Thank you, Lord, for your amazin' gift an' your use of Chief Meyers. Bless him, Lord. I pray he is one of your humble servants," Ollie said, lowering his head in prayer.

"Amen. I'm aware this is a safe place to talk. You worry about my father. Sapros offers handsome rewards to anyone who rats out a rogue governmental employee. My dad is not out to harass those who wish to worship the Lord in peace. He stops those who want to destroy what little someone owns so they can grab more."

"How are ya sure this room is alert-free?"

"Specialized equipment. Something you need to understand, Mr. Johansen: Gifford is ordering my father to send a unit to your café to ensure your appliances are complying with the Help Alert Act. I can install simulated chips, which will display your gear functioning at optimum levels."

"How can I be sure you're statin' the truth? The government swindles thousands of people. Not your father, per se, but he probed Hooper's Cleaners. How can I trust someone who prosecuted a man who operated a church out of his business?"

"Lance Hooper ran a counterfeiting ring and sold the books for a tidy profit. He stole and copied local ads and resold them to covetous customers. After the clerk scanned the improper codes, the charge was accepted, and two days later, the rationing computers rejected the purchase. Once financial security panels discovered the bogus acquisitions, they froze their accounts. The merchant and the government lost revenue. Chatterjee suspended the buyer's purchasing privileges for a year."

Ollie poured two mugs of chicory. "My café does not qualify for sales of rationed items. I consider this as another blessin'. Runnin' a cleaner business is not a restricted operation. So, why did he take a huge risk?"

Justin stirred a teaspoon of honey into a cup of watery imitation coffee. "Hooper's pay scale is a tier four, same as yours. By counterfeiting, his income rose to A."

"Explains things, I suppose."

"Like what?"

"Gifts he offered the investigator afor your father got involved."

"Sounds like he gave a lousy bribe."

"Free dry cleanin' for a year?"

"How much would an investigator save? Ten credits a month?"

"Right, not worth the trouble. About the same as offerin' a cup of dandelion tea with purchase of bosintang soup."

"What are the ingredients?"

"Kaegogi, vegetables, noodles. Elderly Korean an' Asian customers' favorite meal. Inexpensive to make. Keeps people from goin' hungry. What's left over, I take to the ghetto an' distribute the surplus to people. They are near starvin' to death."

Ollie rested his head in his hands. "This area used ta be an upscale shoppin' plaza. This café drew celebrities from New York and Hollywood. Now I serve kaegogi."

His eyes grew watery; his voice broke. "The people...are so hungry they receive enough to survive...provided I bring out the soup."

"Why must they go starving? Are they banned?"

"Chatterjee made drastic cuts in the nutrition allotments for lower-tier workers. Would satisfy me to see her existin' on the meager rations. Gifford too. I can't let them starve. Told your father I check identifications, but I don't. People come here 'cause I will give them a hot meal. No questions asked."

"I guess I better kick off my training as a server, Mr. Johansen."

"Call me Ollie. Might confuse guests hearin' you callin' me Mr. Johansen."

"A moment of your time, Brad Wallace; train Justin to wait on tables."

"Happy to."

Brad opened a cabinet and took out an order tablet. He blew his nose and left a long, wet streak on his sleeve. "Rather self-explanatory. Table number and guests. Tomato soup with a grilled cheese half sandwich is combo three. Should they want extras, make sure you tell the customer each one is a credit. Upcharges would be on the menu except someone tore off part of the menu. So, we tell them."

"Mayonnaise, ketchup and relish a three-credit upcharge."

"Yes."

"Pricey for tier-one workers?"

"Condiments are expensive. Tier-ones order the bosintang soup with a slice of bread, the cheapest item. Comparable to a stew rather than soup; beef, chicken, or pork is a luxury. Kaegogi is cheap. Ollie makes three gallons daily. He never keeps leftovers for the next day. The meat is tender; I can't describe the flavor."

"What is kaegogi? Did he tell you?"

Brad imitated Ollie. "Best ya don't find out, my boy."

"Don't tell me this...is...something."

"Are you wondering if the meat is human? Indeed not. I probed him; he assured me he did not serve cannibalistic fare."

"Rodent?"

"What remains of the animal is larger than a rat."

"Hey, you two. Customers are waitin'."

A male customer stood at the door with his hands cupped to his mouth like a megaphone. "Ollie. A gang of kids outside is demanding food. Those juveniles insisted if you don't give them pie and cake, they will throw rocks through your windows. A darn shame. Must be eight to ten years of age."

"Give those kids somethin' to eat an' the number keep growin,' an' acting worse. Where are the parents?"

Ollie ambled up to the children and rubbed his hands against his apron. "What do you want today, fellas? I got nothin' to give to you."

Chester, a redheaded, chubby-faced boy covered with freckles, stood with his hands balled into fists on hips. His yellow eyes narrowed into a cold, hard stare. "We will throw bricks through your windows until you give us somethin.' Break all the window you got and toss garbage at your customers."

The boys jumped as a deep voice came from behind them. "Excuse me, gentlemen. Did you threaten Mr. Johansen and his patrons? Are you familiar with the term *extortion*, a felony? You pint-sized criminals may spend many years in jail."

"You can't do nothin' to us. We are too young."

"What is your name? You, the one with the red hair, wearing a gray sweatshirt."

The boy turned his head away. "I ain't tellin' you."

"Young men, you used up your last option. Alpha One Actual.

"Sir go ahead."

"Dispatch security vans to my location. I am taking eight juveniles into custody."

"Aye, sir."

"Your parents will pick you up at my office, and you will tell them about your misdeeds. Afterward, I will explain to them how I handle children your age."

A younger child around six with shaggy, light-brown hair thumped his chest. "My pop doesn't pay attention anyhow. If I leave him alone, he does not bother me. Pals with high-ranking people, my pop will make you sorry."

"Who is this person?"

The boy tilted his head back; his broad grin displayed four missing teeth. "Best friends with Meyers; he's goin' to fix you."

"Your name, young man?"

"Topi Fuller. The guys here, they like to call me, Rowdy."

"Meyers will fix me? Tell you a secret; I am not afraid of him. He is afraid of me."

Nine-year-old Quinn spoke, his voice trembled, and his eyes grew wider. "Uh, fellas."

Chester poked Quinn in the side with his elbow and pushed him away. "Quiet. I can manage this guy."

"Stop, Chester. So, you can handle me? By doing what?"

"I got my ways. I can deal with you."

"Are you threatening me? Chief Meyers does not like children to threaten his Marines. Any of you ever meet him?"

Quinn kicked a small pebble while the other boys whispered to each other.

Roger shrugged his shoulders and stared up at the sky. "People say he is all alone in an abandoned bus depot on Smith Lake."

Chester thumped himself on his chest. "No, he doesn't. He stays in an old fishing boat up in Guntersville, where he goes fishin.' Enjoys fishin' for Buffalo. My granddad says Meyers is a damn river liver. Cuz, I saw him."

Rowdy sniffed phlegm from his throat and spat on the sidewalk. "No, Fort Rucker."

Chester rolled his eyes. "Fort Rucker is a Navy base. Meyers is in the Coast Guard."

Quinn tugged on the collar of his T-shirt. "Cripes, guys. Fort Rucker is an Army Base; this guy is a general in the Marines. See his cap with five stars. Uh, fellas. We are Charlie Foxtrot up to our necks. You got no idea who you are talkin' to."

"Ahem, does your father approve of how you talk?"

Rowdy ignored Quinn and continued his taunts. "Meyers is a pushover."

Horace gave the boy a half smile. "How can you be so sure if you never met him? He can be cruel if he chooses to be."

Rowdy stood on his toes, puffing out his cheeks. "Phooey, you got mustard in your shoes. You are jest tryin' to scare us."

"May I beg your pardon? Customers are hungry. Whatever you decide, I'll agree to."

People stared out the window. Servers standing around the windows hurried to grab pots of chicory as the front door opened.

Ollie puffed out a breath of exasperation. "Boys."

The older boys poked each other in the ribs. "Let's jump him. He can't take on us all."

Quinn waved his hands. "Not me. Rowdy, I am telling you we

are in bad trouble."

"He is correct; you are making a grave mistake, gentlemen. This device will slam you flat on your faces if you try to run."

Rowdy's eyes narrowed as he pushed out his lower lip. "Hey, you can't threaten us."

Horace straightened himself, raising his voice. "I'm done trying to reason with you boys. Sit down on this curb. Now."

The boys dropped to the curb, resuming their taunt. "You are a de-spot."

"Despot. No, I am not. Quinton Michael Billings. Come here."

Rowdy nudged Chester. "This guy dealt with Quinn before. Wonder what he did?"

Quinn shuffled toward Horace. "Yes, sir."

"What will your father say after he picks you up from my office?"

He swallowed hard as he stared up at Horace. "What he says, while at your office, isn't what I'm worried about. Once he gets me home...my dad will make me apologize to Mr. Johansen. What else he will do...with me—I did nothing this bad before."

"How did you get off the base without setting off a security alert?"

"Am I in trouble?"

"You are. Better to tell me now before I find out. Quinn, how did you leave?"

"The base taxi requested where I wanted to go. So..."

"How many times did you do this?"

"You don't want to know."

"Tell me."

"I lost count. I went got the guys and—"

Horace stood and rubbed his forehead. "Quinn, sit."

"How come he knows you?"

"Dad is a Marine, and this guy's wife is our cousin."

The first van pulled up; a security agent exited the driver's door and saluted. "General Meyers, sir."

The boys clutched their stomachs. "Are they bluffing us about him being the...? Last week one in California shot three ten-year-old boys 'cause they called him stinky face."

Quinn jumped to his feet to face his friends. "I tried to tell you Charlie Sierras, but you didn't pay attention."

"You fetched us here in the taxi with a golden globe."

"Young man. Sit."

"Aye, sir."

A black-haired boy, Roger, with bright-blue eyes, pointed at Topi. "I never heard of him doing anything mean to children. Once Rowdy's pop speaks to him, he won't be bothering us anymore."

Topi gazed at his feet. "Pop met him a long time ago, made up the story to scare him. I hope he doesn't throw us in prison or kill us or somethin'."

Roger gnawed on his fingernails. "Nothin' scares him."

"Gentlemen get in the van; you will go downtown to wait for your parents."

Horace drove behind the security vans as escort drones flew above. He called Dakota and left her a message. "In late, honey. Arrested a group of boys for extorting Ollie. Love you."

Rowdy and Roger lingered behind the rest. Horace nudged them forward. "Keep moving." The boys crept into the office lobby, poking each other in the ribs. "Sit here, boys. Stay with them and escort them to use the head. Bring the lads in by the parent arrivals. You contacted the parents?"

"Yes, sir. They're on their way, except for Roger Pearson. His parents insisted you keep him. They demanded signing papers to relinquish their custody, almost desperate to do so."

"In my office getting the administrative work ready for the proceedings."

Half an hour passed before the first parent arrived. A sergeant knocked on the door.

"Enter."

"Sir. Lane and Chandler, parents of Topi Fuller, are here."

Horace stood to direct the three to chairs at his desk. "Did the sergeant tell you why I summoned you here?"

Lane wrung his hands. "Our son is well-mannered. No one

complained about Topi's behavior before; he got in with the wrong bunch. The Billings boy is nothing but trouble."

Chandler fidgeted with a three-ring chain. "We don't understand how he got mixed up in this. Rowdy is an honor student at his school."

"Topi claims we are friends. Have we met before, Mr. Fuller?"

"I am a transgender-trisexual. I prefer Mix Fuller."

Horace leaned his head to one side and evaluated the round-faced man. *Pupils are dilated and uneven. An unhealthy sign. What is best for the child is essential.* "Mix Fuller, a response."

"I used a biogenerated uterus to give birth to Topi. Lane is Topi's natural father."

"Where did we meet before?"

"Uh, once at the dedicating of Sapros Towers, we shook hands."

"Hmm, so many people. I'm sorry I failed to recognize you. You must be the person who spilled punch all over my brand-new dress blue uniform?"

His hands waved like a woman trying to dry her fingernails. "Oh no. Not me."

He snapped his fingers. "You altered your appearance. Now I remember at the reception. You dumped sparkling grape juice on me. No worries, the stains came out. Now, to the matter before us; your son stated I needed repair, which you could resolve. Someone with my status would not ignore such threats, regardless uttered from a younger child or not."

Horace thought about his options on how to deal with Topi. *Offer a chance to straighten his life, confine the boy to prison, or take him as a rescue.* "Now, about his priors. Wish to rephrase your statement? I'd rather not report you gave misleading information."

Lane's shoulders drooped. "Rowdy is more than a handful; give him as much freedom as possible and still can't manage him. Despite our attempts, he demands more. We are followers of Sapros's book *In the Spirit of Child-Rearing*. The behavior gets worse."

"Should you continue to follow Aston's advice, your struggle will escalate."

"Our goal is to put him in the Salsa School of the Arts, where he will receive an education and develop his talents. Can't afford the fees."

Perhaps this will solve the dilemma. Base rescue without the legal hassle. "Spring Tree Music Academy or prison. I will provide you with a voucher for his tuition, boarding, meals, including supplies. You are responsible for covering the rest of Topi's costs. My strongest recommendation."

Horace typed out the order and handed the tablet first to Lane and then to Chandler. "Sign here. The base bus will pick up your son in the morning at zero eight hundred hours sharp. Here is a list of items he is not to bring with him. The school will confiscate any contraband."

"We are grateful."

"The academy will report his progress. Make sure Rowdy understands he is not to disappoint me."

Twenty minutes later, Lieutenant Colonel Michael Billings and Quinn came into the office.

Mike saluted. "Sir."

"Please sit, Lieutenant Colonel Billings, young man."

"Sir, I understand my son got involved in criminal activity this afternoon." Mike sat erect with the palms on his legs.

"Do you prefer to tell your father what happened, or shall I?"

"No, sir, he should find out from me."

Mike thumped his hand on his thigh. "Explain."

"Dad, me and the guys went to Little Norway and threatened to break windows if Ollie didn't give us food. We've done this before; we got caught this time."

"After we arrive home, you realize what will happen, don't you?"

Quinn stared at the floor.

"Look me in the eyes when I am talking to you. Now answer so I can hear you."

"Yes, sir, I do."

"Quinn, you are leaving out a detail."

"What else did you do?"

"Dad, I took the base taxi to pick up the guys and take us there. I did this several times."

"First, apologize to Chief Meyers for using up costly resources, including his time. Also, to Mr. Johansen for your conduct. You're too young to find a job to make restitution for your extortion. I will pay for the food you and the other boys stole from him. I'll find a way for you to work off your debt."

"Sorry, sir. I promise to repay you for misusing important time and resources."

"Start by cleaning out all the Charlie Sierra in the chicken pens and not use the term again."

The boy's eyes grew wider. "Aye, sir."

Roger slouched in an office seat for two hours while he tore holes in the upholstery. Horace towered over him.

"Sit up straight. Why did your parents not want to come and take you home?"

"My mom and dad say I cause too much trouble. Next time whoever caught me keeps me. Guess you bein' the security chief an' all kinda got 'em scared."

"So, what should I do with you?"

Roger shrugged. "Dunno. Got no place to go. Put me back where you got me. Been livin' by cheatin' an' stealin' anyways."

"Irresponsible for me to release you back, acting like a coydog. No stealing from anyone."

Horace voiced a number into the holophone. "Colonel, how many beds are available at the Soteria House?"

"Sir, two for girls, one for a boy. How many need a place?"

"One. Roger. His parents relinquished custody. Would you—"

"We can take him, sir. Is Roger sitting on the couch?"

"Yes."

"How old is he?"

"Seven."

"Sir, he is too young for the rescue house. Do you want me to take him to my home where I will give him proper supervision?

Roger, do you want to live with my wife and me? Beats existing like a coydog."

"Sure, I guess. Must I help with cleanin' the house an' all?"

"We call this part of staying in a family home."

"Guess so, but don't boss me 'round none. Nobody bosses me."

"Roger, we will discuss the rules at my house. Disobey them and find out what happens when you do not follow instructions."

"Yeah, what if I refuse?" Roger asked, rolling his eyes.

"Oh, a hooligan."

Roger averted his eyes to avoid an exchange with either man. "So. What're gonna do? I'm a what?"

"Young man, opportunities to straighten out your life don't come often to children your age. We expect success. Don't let yourself down; we will not go easy on you."

Roger stuck his tongue out at him. "So, what? My mom and dad or whatever they call themselves or whoever they share the bedroom with always made threats. Gonna do this or something, blah blah blah."

"I need to finish this work before going home. You, in the meantime, sit right here and write, *I will obey all the rules*, until time for us to leave."

Roger traced his finger along the tabletop. "I never learned how."

"Do you read?"

"No."

"You better not be lying."

He remained quiet and shrugged.

Horace leaned his head back. *Roger is a challenge*. "All right, go to the corner and shove your nose to the wall. Stay put until I say time to go. You are not to so much as to peek at me. Now go."

CHAPTER 7

Later that afternoon, Horace drove down the driveway in Dakota's blue SUV. Solar-panel paint on the roof peeled from the twenty-two-year-old vehicle. "So much fun driving back and forth to Birmingham today. God blessed us with plenty of sunshine. Energy gauge shows half of the power used sitting in the garage."

The guards saluted and opened the gate as the SUV exited and headed to the highway. "Head to where the old Vulcan stood. Since Sapros renamed so many streets and buildings, finding things is difficult."

"I remember my dad taking me there before Randall dismantled the Vulcan and erected the statue in honor of his late father."

"My grandparents told about the turn of the century; attitudes changed. Politics went wild—so much violence between the political parties. Aston Sapros, a third-party candidate, came along, promising greater power...more authority for himself."

Dakota stared out the window and traced the armrest with her hand. "Vote-buying encouraged vicious attacks on people not supporting Sapros. Fear of being discovered kept many from voting. An open election for everyone, a citizen or not, didn't matter."

"Dad told me people protested but did nothing to persuade change. Sapros ordered their arrest and charged them with sedition. Everywhere, streets, buildings, schools, everything is now Sapros.

People didn't understand what happened until too late."

Horace's jaw muscles tightened as he wondered why people would vote away something so precious as freedom.

"Did Spence get Roger settled over the weekend?"

"The two battled a while, with Spence winning out. Roger scrubbing the sidewalks this morning should give him the idea he should comply with the rules. He scours out the chicken coops on the west side this afternoon while Quinn works on the other side."

He rubbed his lower lip with his fingers. "Stubborn little scamp. He is much younger than the others; I worry the teens will torment Roger. Instructors are reminding students of the rules against bullying."

She tugged on a loose string hanging from the sun visor. "Roger can't read anything? How on earth did he manage in school?"

"Don't pull on the thread. What do you think is holding the vehicle together? Roger didn't like school. Current laws don't require a parent to enroll children if the child doesn't want to go. He can't read sight words at the lowest level or identify any letters of the alphabet or count to five. Nothing."

"Mike came down hard on Quinn?"

"Not as much as Nadine did. She applied tough love to where he will remember. Mike took him to apologize to Ollie. Spence and Mike are keeping the boys separated for now. Until they earn my trust."

Horace tapped on the horn. "Something else is broken. Air conditioner works in the winter and the heater in the summer. Windows stuck in the halfway down. The all-essential espresso maker we thought we couldn't live without no longer dispenses. Driverless navigation is useless. Seats quit in my long-leg position, so now you can't drive your car. News scanner refuses to scan. From the appearance of the back seat, we keep two pet lions. We are unable to use the SpeedTubes since the compatibility system crashed during an update ten years ago. Five-hundred twenty-two thousand miles and runs like a dream, a bad one. How can I give up this baby?"

"Yes, you can't let go."

"I delivered Justin in this car and did an outstanding job helping you bring our son into the world. You ought to be proud of me; I didn't pass out when your water broke, baptizing me in amniotic fluid."

"Do I detect a smidgeon of hyperbole?"

"You didn't sit in the splash zone."

"Try pushing an eight-pound baby out of your body."

"As I recall, you reminded me during each contraction. The expression on your face, your cry of joy as I placed Justin in your arms for the first time. Not a neonatal nurse. Our little red-faced boy waved his tiny fists, crying at maximum decibels. God blessed us with a son for getting our marriage back together."

Tears of happiness ran down Dakota's cheeks as she remembered examining Justin's face, hearing him cry for the first time. "A memory I will never forget. I wouldn't exchange what made us late for the world. Funny now, I can't remember what happened. Somehow, you were the reason we did not reach the birthing center in time."

"Storage drive recalls, you couldn't find your purse."

"Oh no. You placed my tote in the security jeep your dad took to visit friends."

She scanned the radio and found a news station announcing Gifford Sapros's trip to Los Angeles, for his anniversary celebration, at the home of Deputy Security Chief Zeke Culpepper. Weather updates, warmer over the weekend, possibility of showers, turning colder by the beginning of the week. In sports, Dancing Spirit won the tenth running of the ostriches in Talladega.

"Waited two hours for him to return so I could retrieve the passkey to the birthing suite."

"You said you forgot."

"Need to keep something over on you, Five-Star."

He slowed as he made the turn into Sapros Park; the aging vehicle protested the climb up Red Mountain. The engine moaned, the brakes squeaked as they bounced along the asphalt road filled with potholes.

"Take the access road past the deserted television stations."

Dust rose as they bumped down the rutted, tree-lined road. Four rows of wooden storage sheds with broken windows lined the street. Tiny flecks of peeling blue, white, yellow, and gray paint hinted at the number of coats on the makeshift houses. Charred remains of three outbuildings, two more with the rooftops collapsed, emphasized the hardships of the people.

Rusty metal roofs, broken picture-frame windows with tattered terry-cloth curtains, doors either absent or hung on one hinge swayed in the breeze. Blue tarps replaced missing doors to keep out the damp elements, showing signs the residents tried to make repairs on their homes to the best of their ability. Pieces of crumbling faux-brick tumbled from chimneys.

A small, thin girl, no more than three, hid behind the corner of a house. Muddy, tangled hair dangled over her pale face, hiding her intense brown eyes. She was dressed in a tattered, mud-stained man's shirt shortened to hang below her knees; a narrow yellow nylon cord created a belt. The child peeked around the corner of a house, gazing at Horace. She stretched out her hand, exposing a tattoo of a Chimera on her wrist while holding a picture frame about the size of a saltine cracker containing a tiny photograph of a couple who appeared to be the child's parents.

A woman's voice caused the girl to jump. "Missy, back in this shelter now." She ran away to the rear of the shed with missing doors and broken windows.

Dakota pointed to other houses farther down the road all in the same derelict condition. Horace suppressed a gag and covered his nose with his hand as an odor of ammonia and feces drifted from the makeshift outhouses, causing his eyes to burn.

The subdued stillness gave an eerie sensation, no cheerful noise of youngsters at play. Barefoot children, their clothing tattered and dirty, walked toward the sheds, emptying burlap bags in a four-gallon iron kettle.

Blue jays warning others of danger disturbed the silence. Ramshackle houses bore a striking similarity to photographs of suffering in Hoover Camps over 140 years ago. Women gathered in front of a shed whispering.

A man in his late fifties, with brown hair streaked with gray and pulled back into a ponytail, came out of the first house. He was clad in a crimson sweatshirt with a white script *A* on the front and faded blue jeans with holes in the knees. "What y'all want around here? We ain't got nothin' to give. Nobody here got nothin' for sightseers."

The man waved his arm at the neglected bronze statue. "Ya came to visit the Vulcan? Gone. Aston Sapros up on his golden pedestal is in bad need of repair. A hole in his chest and a fittin' crack in his rusty behind. Folks say when the wind blows right, the thunderous rumble of farting causes our houses to vibrate. Sets the kids giggling once the old moose starts callin' for a mate. 'Bout all the irritating old toot whistle is useful for anyhow."

Horace swayed and made sounds in his throat. *Don't start laughing*, he thought as he struggled to control himself.

Dakota took hold of Horace's arm. "We got lost trying to find the old trails and found this place —"

"You what? Snoopin' around here? Y'all part of Sapros's government? We ain't feared of him. Ain't scared of Meyers, either. We got no use for him. Round us all up, ship us to Kaegogi Farms. Lucky for us, we are too bony to be of any worth. All we are useful for is the recycle bin."

"Why would he send you to this place?" Horace held his palm out to the man.

"You are investigatin', or somethin'—" The man's eyes shifted as the sound of a truck rumbled up the road.

Ollie parked next to the SUV, rolled the door open, and lowered the lift. "Mind givin' me a hand, mister? This is a touch burdensome."

"Glad to."

The platform rose to level itself to the bed. "What you doin' here?"

"My wife wanted me to visit this place. The poverty is appalling."

"Ducked yar head. Big rascal, aren't you? How tall are you?" He put one of the twelve-quart navy-blue enamel soup kettles on the platform.

"I will move the next two over. Six ten. The doctor said I'm short for my age."

"Huh?" Ollie bent his head back. "Short?"

"My dad tells everyone who asks about my height, saying, 'Horace is short for his age.' He enjoys watching people's reaction."

The people appeared gaunt, wearing dirty old clothing and duct-taped shoes. Women stood in line, balancing empty mixing bowls and toddlers on their hips. Ollie ladled the hot soup and handed pumpernickel bread to the head of each family. "Sorry, no more left."

Justin relaxed on the leather couch, plopping his feet on the white marble Victorian coffee table. "I'm exhausted."

"Feet off the table. So, how did your first day go?"

"Tried bosintang. Somewhat filling. Ever tasted the soup?"

"Once, in Seoul, Korea, at a joint military meeting with government officials. At times you must eat different cuisines as they believe you dishonor them by turning down a meal prepared at a vast expense to the host."

"Expensive? Why so cheap here?"

"Little demand. Majority of Americans find kaegogi distasteful... like eating a family pet. Did you gather anything of relevance requiring my attention?"

"Three female servers say you are 'scary hot.' Jaycee insists your smile almost made her faint. I'm honest. I told them, 'Hey, you're talking about my dad.'"

Horace tucked his lips together, and his shoulders shook. "Other than my being so scary hot, what do I need to know?"

"Other than a health inspection by Chatterjee, nothing worth your immediate attention. Aside from Ollie admitting he lied to you about checking IDs."

"Why?"

"Afraid they will starve, he takes the leftover soup to the banned each evening after the café closes. Ollie is open every day of the week, allowing he can provide them with food."

"Tell Mr. Johansen he will receive more provisions. Obsolete blankets, clothing, shoes, soap, cleaning supplies, rat traps...Find out what they might need. What do the children need? I saw a little girl; would she like a doll? Be vigilant; Brad broke his alert pen the other day. Did he buy a new one?"

Justin opened a Victorian-style glass case and removed a magazine. "I'll take a peep sneak to find out."

"Someone at the ghetto mentioned something strange. Animal proteins for human consumption fall under Chatterjee's authority. Can we find anything about the place? Be careful, belonged to my grandfather Wexler's mother.

"I will. The logo for Kaegogi Farms is on the meat containers. So, I suppose this is where the stuff comes from."

Horace hummed while he searched the Department of Health and Nutrition. "Scary hot, huh? Directives issued by Chatterjee. Kaegogi Farms—access denied? Why? Error code 163 DHN? Means what?"

Justin thumbed through the pages. "In the search section, repeat the code, might tell the reason for the denial. Uh, Marilyn Monroe and the Beatles—what made them unique?"

Horace pushed his reading glasses back into place. "My twentieth-century cultural history serving. Marilyn Monroe, a movie actor, rumored she committed adultery with the president at the time. The Beatles, popular musicians from England. Why do you ask?"

"Their photographs are in this. Articles about the one-year anniversary of the death of Marilyn and the Beatles' new hit song 'Please, Please Me.'"

Horace rubbed his nose with the back of his hand. "You do not possess the correct security rank to continue with this action. Contact IT if you need assistance. DHN enjoys irritating people in a bad mood. Like sticking needles into nostrils."

He called the connection number on his wrist phone and waited for a few moments. "Piper, this is General Horace Meyers, I need access to material on Kaegogi Farms—my security level is Alpha One. Yes, I can wait."

"Tum-de-tum-tum," he sang in a monotone voice. "Wonder what people did before being forced to listen to Sapros's Snappy Words of Wisdom? Yes, Deputy Director Westbury. How are you today? Fine, thank you. Need access to material on Kaegogi Farms. This must be a mistake; got an error code of one six three DHN." *This man's whiney voice is about to rattle my brains.* "The safety of the supreme commander is at stake." His raised voice caused Justin to glance up. "Why is a deputy director questioning a security chief, a five-star general of the Marine Corps. Nobody questions me, including my wife."

He bounced a wad of paper off his dad's head. "Better be glad Mom didn't hear you."

Horace pointed at the ball and the wastepaper basket, held up his hands with fingers spread to signal for ten pushups.

"Anything should happen to the leader of this nation, and I can trace the incident to Kaegogi Farms. I hold you responsible for obstruction. I am sure you don't want me to name you as a conspirator. No need to remind you what happens to government bureaucrats who turn against Gifford. Should I find evidence to make an arrest, I will tell Gifford of your unwavering dedication to avert disaster. Your help is much appreciated. You will receive an appreciation award. Thank you for your assistance.

At the last birthday party for Sapros, he salivated over the gold biplane cufflinks. I hope they are worth the intelligence received. You thought I ordered the pushups?"

"Didn't want to take any chances. Expensive compensation for someone as low-level as Westbury." Justin threw the wad of paper in the wastebasket and brushed his hands off on his slacks. "Wine from Côte de Nuits, France, would do. Must be at least ten bottles down in the cellar. Those cufflinks are one of a kind."

"Jockeying for favoritism, his egotistical ambitions will give me whatever I request."

A five-ping ring tone signaled a call from Health and Nutrition. "Westbury. You are indeed helpful."

"What did they say?"

He wiped his hand over his mustache. "I now hold full access to the Kaegogi Farms files, including the entire Health and Nutrition. Hmm, Westbury cannot grant the authority, only Chatterjee."

"What will you do?"

"For now, data on employees, hours of operation, products in, products out, the layout of the farms, budgets, anything I can find."

CHAPTER 8

Friday, September 29, 2079

Ariella sat cross-legged on a campus picnic table under an old oak tree with branches that hung inches above the ground. Twisted her hair around a pencil to form a bun. Her mouth moved as she read the required reading, *Rules for Pragmatic and Realistic Patriots*.

"You still study from real books?" he asked, shutting the book.

She stifled a cry of alarm as someone she recognized from class snatched the textbook from her. "Give back my—"

"Come with me."

"Please—"

He guided Ariella to an empty bench away from the Sapros Theater Complex. "Quiet."

Acorns under their feet popped as they stepped across the grassy area to a wooden seat.

"I apologize—I can't remember names. I beg you—"

He remained silent as four first-year students strolled by, playing with their gamepads. A junior, with holographic goggles focusing on his adventure, bumped into a professor as she dropped her tote. A thin older man with a charcoal sweater and plaid bow tie flaunted his doctoral Tam with three gold diagonal bars signifying his distinguished doctorate in Saprosism.

"I—I tried, *hicc*, reading, *hicc*, I attempted. Darn it, *hicc*, I can't stop."

"Think about a dead dried-up frog. A cure my grandfather swears by. Works sometimes." The young man placing his index finger on his lips and took a small metallic mechanism from the pocket of his slacks. He took hold of Ariella's arm, guiding her to another spot.

"We can talk here. You take a big risk studying the Tanaka, out where anyone can catch you. Expulsion would be the least of your worries. One of those security drones can focus on what you are reading; you won't be aware those things are around. Are you trying to trap someone for a suggested class project?"

The color drained from Ariella's face; her lower lip trembled.

"I see."

"Please, you wouldn't understand."

"Are you Jewish?"

Her lips quivered. "Messianic."

"No need to worry; you are safe. Study Greek; none of the professors on campus bother with the ancient language anymore."

"You read Hebrew?"

"You are reading from Isaiah, or Yesha'Yahu, if you prefer."

"What did you put in your pocket?"

He gathered a handful of acorns and tossed them to a pair of squirrels. They scampered away to an oak tree to scold him for severe errors in social graces.

"Surveillance detection device helps to find a secure location to talk."

"The other spot?"

"Not a discreet area to talk; before you ask, the second place also unsafe. I am sorry—I didn't introduce myself. My name is Justin Meyers and yours?"

"Ariella Stein. We are in Denson's Sapros Theoretical Ethics class; you sit in the next row."

He tossed more acorns to the jabbering squirrels. A blue

jay landed nearby, picked one up, and flew off, stealing a prized possession.

"I mistook you for being studious, studying bootlegged drivel by Aston Sapros."

"Plagiarized?"

"My grandfather owns an original copy; Aston Sapros didn't write the book—written by a guy named Alinsky or somebody."

"Alinsky? I never read any of his literature."

"Not surprised. My parents considered public school instruction as inferior; so, they educated me. Dad instructed me in Greek, Hebrew, the Bible, and math. Hired teachers taught me science and other subjects. Uh. I didn't mean your education is subpar."

"How did Dad the teacher fly?"

"Patient, willing to work hard with me, and expects me always to do my best. He doesn't let me goof off."

"Sounds like a wonderful Dad. What do your parents do?"

"Employed by the government."

"In what capacity?"

Justin dropped the remaining acorns and brushed off his hands. "Nothing important. At least not to me. Dad and Mom in security. While my grandfather flies around trying to persuade other countries to buy cheap electronic gizmos." *Not the full truth*, he thought; *however, this version will do*.

He handed back the Tanaka. "Be careful. My next class is in ten minutes, afterward to my job. Can we talk after our next Saprosism class over a mug of chicory?"

Ariella strode back to the Sapros Theater Complex and turned. "Mine made sure I got a first-rate education. *Hellēnisti ginōskeis*?"

"Well, well, *Nai*. Yes, I do speak Greek."

"Next time in class."

Horace twisted in the wicker chair against the back wall of the café, nodding to people who entered the restaurant. Justin approached the table. "Today's chipped-plate special is the egg salad sandwich, chips, and a bowl of vegetable soup for sixteen credits."

"Fit for consumption?"

"The horseradish chips are potent today."

"Did the inspectors come in yesterday?"

"I am delighted to say they found everything in compliance."

"Perfect. Yes, the egg salad sandwich, hold the chips. Is Mr. Johansen here? You told him you needed time off for your assignment?" Horace asked. He grumbled, placing the menu in the empty condiment stand. *What did he do with the items sent to him?*

"Yes, he wants to chat with you, I will tell him you are here."

"Which server said I am scary hot?"

"Jaycee, next to the chicory pots with the waist-length cyan-cranberry-and-gold

waterfall-style hair. Why?"

"Ask the young woman to come here for a moment. Rooster tail?"

"Dad. Rooster tails hair is dyed bright yellow and green and is pulled back above the head and droops like as the name says. Sometimes the stylist weaves little cages into the hair with live yellow finches. Waterfalls are similar with little bubble water balls woven in instead, containing blue or green fish. What will you say to Jaycee?"

"Nothing. Ask Jaycee to come to my table for a moment."

"Justin told me...you wanted to...speak to me?"

"Yes, I did. Your hairstyle is most becoming."

"Oh my."

Startled customers glanced toward the serving area. "He is an Adonis. His smile turns me into gelatin."

Horace shrugged. "Teenage girls."

"Dad, what did you do to her? She is sitting on the floor repeating, 'He spoke to me.'"

A loud crash of dishes falling on the floor caused everyone to jump.

Justin bolted away without excusing himself. "A hunch... Jaycee—"

Jaycee's voice drifted from the back. "Ollie, I'm clumsy today."

"You better keep your mind on what yar doin'. You can't be actin' silly every time the SC comes in here. Those smashed dishes are comin' outta your pay voucher."

Five minutes later, Ollie placed the sandwich on the table. "Appreciate allowin' me to speak with you."

"Do not be so hard on Jaycee; put the replacement cost of the broken plates on my tab. She dropped those plates because I teased her. Now, what would you want to talk to me about?"

"First, my gratitude for all those provisions for the Red Mountain community. The expression on their faces would melt your heart. After handin' little Missy a doll, I saw her smile for the first time. Everybody kept askin' who is their angel; many of them dislike security chiefs, so I thought you'd prefer to remain anonymous. Wish you seen the children laughin' an' playin'."

"Whatever else I can do for them."

His breath labored, and his hands trembled. "Need to tell you somethin' about the rat traps. They trap rats for sure. The people are so starved they resorted to roastin' the rodents for dinner. Despite what I take to them, they are still hungry."

Horace stroked his mustache. "May I call you Ollie?"

"Please do."

"Ollie, bring your truck over to Camp Sumiton, gate five. The guard expects you, and she will direct you. Your truck can transport enough food for these people so they won't need to trap...to survive. Why didn't you tell me they are eating rats?"

"After I gave them the traps, they told me. Children are happy they don't hunt rat nests anymore."

He rubbed his face. "Tell them, Jesus heard their cries and told one of his servants to tend to their needs. Must not claim any credit on myself but give my thanks to the Lord for he gave me an opportunity to share what he bestowed upon me."

"How do you manage to do everything?"

"I requested the Lord put me in positions to bring him glory, sharing the blessings given to me. With the help of the Holy Spirit, he enables me to lead others to Christ. The more I prayed, the more the Lord responded to my prayers. Second in command gives me access to storehouses filled to the brim with items that otherwise remain in storage to rot. I buy the necessities and distribute them to the needy."

"You're different from other governmental people. After I read your message on the business card, no one can be sure if someone is trying to entrap them. Pray hard for this government. Pardon me; I shouldn't be discussin' this with you."

"Red Mountain is a greater dilemma. What I'm about to say is not easy; safety will not continue for you or the community. Gifford wants me to arrest somebody on bogus charges. I can delay him a while; the best I can do is buy those people time. Hesitate too much, Gifford will order his thugs from Philadelphia to remedy the matter."

His eyes followed a Hispanic family as they took their seats and bowed their heads in prayer. "Those people next to the window—I will pay their bill. No one prays while I sit in an eating establishment. Sad, so many people believe I'm their enemy. Don't tell them who paid their bill; your best dessert is on me."

"Yes. You were sayin'?"

"Without notice, Gifford sends his people, inflicting devastation. How many on Red Mountain?"

Ollie rubbed his head. "Countin' the kids an' all, must be 'bout thirty people."

"This will take precise prearranging. Be aware—I am putting my life on the line. You understand if we don't manage this with meticulous precision to the last detail—"

"Of course."

"What about your family?"

"No, they, uh, they—"

"I won't make you discuss something painful. This may take four or five days to plan. To make Gifford happy, an appearance of harsh action is necessary."

CHAPTER 9

Meanwhile, Ariella dismounted her cycle and hung her helmet on the handlebar. At the door, she touched the mezuzah, kissed her fingers and whispered a prayer. She placed her thumb on the scanner to enter the house.

"Abba?"

A thin middle-aged bearded man wearing a blue kippah with an embroidered gold Star of David and a tallit draped over his shoulders greeted her with a hug. He pushed his round black-rimmed glasses back into place. "You are home early, my bat."

She fumbled with a ribbon on her lap. "I didn't stop by the library today. I met someone in class." Ariella wrung her hands. "He caught me reading the Tanaka. The guy reads Hebrew and is fluent in Koine Greek. He warned not to bring the book out in public. I am sorry for being careless. He carries a T-35."

Eliyahu took off his glasses. "He didn't turn you in—a blessing. Is he aware you are a T-35 trainer?"

The color drained from her face. "No, Abba, I inquired as to what he held in his hand. He replied the object would help us find a safe place to talk. I didn't tell him you sold the bargain gizmos to the American military."

She patted the bench for Eliyahu to sit next to her. "His grandfather is alleged to push cut-rate widgets to other countries and tries to convince them to peddle theirs to us."

"Ah, appears the young man uses my cheap contraption well. For now, apart from an emergency, you are not to tell what telepathic commands the T-35 follows."

"Yes, Abba."

"Your director called this morning, asking for you to call him. Will he want you to report to him in Jerusalem during the winter break? What if duty extends over Hanukkah?"

"My job is demanding; duty to God and Israel comes first. Why don't you and Ima go with me? We can celebrate Hanukkah."

Eliyahu rose from his seat. "Perhaps, now, my bat, your Ima will be home soon; hurry to help me prepare."

"Let me call the director to find out what's going on. This conversation should keep me for two or three minutes. I'll be in the other room."

Fresh roses and Shabbat candles sat beside a bowl of fruit. A warm loaf of challah bread covered with a blue cloth with words in Hebrew, *Remember the Shabbat*, sat next to the fruit. Silver grape-patterned wine goblets placed next to the gold-trimmed white porcelain plates completed the Shabbat setting. Eliyahu nodded his approval.

Ariella came out of the den with slow, measured steps into the dining room. "I'm sorry—I leave for Jerusalem right after Shabbat; I return for class on Tuesday afternoon. My commander gave me an assignment."

"What is troubling you, my bat?"

"Ima is home now; we must not discuss work during Shabbat."

TUESDAY, OCTOBER 3, 2079

The security chief's office sat on the top floor of the forty-story Sapros Defense building. Horace read over arrest affidavits from the weekend. *One hundred homicides, ninety-five auto thefts, two armed robberies at the same food services facility on the same day. Eight sexual batteries and fifteen church services.* He sipped on a cup of coffee. "Spence. Do any of these detentions require my attention?"

"Only the two pastors arrested last night in Georgia. Security transported them here; they are ready for you to interrogate them. Both men visited us twice before, sir."

"Bring them in. I'd rather contend with murderers than pastors. Murders know what I will do with them. Pastors assume what I will do."

"Gentlemen have a seat. Coffee while we talk? Real coffee."

The older man wore a jet-black toupee, which reminded him of a pile of black Spanish moss on top of a honeydew melon. Pastor Lucas Hustad slapped his fingers on the desk. "We will not allow your bullying to keep us from preaching the Word of God."

"Enlighten me. How did I persecute you? Last time you came to my office, I promised you my squads would not bother you. I did not persecute you in the past, nor now."

The lack of sleep and intense interrogation from the previous night exhausted the men. Unshaven and eyes bloodshot, the two men resembled street tenants rather than pastors. The younger one with a full head of curly brown hair pointed at Horace. "Not in person, but your Marines harasses us daily. Your people attended church Sunday morning in civilian attire. Took us into custody right after services concluded."

"Can you identify these people of mine? I gave a direct order to them not to disturb churches as they are the least of my troubles."

Horace flipped a lever; a wall panel opened, revealing the former living quarters of General Brinkman. "Please—go into my private lounge; make yourselves comfortable or browse around while I decide what to do with the both of you."

Lucas roamed around, viewing diplomas hanging on the moss-colored walls. "Stephen, this Meyers guy received a doctorate in theology and apologetics, doctorate in military management, master of divinity in military chaplaincy, master of divinity in biblical languages, and a bachelor of science in Christian leadership and management. I received a two-year diploma from the same university; wish Sapros allowed us to travel to New Liberty."

"Real books. I daydream of diving into books such as these. You can't find them anymore. Copyrights on these are long before 2060.

In this glass case, a first-edition book from Arthur Pink. *Gleanings from Paul.*"

"Gentlemen let us discuss your situation over lunch. Grab a plate, go to the buffet, and join me at the conference table."

"Impressive credentials. How did you end up here?"

"I will give you the shortened version. The Southern Baptist Convention ordained me after I earned my bachelor's degree and pastored a church for two years. After my first tour, I became a candidate for the chaplaincy, afterward going into the seminary full-time. Received my last doctorate two weeks before Sapros forbade travel to New Liberty to attend Christian universities. Gifford sought what would soothe my anger. Years before, he asked me how much power I would like. Held him to his promise, and he promoted me to a five-star general. Other than God, only Gifford outranks me."

"I assume you are a true man of God."

"What matters is how the Lord sees me."

"Are you filing criminal allegations against us?"

"I read the summary; my finding is you failed to produce proper authorization for a gathering. The investigators stated a neighbor accused you of conducting services. Therefore, no proof you violated the religious law—in simple terms, a permit violation. I am issuing you a written warning to obtain a license for a gathering. A birthday party, anniversary party, knitting groups, chili cook-off, or chicken-feather-plucking contest, anything. My inspection and approval are required. Now, listen, once I conclude my review, I will note no infringement of the law transpired throughout my investigation. Understand?"

"Do you mean we can continue services?"

"Gifford did not authorize me to allow this activity. I am stating if no obvious violations occurred during my inspection, I could not file any affidavits. My advice is to vary the day of the week, locality, and types of parties you conduct to help to reduce the number of meddlesome nosy neighbor stories."

Horace wrote a note on the back of his business card. "One word of instruction. On a chicken-plucking contest. Make sure half-naked chickens run around, should a surprise inspection take place."

"Worth remembering. You have been kind to us."

"Here is your warning. Read the document in full."

"This gift is more than generous."

"Notify me once you obtain your permit. Prepare for an inspection. My preference would be to a chili cook-off than seeing a bunch of butt-naked chickens squawking around."

Wednesday, October 4, 2079

Eliyahu's heart bled for his daughter as she dabbed her eyes with a tissue. "My bat, what is wrong?"

"I go back to Israel during the break. Did anybody call?"

"A young man named Justin. I told him you requested no disturbances while you studied. The young man must think this is all you do. About getting your project assignment Tuesday."

"We find out in the next class our assignments from the professor. Justin and I plan to band up together."

"Ah, you like this boy? Is this young man Messianic?"

"Yes, Abba, I like him; no, he is not Jewish or Messianic."

"Don't allow this relationship to grow out of hand. As the Torah says, 'You are not to plow with an ox and an ass together.'"

"Abba, I met the guy last week. You are behaving like we are getting married. Uh, which one am I? The ox or the ass?"

"My dear bat, a father cannot be too careful. As a young man, I found the prettiest woman in all Israel; her father probed me about my intentions the first time I came to her house. Ah. Not yet a yeled of sixteen. I stood like a bumbling fool, stammering about, a borrowed book in my hand."

"Sav Katz?"

"Mahar in criminal interrogations; when your mother caught her father talking to me, she came into his den rescuing me. Not funny at the time, but now...ah. Your mother later teased me about my expression reminding her of a yeled with crumbs all over his face after eating the last knish. Now I'm a father of a beautiful daughter;

I too will develop into mahar in interrogations."

"Abba. I am not planning to marry Justin, only work together on a college project."

"Today a college project, tomorrow—"

She tilted her head to the side in mock disapproval. "You sound like Savta Stein."

"An outstanding woman of wisdom, your savta. Do you plan to visit her while in Jerusalem?"

"Savta invited me to stay with her and Sav over Shabbat."

"I am glad; they always enjoy your visits."

"My commander advised me the relations between the US and Israel are becoming intense. Rumors are circulating Sapros may expel all Israelis."

Monday, October 9, 2079

Horace stood by his desk as he studied flashing images across multiple monitors from various sectors in the city. Automated trucks ditched merchandize in front of abandoned stores. People trampled each other to snatch up the goods before protection drones arrived to disperse the mob. Street hawkers beckoned to people to buy their high-in-demand black-market ware. Bibles or, for those with fewer credits, a page or two from the Scriptures. Ribbons, graphite pencils, handmade paper, and quilled pens items without traceable alert chips soon sold out.

Someone from an upper-level window dumped a chamber pot on a senior man as he walked on the street. Cyborg police officers chased children for stealing from vendors. So far, a routine day.

"Morning, Spence. What happened over the weekend?"

"Sir. The weekend reports from the quadrant sectors might displease you."

"Bad?" He read the memos from area officers across the quadrant. "This is wonderful. A cyborg officer shot a fleeing shoplifter who stole two packs of cornhusk cigarettes. Geez. Four hundred homicides, thirty-six suicides, thousands of armed robberies, one hundred two kidnappings of a child under the age of ten. Here is an improvement: only fifty arsons to abandoned buildings this weekend. What are the investigators doing? Oh, this explains everything. Nine hundred allegations of church services with captures."

Horace slung the tablet on his desk and slammed his fist into his hand. "Dammit! What is up with all the investigations of—How many times do I need to tell those skates to leave churches alone? Crime is up to the exosphere, which is where I'd like to punt those shirkers. All they do is chase easy takings, like toddlers scooping up pails of sand at the beach. Those district commanders are due here in forty-five minutes; they are about to face one fire-spitting general."

"Yes, sir."

"One more report from any of them, I will give their entire unit a big chicken dinner for disobeying a direct order. In the meantime, advise those skaters to cease all these so-called criminal church investigations at once; I do not mean five minutes from now."

"Aye, sir," Spence spoke into the conference holophone. "Papa is not a happy man. A hint to those willing to listen, you better move your butts here; furthermore, halt those church investigations. Papa is ready to go for hot."

The holophone rang with the symbol of a red-and-gold Chimera appearing on the holopad. "Dammit. Goofy Soup is calling."

"He calls to brighten your day."

"Geez, now what." He remained at attention, saluting. "Supreme Commander, I am honored to be of service to you today."

Gifford appeared, draped in a Greek-style white toga with a red cape, and gold laurel leaves resembling a crown sat on his bald head. A Chimera medallion on a pencil-thick gold chain hung above his midsection.

Gifford extended his right hand over his eyebrows. "Meyers. Congratulations on your efforts to reduce the crime rate in your quadrant. Despite increasing illegal church services and other abuses of the law. Meyers take an assignment. Are you familiar with a secret community of people on Red Mountain?"

"Yes, I am aware of a community surviving in extreme poverty near your grandfather's shrine; whether they are banned or not... What is the difficulty? They maintain rights to live somewhere, do they not, Supreme Commander?"

"What concern do the banned inhabiting somewhere matter? Those people existing somewhere is not the obstacle."

Horace stared into the holographic camera. "What is?"

"Someone is assisting them by distributing food." Gifford's face flushed into a deep crimson.

"Yes, an individual is helping the Red Mountain community; the law expresses one cannot sell or trade any materials to a banned person or persons in a business transaction. Part one is clear. Federal regulations do not include any person or persons who give away items without compensation, including deeds of charity. Without this clause, no one defied the law. Scrutinized those rumors myself. Yes, someone gave out a simple meal to the people. The community gave nothing since they own nothing of value to give. No violation of the law by either party."

"They will never realize the importance of paying me my rightful allegiance if people continue feeding them."

"To attain loyalty from people whose stomachs are empty is nearly impossible, considering they hold you responsible for their hunger."

Gifford struck the desk with his fist and pointed at Horace. "Do something before this gets out of hand. Send drones to do surveillance on Red Mountain; those rogues need dealing with."

"On what grounds?"

Gifford's face flushed; he exploded with several well-chosen expletives. "Make something up if you must; I don't give a rat's behind what charges you conjure up. Make blasted sure you do the job."

"I will explore further."

Gifford rasped for breath. "What about...Ollie's Little Norway? What is...going on?"

"One of my investigators is on a covert assignment; he advises on no unusual activity. Other than Ollie Johansen being short on supplies for his restaurant."

"Find something. I couldn't concern myself less with what you find. Find a one-day overdue library file. Uncover anything." Gifford's image disappeared from the holopad.

"Ahem. Gifford is in a pleasant mood this afternoon. Guess I should give him a gift for requesting my ever-so-loyal services. The Italian humidor with gold-leaf-wrapped cigars should do the trick. Any chance he will drop hot ashes on his toga, setting himself on fire? In the meantime, instruct him how to salute. He looks like he is trying to keep the sun out of his eyes."

Spence tossed his security fob in his hand. "Goofy Soup would change how the military salutes. Like everything else he changed."

"Crazy bird-sniffing—no count—pond-scum skimmer."

"General, such language."

Horace shuffled through his desk drawer, mumbling inaudible comments, and found a purple-head-shaped stress reliever toy having an uncanny similarity to Gifford. He squeezed the ball in his palm until the head screamed, "Ouch."

"Ready, Mr. Goofy Soup?" Horace's jaw ached as he clenched his teeth and threw the head across the room.

The head hit the wall and bounced on the floor and squeaked out the words, "Ow—Ouch—Ow—Ouch."

Someone banged three times on the office door.

"Enter."

A female private marched to his desk, saluting. "General Meyers, sir. An envelope came for you."

"How long since you graduated from recruit training, Private?"

"Three weeks. My first assignment, sir."

"You need not pound on the hatch; a simple knock will do."

She picked up the head to return to Horace. "Aye, sir. Bought one resembling my former DI."

"Thank you, Private."

Horace slit the envelope open. Photographs tumbled out, as did a written report on Kaegogi Farms. Violations were unaddressed by the administrators in charge of the facility. Breaches in procedures included dog pens often left unsecured, no guard posted at the gates, unauthorized personnel allowed access to the breeding sites, animals unaccounted for, plus malnourished dogs wandering loose on the property. Unsanitary conditions in the kennels, refrigeration, and research labs. Other infractions included allowing undocumented workers into the feed preparation rooms, including nonoperational identification thumbprint scans.

Memos from Chatterjee to Gifford stated she did not believe the mentioned breaches warranted an inspection by her office. Security investigations transferred to SC Meyers for his assessment, dated and signed April 26, 2072.

Horace swiped through supplementary electronic memos locating one sent to him from Chatterjee, dated April 28th, 2072:

To Security Chief Meyers,

Multiple security breaches require your attention, reference Kaegogi Farms. Consult attached copies of violations.

Should you need aid from my office in conducting your investigation, do not hesitate to call.

Signed, Nutrition Chief Manju Chatterjee, United States Navy, carbon copy to Supreme Commander Gifford Sapros. A small notation on the memo stated, *delivery failed*.

Horace drummed his fingers on his desk. "Now, I need someone to investigate the place without arousing suspicion. Who is available?"

The computer displayed available low-level personnel. "Koslov is on parental leave until March. Karppinen is on assignment in Japan until July. Dahn is also in Japan. Zuniga is transferring to Southwest Quadrant next week. After about a week out with them, I suspect she will come back. Zimmerman is finishing flight school. On vacation leave, Hastings and Carson. Finney broke both of his legs and is assigned to security monitoring. D'Angelo is available, although I do not trust him not to tip off the farms ahead of the investigation. Not low-level, Major Rios; if she did find something, she'd fill my office full of dogs and puppies—she is too soft-hearted." *Lord keep her from hardening her loving heart.*

"Spence."

"Sir."

"How many people are waiting for the meeting?"

"All present. What do you intend to do?"

"Give them all a first-rate butt chewing they won't forget. Plus, rank pay reduction disciplinary action. Those brainless clucks better pray I won't come down harder on them. Let's go."

Spence flung the door open. "Attention!"

Horace stood at the podium and glared at the saluting officers, waiting thirty seconds before returning their salutes.

"Take your seats. Did everyone enjoy the day off yesterday?"

"Yes, sir."

"Excellent. What progress are you making in lowering the number of burglaries, robberies, kidnappings, sexual assaults, and such?"

Second Lieutenant Beckfield from the Nashville district stood. "Sir, we are shorthanded; therefore, we cannot cover all the crimes."

"How many of your people are investigating churches?" Without looking up at the officer, he swiped through the electronic files.

"You ordered us not to poke around churches."

"Why did I receive eighty-five reports from your district this weekend, Second Lieutenant? Your approval is on these affidavits."

"Yes, sir. I accepted them. I did not order the investigation of churches."

"Why did you not order the investigators to use their energy elsewhere?"

"Poor judgment on my part."

"Did I give you a warning twice before? Second Lieutenant?"

"Yes, sir."

"Do you consider continuing to conduct church investigations after two warnings disobeying a direct order, Second Lieutenant?"

Sweat glistened on his forehead as he shifted his weight and took a breath. "Yes, sir."

"Can you give me any reasonable explanation why you defied my orders?"

Beckfield said, gritting his teeth, "None you might find acceptable."

"You may sit, Second Lieutenant."

He slapped his palms on the podium. "After investigating the reports, each of you disobeyed my direct order. Did a three-star unload a bunch of Cat Nines on me? Dammit, I expect better out of my commissioned officers, or am I shooting at imaginary pigeons? The people we swore to protect deserve better than what we give them. To allow these crimes to escalate is a dereliction of duty. Your duties do not include harassing the religious."

Horace picked up a bottle of water and took a sip. "You must prevent people from committing acts of violent crime. By permitting them to skate on easy targets, you became part of the predicament. We took an oath to protect the citizens in this quadrant. Each of you realizes the seriousness of your foolhardiness, you will receive a reduction of one pay-grade, effective on your next pay voucher. Also, a written dressing down in your file. After one year, provided you do not commit any other infringements, you may petition me to remove the letter from your record. Any further violations occur, the offender will receive a one-month suspension of duty. A third offense, dismissal from the corps. Do you understand?

"Yes, sir."

"Dismissed."

Horace reentered his office, with Spence following. He pulled Mr. Goofy Soup from the drawer and slammed the ball against the wall. "Make sure those disciplinary action papers are in electronic courier. I am going out on patrol if nothing else to regain respect from the community."

"Sir, someone should go with you. Cyborg police officers go in pairs."

"Are you volunteering?"

"I guess I did, sir."

CHAPTER 10

Tuesday, October 10, 2079

"Listen up, class," Professor Thomas Denson said, elevating his voice over the din of the students' jabber. He grasped the podium with a tight grip on the motto "Promoting Better Citizens for the Supreme Commander."

Denson tapped a Victorian-style brass bell to gain the attention of the interns. "Pair up. Anyone without a partner, I'll place the extra person with a group. Anyone not paired with a coworker?"

"Excuse me. I need one, Professor."

"Jenkins will work with Meyers and Stein. Each group is assigned to a specified governmental agency."

The professor picked up a stack of papers. "Find out what you can about the organization, spending three weeks working on your assignments. The bureau director will assign each of you a different task. Each team will give a presentation on what you discovered from your experience."

Denson ambled down the rows of desks, distributing the assignments; his lorgnette glasses dangled on the end of his nose. "You're not to pull strings to switch your assignments, Mr. Meyers, Ms. Stein. You receive your projects from me, not SC Meyers or Ambassador Stein. I expect each of you to make an inspiring presentation. The university is offering you an opportunity of a lifetime, so don't squander your chance."

Justin opened the folded paper, whispering to the other two, "Fort Oglethorpe."

"Fort Oglethorpe?"

A pungent odor of raw onions caused Justin to choke when Silas rose from his seat. "An old Army post in Georgia opened over a century ago, near Chattanooga, Tennessee, and shut down after World War II. Other than the necessary knowledge, I have no idea. We report to this site first thing Sunday morning. Zero eight hundred hours. They will board us on a bus, taking us to a place called Camp Chickamauga, located in the former national park south of Oglethorpe. They will serve a full breakfast in the private dining hall. We will attend an orientation to pick up our work assignments. After lunch, a tour of the camp. A little over a two-hour drive if we take the interstate the entire way. Provided we don't run into traffic obstacles along the way," he said, sliding his foldable tablet back into his backpack.

Ariella bit her lower lip. "My father will worry about breaking Shabbat if we leave before dawn."

"Don't miss your beauty rest, cupcake."

"Able to get up. Don't cross me; you are qaton."

Silas wrapped his arms around himself. "I am so scared. What did you say?"

"Come on, you two. We need to work together on this, no more cupcake or qaton stuff."

"Let's go to the library to find out about the Chick camp. Sorry, man. Expected at a dentist appointment over in Hoover. Traffic on 280 is terrible. Can't stay."

"Yeah, yeah, go on. I'll be in touch with you when we go up," he called as Silas hurried out the door and jogged down the corridor. Justin held out his hands and waved them. "I hope he doesn't behave cocky the entire time."

"Ought to put him into a full nelson. You better believe I can."

"What's the matter? You act as if you are ready to explode."

"Something I need to manage."

"Anything I can help you with?"

Ariella gazed at a flock of Carolina wrens flying overhead and remembered the times she wished to escape. "How sweet of you, but no. My handling of this situation is a pleasure."

Electronic doors opened to the library. They dropped their tablets on a computer table. Justin sounded out each syllable into the search engine. "Camp Chickamauga. A federally sponsored camp with state-of-the-art academic preparation for meeting today's life challenges. Administrator Alice Cummings, instructors, support personnel, and so forth. Holophone number. Not a lot in the way of graphics—we need a layout of the facility. Here's the key dining room…Wooded trails. Last update on the site more than two years ago."

"Did the government close the camp down? Denson is testing us if we will make other arrangements. We are hunting for information; call them to find out what they say. Professor Denson, for unknown reasons, holds biases against our fathers."

Ariella tapped the number on her wristband phone. "It's ringing." She changed her earpiece, humming a tune playing while on hold. "Yes, this is Ariella Stein. I am a student at Sapros University Birmingham. Dr. Denson assigned three of us to Camp—What? Yeah, I can hold." After a five-minute wait: "Yes, correct, Ms. Stein. Yes, Mr. Meyers. Yes, Mr. Jenkins. Any idea what we will do once we arrive?"

Scribbled notes while she spoke to the person on the other end of the phone. "He is finding out from his supervisor about our assignments."

"Mr. Jenkins not yet assigned. Mr. Meyers will catch up backlog records."

Justin leaned back in the chair and grabbed the table to keep from toppling over.

She lifted her chin and poked him in the side with her pen. "What is the compliance force? Make sure residents complete their studies. Yes, attending Sunday morning."

The two exited the library, wandering to the parking deck. Ariella swung her leg over her cycle, waiting for Justin to say something.

"You're not happy with an early-morning start."

"No, I am not."

"Look. Hey, Silas, what about your dental appointment?"

Silas pressed his hand against his stomach. "Got canceled—the dentist got called away. Glad I didn't tangle with 280."

"Don't you live off 280?"

"North Lake Cove, but I'll wait here until after the rush hour."

"You have a long time to wait."

"My studies should keep me busy. Catch you Wednesday in class."

"He doesn't appear concerned much about the project," Justin said. "Always in a hurry about something."

"Let's go for a cup of chicory. Where can we find a decent cup?"

"The Chicory Pot."

"Not far. Hop on."

Ariella whizzed through the traffic, dodging exiting students. She stopped at a light. "We will find a place to talk. Got the gizmo doodad with you?"

A charcoal-gray-and-yellow traffic enforcement drone hovered over the intersection. With a sudden jerk to the right, the drone sped off chirping, detecting a vehicle running a red light.

"Doodad? I always keep the gizmo doodad on me." He held to the seat as Ariella's acceleration caused everything to whiz by in a blur. With chicory and creamers in a bag, the two sped off, searching for a safe place.

Justin tapped on her helmet and nodded to the three police officers. "These are all risky, three cyborgs with dogs. Let's not attract their attention. Wonder why the city allows three of them together; they aren't meeting for a chicory break. Incredible how human they appear."

"Did you see them laugh? Are you sure they are 'borgs?"

"Birmingham is cutting back on human officers; most of them are cyborgs. I understand laughing is a sign of central control databank failure."

"What does somebody do with a malfunctioning cyborg?"

"Might go to my place. My father is home; you will like him."

Wrought-iron gates swung open and allowed Ariella to enter; she slowed the cycle again, waiting for the garage door to open.

"Beautiful place."

"The manor is perfect for the Israeli ambassador."

"Eliyahu Stein?"

Ariella opened the door. "Abba, I brought a friend home with me."

Eliyahu clasped his hand in a firm handshake. "Ah, my bat, you are home. Justin Meyers how is your father?"

"He is doing well; thank you, sir, for inquiring."

"Abba, you met Justin?"

"Your father comes to my home on many occasions to discuss matters with my dad and grandfather."

"Yes, your grandfather negotiates with me to sell cheap gizmos from Israel."

"Uh, I didn't mean Israeli technology; they are the best of the best."

"So, Justin, why did my bat bring you here?"

"We need a safe place to talk, Abba."

"This is a safe place. All appliances came from Israel. No eavesdropping chips here, I can assure you. Anything I can do to help?" Eliyahu sat at the table, waving for them to join him.

"Abba, for an assignment for a class project, I report Sunday morning at eight. To arrive on time, we must leave ahead, before Shabbat ends."

"So, if you obey mitzvot, it will make you late to your assignment. To reach your appointment on time, you break mitzvot. Any other options, a transfer closer to home?"

"The camp is the closest one. The professor warned us not to change anything, or, as I quote the instructor, 'use our parents to pull strings, or rank, depending on your situation.'"

Justin sat back in his chair. "I might suggest a solution. My dad might—I am stressing the word *might*—allow the use of the helicopter to transport us, including our cycles, on time."

"What about Silas?"

"He made so much noise about going early, let him worry about himself. I need to go to work, so better take me back."

The pair rode back in silence; Ariella pulled up beside Justin's cycle. "Thanks for the lift." He found Silas's late-model cobalt Aston Ranger, with dark-tinted windows and a double spoiler on the rear trunk.

"Wonder why he hasn't gone home yet. Guess we should go talk to him."

Ariella shut off the cycle. "Why haven't you gone home?"

"I enjoy hanging around for a while. The weather is beautiful; I enjoy reading and getting away from people. Until classes let out, the parking lot can be the quietest place on campus. Provided the eavesdroppers don't come by, reminding me I am not to linger in one spot for longer than ten minutes, encouraging me to move elsewhere," Silas said, mimicking the drones. "You are in violation of campus code sixty-two–twenty-one, loitering after warning. The university will levy a penalty of twenty-five credits for lingering in the parking areas. Move to another place."

"Why don't you sit in your vehicle? More comfortable than standing. Heat signatures attract drones."

"Yes, I am aware what they can and cannot do. Scary, realizing what those objects do."

"Like what?"

"Not the ones here. Military-grade drones are…My vehicle is too cramped."

"No room to spread out to study?"

Stuffed his hands into his gray jacket and pursed his lips. "Yeah. Hey, when you depart for Fort Oglethorpe, do you mind giving me a lift?"

"I thought you'd drive your vehicle."

"A guy is installing a new custom spoiler; won't be ready until a week after the project is due."

"Well, we leave from Ariella's. So, I will pick you up at your house in Greystone and drive back north of Birmingham."

"Don't come over to the house. You can meet me here. Two-eighty is a terror to drive. I need to call the guy doing the installations here."

"So early in the morning? Roosters are still sleeping."

"Here come those annoying drones again. Hey, I'm leaving."

"I will call you before we arrive to pick you up."

Justin sat at the dining room table and stirred a bowl of lobster bisque. "Dad, are you familiar with a place called Camp Chickamauga in Georgia, south of Fort Oglethorpe? Two others work with me on the class project."

"The camp is a reeducation penal complex for dissenters. Your sister worked at one—you remember what happened to—"

"Yes, Mom."

"Encourage him to modify your assignment. Who is your professor?"

"Dad, Dr. Thomas Denson called Ambassador Stein and you by name, making sure parents are not to interfere."

"Must be trying to worm his way back into Gifford's malevolent kindness."

"One thing you can do to help with Ariella. We must leave before daylight Sunday; she breaks mitzvot if she goes before sunrise. Can Grandpa take us in the helicopter to Camp Chickamauga? Need to pick up from the university someone named Silas Jenkins. Will need a helo to transport cargo, ourselves, and two cycles."

"Tell Mr. Jenkins to wait at the Sapros Theater Complex parking lot in the helo area, and we will pick him up at zero six thirty hours. Ariella at zero six forty-five. Your grandfather and I will fly the three of you to your assignment."

"Where is Grandpa Andy?"

"He went to visit friends over in Greystone. He'll be back later."

CHAPTER 11

Sunday, October 15, 2079

Silas stood under a gazebo in the waiting area for the helicopter. A security drone with a flashing orange strobe approached and warned, "You are not to loiter around campus. Move to another location, or the university will penalize you twenty-five credits. Why are you here, Student Jenkins?"

"A helicopter will land soon to take me to another location." Silas stuck his hands in his empty pockets, searching for his Aston Ranger security fob.

"Name of the pilot?"

"Anderson Meyers."

"Stand by." The drone, shifting positions, sent signals. "Confirmed. Arrival time is two minutes."

The helicopter hovered over the parking lot for a moment and then landed on the helipad as Silas slung his backpack over his shoulder. A burgundy helicopter with a gold horizontal stripe with the emblem of the security chief on the door opened, with Justin waving for him to enter the craft.

"Thanks for the ride. This helicopter is huge."

Andy checked the gauges before the craft rose. "Our pleasure. Not the largest but fills the bill for what we need today."

"Silas, this is my dad, Horace Meyers, and my grandfather, Anderson Meyers. You can call my grandfather Andy, if you like; as for my dad, he prefers people refer to him as Security Chief, General Meyers, or sir."

"What people refer to me when they believe I can't hear them… is another matter."

Sunlight illuminated the sky as the helicopter rose into the air, turning northeast. Andy circled the tow truck; he changed directions and headed to the northwest. "Someone is getting their Aston Ranger repossessed. What a shame."

Silas placed his fingertips on the window. "Yeah, for sure."

"We land soon. Still, ample time to fly the three of you to Camp Chickamauga, unload the cycles, and chat before you report."

Justin held the door for Ariella, helping her secure her cycle into the cargo hold. She buckled herself in, placed on a headset, and waved to her father. "I'll be home in three weeks, Abba. Tell Ima I love her and will keep in touch."

"Sit back and enjoy the ride. The weather today at Camp Chickamauga, high today seventy-six with clear skies. Arrival time is about thirty minutes. Gives me pleasure to say to passengers who are not government executives or family sick of hearing weather advisories."

Andy gestured to a drone flying next to the helicopter. A speeding remote aircraft, with flashing green lights, darted in and out of the flight path. "Air traffic is heavy over here. Stupid RA vexes the last nerve in my soul, getting in the way. Traffic condition drones cause more glitches than they relieve."

The blades on the helicopter slowed to a stop. Justin pushed the door open to assist Ariella and Silas.

Andy pressed a lever, opening the back to allow removal of needed equipment. "Unload the cycles out of the back."

"Aye, sir."

Horace climbed out of the helicopter and reached into his jacket pocket. He held out a small burgundy box, "Silas, I wish to speak to you for a moment. Something for you to earn."

Inside the box lay a new security fob to a bright-red solar cycle with jet-black trim. "Sir, words fail me. You must be ragging me, an Aston Spider 332 SCX. I must be dreaming."

"Listen, Silas. This cycle is on loan. Now, hold out your right thumb; I am placing five hundred credits into a new account for you. You must straighten out your life. No more gambling, drinking, drugs, and whatever other reasons your parents kicked you out of their home. You lived on Red Mountain a short time. You can make something of yourself. Now, do you understand? One bad report comes in on you, the deal is off. I will take back the cycle; whatever credits you used, you will repay me. You do a first-rate job; the bike is yours to keep. Understand?"

"Yes, sir."

Justin pointed to a station nearby. "Requires a quick charge; plenty of stations around here."

They listened to the sound of sports whistles blasting away the relative silence. A recorded message over the loudspeaker blared. "Welcome to Camp Chickamauga, college interns. Breakfast is provided in the private dining hall at the Sapros Suite in about twenty minutes. Bring your identification and assignment tablets with you."

"Well, Dad, time to report. Thanks for bringing us, Grandpa Andy."

"Grateful. My father is passionate about Shabbat."

Silas ran his hand through his hair. "Thanks."

Horace shouted over the beating of the helicopter engine. "You better be moving; don't be late on your first day. Keep in touch with me, all three of you. Contact me if you need anything."

The three trod to the Sapros Suite, meeting a crowd of apprentices from a range of universities in the Southeast Quadrant. They chatted among themselves, pulling out expandable tablets from their belongings. At the podium, a tall, athletic woman, wearing an Aston University sweatshirt with matching shorts, stood four or five inches taller than the two men next to her. Director Jack Williams, still in his twenties, combed his moussed hair across the top of his head. His eyes narrowed as he leaned toward the other man, whispered, and the man nodded.

Dean of Internees Frederick Phillips wore his shirt tucked in, accenting his abdominal obesity. He smoothed his mustache with his fingers, anticipating for the woman to introduce herself to the students, and mouthed the words, "I'm fine."

"My name is Alice Cummings. I am the educational advisor here. Welcome to Camp Chickamauga. We hope your three weeks here is both educational and rewarding, assisting the campers in their progress. Now, form a line and enter through the double doors to find your assigned seating. We assigned seating, so do not sit with your classmates; you will work with other interns."

The dining hall was filled with a collection of mix-and-match pieces of furniture from the brashness of Victorian to the simplicity of early American, castoffs from wealthy donors. Justin wandered through the rectangular tables and found his name with five other students. "Atlanta, Nashville, Tampa, Baton Rouge, and Jackson."

Silas walked the room to locate his assigned place near the noisy kitchen. A male student wearing a pink feathered cape ignored him as he tried to welcome the creature. He waved off the sizable pink bird, took a seat at the table, and sipped on a goblet of water.

The trainees filled the dining hall and stood beside their chairs, pausing for the pledge and a request for the blessing of the meal. Camp Director Jack Williams strutted up to the stage and spoke into a microphone. "All stand to face the portrait of Supreme Commander Gifford Sapros to recite the pledge."

"I pledge my allegiance to Supreme Commander Gifford Sapros, the protector of our nation. He is our wise and noble leader. He alone understands what is best for our country. We are a nation of unity, of one mind. We fight against those who challenge our values, our reasoning, and our grand leader. We will protect our land from seditious ideas, coming from those who desire to destroy our beliefs. Let us not be defeated; help us, our supreme commander."

"Now we shall sing our national anthem, 'Imagine.'"

Justin bowed his head and remained quiet. A chorus of voices filled the dining room as he kept silent, remembering what his grandfather had told him about Aston Sapros replacing the "Star-Spangled Banner" with the song "Imagine," written by John Lennon, as a better representation of the beliefs of the American people.

"Now for the blessing. Mr. Phillips, please ask the blessing of the supreme commander for our bountiful breakfast."

"O absolute and mighty supreme commander, we give our thanks for providing us with a lavish meal. We ask you to bless our efforts in our tasks today, so each resident will develop into a better citizen educated in your methods as we help other youths to remember your ways are greater than our ways. We thank you again, our supreme commander."

Justin shivered as he envisioned a thousand eyes glaring at him, accusing him of treason for refusing to take part in the blasphemous pledge, national anthem, and prayer.

Attendants carried out covered plates and set them in front of the students. A server lifted the stainless-steel cover; the plate was filled with vegan bacon, scrambled eggs, home fries, a sherbet dish of fresh strawberries with cantaloupe, a buttered English muffin, and a selection of real coffee, milk, and orange juice. Around the clatter of plates, the constant conversation challenged those who sat near the stage.

A young female from Tampa raised her voice above the din of the students. "I am Patricia DuPont, from Aston University, Tampa, but you can call me Kitty." Yellow cat eyes and five-inch long whiskers added to her feline features. She tapped a bell tied to a pink ribbon around her neck with her long fingernails resembling cat claws.

"Early-entry intern students like me are still in high school. My major is in criminal psychology, minoring in Saprosism. My mom is a psychologist at Aston House for Insane Criminals. Many of her patients are delusional; she claims they can lead healthy lives once medicated with intensive treatment. Those who cannot remain at the hospital or if they become harmful to society—my mom petitions Health Services to euthanize them."

She poured chocolate syrup and milk into a saucer and lapped up the mixture. "Mother claims putting them down is more humane than allowing them to suffer from religious schizophrenia."

Kyron Abercrombie, a dark-skinned young man in his late teens from Baton Rouge, poked at his food. "What do you mean, religious schizophrenia?"

Kitty shrugged her shoulders and licked her palm. "Simple. Those who believe in a god, any god, have religious schizophrenia. Clinical professionals reported unfortunate cases for over fifty years. Earlier this century, most doctors ignored the syndrome because several suffered from the same delusions. Now, with a better understanding and successful therapies, diagnosis is seldom rejected."

"For those with less advanced symptoms, recovery comes right away. On occasion, the patient may require electroshock therapy, plus a potent dose of an antipsychotic cocktail to make progress. Many will improve in weeks; others may take months or a year—"

Sybil Chambers, a journalism major from Nashville, dropped her fork on the table. "My mother received treatment a while back. Before Sapros Psychiatric Hospital admitted her for the treatment, she loved studying the Bible, talking, and singing, and she loved Jesus. Now, she doesn't do much of anything aside from watching the *Sapros Praise Hour* on telemonitor. She doesn't discuss the therapy she got when she does talk."

"Success stories like your mama's thrill me. Thrilled she received treatment before her condition caused permanent damage."

She caressed Sybil's arm with the top of her head. "Now she is recovered from her delusions."

Her voice rose an octave. "You don't know what you are talking about. Your better-than-thou attitude, doing your so-called humanitarianism on individuals, who are no bother to you or anyone, reeks with hypocrisy. Nothing but a self-prominent Sapros worshiper. You profess you don't believe in a god yet pledge your allegiance and pray to his likeness to bless our meal. What is Gifford to you? Dare you call anyone delusional? Impersonate an ordinary alley cat with your nymphomania of Gifford Sapros. He is your god. Worship him. Don't force your delusions on me. Yeah, I'm the delusional one."

Kitty bared her pointy cat-like teeth. "I am a Siberian."

Justin moved his palms downward for Sybil to lower her voice. The sound of their heavy footsteps on the marble floors grew louder as they approached. "You are attracting attention; security is on the way to this table.

Sit on ice. Bots won't take aggressive action."

Kitty pulled her legs up to her chest and wrapped her arms around them. "I'm about to cough up a fur ball."

"Sybil Chambers come with us. Do not resist." Machine-like voices echoed in unison. A thin yellow beam of light rotated around their helmets, providing them a three-sixty-degree of observation ability.

"On my Granny's grave, I won't."

One guard aimed a fist at the young woman. A yellow beam of light shot out, striking Sybil below her throat. She stumbled backward and collapsed on the floor, unable to move. The guards hoisted her up by the arms and legs, taking the unconscious woman out of the dining room.

"I am not a Gifford worshiper. I hate Gifford Sapros."

Justin arched his eyebrows. "Did you say something, Kitty?"

"I hate show-offs."

Cummings waved her finger like a metronome. "Students. Let this be a reminder to each of you to obey all the rules of the camp. We do not tolerate any subversive talk about our supreme commander. You can be confident we will take appropriate action managing the young woman."

Later, during the afternoon break, the three sat on a bench under a tree. Sweat beaded on Silas's forehead. "What, in the name of Sapros, happened at your table? I heard her shouting all the way where I sat."

Justin gestured with his head to the hovering security drones. "She is anxious about being here at the camp."

"Yes, a big adjustment." Ariella held the T-35 she kept hidden from Justin. "We should encourage the others to give their support to Sapros, so they may avoid the same fate." The drone flew off to another cluster of students until making another pass.

Ariella stood, signaling for the two to come with her. "We can talk here. Stay alert for those drones."

"What kind of place is this, Justin?"

He shielded his eyes against the sun to search the sky for any drones. "This is a reeducation camp, one of the worst. We didn't learn much about this place from searching the online literature. My mother is familiar with this operation. My older sister worked at a reeducation camp and went missing, and later we received a letter informing us of Kassidy's death. Fault Denson for assigning us here, not allowing us to change our assignments from this maggot farm."

"What is your job assignment, Silas?"

"Drones and security bots need reprogramming. My expertise in cyborgology impressed the director. Surprised this place would consider me, after working at Aston University, Columbia. Bypassed their security software to change a grade for a friend. They listed all my minor traffic infractions except hacking. Weird; the violation doesn't show up on my criminal record. A background check listed the charges two weeks ago."

"My dad may have intervened for you, correcting your problem."

"He expects me to make something out of myself."

"My dad is straightforward. He means what he says."

The shrill blast of whistles caught everyone's attention. Witch Cummings, as students referred to her, blew her whistle with three long, sharp bursts. "Students, the minute you hear this signal, present yourself here for announcements. You received your duty assignments. Report to your station to begin your job."

Ariella proceeded to the administration offices, Silas to the security department, and Justin sulked to the central office.

A bony middle-aged woman, with salt-and-pepper hair styled into a French twist, sat at a desk. The thick lenses of the diamond-encrusted gold-rimmed glasses gave her an owlish appearance. She did not rise to her feet and spoke with a military drill instructor's voice. "Refer to me as Records Director Wentworth. I will state the rules once. I do not tolerate lateness, laziness, or the spreading of gossip. Work at your job station until I say you may take a break or until dismissed for the day," she said, directing attention to a nearby table stacked with file boxes overflowing with documents. "Those white forms must be arranged in alphabetical order, the duplicate yellow copy filed by the camper number. Those files go into the orange file cabinets, while the camper digital files go into the blue cabinet. Do you understand so far?"

"Why do digital files go into a cabinet?"

"Meant to say, binary files. Do you understand my instructions?"

Justin nodded.

"Can't hear your head rattle, boy. Reply with an audible voice."

"Yes, ma'am."

"Use my title when you're speaking to me as Director Wentworth. Also, if you have questions, stand at my desk and remain silent until permitted to speak. Do you understand?"

"Yes, Director."

"Now, take one of those boxes and put them where they belong. In the event you find any loose documents, put them aside until locating the folder holding the paperwork."

Boxes sat on the file cabinets plus any other place someone might pile a container. Papers of various sizes and colors overflowed, spreading over the floor.

Justin found a three-tier organizer, labeling one tray for white papers, the other, yellow. He pulled a box toward him, struggling with the packed files. "Figures, a file, no documents. Need another label.

Now this is getting better. Documents don't correspond to the name on the file or match anything else. My empty basket will multiply exponentially. Two white papers and no yellow copy. Hello, a pink discipline form. Sheesh, need another basket."

Justin yanked out files, categorizing them into the appropriate basket. A blue document, an empty folder, another pink paper.

"Well, at last, a file with both sets of documents. Can't complain about not being busy." He slid the file into an empty box sitting in a chair next to him. A file of intake photos spilled from the next folder, with their camper number and no other identification. "Horseradish. How did I chance this secure job?"

Blanche rapped on her desk with a ruler, pointed to an additional stack of boxes next to the break room door. "Best stop talking to the sky, young man, and do more work."

"Yes, Director Wentworth."

Reclined in an oversized wine-colored leather executive chair at her Bubinga wood desk, Wentworth talked to someone on her wrist phone. "He's working hard, talking to himself a lot. One thing, well-organized, finding empty wire baskets in which to place the stray files. Oh, I would be pleased to dine with you this evening. Our night."

Wednesday, October 18, 2079

Ariella sat at a plastic folding table well supplied with green clipboards, a pencil holder with five pens, plus two organizer baskets. The blue form indicated the campers met compliance with assignments; the pink specified those in violation. Blue forms granted the camper the privilege to go to the camp canteen for a single scoop of frozen sweetened watery milk, masquerading as ice cream. "A potion best savored if allowed to melt and poured over the roots of an artificial plant."

The discipline form listed the penalties; consequences increased in severity with the age of the camper and the number of penalty points. A minor offense such as turning in an overdue class project might result in being restricted to the cabin for the weekend or a work detail such as scouring sidewalks with a small scrub brush. Execution was reserved for the obstinate teen campers who refused to comply with regulations.

The Behavioral Compliance Office door opened, and two girls crept in, holding goldenrod sheets of paper. The first, no older than twelve, handed Ariella her referral. A red *X* marked the failure to turn in an essay assignment. "Report to Educational Advisor Cummings for disciplinary action."

"Ms. Stein, my second time to Behavioral Compliance."

"Why didn't you learn from your punishment the last time?"

"We turned them in. The instructor threw them away and gave us these yellow papers. You don't know what Advisor Cummings does to girls."

"What does she do?"

The other girl, her voice at a whisper, said, "May I say something? Don't report me, please, for saying bad stuff about the staff."

Ariella signed the forms. "Better to remain quiet. Cabin restriction for the weekend. Don't come back here with another violation or expect to spend three days with me doing military calisthenics."

"Thank you. Better this than Cummings."

"Director Summers. I need a break; back in twenty."

Ariella spotted Silas under a tree with a robotic guard. "Silas, your skills, please."

He bowed and swept an invisible cape. "My lady. The drones, they won't bother us; besides, the bots don't gossip. These are first-generation robotic technology, more like children's toys than useful tools."

"Are recording systems installed in the guards?"

"Yes, why?" Silas asked, adjusting the guard's electronic panel.

"Do they record all incidents?"

"Not unless someone programs them to document an event."

"The mechanical creatures, when they escort a female camper to Advisor Cummings, does the robot stay with them?"

"Yes, most of the time. On occasion, the guards returned; the female did not. Yesterday, a black van parked next to the central office. Two male guards shackled Sybil, shoved her in the back, and drove off."

"I didn't find a discipline referral, but she is not a camper. Did she do something else for them to haul her away as a prisoner? Do the bots record what happens when someone is in with Cummings? Can anyone tell they are in recording mode?"

"By setting them for surveillance mode, once entering her office, the recording will continue until leaving. Is something going on?"

"Strange, in the process of referring two campers to Cummings, they reacted with fear. I don't believe they faked fear to wiggle out of whatever punishment she might give them."

"By adjusting the bots' programming, they'll report to me. As often as one of those robots escorts a female camper to the witch, we won't wait long."

Justin pulled loose white and yellow papers and placed them in the nearly overflowing baskets. "Been shuffling these stupid files for days now and yet put ten complete files together. Now, who still uses this antiquated paper system? Pink again. Whoever's responsibility to sort these forms, I wish—"

He gasped as he read the name on the paper. "Kassidy, here at this camp?"

Justin glanced over at Director Wentworth, in a captivated conversation with Advisor Cummings. "Yes, I enjoyed last night so much. Oh, you are so bad. You are awful."

Justin slipped the paper into his pocket. "Alice Cummings referred...Camper Meyers? ... to her office for disciplinary action. Violation of a direct command from the educational advisor."

Justin stood at the director's desk and remained silent for her to respond to him. Wentworth chatted with the advisor. "A camper came in your office needing disciplinary action? I will talk to you later."

Her chair squeaked as she spun around to face him. "Well, Meyers?"

"I need to take a break, Director; I worked through lunch, which ended two hours ago."

"Take the rest of the day off. Be back an hour early tomorrow."

"Thank you."

Justin shut the office door and wandered to a concrete picnic table and sat under an oak tree. He took the pink form from his pocket to reread the paper. A security robot stood by. A thin white light in his visor rotated. "Are you in need of assistance, Student Meyers?"

Justin blinked. "Um."

"Notify Silas Jenkins for you?"

"Why contact him?"

"One of my functions. I am programmed to assist you."

"Did my father—why am I asking you about my dad?"

Light on the visor continued at the same tempo. "What is your father's name?"

"Horace Meyers."

"Stand by." The unit sounded like a clock running too fast. "Yes. Horace Meyers, security chief of the Southeast Quadrant."

"Did my father send you with your services?"

"Negative. Silas Jenkins encrypted me to assist you. Do you want to contact him?"

"Yes."

The light on the bot's visor changed from white to blue, now rotating at two-second intervals instead of four. "Silas Jenkins will meet you here in one minute twelve seconds."

Silas took a seat on the other side of the table. "So, how do you like your bot? Make sure you keep your identification device with you, so they will recognize you as an Alpha leader."

"What is this thing's name?"

"The robot?"

"No, the picnic table. How do I gain the bot's attention?"

He handed him a blue piece of plastic with a small white chip. "Use this. All you do is press the chip for a response. Don't do this often and give the idea you and this android are best buds."

"Best buds? What? You mean like making a foursome going out to dinner with Ariella and her bot? Someone might think I prefer computerized nonhuman company."

"Bots don't eat, do as they are programmed. They can play the guitar or card games, recite all ninety-four verses of "Ode to Gifford" in ten thousand languages. Don't expect them to do something that takes reasoning skills, like standing out in the pouring rain might cause them to short-circuit. Not much vocal talent, unless you enjoy monotone off-key singing. These machines are so old, surprised they still operate."

"This device contacted you. Can I communicate with anyone outside of the camp, my dad, for instance?"

"The best way to make a call. These guys can bypass the communication system here."

"You need to talk to your dad?"

He handed the pink form to Silas. "The person on this document is my sister. Despite my dad's connections, the leads go nowhere. She worked at a camp, from the paperwork, this one. Someone notified us she died."

"Ariella needs this. A bot produced surveillance regarding Advisor Cummings. She suspected abuse, and those suspicions are correct. One sick—"

He took out his wrist phone and tapped four buttons. "How soon can you come to our position, Ariella? I'm in possession of the evidence you requested, and Justin needs your help on something… Yes, coming."

A female approached from behind them. "Well, hello, you two. Missed visiting with you the past couple of days. Lonesome without you at breakfast; Kyron doesn't want to talk much. Can't get him to say more than 'uh-huh'…Shy, I guess. Hoped we could get better acquainted."

Kitty tugged on a new jacket she wore over her translucent body stocking. A silver glittering cat-ear headband completed her feline costume. "Say hello to a full-time camp counselor. She assigned Sybil as my first patient. Sad to say, I recommend her to an advanced homeopathic treatment center. Pitiful—she is in the later stages of acute deteriorating religious schizophrenia, or ADRS, for short."

"What is this treatment center called?"

"Kaegogi Farms is a state-of-the-art rehabilitation center. They use drug and animal therapy to assist struggling clients to overcome their delusions. I am sure Sybil will respond well to her treatments."

"Kitty, any possibility for Ariella and me to take a tour of this facility? An opportunity like this one will supplement our class presentation. We would be most appreciative if you arrange this."

"The SC's office must grant a clearance. Cyber forms will take weeks for approval. Once submitted, the internship ends before the authorization comes back. My mother can sweet-talk Chief Meyers to move matters quicker. Enough time to make a quick trip to the litter box before scratching up my next client. Know something for you tomorrow. Meow."

Ariella laughed until she doubled over and sat on the ground. "Why is she in a cat costume?"

"You should try having breakfast with her. She puts her face down on the plate and laps up milk with her tongue. Picks up a bite and chews with her mouth open."

Ariella hid her mouth. "With those teeth, how else can she chew?"

"Hey, I am stuck with a guy who wears a pink bodysuit; at least his costume is less revealing. Claims to be a flamingo." Silas took long, slow, striding steps, bringing his knee to hip level. "He complains because he wasn't served raw shrimp for breakfast. Much rather dine with Kitty."

"My table is boring unless someone is a closet kangaroo or a unicorn," Ariella said. "Why didn't you tell Ms. Meow who your father is?"

"Feed her control obsession. My dad will handle everything. Smarty Paws will think she arranged everything, trapping herself in a ball of yarn."

"The name Kaegogi Farms sounds unnerving," Ariella said. "What is this place?"

"Not sure, except this facility is not a medical anything. By getting

Kitty to arrange a tour, it provides reconnaissance for my dad."

"What, Silas? You didn't request me here to gawk at Hissy-Kitty."

"The robots provided plenty of information on Cummings. Justin needs your help concerning a pink discipline form."

"Anything useful on Cummings?"

"This is what the bot recorded. Changed the bots' programming, so they will no longer respond to commands from Cummings or anyone else." A three-dimensional display projection of Alice's office showed the administrator standing over a camper tied to a chair.

Ariella's eyes watered. "The hag using a metal-studded belt on a child is beyond disgusting. What the witch commanded the cyborg do is straight-out depraved. Silas—"

"Done. Time is passing too slowly for our time here to finish. I'm ready to leave out of here."

"Now, about the discipline referral?"

"On my sister. She worked here and later went missing. Today I found this stuffed in a pile of papers in Records."

Ariella read the paper. "Few years old; possible administration purged the files. This facility does not keep much once a camper turns twenty. Accessing the archived data is one possibility."

He opened the chest section of the mechanism. "Equipped the bots with an accessible computer. This is a different system than you are accustomed. Call this one Gerry; he is a functional fifty-year-old geriatric bot. Often the lower the technology, the higher the security. Can't hack someone writing a note on a piece of paper with an old graphite pencil. Type in the name you want for a record search; press print. Go ahead; warmed up and ready."

Justin tapped his sister's name with one finger and pressed Enter. "Wow, I saw one of these in a museum." The screen lit up with Kassidy's name and holo identification, along with other unusual codes. "All files are in the Records and Property archives. Federal law requires data on employees and campers remain accessible for ten years after the organism's death."

Justin stiffened himself; the three walked over to the Records building, and the automatic doors slid open for them to enter.

"Guess we should get this done."

Justin stood at the director's desk for her to speak to him.

"Meyers, I gave you the rest of the day off. Why are you here?"

"Director allow me a favor to examine the archives. I need to find out what happened to somebody."

"Is this person a relative?"

"My sister worked here at one time, so please, may I check if I can find any leads?"

"Fine, you may go inside." Wentworth slid open a drawer and removed an electronic card. "Hand me your cards to adjust your security level; if not, I will let you in using my passkey."

The director took the three cards and waved them before the scanner; a soft ping sounded as the security beams turned off.

"Director, should I find a file box with my sister's personal effects in them—?"

"Sign the cyber forms releasing the property. In the back are tables and chairs, so you can go through everything."

They twisted along the dark passageway filled with overflowing boxes. Old leather, with a hint of dried roses and lavender, scent permeated the hallway, causing Ariella to rub her nose and eyes. Silas pulled a penlight, scanning the labeled boxes. A chamber filled with file cabinets sat on a massive roller wheel. Justin touched the *M* button on the control panel; the files rotated and squeaked to a stop.

"*Ma* through *Me*...Her file is here." He held the folder against his chest. "Please give me a resolution."

Ariella and Silas sat at his side; Justin read the file before him. "Kassidy's job application, employment identification card, a written warning for proselytizing campers, and termination papers with a transfer to camper status. The date is getting closer," he said, highlighting the date on the pink copy of the discipline referral. Another written warning against proselytizing. Justin flipped to the next page. "Failure to obey a direct command...Oh no."

Silas rested his hand on Ariella's shoulder. "I'll give you time alone with him."

Her hand dropped as she read the paper, disciplinary

recommendation, *EXECUTION*. She turned to the next page. "The death order with an execution date is here. I'm sorry, Justin. Over three years back, on Gifford Sapros' birthday. Signed by Matthew Skyler O'Connor, executioner."

"How do I tell my parents what happened to her?"

"Quick and brief. Sounds harsh but dragging out the news is worse."

"We did not expect something like this happened to her. The only comfort I can give them: she did not back down from what they taught her." He held his head in his hands to hide his tears.

"Here, Justin—I found your sister's belongings." Silas set a cardboard box on the narrow table.

Envelopes ready to mail and bundled with twine lay in the box. Justin cut open the binding, sorting out the letters. "Eight sent to Dad, six to Mom, five to both Mom and Dad. Here are two written to me."

Ariella placed her arm on his shoulder. "Do you want us to give you privacy?"

"No. No. Please, stay here."

He unsealed the envelope, reviewing the letter. "No date."

Justin,

Terrified campers fill the facility, more than I can count. Many of them, their one crime is loving Jesus or following whatever belief. My heart breaks for them. I do what I can by sneaking a crumb of extra food to them, praying for them, and trying not to make promises I might not be able to keep. Please pray, Justin; the directors are scrutinizing my every single move. I wrote to Dad, but he doesn't call or write me. Tell him about the trouble here. Alice Cummings is blocking my letters. Otherwise, he would have me out of here long ago.
Love,
Kassidy

"Here is another one."

Justin,
   My time is short; they're coming in the morning. Remember how we once sang "Three Blind Mice" as children. Remember this time and keep it in your heart always.
Love,
Kassidy

"I wonder what she meant by singing 'Three Blind Mice.' I don't remember singing the song with Kassidy. Too young to remember, I suppose."

A trinket box inlaid with mother-of-pearl swans and pink coral butterflies lay on the bottom of the box. Inside, he found a gold heart-shaped locket with a tiny engraved cross on the front. "My parents gave her the locket as a gift before she left for college. Two medals for an outstanding scholar award from Gifford Sapros. I gave her this silly glass with a tarantula inside years ago. Kassidy opened her present, screamed, throwing the paperweight across the room, almost hitting Dad. The thing hit the floor, spun around, and rolled under the sofa. Mom made me go crawl under the sofa because Kassidy thought the paperweight broke, letting the spider out."

Justin gathered Kassidy's personal effects and carried them to Director Wentworth's desk. "Found my sister's belongings. May I take them home?"

"Meyers, Ariella should go with you."

"Most kind, Director."

CHAPTER 12

Friday, October 20, 2079

Horace pivoted back and forth to the refrigerator and sat at the table for a moment and paced again.

Dakota copied Scripture verses in her notebook. "Do you want something to eat? You skipped lunch. Gifford's delay is agonizing."

"I can't eat so much as a raisin. Gifford promised to call back within two hours, three days ago. I tried contacting him, but his secretary insisted his wonderfulness went out of town and won't be back for another week. Somehow he tries to find a way for me to finish his immoral acts for him."

"News from Ollie?"

"Left a cryptic message this morning, stating he padlocked the café to go out to Red Mountain. Did he mean moving to Red Mountain or taking supplies out? Tried to call him back, got voice messaging." Horace slid onto the table bench and moved a stack of papers to open a small box of identification cards. "New identities, along with secured passages to relocate to New Liberty."

"What are you waiting on Gifford for?" She took the paperwork from his hand and read them. "You don't need his approval for issuing passages."

A loud pinging sound from the holophone with the emblem of the Chimera appeared. "At long last, let us hope his mood is cooperative today."

"Supreme Commander, I am honored to be of service to you today."

Gifford, robed in his usual Greek philosopher apparel, sat behind a gold-plated desk about the length and width of a double-sized bed. He curled his lips and smirked. "You might find a bit of news enlightening; Chief Chatterjee conducted a raid on Red Mountain this morning. Chatterjee apprehended all those rebels, including the traitor Ollie Johansen."

"Yes, I do." *Please, Lord, help me stay calm.* "How may I be of service today?"

"I am turning your property into a holding facility. Take them into your custody. Treat them as enemies of the State."

Horace remained expressionless. "Sir."

"I am sure you are grateful for the distinction I bestowed upon you. Two buses with dissidents will enter your compound with extra guards."

"Provided you approve, my staff were trained by the Chimera Elite Squad; I demand the best." *The finest come from my teams, not yours.* "Wouldn't want to burden your security crew. Trustworthy people are difficult to find nowadays."

Gifford held up his right arm and exposed two scars three inches long. "So true—I have the same challenges myself. Which entrance do you prefer the delivery made?"

"From Interstate 65 take the Sumiton Bypass, head south on Randall Sapros Corridor, to exit fifty-one. Travel three miles to Pine Estates on the left. Go right on Coal Mine Village; the sentries at the gate will allow the buses to enter. Pull up to the pavilion; my detention guards will take custody. Do any of the prisoners need medical attention?"

"One or two. Nothing life-threatening."

"How soon will they be arriving?" *Goofy Soup forgets we track all Chimera-owned transports.*

"Their arrival time is forty-five minutes. Chief Chatterjee will transfer the prisoners over to you. Make sure they are eliminated, so they will not cause me any more difficulties. Have a good day, Meyers."

Horace paced the kitchen again. "Why does this give me the feeling everything is too simple?"

He checked the food inventory list. "We can supply enough chow to last them two weeks. Now to move them to Iowa without delay."

"They will need warmer clothing, Five-Star. Winters in Iowa are brutal," she said, flipping on the security monitor to the entrance gate guarded by two sentries. "Did you notify the guards to expect guests? They are not anticipating prison buses."

"Lieutenant Colonel Billings."

"Sir."

"Mike, two prison buses will arrive within the hour at the Coal Mine Village gate with guests. Make sure you alert personnel. Chief Chatterjee will transfer custody over to me. Are the guesthouses ready?"

"Always, sir."

"Thank you, Mike."

A cloud of white dust signaled the approach of the buses as the group waited at the pavilion. Four guards disembarked, wearing black ski masks. Two guards saluted and handed him a tablet.

"Your signature."

Horace recognized the guard with a brown left eye and hazel right eye. After returning the electronic form, he wondered how much information Brad had gathered on Ollie and his activities.

"Give me a copy of the transfer, a full report on the raid, and arrest of all involved. You bought a new pen?"

Brad removed a memory card to hand to Horace. "Among the best."

"The prisoners, I do not want this to drag out all day."

Brad signaled to someone on the first bus. People stumbled out of the bus as the doors swung open. A woman with bruises on her face and a cut on her lip fell as one of the guards pushed her down the steps. A man with bleeding scrapes on his arms and legs lifted the woman to her feet. Missy got off the bus with a swollen arm held in an odd position.

"May I hold you, Missy?"

She nodded. "I want my daddy."

A boy of about ten exited, his nose swollen, and eyes blackened. The final passenger, Ollie, stumbled as blood trickled from his mouth, eyes red and puffy. Brad shoved Ollie to make him move faster to the huddle.

A plump woman in her late thirties, hair dyed fuchsia with flecks of emerald highlights and a purple Chimera tattooed on her left wrist, approached. "Meyers, these prisoners are now in your custody. Give the supreme commander an account once you dispose of these prisoners from society."

"Chief Chatterjee, I am not accustomed to someone of a lower rank using a disrespectful tone of voice while addressing me. Must I remind you of my proper title and rank? You are a Captain in the Naval Civilian Corps. Use the salutation *sir* and my proper title when speaking to me. How long did you serve Sapros?"

"At the age of thirteen, Supreme Commander Randall Sapros requested my services. By the time I was fifteen, he had named me deputy paramour to oversee his stable mares."

"What about Gifford?"

Chatterjee sneered as she displayed several missing teeth and an *X* branded on her tongue. "Preposterous thinking. Everyone can see I am too old to be one of Gifford's many paramours. He prefers younger and more diverse alternatives among his many lovers."

"What about the *X*? What did you do to earn a branding?"

"Disobedience. Gifford enjoys certain types of explicit sexual entertainment, which I did not want to get involved in. He punished me by marking me as a bigot for refusing the overtures from his females," Chatterjee said, clapping three times. She and the guards boarded the empty buses for Birmingham.

He guided an older woman to a bench. "Call the health crew

out here now for a triage unit. Tend to the worst injured first. Take a seat; assistance is on the way."

Medics hurried out of elevated shafts disguised as small cottages. They pushed power wheelchairs and gurneys to transport injured prisoners to the medical clinic. Later they returned to assist more people.

Horace sat next to Ollie. "Two more days and everything—Sapros got impatient and jumped ahead. Difficult, but I can still move you to safety."

"Brad."

"Yes, I recognized him."

"He followed me outta Red Mountain last week an' witnessed me givin' out soup ta the community and reported me. Now he is workin' for Chatterjee, with a promise of promotion from Sapros." Ollie held a blood-stained cloth to his mouth.

"I told Sapros myself I investigated Red Mountain, and no criminal violations occurred. He demanded I go out to arrest you on spurious charges. Gifford ordered Chatterjee to do the job instead. Now I need to work out a way to get everyone out of here safely and appear I did my job."

A medic knelt beside Ollie. "What happened to you?"

"A guard came up an' hit me in the mouth with a small metal baton," he said, flinching as the cloth touched his mouth. "Brad did this."

"Come with me, Mr. Johansen; we will fix you up." A guard led him to the guesthouse with the medic close behind and took an elevator to the underground hospital.

Dakota's voice quivered. "Times are getting dangerous?"

"We might be in for a battle for our lives."

"What are the plans?"

"Try to keep business appearing normal as possible. I do not want Gifford becoming any more suspicious than he may be. Our last conversation about Red Mountain was, let us say, unpleasant."

Missy kicked at a medical staff member as she wrapped her uninjured arm tighter around Horace's neck. "I want my daddy."

He cuddled the girl. "Missy, we will make your arm better. I'll carry her down to the clinic. What about the parents?"

A guard read the list. "Someone abandoned the girl at the community. Everyone takes turns minding the girl. Sometimes a man and woman come to see her and give a few provisions for her. She cries after they leave."

"Missy, who put the tattoo on your wrist?"

"Giffy did. Daddy got mad. He punched Giffy in the face."

"Where is your mommy?"

"Daddy hides Mommy from Giffy. He hides Aunt Tisa and me. Giffy and Aunt Tisa's mommy make her cry a lot."

Ariella strapped on her helmet. "Can you hear me?"

"Yes," Justin said, straddling his cycle. "Did you input the coordinates?"

Ariella rolled up beside Justin. "Are you ready?"

"How can anyone prepare for this?" Justin let off the brake as the two headed for the exit. A crisp cool breeze blew maple leaves across the two-lane road; pine cones cluttered the ground along the way. They slowed to allow two speeding security vehicles going southbound to pass them.

"The navigator says a restaurant of interest is ahead. We should stop."

"No, I am not hungry, and I need to get home. Aunt Maddie will feed us with more than enough food."

"No, Justin. The name of the restaurant."

They slowed for a sharp curve as Ariella pointed to a heart-shaped red wooden sign: *Three Blind Mice*. Justin switched his cycle over to manual and turned into the gravel parking lot.

Ariella stopped beside him and took off her helmet. "Worth a try."

The pair entered the empty dining area; a server waved her hand. "Sit anywhere you like, if you can find a vacant table."

Justin brushed the dust from his jeans and pulled out a chair for Ariella. "A glass of lemonade."

"Same here."

Antique clocks, hearts, and little stuffed mice added charm to the restaurant. A vintage grandfather clock stood on the other side of the room with steady tick-tock sounds. Holographic white mice wearing dark glasses ran up the side of the timepiece. A cobalt glass music box sat in the corner playing "Three Blind Mice."

"Employed here long?"

"Ten years when this place opened."

"Ever met a Kassidy Elizabeth Meyers?"

"A Kassidy worked here as a night manager. One night a sleek black limo came up; two Sapros defense agents got out and shoved her into the back seat and drove off. She resigned the next day."

"How long ago?"

"Six months at the most. Not long after the tornado went through Huntsville."

Justin pulled a holograph out of his wallet. "Do you recognize this woman?"

"Of course, Kassidy."

"You are a tremendous help."

Three hours later, Justin and Ariella stopped at the entrance. The drop gate remained down as a security guard approached them. "I need your identification."

"Come on, Murry; we went through recruit training together. You are aware the general is my—"

"We are in an elevated high-security protocol. I am required to ask for all identification."

"Well, here, along with the ambassador's daughter. I have vital information for my dad."

"Sorry, general's orders..." Murray said. "The general's son is requesting authorization to enter, an urgent matter for the chief."

The gate lifted; the cycles continued along the driveway up to the Tudor-style house. Ariella gazed about the property. "I thought the Israeli compound took up a significant amount of property—this is gigantic."

"This is a small portion of the entire property. My dad might let me take you for a tour. Hope this is a drill, or we won't be doing anything during our time off. Do you ride horses?"

"I love to."

A guard greeted them as the two approached. "The chief is down at the guesthouses. Chatterjee delivered about thirty people as prisoners; they are now in the general's custody."

"Explain."

"About three hours ago, the chief transferred the guests to the medical facility; medics are treating injuries sustained during their arrest. Ollie Johansen is among those arrested."

Justin sat on a stone bench in the flower garden. "Ollie. On what charges?"

"Treason, aiding and abetting dissidents. Anything Chief Chatterjee conjured up."

The guard cupped his hand to his ear. "The general is on his way."

Justin stood and smiled as Ariella's mouth dropped open at the massive room with a twenty-foot ceiling and a wide sweeping staircase.

"You and your friend make yourselves comfortable in the dining room. Are you hungry? The staff tells me dinner is ready in five minutes."

"Thanks, Aunt Maddie."

Justin waved for Ariella to follow him into a room with a long banquet table set with the burgundy china embellished with a gold emblem and Waterford beverage glasses. A shiny copper pot hung over an open crackling fire, releasing a scent of apples, cinnamon, and nutmeg and causing Ariella's mouth to water. Nearby, four overstuffed chairs with pillows, a serving table with a pitcher of cider, and a plate of small sugar cookies tempted them.

The hard-stone floor betrayed Horace's military-style footsteps entering the room. Dakota took his arm for support.

"Justin, you gave us short notice. Is anything wrong?"

"Sorry about coming home with so little warning, Dad. What about Ollie and the other people arrested now in your custody?" Justin sat and listened as his father explained what had happened.

"Now, what brings you home a week early?"

"A couple of issues. I need a written consent from your office to take a tour of Kaegogi Farm."

"Perfect timing—you both can do me a favor during your tour and help inspect what may be significant violations at the facility. Encounter problems, and I'm two minutes away by helo."

"Now for the other thing I need to tell you about."

"Which is?"

Justin glanced downward and over at his mother as Dakota twisted her wedding ring around her finger.

"Tell them, Justin," Ariella said, whispering.

Justin opened a sack and pulled out a file folder and handed the trinket box to his father. "I found information on Kassidy. Before I show you what I found, I believe Kassidy is still alive. I found a woman who identified her holograph. She claims she worked with her within the last six months."

Horace lifted the lid and held the items close, kissing each piece before passing them to Dakota. He used his thumbs to move the swans and butterflies to unlock another part of the box.

"Didn't know about the secret compartment; did you find anything?"

He read the piece of paper. "Marriage license, between Kassidy and somebody by the name of Matthew Skyler O'Connor."

Justin took the paper and dug into the file to pull out the execution warrant. "What? The date on this certificate is two days before Kassidy married him?"

Ariella took the papers, looking for more details. "None of this is making any sense."

Horace held out his hand. "Hand me the folder. Kassidy married the man who executed her?"

"What?"

"Dakota, Kassidy married the man two days after he executed

her. The date on the certificate is over three years ago; Justin found somebody who worked with her earlier this year."

"Mom, Kassidy is still alive. Dad, how do we go about finding her?"

"The Lord led us this far; he will bring her home."

"Why did Camp Sumiton get classified as a prison?"

"Gifford declared the compound a holding facility until we processed the people. All the people Chatterjee transported received injuries; several people required surgery."

"A surgical department here? Where?"

"My son can take you down later and show you around. You will find this facility impressive. We did not inform the Supreme One we converted the old coal mine shafts into useful purposes. They are over one hundred years old."

"Go visit Ollie down in the infirmary. He'll be happy to see you."

He strode down a passage and stopped in front of double doors with the corps' emblem carved into the oak panels. Justin waved his hand over a sensor for the doors to slide open. "Ariella, this is impressive."

"An elevator in a house?"

"Necessary for this size. Plus, my mom requires assistance walking, so she needs elevators."

Justin and Ariella stepped in, and the doors closed and opened to a family room, kitchen, and additional bedrooms. "This is in case of inclement weather or many guests."

Ariella followed him down a passageway into a master-suite bedroom; he unlocked a dressing room door and moved to a full-length mirror set in French tile. A five-foot-tall gray soapstone cat sat to the right of the mirror; Justin touched the right eye, the left eye, and the nose. The mirror glided to the left, revealing another elevator.

"This leads to the infirmary and access points to other sections."

The two stepped into a state-of-the-art clinic complete with waiting areas, labs, and other diagnostic specialties. "We live so far from quality facilities; my grandfather built this during his tenure as a senator. My dad decided to expand the medical center soon after he became security chief."

"Where may I find Mr. Johansen?"

"Room three. He is up to visitors and is talking more than when admitted. A lot more."

Justin knocked as Ariella remained outside for him to finish getting dressed. He gestured for her to come in with him.

Ollie sat on the bed; he grinned to show off his repaired teeth. "I am amazed such thin's existed, but I never thought how fast an' painless. An', Justin, who is your female friend?"

"Ariella Stein, a classmate. Chatterjee arrested you along with other people?"

"Brad went mole and reported me to Chatterjee. She an' her comrades in mayhem came out to where I gave out food to the hungry. Gifford declared givin' food away to the starvin' illegal."

A man with payees and a full beard passed by the open door. "Ariella Stein? Please speak to your father. I am Israeli. I need to go home to Israel; I need his help."

"Who shall I say is requesting my father's help?" Ariella took him by the hand and led him to a chair.

"Yosef Rabinowitz. My family is in Jerusalem; I am not able to speak to them. Guards arrested us, took my passport, and deleted the cyber chip. They swore I'd never set foot in Israel again."

He bowed, praying in Hebrew. "Adonai, master of the universe, we come to you in the name of Yeshua the Messiah. Show compassion on your children, humiliated and disgraced, torn, crushed, taken captive without cause, sold without money. We cry out in prayer and seek permission to plead with you."

Ariella whispered, patting his hand, "I will contact my father."

She stood and slipped back into Ollie's room. "Is a holophone available? My wristphone won't connect."

He beckoned her to follow into the well-lit hallway, Justin pointed to an office door. "Go in the office; call the numbers fifteen, three, six, one, one for a secured line. Say, 'Call Israeli ambassador,' the direct line to your father. Your dad might think the chief is calling, so make sure you are in front of the screen when the light at the top turns on."

Ariella called the numbers Justin gave her. The light came on as her father appeared on the holopad. "Why are you using the emergency line?"

"Are you aware of what is happening here?"

"I spoke with him about half an hour ago, so I am mindful of the circumstances. So, my bat, what brings you to call me from Chief Meyers's home?"

"One of those arrested is an Israeli, Yosef Rabinowitz; he is soliciting your help to get him to Israel. Guards confiscated and destroyed his passport during the raid."

"The Lord gave a solution; be there within the hour."

Ariella disconnected the call and found the young Jewish man in prayer. "My father is on his way."

"Toda. Toda."

"Any others who are Israeli here?"

"No. These people took me in; they begged me to become their Bible teacher. Rabbi Yosef."

Ariella and Yosef talked longer; both stood, hearing someone speaking. "Ambassador Stein, so happy to meet you again, sir."

"Abba, I'm over here."

Eliyahu embraced his daughter. "Where is this Yosef fellow?"

"Shalom, I am Yosef Rabinowitz."

"Yes, I can return you to Israel. The others, do they request asylum? I can transfer them to New Liberty, continuing to Canada, where they will receive a visa for Israel. They must understand, once they leave, they may not be able to resume their former lives."

"I am unable to speak for each one. These people lost everything. Chatterjee burned down their shacks they called home, including what little they contained."

Horace greeted Eliyahu. "Everyone is in the conference room. We must explain all the risks of their alternatives, staying here, staying in New Liberty, staying in Canada, or continuing to Israel."

Horace looked down as Missy tugged on his trousers, staring up at him with sorrowful brown eyes. He smiled as he lifted the child to cradle her.

"Chef Meyers. Those men broke my dolly." Missy's arm hung in a sling with a blue nylon support brace decorated with bright-teal and pink ponies.

"Sweetheart let's go to the toy room, and you can pick out a new one." The lights came on in a room filled with dolls, rocking horses, red, blue, green, and yellow balls, teddy bears, a six-foot-tall stuffed giraffe, and an assortment of other brightly colored toys. "Which toy do you like?"

"Chef Meyers, the pink princess." She held her hands out to a doll the same size as her.

"Do you promise to take loving care of Princess Lisa?"

Missy grinned and hugged the doll. "Tank you, Chef."

"My pleasure, sweetheart."

Dakota approached, touching his shoulder. "Why don't you give me Missy; I will keep her while you meet with the adults. We will keep the children entertained while you talk to the others."

He handed Missy to her, turning to go to the conference room. Missy laid her head on Dakota's shoulder. "I want my...daddy. I want...Mommy."

The men's faces paled. Women dabbed their eyes with tattered dish towels as they followed the men into the meeting room furnished with cherrywood tables and conference chairs. In whispers, they questioned their fate. Soft sobs rose as Horace and Eliyahu entered.

"Permit me to introduce myself. I am Security Chief Horace Meyers; don't be frightened of me. I desire to help you. Some options are available to you—not the preference you'd prefer but is an improvement over what Sapros wants me to do with you. My orders are to remove you as a problem for Sapros. How I fulfill his order is my decision. The first option is to stay here. He is expecting executions when he returns. The method is his pleasure. Do not choose this option. Option two, with the help of Ambassador Stein, getting safe passage to New Liberty. This alternative will give you a chance to live a normal life. Be advised: bounty hunters possess no qualms about kidnapping and returning you to the US to prison for immediate execution. Next possibility: you continue to Canada. They agreed to allow you into their country. Here again, the bounty hunters still hold the advantage of forcing you back here. The final and safest alternative is to go from Canada to obtain a visa and enter Israel under their protection."

Eliyahu nodded. "My country gave emergency powers to assist you from here to Israel following this route and receive new identities once you are in Canada. I will give you instructions on what to do and what you must never do once you depart this property. Any questions?"

A woman stood. "Will we ever be able to talk to our relatives or come home again?"

"For your protection and the others, we must say no. Computer experts eliminated your identities from the federal data systems as we speak, and you, in a sense, no longer exist. The plan is not fail-safe; instead, a chance to live an unregimented life."

"Remain calm." Eliyahu said, "I will travel with you to Israel, your new home. We will assist you with studying Hebrew, finding a place to live, and getting a job or acquiring a trade."

Horace stepped forward. "Does anyone wish to remain here? I recommend you do not. We can transport you to Iowa, but my best recommendation is you go on to Israel."

A man stood in the back pointed. "Y'all tryin' to rid us. Ain't ya. Us believers too much trouble, for ya."

"You are?"

"Why are you making who I am your business?"

"Mr. Mahoney. Yes, I am aware of who you are, and you can quit the ersatz hillbilly vernacular. By your expression, you understand what I'm talking about; am I correct, Dr. Victor Mahoney?"

Victor nodded. "All we experienced is suffering, not being able to trust anyone. Students conspired against me before the name change. Most troubling is finding myself face-to-face with Meyers."

"Mr. Mahoney, I am not your adversary or enemy. We are trying hard to save your life and the rest of the community."

Ollie stood facing Victor. "This man helped out your community more than you realize. We would be dead if he did not step in."

"Don't give me credit for the Lord's victory, Ollie. I am his servant. I was given a position I did not want, but where the Lord wanted me. Placed somewhere else, what help could I be to you or anyone else?"

Monday, October 23, 2079

Justin knocked on the exterior wall and tossed a catnip mouse to gain Kitty's attention. "Hey, Kitty. Wake up—you are in a dream world somewhere."

She sat in her open office with floor-to-ceiling windows allowing the sunshine to illuminate the room. Against the white wall sat a blue five-section sofa with fluffy cushions. In the corner stood a cat stand, with two black Persian cats sleeping on the top level. Wedgewood blue empty shelves ran from the floor to the ceiling for the cats to climb. Wicker baskets matching the color of the shelves lined the window walls, accenting the decor of the office. A five-foot-by-three-foot sign hung over her desk; in bold red print, it stated: *NO DOGS ALLOWED.*

"Sorry. Glad you are back. Did you get your clearance from the security chief?

Got the authorization for you and Ariella to visit the facility. Though, I am required to escort you." She stood licking her hand, peeking through her long bangs at Justin.

"Top idea. Also, SC is dispatching one of his investigators to make sure they are complying with the current rules and regulations." He set a golden box with a bright-red bow on her desk. "For you to enjoy."

Kitty slid the bow off the box and opened the lid. "How did you guess chocolate strawberry-filled mice is my favorite?"

"Lucky assumption."

She nibbled the head off and slurped out the strawberry filling, licking her fingers. "This is yummy."

"Major Rios is waiting outside; she will go with us to Kaegogi Farms."

"I can't go now; I'm not properly groomed—"

"You're heading to a treatment facility, not a cat show."

"I'll drive the van."

"Major Rios requested cargo trucks including additional drivers. We will ride with them."

"Drivers? How many does she need?" Kitty threw her hands in the air. "Why so many Marines?"

"Something about if she finds any violations, she can take immediate action."

"I'm sure she will not. Kaegogi is one of my mother's top facilities."

"Lovely workplace, Counselor DuPont. We are ready to leave." Gabrielle strode into the office with Ariella.

"Don't call Kaegogi. Orders are to do a complete inspection of the facility; they do not receive a warning. To tip off an industrial unit, in any fashion, is a federal violation."

"No calling my mother."

"Let's go."

"Hiss. I'll drive."

"Don't give me your nonsense; you are not driving anything; move your skinny little butt to the van before I find a vet to spay you."

Kitty tossed her head back as she stomped to the van; she spun around and hissed at the major.

Another two investigators joined along with Alice Cummings. "Advisor Cummings, you are going?" She ran to the director. "Protect me, Director; she is mean."

"SC demands information on the campers we sent to Kaegogi. I told the investigators we would be most happy to cooperate; so many of the campers are a threat to the public. Meyers promised an appropriate reward for our efforts in protecting the citizens once the investigation is complete."

Kitty peeked out from behind Advisor Cummings. "I am sorry for my rudeness earlier. I do want to assist in any way I can. So many of these campers are in desperate need of psychological services."

"We'll start soon. Justin, Ariella, I need to speak with you for a moment," Gabrielle said, waving her hand for the two to follow her a short distance away. "Wear these caps; the mini-cam will record and stream the feed to Delta Squad. The general is nearby with the team. Let's go."

The driverless black vans merged into the SpeedTube heading north. Kitty nibbled on a mouse, offering one to Justin. He waved her offer away, as did Advisor Cummings.

"Kitty, did you refer any additional campers to Kaegogi besides Sybil?"

"Two, they are most difficult cases."

Advisor Cummings nodded. "Kaegogi is our last resort when all our attempts at rehabilitation fail."

Gabrielle turned the seat around to glare at Cummings. "What methods do you use to correct the campers' behavior?"

Lights in the SpeedTube flashed by in a blur. "Restriction to their cabins, take away privileges, once or twice, I might give them a swat or two."

Under his breath, Justin grunted. "Swat or two? More like beating them half to death."

The transport slowed. "Estimated time of arrival is three minutes," a female voice said. "Now arriving at the destination,"

Ariella positioned her pack over her shoulder. "Set to go?"

He unbuckled the seat belt and slung his duffle bag on his shoulder. "Ready and recording for our class project."

Driverless trucks backed to loading docks with robots putting foam containers into a refrigerated trailer. Others loaded vehicles with wooden crates marked in black letters: *furniture*. To the west of the platforms, ten thousand-gallon tankers filled up with unidentified material ready for shipping. A cyborg greeted the passengers as the doors slid open.

Three stars tattooed on his right cheek identified the android as a class four. His facial features bore no expression. "Good morning; my designator is Elliott. Welcome to your tour of Kaegogi Farms. We hope you enjoy your visit here. Do visit our coffee shop to sample our products."

Gabrielle marched up to Elliott and placed her thumb on a panel on Elliott's right sleeve. "I am Major Gabrielle Rios; we are here to inspect the facility."

His unblinking eyes stared straight ahead. "Understood. How may I help you?"

"Where do the clients go once sent here for therapy?"

"This is a food production facility. We do not house clients at this location."

Kitty jumped and glanced around as barking and growling came from another section of the farm. "You keep dogs here?"

"This is a dog farm. What you hear is from the breeding and nursery kennels. Today, we house 507 puppies. Please follow me, to the kennels."

Kitty arched her back. "Rather stay here, if you don't mind. I don't like dogs."

Gabrielle glanced at the colonel. "Do you want me to remain with her?"

Colonel Harris held Kitty's arm. "I'll babysit her, Major; easier for me to run her down should she bolt."

Elliott guided them toward the kennels. Dogs barked louder as they approached.

Ariella tapped on Gabrielle's shoulder. "What is the green building used for? Need to get inside."

"Food prep room for manufacturing dog feed. Restricted to authorized personnel. The building is not an approved setting for the tour."

"What about the blue building?"

"Organic recycling building; nothing goes to waste here."

Ariella covered her nose as odors grew stronger. "What do you recycle?"

"Recycle materials into useful products, furniture for office and educational buildings."

"What kind of materials? Is the recycling building part of the tour?"

"The recycling building is not part of the tour."

Justin covered his nose with a rag. "What a horrible odor. The stench is making me sick. Blasted flies. Must be a hundred buzzards perched on the roof and circling."

Ariella placed a cloth over her mouth and nose. "Recognize the odor. Major, I need access to that building."

"Food prep section is not part of the tour."

Major Rios nodded her permission. "This is an inspection, not a visit, Elliott."

Odor poured out as the kennel doors swung open. Mother dogs corralled in ten-feet-by-ten-feet pens stood and guarded their puppies and growled as they approached. Gabrielle neared the pen. Female dogs lunged at the wire fence, nipping at her.

"Relax, little mamas; nobody will harm your babies. Elliott, why are the dogs so stressed? Why are they not socialized?"

"Let us continue the tour."

Gabrielle crossed her eyes. "Elliott's one-track memory drive is beginning to scorch my sanity."

Shrill screams came from the food prep structure and caused everyone to jump. Justin sprinted to assist Ariella. Her face paled as she supported herself against a fence.

He spun around to where she pointed. "Ariella, what's wrong?"

Ariella wiped vomit from her lips. "Inside—They made me stun them. Those murderers, I killed them. Those butchers kept coming after me after I stunned them. Yeshua, please help."

Investigators ran into buildings while the distant sound of helicopters and sirens grew louder. Gabrielle pointed at Advisor Cummings. "Don't you move." She spoke into her microphone, not taking her attention away from Alice. "Colonel Harris, sir. Can you make sure Kitty Cat doesn't run off? She might need a leash."

Five investigators backed out from the building. "This is a

major crime scene; cordon off the area. Multiple casualties. Five or six inside still alive and require immediate attention. We have neutralized the suspects."

Fifty investigators searched for victims and arrested the farm administrators. Shouts came from different areas, calling, "Over here. Over here. More victims."

Other officers chased ten people from the food prep room in white coveralls splattered with wet crimson stains. "Freeze!"

Thud—thud—thud. The suspects collapsed as an investigator fired three pulse blasts.

"Justin. Ariella." Horace took hold of the pair. "Are you injured?"

Ariella trembled and leaned against a post and then slid down until she sat on the ground. "I needed to make them stop. Those thugs killed—"

Horace knelt beside Ariella. "We saw everything from your feed, cutting our ETA. We recorded enough to shut this place down and Camp Chickamauga. Security is apprehending the workers as we speak."

"Silas?"

Horace lifted Ariella to her feet. "Thanks to him, he gave us the evidence we needed."

"Get investigators to check the blue building and ascertain what else is happening."

"Aye, sir."

Numerous buses, emergency medical and authorized vehicles from the Department of Health and Nutrition arrived as Chief Chatterjee confronted Horace.

"Will she be a problem?"

"Chatterjee will distance herself from this fiasco as much as possible. Sapros doesn't give a bag worth of peach fuzz how these establishments conduct business. His primary concern: underground media outlets reporting what happened."

Ariella swayed and held on to the bench. "They killed—I had… no choice—"

He put his arms around Ariella and held her tight. "You stopped the cyborgs. You did not kill any humans. One heck of a blast you kicked on those 'borgs."

"Wish we engaged sooner. Sybil is she—?"

"No word yet. Major Rios notified me they found several people alive in holding pens."

Justin jolted when Major Rios shouted.

Gabrielle jerked Alice by the arm. "You monster. Come with me. I might let you taste the evil treatment you inflicted on others. We will start by using robots on you."

"Major, I will take Cummings into custody. Tend to the survivors. Trust me; Cummings will receive her reward." Horace spoke into the microphone, "Colonel Harris, bring Ms. DuPont down here."

Spence took Kitty's arm in a firm grip. She planted her feet together, locking her knees. "I'm not going anywhere."

He turned her to face him. "You insist. I'll handle you the same as my son, Roger."

She gasped as he picked her up and placed her prone over his shoulder and walked to the general where he dropped her at his feet. "Hiss."

Horace took her arm. "Enough."

"Security Chief Meyers. I am so glad you are here. Appears a huge misunderstanding occurred. In no way am I involved with this facility. You are an honest man, and you wouldn't allow someone to accuse an innocent person of wrongdoing."

Justin held his breath. *Don't try to seduce my dad, Kitty. You are inviting trouble. Keep calm, Dad.*

"Ms. DuPont. You are trying my patience. I am fighting the urge not to give you what you deserve."

She tickled his nose and traced her costume tail down his torso. "What will you do? You are one handsome stallion. I'd love to scratch you up."

"You are about to find out."

Kitty gasped as he heaved her prone over his shoulder and took long strides to the kennel.

"Please don't."

Her eyes widened as he dumped the kicking bundle in an empty cage. He stepped back, locking her inside. She cowered in the center of the cage, screaming as dogs barked and lunged at the pen.

"You can exit if you start behaving and cooperate."

"Anything. Let me out of here."

Horace opened the cage. "Come on out. I warn you: don't try anything stupid."

She crawled out of the pen on her hands and knees, using the cage to stand. Kitty leaned on the outside door of the kennel, breathing hard. "What do you want...from me? Don't put me...back in with those dogs."

"Come with me. Sit here."

She sat on a wooden bench, holding her stomach, as Major Rios approached them with robotic guards. "Major Rios and I will investigate the criminal activity at Camp Chickamauga and how campers ended up at this place. The guard is here to record your statements. Do you understand?"

Kitty studied his necktie clasp to avoid eye contact. "Aren't you required to advise me what my rights are? What about my right to remain silent? I am unaware of campers sent here."

"Are you referring to the now archaic Miranda warning? No, the government denies all your rights. Accused criminals lost all rights a long time ago. I can help you if you cooperate with me. Now, you claim you are ignorant of campers sent here—what about college interns?"

"No."

"Play recording sixty-two."

The guard's screen lit up, showing her discussing sending Sybil to an advanced trauma facility.

"Now, what is the name of the facility you sent her to?"

"Advisor Cummings made all those decisions. I suggested a place for the camp to transfer her."

The image displayed her speaking with Justin and Silas about where she sent Sybil. "You promised me your cooperation; so far everything you claim is a lie. Tell me the truth."

"Sybil is alive. She is in critical condition and is talking to an investigator informing us of what you and Advisor Cummings did to her," Gabrielle said, snapping a set of flex cuffs. "A tidbit for you: Advisor Cummings is placing full responsibility on you for sending Sybil here. She insisted you chose the place because your mother started the so-called animal therapy."

"I need to talk to my mom. I won't answer anything until I do."

"You can't talk to her, as she is in custody. Your mother is facing prison for falsifying documents. She did not graduate from high school, let alone anything else. Apparently, you are aware of those falsehoods also. Anything you need to inform us? Better to disclose them now."

Kitty fidgeted with her costume. "What do you want me to tell you? I'm cold."

"Would you bring something for Ms. Dupont to wrap around herself? A little cold out here for what she is wearing."

Elliott marched toward them and stopped next to Kitty, dropping a fleece blanket on her lap. "Would you like to continue the tour? You must experience the fine dining facility and sample tour favorites. Our chef's choice today is kaegogi country meatloaf, with mashed potatoes, fresh carrots, salad, and beverage, for three credits."

"We will not need your aid any longer."

"Should you decide you need my services, give the office a call."

Horace knelt, turning Kitty's face to force her to make eye contact. "Understand, I am authorized to order you to the prison of my choosing. One preference is leaving you here; this might be the ideal place for you. However, I am making you a proposition, on the condition you are truthful. I may reconsider and imprison you someplace more tolerable than here. Lie, the offer is repealed, and I will find a prison worse than here to send you. Now, talk."

"I promise not to lie to you," she said, rubbing her nose. "Yes, this place slaughters dogs for human consumption. Yes, I did recommend Advisor Cummings place Sybil here. Alice cautioned her violations did not necessitate such action. My mother never graduated from high school, but she worked hard, moving up the ladder, doing sexual favors for Sapros. May I have a tissue?"

Gabrielle opened a pouch on her utility belt and handed tissues to Kitty. "Here. Anything you can tell us to help the investigation. You can still help others and yourself."

"I'm scared. All my life Mom claimed Gifford Sapros is my father. She claims he ordered her to obtain an abortion, but she ran away and hid until my birth. Gifford Sapros never accepted me as his daughter. I hope I'm not his daughter. Alexander, my half-brother, is a bit older than me. He is around twenty, and I am seventeen. Gifford...I sunk these teeth into his arm."

Kitty exposed her cat-like teeth. "Gifford whipped me on my shoulders and head with an old, heavy extension cord. Alexander hid me under his bed until I was too big to fit anymore. Afterward, he hid me in his closet until he found someplace safe, sending me to school in Tampa. Little did I realize this was where I would find myself. He wanted his father-in-law to take me in but feared this would cause problems if Gifford found me. Called him an honorable man."

"What is the name of his father-in-law?"

"I don't know who or where he is. Alexander told me his father-in-law would provide protection."

"At what age did Gifford start to abuse you?"

"As long as I can remember. The reason I wanted the cat teeth. I hated myself and thought I'd be more exciting and attractive as a cat. People made fun of me instead. Mom explained people could refer themselves to any species they want. I became determined at the age of nine; I wished to become a cat. My mother supported my fantasy. She found a dentist willing to implant cat teeth, for a price. Now, I realize how absurd—Once I got older, I kept them because they served a purpose, defense. Sybil is right, anybody who imagines they are a cat must be delusional."

"You acted like a devoted supporter of Sapros."

"Used stunners on me if...I didn't obey. The pain was—"

"Are you trying to make me sorry for you? Did he leave marks on your body where he stunned you?"

"The marks won't show where he used them. Please don't ask me to describe what he did."

"Are you trying to gain sympathy from me to let you off easy?"

Kitty tugged at the ribbon around her neck. "I guess. I don't understand myself. I—I...No, too late, I guess."

"For what?" Horace took a seat on the opposite bench.

"Nothing. I let my mouth run too much."

"What would you change if you could?"

"Be someone else."

"Do you consider Sybil delusional? I am waiting for a reply."

"Never understood anyone like her. Tried to shake her beliefs, but each time she countered my taunts. Pushed her too hard on the first breakfast, but later she tried to reason with me to understand what I am rejecting. She made me angrier. Sybil's claims are the one thing to hold on to."

Horace took hold of Kitty's hands. "Are you telling me what you think I want to hear or gain my sympathy?"

"Both, I guess. I'm too scared to know what you want to hear." Kitty pulled the burgundy blanket around her tighter with her left hand. "Rather run away and hide. Like a cat, run from danger and hide."

"What are you hiding from—your past or something else?"

"Did too much stuff to undo. Now facing criminal charges for all the things, I did and face the same penalty."

"Correct—you are. Before I tell you what price you will pay, anything you'd like to say before I announce your sentence?"

An investigator approached. "Excuse me, sir. The blue building is a recycling plant. They recycle human bones into furniture using polymers. Recycle Building A is secured for forensics to identify unrecycled human remains."

Kitty screamed, curling up into a ball. "I did not know. I didn't know."

Horace sat, putting his arm around her. "I believe you. Now, what do you want to say on your behalf?"

"Sir, I realize what freedom you carry in sentencing, I'm aware you can execute me right here where I sit and walk away pretending nothing happened. I'm terrified more than anything I have ever felt before. Should you find compassion in your heart, sir...the smallest speck. Please don't say it's too late."

"Yes, I will give you more mercy than you deserve. I am sentencing you to my detention center, confined for an undetermined amount of time. While you are at the detention facility, I expect you to follow the rules."

"What is the place like?"

"A clean and safe place for you to rehabilitate into a productive person."

"Like a reeducation camp?"

"After spending a day at the compound, comparing my facility to a reeducation camp is insulting. No camp directors to abuse you; no atrocious penalties for breaking an unwritten minor rule or otherwise. Do I expect better out of you? Yes, I do. You are to obey the rules of my home. What do you say?"

She nodded. "You have been so kind. Uh, any possibility to see Sybil?"

Gabrielle squeezed Kitty's hand. "Not yet. Sybil is en route to the trauma center at Camp Sumiton. Medical staff believes she will make a full recovery from the mental and physical distress she received. You may be able to speak with her, supervised, soon."

"Uh, I don't understand what I'm asking. I need to talk to Sybil."

"What would you ask her?"

"For her to tell me how, despite all she went through and what her mother endured, she still believes in God. Either God is real, or she is delusional. Well, I'm beginning to doubt, and this Jesus is more than being a made-up story like childhood tales. I want to hear her tell me about the Jesus she kept talking about."

"Jesus wants to forgive you."

Kitty's head bowed, her voice trembling. "I did too many horrible things. Jesus could never pardon me. He knows what I did to Sybil."

"God wants to offer mercy for everything. Let me tell you

about a man named Saul. He hated Christians; he believed he did the work of God by arresting and imprisoning them. Something happened the day he traveled to Damascus. He had arrest warrants in hand for any Christian he found, and the Lord Jesus appeared in a brilliant, blinding light and stopped him. He identified himself by questioning Saul as to why he persecuted him. The Lord made a point; Saul tormented more than Christians. Saul harassed God himself. Jesus forgave Saul for everything he ever did. He offers the same mercy to you."

"I am so scared."

"He understands you are," Horace said, taking a tissue to wipe her tears. "He loves you so much; let him help you."

"What do I need to do so he will forgive me?"

"Admit you are a sinner, ask God to pardon you, accept his mercy, and confess Jesus is the Lord of your life."

"Does God require payment for my sins to earn his forgiveness?"

"Jesus paid for your sins over two thousand years ago. You could never pay for your sins, including the tiniest one, which is why he went to the cross and died for you. Jesus conquered death by rising from the grave. His offer of salvation is free; the only stipulation is you must believe and accept his gift."

"How can he forgive me for sins committed before being born? Or coming along?"

"Jesus knew you'd one day come into this world and need his forgiveness. He knows everything about you, right down to the number of hairs on your head, all those eons ago. Nothing you did took him by surprise. Do you realize whom Jesus thought about when he hung dying on the cross? He thought about you. He thought about every person ever born and yet to be born. He prayed for you in the Garden of Gethsemane—he prayed for us."

She swayed back and forth, holding herself tight. "It's almost like something is trying to tear me apart. Part of me wants to rush to this Jesus you are talking about; the other half wants to run away."

"This may be difficult for you to understand; a battle is taking place over your immortal soul. God wants you to come to him; the devil wants you to remain in this dark world away from God. Both are talking to you; listen to God. May I say a prayer for you?"

Kitty nodded and covered her eyes with her hands.

"Heavenly Father, please rebuke Satan and send him away from this lost child. Help her, Lord, to see her need for you. Touch her heart and calm her soul, so the fear in her heart will flee and she will know the peace only you can bring her. We pray this in Jesus's name. Amen."

Justin sat beside Kitty. "We are praying for you. We are not ganging up on you; we want you to give your life to the Lord. The way Sybil did. Before she left; she wanted me to tell you she forgives you."

"I need to ask her for forgiveness, yet she did. I want God to forgive me so bad," Kitty said, covering her eyes with her hands. "Please forgive me, Jesus, for all the horrible things I did. I want you in my life. Help me be the person you want me to be. I believe in you. Lord Jesus, please save my soul." She looked around and smiled. "Never felt like this before. Somebody lifted a ton of weight off my shoulders."

"You have become a new person," Justin said, embracing her. "Kitty, Jesus washed your sins away, and you now stand justified before God."

"The nickname is as fake as the life I led for all these years. Call me Patricia. Your detention center is the place I am meant to go rather than the other places you mentioned."

"I'm more than happy to bring you to the compound," Horace said as he embraced her and kissed the top of her head. "You must serve your sentence and grow; in time, privileges will match your growth."

"I wish my mother had refused me getting these teeth. You must be thinking about my ridiculous costume."

"We are not laughing; however, we can help you with the dental and other difficulties."

Ariella scowled at the happy group. "What is going on? We came from a horrific crime scene, and you are smiling. Now is not the time to be acting like a party is going on."

"The angels in heaven are shouting for joy, Ariella, celebrating the birth of a new child of God, born this hour."

"Kitty?"

"Call me Patricia." She took the blanket to cover herself. "I need something different to wear. What I have on is too embarrassing."

"Now I know why I thought I needed to bring extra clothing with me. So, you could wear warm clothing. Come with me, and you can change your clothes. How do blue jeans and a sweatshirt sound?"

"Snug and cozy; you are so kind, considering the awful things I did."

"This is what forgiveness is all about. Adonai who forgives all the sins we commit, we should forgive others." Ariella took long strides to the van. Patricia followed, pulling her costume tail from clutter.

"Now we will contend with Cummings." Horace's smile faded, turning to Gabrielle. "I hope she thought about what lies ahead and is willing to cooperate."

"A resilient one. Before I came over, the accused made demands to go back to the camp. With all the evidence we gathered, what do you plan to do?"

"Transfer her to Southwest Quadrant to one of their facilities. She will not be able to abuse any more girls."

An investigator handed Horace a complaint affidavit and stood by for instructions. "You took the security videos into evidence?"

"Yes, sir. All in the report."

"Bring Cummings to me."

"Aye, sir."

Three Marines dragged Alice across a field and shoved her into a chair. She struggled to get on her feet, swearing at the men restraining her.

"Release me from here."

"Well, anything to say in your defense, Cummings?"

"I got a job to do at the camp."

"First, I need you to explain something. In the past five years, you sent at least fourteen pregnant girls here."

"They must have seduced the male guards."

"The girls played around with the bodyguards and got pregnant? Bot guards are not capable of procreation; explain again how these girls got pregnant? Male campers are in a secured area and can neither sneak in nor out of their assigned area. Let me ask you again, who impregnated these girls?"

"Jack or Fred called in girls for sex." Alice held her palms upward. "I'm sure they did."

"Why did you not report these violations?"

"Girls will consent to anything if they might gain favored treatment or be released early."

"Did you ever wonder why the camp allows two males direct interaction with female campers?"

She gave no response, continuing to stare at the doctor.

"I read in your health report you refused checkups since you became employed at the camp. Regulations require an annual exam. I obtained Dr. Sherry Grassley, a member of my health staff, to do a courtesy exam. For your information, I can order you to submit to one. She examined both Jack and Fred; neither one is capable of fathering children since they are both transgender. Also, you need to know, Fred is pregnant. I suspect child support might deduct credits from your pay voucher...I ask you again; how did those girls get pregnant?

"No idea."

"Advisor Cummings, I am Dr. Grassley. General Meyers ordered me to give you a health check as a courtesy to keep your records up-to-date. Failure to make your annual health exam is risky; cervical cancer is on a perilous rise."

"I got a right to refuse," Alice said, glaring at the doctor.

"Explain how your DNA happens to match the paternal DNA of the pregnant girls' babies?"

She remained silent, continuing to stare at the doctor.

"Dr. Grassley geld him."

"Sir?"

"Turn that thing into a gelding. Now, doctor."

"Aye, sir. I'll get my equipment. The procedure will take ten seconds to finish."

"Yes, I impregnated those girls. Yes, I declared myself as a woman, to get near the girls. Please don't castrate me."

Horace tapped a stunner with his hand. "What if I show you the same mercy you gave the girls?"

Cummings paled. "You couldn't. Wait. An autographed first-addition, Aston Sapros book, *A Christmas Carol*, I'd be more than happy to give—"

"Aston Sapros never wrote an original piece of work. I prefer the Dickens version of the tale. In Aston's version, Ebenezer Scrooge gains control over the three spirits; they convert to his philosophy and admit they are frauds. Cummings, you're not able to come up with anything making me forget about your crimes."

"You got no proof I did anything wrong. Those girls consented," Cummings said, pointing her finger.

"What makes you think I lack evidence?"

"You're trying to trick me into a false confession."

Horace signaled to the doctor and four assistants. "To some degree, the penalty might be lessened. I show compassion to people who give me a reason. Due to you offering me a bribe, you lack a strong defense."

Alice held up her hands. "Wait. I can give you the information you want."

"Which is?"

"Kassidy. I know where she is and who owns her."

"Tell me about Kassidy."

"She is your daughter and is missing."

"Don't give me a bunch of bilge. Tell me something I don't know."

"Search no further than Alexander Sapros."

"Why should I trust you, Ian Knupp?"

"Who told you my real name?"

"DNA does not lie."

"I sold Kassidy to Alexander."

"I found a marriage certificate saying she is married to Matthew Skyler O'Connor."

"While working at the camp, Alexander used the name to be incognito. I took Kassidy into custody for execution on the charges of proselytizing. Wealth and power buy Alexander whatever he wants. You want Kassidy back; you must ransom her from the Legatee."

"Knupp, I keep my promises—you are free to go after the doctor turns you into a gelding." Horace smacked Justin on the back. "Let's go home." As they jogged to the waiting helicopters and vans a high-pitched shriek came from the kennel area causing the dogs to howl.

Horace slapped the side of the van. "Once you get squared away, I will give duty assignments and assign education and other tasks. We will discuss this more when you reach the compound. May I welcome you to the Southeast Compound in advance."

As the blades rotated, Horace sat back and nodded to his father. "Let's rescue Silas; I'm sure his hands are full, and he is ready to escape from coo-coo land. He collapsed the security system by programming the bots to sing all verses of "Ode to Gifford" in all languages. Enough time for Squad B to secure the facility," Horace said. "Eighty-six years before anyone can gain control of those bots again. What is Elliott doing in here?"

"I brought him in here," Ariella said, "because Elliott might be useful to Silas."

"Would you like me to take you on an aerial tour of the facility? One of my functions is flying helicopters. After which you can feast on our delicious cuisine at Brasserie."

"Tours and food again, Elliott," Horace said. "What information do you have on the supreme commander?"

"The supreme commander is not on the menu at Brasserie, but if you place your request in advance, our chefs will accommodate your request."

"Wait a minute," Horace said, sliding the passenger door open and getting out. "Elliott, go back to the central office and wait for your next order."

"But—"

"Wait, I will handle this, Ariella," he said, unstrapping the cyborg.

"Have a pleasant day and see you soon," Elliott said, stepping military-style down the path to the offices as the helicopter ascended into the air.

"Silas will manage without Elliott. What made him think he could take a piece of government property?"

"He powered down Elliott's defense mechanism to focus on the tour and not on our investigations. Otherwise, game over when I came out of the food prep building. Per Silas, Elliott is a sophisticated piece of machinery. Reactivated, he will replay everything, starting from our arrival."

"Can this day get any crazier? Major Rios is collecting puppies; now Silas is acquiring a cyberbot for whatever purpose. Turn the wind machine around, Dad; let's go pick up Elliott. Major Rios," Horace said into the radio. "Elliott is at the central office, get him to the helipad."

"Aye, sir. Anything else I can do?"

"What are you doing about the dogs?"

"The adult dogs are too wild; Dr. Grassley is putting them down. The puppies are eager and friendly; Patricia is playing with them. They don't scare her like the adult dogs. She is helping us load them into the vans, and we will take them."

"Major Rios, how many?"

"I called for extra cargo vans to transport them."

"Major. How...many...puppies."

"Too much noise, sir, I'll meet you when you land."

"I will regret this. Sixty bundles of energy, all running and yapping over the place, digging holes and whatever else dogs do."

Justin opened the sliding door, allowing Elliott to enter the helicopter. Patricia deposited an excited golden-haired puppy into Horace's lap. "No, your kissing up to me isn't working."

"I call her Sunny because she likes to play in the sunshine."

"How many? Major."

"Five hundred."

"Did I misunderstand, Major? What are we to do with five hundred—"

"Better get this bird back into the air—stand back."

"What will I—Oh! My new trousers. Naughty Sunny."

"Anyone wanting to visit the nursery, ask me to arrange a tour of the puppy kennels."

"Thank you, Elliott."

CHAPTER 13

Later that evening, Horace read a verse from the Bible to Dakota. "'In peace, I will both lie down and sleep; for you alone, O LORD, make me dwell in safety.' Psalms 4:8."

He passed his hand over a sensor to turn off the bedroom light. "Is Ms. DuPont settled in for the night?"

Dakota yawned. "I gave her new pajamas and clothing; she appreciated them. The size of her bedroom amazed her. Twice the size of the two-room apartment she and her mother lived in. Her light went out an hour ago. Poor thing, she is exhausted."

"Maddie will keep her breakfast hot," Horace said, checking the time. "Almost zero one hundred hours. I will allow her to oversleep."

"I thought you planned to place her in detention or the rescue. Why into the house right next to our room?"

"Right after she accepted the Lord and I hugged her, the detention center and the rescue cottages felt wrong. The Lord urged me to put her here with us."

"For reasons we do not yet know."

Dakota threw off the blanket and fumbled for her cane. "Did you hear a noise? Sounded like someone banging on closet doors. Patricia is screaming."

He put on his robe, grabbed his sidearm, and he bolted out the bedroom door, with Dakota behind him. He knocked and opened the door as she screamed.

Dakota waved the sensor light. "She hasn't slept in her bed."

"Why did you barricade yourself inside the closet?" Horace jostled the doorknobs to the closet.

"Get away from me. Stay away from me. I'll bite you again."

"Wake up, honey. You are having a nightmare," Dakota said, tapping on the closet door.

Moments later, the sound of Patricia shoving away boxes came from the locked closet door. "Sorry, a bad dream."

"Why are you still wearing your clothes and shoes? We gave you everything you need, including pajamas. They are yours."

Patricia cowered back into the corner of the closet. Her eyes shifted from one to the other. "I always sleep in my clothes in case of an emergency."

"What kind of emergency?" Horace reached out his hand and helped Patricia to stand.

"Easier if I need to run."

"May we sit with you?"

She nodded, curling up into a ball, tucking her legs up to her chest, wrapping her arms around her knees.

"Did you forget where you are?"

"Too dark and scary. Somebody tried to grab me."

"Ms. DuPont, I promised you. You are safe here. You don't need to be afraid anymore."

"I'm afraid to go to bed—terrible things happen."

Dakota went over to the bed and removed a down comforter. She placed the soft cover over Patricia's shoulders.

Maddie stood at the end of the sofa. "Would you like a mug of cocoa with marshmallows?"

She stiffened her body as Maddie stroked her hair. "I'm sorry, Patricia. I didn't mean to make you uncomfortable."

"You are trying to be kind."

"From the medical findings, I can speculate what happened to you in the past. Would you like to tell Dakota or me about what occurred? Who branded a star on your tongue?"

Tears poured down Patricia's cheeks. "I can't."

"Gifford abused you. Is this why you are so frightened?"

"Don't make me tell you."

"God sent an army of angels to guard your room. He will keep you safe. Psalms 34:7: 'The angel of the Lord encamps around those who fear him and delivers them.' Can you sleep in your bed now?"

"No. I prefer the closet."

"More comfortable in your bed, with plenty of fluffy pillows."

"I'm not safe."

Horace ran his hand through his hair. "Security is tight here; no one can come near you."

Lines formed on her eyelids as she held her eyes closed. "Yes, they can. He refused to stop. I begged him to stop. He kept—"

"Who is this animal?" Horace knelt beside Patricia's chair.

"I. Can't. Tell. You."

"Alice Cummings?"

Patricia shook her head.

"I am the security chief for the Southeast Quadrant. I can make sure this person pays for what he did to you. All you need to do is say his name. I guarantee he will never bother you again."

"He is violent; you can't fight him. I tried. You won't be able to stop him."

"The only person in the country who controls more power than I do is Gifford Sapros himself."

"I can't; I am terrified of him."

Maddie carried in a tray with a white mug decorated with yellow roses and a chocolate chip cookie on a matching plate.

"Take it away. It scares me."

"Honey, I will. Andy and I will pray for her."

"Why did the cocoa and cookie upset you, Patricia? We want to help you."

Horace called the clinic. "Ask a doctor to come to the house. Ms. DuPont is having stress-related difficulties."

Dakota snapped her fingers. "Be right back. I might have something helpful for you."

"Did the cocoa and cookie remind you of an unpleasant experience?"

She sobbed as she rocked. "Brought them to—"

"I can stop Gifford."

"No, he will destroy you."

Someone rapped on the door; a man in a knee-length white lab coat walked into the room. "General Meyers, I understand Ms. DuPont is in distress."

Horace took the folder from the doctor. "Is this the final medical exam?" He closed his eyes and gulped in a breath. "We will see to her receiving the treatment she needs."

The doctor sat in front of Patricia. "Can you look at me? Fine. Can you follow my finger with your eyes without turning your head? Excellent. Let me check your vitals. Hmmm, respiration elevated somewhat; her oxygen level is below normal. Patricia, can you take a deep breath and hold? Now give me a slow exhale. Now inhale; now exhale. Her oxygen level is improving. Her heart rate is back to normal. She needs a restful night's sleep."

Dakota returned to the room; she held a giant teddy bear under one arm.

"Blurty, you thought of the perfect thing."

Horace took the five-foot royal-blue teddy bear dressed in a white shirt. "For you."

Patricia took the bear and held on tight. "Bear hugs from Jesus. Thanks."

"Do you think you can go to bed now?"

"I am acting like a two-year-old. Would you and Dakota sleep in my bed while I take the sofa?"

"More comfortable in your bed."

"Please. I'll try to sleep in the bed; I am too scared tonight."

"All right, we will."

"Lights off," Horace said.

"Chief Meyers?"

"Yes, Ms. DuPont."

"Are you armed?"

"Yes."
"Are you always armed?"
"I am never without my sidearm."
"Dakota, are you armed?"
"Yes, honey, I am armed."
"I can sleep now."

Tuesday, October 24, 2079

As daylight filtered into the room, Horace got out of bed and read a handwritten note on the empty sofa.

Chief Meyers,
Went to clean the kennels. I'll be in time for breakfast and to attend the Bible study, as you instructed me.

Dakota sat up, yawning. "Where is Patricia?"

"She went to clean the kennels."

They went downstairs, hearing Maddie's raised voice. "Stop right there, Miss Dirty and Grimy. Don't track dirt over the floors. Remove your shoes and march upstairs and take a shower. Breakfast served soon."

Covered with dirt, Patricia picked embedded hay from her hair. She brushed the dust from her slacks and removed her shoes and placed them in the corner.

"Um, please explain how you got so dirty cleaning the kennels?"

She jumped, hearing his voice. "Not from the kennels. They are easy to clean. I got dirty cleaning the stable."

"Clarify how your face and arms got dirt all over them."

"I hugged and kissed the horses. I'll bathe them after Bible study and take another shower, so Mrs. Kramer won't need to scold me."

"Ms. DuPont, I did not assign you to clean the stables. Why did you take on extra chores? Extra work will not speed up your release date."

"I enjoy being around horses. You are right; comparing this place to a reeducation camp is an insult."

"I'll buy you some boots, so you won't mess up your new shoes. Now, scoot and wash up."

Patricia slipped into the house wearing a pair of new jeans and a black sweatshirt falling off her shoulders and reaching her knees with the word *Marines* in gold lettering. She held Sunny under one arm while she held the bottom of the shirt secure with the other. Patricia glanced around the room and stairs before she crept toward her room.

"Ms. DuPont, I need to speak to you for a moment."

Patricia jumped. "Sir."

"In the sitting room. Sit on the couch."

"Yes, sir."

Horace came out of his den with a paper, looking over his black reading glasses. "Here are the house rules I expect you to obey while you are living under this roof. The first rule, you are not to bring pets into the house. One of the stable workers will build a dog house which matches this house for Sunny to sleep and play in. Now, take Sunny outside."

"Yes, sir."

Patricia coaxed the puppy to follow her outside; she inched back into the room and slouched on the couch.

"Why are you wearing one of my sweatshirts? They come in your size."

"Smelled your aftershave when you arrested me at the farm. Your scent on the sweatshirt gives me a sense of safety."

"Go ahead, if wearing my sweatshirt helps."

"Thank you."

"Ms. DuPont, before I go further, do you need to tell me anything? Now is the time to inform me, not later. You lie for any reason...Did you perjure yourself about anything?

"No, sir," Patricia said, scratching her neck.

"You don't need to fear me; you better be stating the truth. I expect you to give proper respect to the members of the family, which includes Justin. Refer to me as Chief Meyers, my wife as Mrs. Meyers, not Dakota, my father as Mr. Meyers. Justin...call him Justin."

Patricia rubbed her stomach. "Yes, sir,"

"Are you having problems? Why do you keep holding your stomach?"

"Uh."

The back door opened; Sunny came running in, barking at Patricia. A gray-and-white long-haired kitten, about three months old, escaped from under Patricia's sweatshirt. "Ow." Sunny pursued the fleeing feline up the stairs into one of the bedrooms. She froze with her feet planted flat on the floor and waited for him to react.

Horace sat in a chair pressing his fist against his mouth. His dark eyes penetrated her as he tried to decide what disciplinary action to take on the rule violation. Patricia sat still as seconds passed.

"Well, Ms. DuPont, as long as you are here, life will never be monotonous," he said, moving his hand to reveal a smile. "Let me find something to tend to your scratch."

Tuesday, October 31, 2079

Ariella stood in front of the class explaining her job at Camp Chickamauga. "My assignment in the Behavioral Compliance Office led us to discover horrendous activities at the camp. Details of what we uncovered at this so-called reeducation camp are too explicit to show on the holographic projector. Through the efforts of this team—Justin in the record section, Silas programming computers, while I worked in compliance—we assisted SC Meyers to scuttle this camp and farm," Ariella said, pointing to the offices and the deceptive tranquility of the camp.

"The backlog of files kept interns busy," Justin said, directing the students' attention to stacks of scattered files. Those camps will no longer abuse interns, as my dad locked them down. Carelessness plus sloppy file keeping gave us a piece of a puzzle, leading to the closures, saving hundreds if not thousands of lives."

"Meyers, I assigned you as a camp cook, not records. I told you your father could not change your assignments. Should I discover either of your parents changed your duties at the camp, the three of you will receive a failing grade."

"Professor Denson. Neither my father nor Ariella's changed anyone's assignment, including Silas's. Now, may we continue our presentation?"

"Well, Jenkins, your turn," Denson said, rubbing his temples nodding to Silas.

"Elliott tell the class about yourself."

"Good afternoon. My designer is Dr. Edgar Neuhauser, chief engineer of the Cybernetics Institute at Aston University. I am a tour guide and chief security droid at Kaegogi Farms. We offer three tours each day. Do any of you have questions?"

"Elliott, explain: what is kaegogi?"

"Kaegogi Farms raises quality farm-bred dogs for human consumption. Preparation of canine meat and beef are the same. Production of kaegogi is less costly than beef products, considering the number of puppies born in a litter versus births of cattle."

Professor Denson stood, raising his voice. "Enough. I did not assign you three to do a secret investigation. What the three of you presented is a collection of fear-mongering nonsense."

"Upon recognition of criminal violations taking place at the facilities, we reported them to Chief Meyers, and he took appropriate action," Ariella said. "Professor Denson, you assigned us to report what we gathered from our experience, which the three of us are now doing. Do you want us to continue our presentation? I can show you everything we found. Let me warn you: the holograph may be upsetting to some here. Throughout my time working in defense, I witnessed a lot of horrific scenes; this is the worst yet. People working at these facilities possessed no more compassion than this cyborg. Provided you can stomach watching a holographic video of a female hanging from the rafters slit from the abdomen to the throat with her bowels tumbling out, along with numerous grisly scenes."

"Why did they do this?" asked a male student, sitting in the midsection of the class.

"Kaegogi Farms is an execution camp for accused dissenters.

The accusation of dissension may come in many forms."

A classmate raised her hand, shut her eyes, and then covered her ears. "Why executions at a reeducation camp?"

Ariella glared at the professor; her eyes narrowed into thin slits. "Do you want me to tell them? The government kept the truth hidden for years. Go ahead and threaten us. Chief Meyers condemned both places and is continuing his investigation. More than a few college professors are on his hit list for helping feed, and I mean in the literal sense, naïve students into the system. We rescued fifteen survivors."

"In my possession are dossiers," Silas said, "on several college professors at numerous universities in the Southeast Quadrant. All information is in unsecured data files. Your's professor could be the most peculiar."

"Why are nine seats empty? Why did they not come to class? Instructors assign certain tasks to keep control over what one finds out," said Justin. "Your mistake, Professor Denson, was you did not verify having links to the project areas. Somehow, our assigned duties stationed us in the perfect place to discover what secrets they held."

Denson slid off a wooden table in the classroom. "Class dismissed. You'll find your grades posted by the end of the week. I hope you gained knowledge from this course," He said, hurrying out the door; his footsteps echoed down the hallway.

Justin chased after Denson as the double doors swung open for him to exit. Two security Marines blocked his escape. Now handcuffed, Denson was escorted by the Marines to a waiting van bearing the emblem of the security chief's task force. As Justin returned, students rose from their places, talking to those around them, wondering why the professor had left in a hurry.

"No word from my boyfriend in days. I tried to call; someone answers his phone, says he is busy and disconnects. After what you told us about this camp and the farm, I am afraid," a female student said.

"Give me the names of those missing from this class. I will check the list against the casualties."

"Two from the same team went to a camp in Tennessee; my teammate went missing in Kentucky. One morning, a director informed me, Jerome went absent. Strange—his car still sits in the parking lot. The professor swapped me around with Savannah's male friend, who went to Tennessee. Guess I'd be missing too."

"Give me their names and their assigned locations; my dad can check into what became of them. Try not to worry; we will locate them." Justin put the names of the students and whom to contact into his computer notepad. "The next of kin, in case, well, in case."

Elliott followed the three walking to the parking lot. Justin mounted his cycle as the black security van exited the parking deck, turning to the roadway. "Let's head back. I am sure my dad can use our help."

"I need to go home. I'll call you, Justin." Without looking back, Ariella headed north to her home.

"Are you coming, Silas?" Justin took his helmet from the handlebar.

"Where is Kitty?"

The engine of Justin's cycle hummed. "She prefers Patricia. You won't recognize her. After she got her teeth fixed and got rid of the silly cat getup, she is knock-down gorgeous. How do you like the bike?"

Silas mounted the cycle, with Elliott sitting behind him. "This rides like a dream. I can't thank your father enough for the opportunity to prove myself to him."

"My dad wants to talk to you about taking on more responsibilities, if interested." Justin and Silas rode from the parking deck on their way to the compound.

A guard waved the two to continue up the driveway. They circled the entrance to the house.

"What does your dad want me to do?"

"He intends to talk to you about job ideas, enlisting as a Marine." Justin hung his helmet over the handlebars.

"Is he running a puppy mill? Hey, those dogs aren't about to become one of my responsibilities, are they?"

"The farm offers an exceptional tour of the puppy kennels if interested."

"Yes, Elliott, we will take the puppy tour later."

"Puppies will not be one of your responsibilities. Elliott needs reprogramming, well, come on. I think someone else got puppy duty."

"Hey, I'm home," Justin said, opening the door, "and got someone with me. Hey, Patricia, are you in here?"

Maddie greeted him with a hug and welcomed Silas. "We heard so much about how you work with cyborgs."

"This must be your mom. May I introduce this pleasant fellow, Elliott; he is a cyborg, and he doesn't cause any trouble."

"Glad to meet you. Are you interested in a tour of the facility?"

"You can ignore Elliott; he tends to have a one-track memory drive. Gets insistent on convincing people to take a tour of the kennels." Silas pushed back a lock of hair from his eyes. "He isn't cognizant we left the farm."

"This is my aunt Madeleine Kramer; she is the executive chief of staff. Aunt Maddie, where are Mom and Dad?"

"They are with Patricia, helping round up puppies. Several of them proved to be savvy escape artists when she opened the gate to the new kennel."

"What did my dad do with Sunny?"

"Your dad found her sleeping in one of his covers. He softened up a lot. Sunny curled up on his cover with her head hanging over the edge. Ask him to show you the holographs he took of her."

"We are talking about my dad?"

"I know, for years he declared"—she lowered her voice— "'No pets in the house.' Now, Sunny and Leopold."

"Leopold?"

"Our guest smuggled in a kitten by wearing one of your dad's sweatshirts. He made Patricia put the puppy outside. Sunny got back in and tattled on her. To the horror of our guest, Leopold took off across the room like a streak. Poor kid, she sat petrified until your dad told her our home would never be dull while she is here."

"Maddie, I caught Leopold climbing the hat tree to knock the dress cover to the floor to use for a bed. Happy to see you again, Silas," Andy said. "My son will talk to you when he comes in. How does flying helicopters appeal to you?"

"Helicopters? Never thought about flying. Strikes my interest—I'm accustomed to working with computers and staying on land."

"This helo will almost fly itself with the central processing unit they install now. A new challenge."

A familiar female voice came from the back door. "I am sorry, sir—I didn't mean to let the puppies escape."

"A certain son of mine let the horses out once. Five mares are easier to corral than a multitude of yapping furbabies."

"Man, Dad hasn't forgotten about what I did yet. How old? Six? You laugh. Dad didn't act like my letting the horses out as funny."

"You terrified him, letting the horses loose. He thought they might trample you; he didn't want you letting them out again."

"Yeah, I know now. I hoped Dad forgot."

"Chief Meyers arranged for the doctors to replace my cat fangs. No more cheek implants, whiskers, or cat-eye contacts. I am an ordinary woman now."

"Ordinary? You are the most beautiful woman I have ever seen. What a change," Silas said, gawking at Patricia from head to toe.

Patricia blushed and glanced at the floor. "You must have thought I looked ridiculous."

"You need someone to believe in you." He thought about the chief's words of encouragement to him three weeks earlier.

"I found someone, or should I say he found me, praise God. I believe in him. Jesus saved me, Silas."

"I need to tell you something, sir. Drugs did not get me kicked out of my home," Silas said. "A made-up excuse. They thought my being a doper as less embarrassing than to tell everyone I became a Christian. I let God down, not acting Christlike the past few weeks. I prayed, promising God, with his help, I will do better."

"I hoped you'd be honest with me. The community selects who

may live among them."

"What became of them? I know Chatterjee raided the place."

"They are safe in Canada, waiting for acceptance into Israel. Ambassador Stein estimated in another week they should be on an airliner to Tel Aviv."

"Dad, students are missing from our class. Here is the list of names; can you check on their whereabouts?"

"Let me run these names through comparing them with the casualty list." He spoke into the computer; a list of victims appeared on the screen. "Four are here on rescue status recovering in the health center. The two from Tennessee, both assigned to a midlevel facility. They both checked in for work this morning."

"We presumed they'd be back in class today. Not returning to get credit for the project makes little sense."

"One became the director of rehabilitation; the other, dean of academics. Not bad for students not finishing their degrees. Wonder what they did to gain those positions? Well, at least they are found."

"Thanks, Dad."

"Son, Jaycee is on the victim list. An investigator found her; she died in his arms."

"This whole thing is one horrible nightmare. I hate Gifford more for this. Jaycee told me at Ollie's; her professor assigned her to someplace in the mountains of Eastern Tennessee. Wacky but sweet. I miss Jaycee."

Major Rios came in, clearing her throat. "Excuse me, Chief, but Sybil is requesting a visit from Kitty. I'm sorry, Patricia—I thought you would prefer to tell her. I didn't tell her what happened."

"I am excited to tell Sybil."

"Ms. DuPont, a small favor when you pay a quick visit to Sybil. Go to the blue cottage and ask for a woman by the name of Chole. Take her for a checkup. At admission, ask for room six."

"What's going on?"

"Don't ask questions. You are still on probation level one here. Now do what I tell you. Go on. When I give you an order, you respond, 'Aye, sir.'"

"Yes, sir. Aye, sir."

"Probation level one?"

"Something to concoct as I go along. The compound is a certified holding facility; however, Ms. DuPont is our sole detainee."

"Who is this Chole?" asked Justin.

"Sybil's mother. The doctors found the reason for her near-catatonic behavior. A treatment center inserted a microchip, keeping her sedated. Once they removed the chip, she regained her strength and begged for Sybil."

CHAPTER 14

Monday, November 6, 2079

Patricia sipped on a cup of chocolate-mint coffee, reading a textbook on the Gospel of John. "Compare the I AM sayings of Jesus to Exodus 3:14. God said to Moses, 'I AM WHO I AM.' And he said, 'Say this to the people of Israel: I AM has sent me to you,'" Patricia said, flipping the pages to John 8:58. "Jesus said to them, 'Truly, truly, I say to you, before Abraham was, I am.'"

Horace took a seat on the other side of the table. "Are you confused?"

"Not sure what Jesus means by 'I am.'"

"Many people become confused by the term. The Gospel of John, despite the apparent simplicity, is profound. The writer is trying to convince the Jews that Jesus is more than a prophet. He is God himself; Jesus proclaimed he is God. Why are you starting in section eight instead of section one?"

"Caught my attention, so I dove into what I thought as the most exciting."

"Before you learn how to swim?"

She hugged her new Bible, her face beaming. "This is all so new, I wish to understand everything at once."

"John packed his writing with riches for you to uncover. I am proud of your enthusiasm; continue to dig."

"You make the Bible sound like a bottomless treasure trove, and I am waiting to find golden nuggets and gems," she said, reading the first five verses of John.

"For where your treasure is, there your heart will also be."

"Oh, you quoted Matthew, 6:21. My memory verse for today."

Puppy barks came from another room. Sunny came dashing in with Leopold close behind. Leopold jumped on Horace's lap and climbed to his shoulder.

"Careful with the claws, Leopold."

She scooped up the two. "I'm sorry. I didn't mean for Sunny and Leopold to become a nuisance. I'll take them outside for a while."

Dakota leaned on her cane, nudging him. "This morning, I found Sunny and Leopold used the chief's cover as a bed last night."

"Sorry. I will make sure the pair don't trouble you."

"You need to hear the rest of the story. Sunny and Leopold slept on the chief's stomach. Mr. Prim and Pompous faked sleep, but I caught him smiling, scratching Leopold's ears. You can't let Sunny sleep on you; full-grown she will weigh around sixty pounds," Dakota said, massaging the nape of his neck.

"She cries when I put her on the deck. Unless she becomes too excited, Sunny is learning to let me know when she needs to go out. I am teaching Leopold to use the toilet but not to flush. Fascinates a cat." He made circular motions with his hand. "They like to watch the water go around and around.

I called Alexander Sapros. He meant to call back but needed to find a secure location before calling." Horace pulled Sunny up to his lap to keep her from chewing on his suede tactical boots.

Patricia scanned through family holographs, tracing her finger across one with a young woman. "You met Kassidy Sapros?"

"Kassidy is our daughter."

"Yes. Alexander's wife. They hid me from Gifford."

"Are you sure this is the woman with Alexander?"

"Yes, sir, I am sure. Please don't tell him about me. Should Gifford find out, he would come after me. Alexander would not betray my whereabouts."

The holograph pad lit up with Alexander's emblem. Patricia trembled as she hid behind a desk, peering out.

"Thank you for calling me back, Legatee."

"You are welcome, sir. Excuse me for not answering your question. My father is a suspicious person. Now to your request: I am sorry I know nothing about your daughter."

"Are you acquainted with an Alice Cummings, also known as Ian Knupp?"

Patricia gasped and ducked behind the desk. "Ian? My uncle Ian is Alice Cummings?"

"Should I?" he asked.

"Cummings insisted you married my daughter. He claimed you bought Kassidy from him to keep her from being executed and says you went by the name of Matthew Skyler O'Connor when you worked at the farm. I have an additional witness who knows of your marriage."

Alexander stood at an angle, scratching his left ear. "No, I don't know what you are talking about. He is one of my bodyguards; he hasn't gotten married, at least not to anything human."

"Please tell us if she is well. Why did someone give me false information? For so long we have been led to believe our daughter died." Dependent on his military training to remain calm, he kept hands behind his back. In his peripheral vision, Patricia peeked out from behind his desk, motioning to him.

"I'm without explanation as to why someone gave you incorrect information. I can only imagine how difficult this must be for you."

"Can you tell us anything about Kassidy? Not knowing is breaking our hearts."

Alexander scratched his ear again. "Sir, I met your daughter once, for a moment. May I assist you further—"

"Enough, Alexander. Monitor off."

Dakota's voice broke. "Five-Star, Alexander met Kassidy many times. Why is he not telling us the truth?"

"He knows where Kassidy is. What I don't understand is why

Gifford and Alexander are keeping her from us."

"Can you ask Knupp for more information?"

"I doubt he will speak to me after I ordered a veterinarian to make a gelding out of him."

Patricia covered her face with her hands and remained silent.

"You did what? Why?" Dakota asked, steadying herself on her cane. "How could you be so cruel?"

"For raping fourteen-year-old girls. Blurty, you would accuse me of being too kind. Cummings should not be breathing, let alone singing soprano now. First, he raped them, and then he sold the girls he impregnated to the slaughterhouse." Horace hid his face in his fists. "Can't remove those images out of my mind. Knupp got his freedom and won't be able to rape anyone's daughter again."

Dakota laid her head on his chest. "Where do we go from here?"

"Blurty, I don't know. Provided Ms. DuPont's information is factual, we will celebrate Kassidy's homecoming before the supreme commander's birthday."

"Chief Meyers?"

"Yes."

"Alexander scratched his ear; he is trying to tell you: he and Kassidy are in danger. Kassidy taught me if I got into trouble, call them and scratch my ear. They'd send help."

"Our secret code. Thank you for telling me."

"Sir, something you need to know. Alexander and Kassidy have a daughter they keep her hidden from Gifford. Her name is Melissa; we nicknamed her Missy."

"Are you Tisa?"

Patricia nodded.

"Dakota, the three of us need to pray for Kassidy and Missy."

Friday, November 10, 2079

"Mrs. Meyers, my dress is beautiful; what is this occasion?" Patricia spun around in her royal-blue gown with sparkling gold beads. "I feel like Cinderella."

"The chief yakked about this banquet for a month now. The Marine Corps Birthday Ball, their 304th. You have not paid attention."

"Since I am not family, I thought I would not be going. Planned on staying in my room, studying. Other rescues aren't going unless they are part of the cadet program. I haven't taken the entrance exam yet."

"The chief requested Silas as your escort."

"What will he be wearing? Blue jeans?"

"Not unless he wants inconveniences with the chief. Don't worry; he won't embarrass you."

"Silas or Chief Meyers?"

"Excellent point."

Someone tapped on Patricia's door. "Chief, you are so manly in your uniform with your fancy sword."

"This sword? Only carry this thing when I am in the company of beautiful women who need my protection. Blurty, you are stunning; you will outshine all the women. Shall we go down? The limo is waiting."

"Five-Star, you are such a flatterer."

"Let me go down first; I would like to see you and Mrs. Meyers come down." Patricia lifted the skirts and rushed down the stairs.

"Hey, Cinderella, you have six hours before midnight. Why are you wearing your jogging shoes?"

"Ahem, the limo is waiting, sir."

Patricia reached out her hand. "Silas?"

"Meet Private First-Class Silas Jenkins."

Silas offered his arm. "Ma'am."

Horace extended his elbow to Dakota. "Not a ma'am."

Patricia scanned the front lawn. "Where's Justin?"

"He is supposed to be on his way with Ariella."

"On his cycle?"

He winked at Silas. "No, he took the Sagitaur."

Silas's mouth twisted into a smile. "The Sagitaur will grab Ariella's attention, as well as the city of Birmingham's."

"Fancy? What is a Sagitaur?"

"Fancy price tag. Not a comfortable ride or sporty; however, the military device is enormous."

"Sagitaur? Sounds like some kind of dinosaur. Garrrrr."

Dakota balanced herself on Horace's arm as they descended. "Ariella ought to give him a first-class stun-bop if he escorts her in one of those contraptions."

"He took a driver; they are picking her up in the spare limo."

Saturday, November 18, 2079

"Sweetheart, the chief wants you to join us for a family picnic. Justin invited Ariella, and Silas asked about you."

"Where is this picnic place?"

"Not far—down to the forks of the river. Most relaxing and peaceful unless somebody drives past in a Jeep, several tanks rumble by, or a platoon on a jog doing cadence. Or helicopters vibrating overhead. Other than all the distractions, peaceful serenity."

"Major Rios pointed out the rivers when she transferred me to the house."

"Horace is itching to grill steaks, and he brought a couple of gallons of hot chocolate in case you get chilled. Maddie made all the fixings. Andy is bringing fishing poles for anyone who wants to fish. Wait until you taste his renowned campfire chocolate marshmallow melts."

"Should I change? I don't know what I'm supposed to wear."

"What you are wearing—the sweatshirt and blue jeans are perfect."

"We loaded the bus with picnic chow," Horace said, entering the house whistling "Count Your Blessings." "Now will my family get on board?"

Patricia sat on the bottom step of the stairs with her head hung.

"Come on; you are holding us up."

"I'm not family."

"While under my roof, you are family—now, get on the bus."

Justin took a seat beside Ariella, Andy next to Maddie. Dakota sat behind Horace. Patricia slid into place behind Justin and Ariella. Silas sprinted into the bus, taking a spot beside her.

"Want company on the trip?"

"Silas, we are less than five minutes away. But I would love for you to sit beside me."

"Have you ever learned how to fish? Chief Meyers provided live and artificial bait."

"Live bait? Like worms and minnows? Don't their guts goosh out when you stick the hook in them?"

"How about live crickets," he said, glancing into the rear-view mirror. "Cricket guts burst better."

"Behave yourself."

"Come on, Blurty—fishing with slimy bug guts is fun."

"Five-Star, you are worse than a ten-year-old. Stop tormenting Patricia."

"I'm sorry. Part of fishing is getting worm guts all over your hands."

"You missed the turn. See what happens when you pester instead of paying attention to what you are doing."

"So, my drill instructors screamed at me during recruit training with their hazardous elevated levels of sodium-packed language. Give me a second to back up here and turn around by this machine barn; we are here."

"Dad why not say they swore at you?"

"Too boring."

Dakota opened the van doors and removed a picnic basket. "Spence, Colette, and Roger are here. He is showing Roger how to start the fire pit."

"Let me help you, Mrs. Meyers," Silas said, taking the basket from her.

Patricia wobbled down the muddy incline where the two rivers met. "Why so much colder standing here than back at the picnic table?"

"The turbines are on up on Smith Lake, north of here."

"Is the lake part of the base?"

"Yes, the US government bought around fourteen hundred square miles of land about twenty years ago to make up the entire base. The original property contained about two hundred acres belonging to the Meyers family."

Silas set the picnic basket on a table and jogged back to the van to bring an assortment of new fishing rods, placing them against a historical marker near the bank. Spence followed, carrying a bucket of worms and a box of chirping crickets, and set them next to the fishing rods.

Roger trailed behind Spence. "Did you ever catch sharks in the river?"

"Something the length of a boat, but never any sharks."

Silas searched through the assortment of different fishing poles. "Any experience fishing, Patricia?"

"On holographic games."

"Not the same thing—too easy to catch the fish. I'll start you on something easy. Here, this is a push-button reel. I baited the hook for you this time. Now, this is how you point and cast. Your turn. Point and cast."

"Like this?"

"Well, somewhat."

"A fish is tugging on the line, Silas."

"Yank the rod and reel in. Do you still sense pulling?"

"Like, going the other way?"

"Keep reeling in."

Patricia spun the handle toward her. "Did you see the fish jump out of the water? Looked like a tarpon, from my fishing games."

"Might be a shad—fun to catch but too bony to eat."

"Those fish have icky guts," Horace called out. "Makes them a favorite for bait."

"Turn the handle away from you."

"The tugging stopped. Is the fish dead?"

"Got away. Reel in, and I will change the lure to a silver spoon, attracting more shad."

"Mrs. Meyers allows the chief to use expensive silverware as fishing lures?"

"The chief might try, but he knows not to utilize our silver as lures."

"Blurty caught me once."

"He is silly. He never tried using the picnic wear."

"Try a shiny spoon with multiple hooks. Point your rod. Cast. Reel in quick and jerk as you reel back in. Turn the handle away from you this time."

"This fish is fighting hard. Must be a monster," she said, allowing the fish to flop on the bank. "What do I do now?"

"Let me show you how to pick up the fish and remove the hook. You don't want to stick your finger with the hook or get jabbed by a fish fin."

"Your job is to remove the fish from the hook."

"Tell you what: when you catch one worth keeping. I will remove the hook for you."

"Sounds like a deal: I capture; you clean."

"I clean; I eat."

"Better deal—I hate eating fish."

"Attention, everybody, the steaks are on. Let me know how you like them. We have chicken, kosher hot dogs, or hamburgers if you don't want steak." Horace wore a black chef's apron with words in red letters, *Cooking for Hungry Marines*.

"Hot dogs, please."

"Okay, Roger."

Justin sat with Ariella under a shade tree. "You are quiet today. Something wrong?"

"Stuff I'd rather not think about."

"The farm?"

"No, other factors I can't discuss yet."

"I'd like to help."

"I would like to talk about the circumstances, but I can't."

"Concerns your father?"

"In a way. Those steaks smell wonderful. I'm getting hungry."

Laughter drew everyone's attention. "We will get this one mounted, Patricia."

Horace flipped a steak. "What did she catch?"

"Somebody's tactical boot. The tag says, *The property of General*

Horace Wexler Meyers, United States Marine Corps."

"Does not. *General of the Marine Corps, Horace Wexler Meyers,* provided I placed a name tag on my boot. Did everyone think I never learned to ride a merry-go-round horse? Is it because I'm too short for my age?"

Silas poured water out of the boot. "Oh, wait, I found a little red horse inside. We'll let the fellow go."

"Not bad. I caught the seat of Blurty's pants once. Fortunately for me, a heavy test line kept her from getting away. I thought I snagged a whale."

"Five-Star."

"Are you telling tales like Mike?" Spence asked, patting a small football, waiting for Roger to run out to catch the pass.

"Hey, everybody, Patricia caught a walleye. Now to show her how to clean the fish. What's wrong? You are turning pale."

"Get me away from those fish."

"Let me help you back up the bank." Silas put his arm around her waist and felt her body stiffen.

"Don't. I'm sorry. I didn't mean to push you away."

"I am the one to apologize."

Horace smiled as Silas and Patricia sat at the picnic table. "Would flight training be of interest to you?"

"Yes, sir."

"Food is ready; head for the chow line. Dad, would you ask for the Lord's blessing?"

After the prayer, Andy called out, "Take a plate and grab a heap of food. Maddie made enough to feed at least half of our personnel."

Horace twirled the meat fork like a baton. "Come on Justin, Ariella. Step in line. Silas piled enough chow on his plate for an entire platoon."

Patricia smiled. "He must mean the anorexic platoon."

"Or one hungry Marine."

"Go easy on those beans, Silas. Unless you want to sound like a one-person snare-drum corps."

"Five-Star will sleep outside tonight. I told you not to put so many of those hazardous combustible beans on your plate."

"You two can form a two-man marching snare-drum squadron," Patricia said, before taking a bite of the hamburger. "Minus the drums."

"These beans are not for me," he said, dumping them on Dakota's plate. "The extra beans are for you, honey."

"Don't honey me. You will sound like a like a bunch of firecrackers popping off."

He scraped the beans on Dakota's plate. "Here they come. Remember, take all you want; eat all you take."

"Oh, returning these beans back at you, mister."

"Do they always tease each other? My mom, Gifford, or one of her many boyfriends always fought…I never enjoyed myself more than today. Thanks, Chief and Mrs. Meyers, for allowing me to join your day."

"Our pleasure."

"Would you go to the van and bring my Bible from the compartment in the driver's hatch?"

"Glad to."

"Go slow with her; she is a long way from being ready to begin a committed relationship," Horace said.

"She will not receive any pressure from me. I understand her reluctance with trust."

"I am her custodian, not her father."

"Why didn't you place her in the rescue cottages?"

"She suffers from a situation the guest cabins are not equipped to handle," he said, wiping his mouth with a napkin.

"Are you done talking about me?" she asked, returning with the Bible.

"Thank you. What makes you think we discussed you?"

"My mother used the same trick, shooing me out the room so she could talk about me. But whatever you talked about…than anything, my mom would say."

"I gave Silas advice."

CHAPTER 15

Monday, November 20, 2079

"Mr. Meyers, may I speak to you?"

"What's on your mind?"

Patricia sighed as she examined the rectangular music room with a flat ceiling. Brass, reed, string, and percussion instruments sat ready for entertainment on days guests should come to visit. Photographs of Andy with a full head of black hair hung on the wall. He played an acoustic guitar for a woman and a small child seated at his feet. "Who are these people with you?"

He nodded as he played the piano. "Horace at three and my wife, Lila, our last photograph of us together."

"What happened?" Patricia stood looking at the picture, examining the woman's smiling face.

"The Lord filled Lila's life," Andy said. "One day, a beautiful spring morning."

He bowed his head and stopped playing. "Lila left to join a committee of Christian women. About an hour later, one of her friends called, asking if she forgot about the meeting. The police searched for her, finding her body the next day about half a mile from where the meeting took place. Took a year for security to catch and execute the man responsible. My sister, Maddie, came to take care of him during my time as a Navy pilot and later after I became a US Senator in Philadelphia."

"I'm sorry. I didn't know," Patricia said, touching his shoulder. "What is the name of the beautiful piece you played, Mr. Meyers?"

"*Rondo Alla Tura*, by Mozart. Mr. Meyers is too formal. Andy will do."

"May I talk to you about something?"

"You asked me a moment ago—is something troubling you?"

"Promise not to tell Chief Meyers?"

"Well, honey, depends on what you say. Now, if this involves your well-being, I must let my son know."

"Everyone made me feel like I am part of the family and not a prisoner. I pretend Chief Meyers and Dakota are my parents. Now, if God would let me pick out a new father and mother, I would take them. Mrs. Meyers, not Dakota." Patricia shook her hands in front of her face. "A silly dream. Promise not to tell them?"

"I won't. You are not a prisoner. My son prefers to use the term *rescue*. Why don't you pretend I am your grandfather? How about Grandpa Andy, like Justin?"

"I would love to, but I won't…Well, I can be obnoxious if he got angry enough to send me away…. Jesus is all I have. The clothes I wear are not mine. I love the giant teddy bear Mrs. Meyers gave me. I need something to hug me—"

"Honey, you have us. Jesus brought you here, so you became part of our family. My son does not intend to send you anywhere. The chief hasn't sent anyone away in years; those he did, he let them come back when they apologized, often as soon as the next day. You produced a change in him. The sound of my son whistling through the house—well, that's not happened since before Kassidy went missing. We know she is with Alexander. My son is whistling again. He is happy."

Andy plucked at the keys, nodding his head. "Do you play?"

Patricia's traced the lid with her finger. "Not like you."

He took out sheet music from the bench. "Can you play this?"

She hummed several bars. "*Moonlight Sonata*, Beethoven. Yes,

I never played on a concert grand before, only a spinet, when my mother allowed me to play. A Steinway. I never dreamed someone would let me touch one." She sat on the bench, taking a breath. "The palace has a beautiful piano, but Gifford never allowed me to play. The little spinet never sounded like this."

"Ahem." Horace stood behind Patricia, tapping her on the shoulder.

"I didn't hear you come in."

"Son, I gave her permission," Andy said, laying his right hand on Patricia's shoulder.

"She may play the piano all she wants. You need to keep track of the time; you are late for class. Now, don't cry. Go to class and apologize to your instructor."

"Yes, sir." Patricia rose from the bench and darted out of the room. "Thanks, Andy."

"Refer to my father as Mr. Meyers, young lady," Horace said, placing his hand on his hips. "Go to class, now."

"Yes, sir."

"Son, I told her to use Andy."

Horace hesitated as Patricia left the room. "Why does she tug at my heart so much? The time will come for her to leave. Dakota, and I...we dread the day."

"Interesting," he said, playing *Moonlight Sonata*.

"In what way?"

"She fills a void in our lives, and we fill one in hers. The Lord sent us Patricia for a reason. I don't know why, but he did. Why do you keep calling her Ms. DuPont? You made her like family except for saying her first name."

"Dad, if I use her first name, I will have to fight Renee."

"God will answer the prayer."

"This whole thing is killing me. I transported many teenagers to this compound and cared about them all. Gave them a safe place to stay, taught them about God, and most of them stayed and became my best and most trusted Marines. Not one of them captured my emotion like Patricia. She needs a father, and mother; I cannot allow myself more."

"You love her as your daughter, don't you?

"Don't tell her; we discussed this."

Andy nodded as music filled the room. "Interesting."

"Why do you keep saying interesting?" he asked, picking up a cello to accompany his father.

"Go talk to her before you explode. She needs parents—be one to her."

"To allow myself to love her as my own and she leaves would break my heart. I can't risk losing another…"

"Did you hear yourself? You cannot bear losing another child. Too late, son; you thought of Patricia as your daughter when you brought her home."

"Trained Marines control their emotions."

"Love is a difficult emotion to control. You, my son, have adopted Patricia into your heart, mind, and soul. Regardless if you want to accept the fact or not, you love her as much as you love your children."

"I am a five-star general of the Marines assigned as security chief of the Southeast Quadrant, acting like a, like a—"

"Father. Patricia won my heart; I love treating her like a grandchild. Horace, the change in you since she came here is remarkable. You whistle "Count Your Blessings" in the morning before you go to the office and come home whistling the same hymn. She is a blessing to our home. Why don't you petition Renee for custody?"

"Ms. DuPont is almost too old, becoming an adult before the petition goes through the courts."

"Talk to her. What does she want? She is at the age to decide whom she wants as a parent."

"Biological parents possess stronger standing over adoptive parents. Does not matter what the child wants."

"Use your position over Renee. The Lord sent her here for a reason; he wants you to adopt her. At least give her parental love. She is a poor excuse for a mother."

"She still loves her. How can we ask her to toss her mother aside?"

Andy played *Moonlight Sonata*. "You won't be requesting her to cast her mother away; you will ask her to let you and Dakota in. Pray. The Lord will make a way."

"You always have wise advice, Dad."

"Now you and Dakota go talk with the Lord. He answers prayers; he is waiting for you to ask."

Horace nodded. "Thank you, Dad."

Jarrett Ellis sat across the table from Patricia. "I don't delight in conveying negative assessments. You neglected your assignments and are late for lessons. By not completing your tasks and failing this course, you will hinder yourself getting released soon."

Patricia shut her eyes, crossing her arms. "I know."

"Wait a minute—you smiled. You want the chief to extend your incarceration. How long is your sentence here?"

"Whenever he decides I can go. Chief Meyers quizzed me on my assignments; he expects me to make better grades. Furious, yes. Should have made a perfect score on this test."

"Patricia, you are brilliant. More disappointed in you than mad. Good reports make him brag." His hands rose to shoulder level. "Now why are you crying?"

"Don't know why I cry so much. At times when I see the disappointment in their eyes, it hurts; when they reprimand me, it hurts."

"Chief Meyers said you are seventeen. I'm suspecting you are younger than you claim. How old are you? Fourteen?"

"Please don't tell him I lied about my age. He warned me about lying to him, if he finds out..."

"I'm sorry, Patricia; fourteen is too young to take this class. Once the chief discovers I kept this from him, my position here is history."

Jarrett spoke into the intercom. "Sir, would you come to the study?"

Patricia laid her head on the desk, listening to Horace whistling as he strolled up the long hallway.

"What can I do for you? Ms. DuPont why are you crying?"

"Tell him."

"I lied to you," she said, looking away from him.

"About what?" He sat beside Patricia, turning her face with the tips of his fingers.

"Stop calling me Ms. DuPont. It hurts. My name is Patricia."

"I'll leave you alone to talk to her. Get in touch with me when you decide what you want to do about Patricia's classes, sir."

Horace waited for Jarrett to close the door. "All right, Patricia." He took her hand in his. "What did you lie about? Why do I need to call Mr. Ellis about your classes? Stop crying; you are seventeen years old."

"No, I'm not."

"How old are you?"

"Please don't send me away."

"What makes you think I would?"

"Thought fourteen-year-olds were not old enough."

"I gave too many excuses for your behavior. Patricia, if you lie again, I will—"

"Won't be necessary."

"Do you need to tell me more?"

"Yes, sir, I am failing my class. I didn't do my assignments, was late to class many times, and failed tests on purpose."

"Why?"

"To make you extend my sentence here," Patricia said.

"Do you want to be free again?"

"No. Where would I go? My mother is in prison for the rest of her life. I refuse to go back to Gifford. Alexander can't keep protecting me."

"I wouldn't send you to your mother or Gifford. Now, tell Silas you lied about your age."

"Please, don't make me."

"I won't make you. Your choice is to tell Silas yourself, or I will."

"Let me. Otherwise…"

Horace pressed his microphone. "Private First-Class Jenkins, I need you in my study for a moment."

Minutes later, he marched into the study and saluted. "Sir. You wanted to see me."

"At ease. Tell him."

"About my age. I'm fourteen, not eighteen. I'm sorry."

"Do you need me any further?"

"No, you may go."

"Aye, sir."

"Let me stay here," Patricia said. "Don't send me away."

"I need to discuss this with Mrs. Meyers. We will tell you what we decide."

"Please."

"Now, go to your room for the rest of the day. Mrs. Kramer will bring you a peanut butter sandwich and a glass of milk for your supper."

"Yes, sir. I'm sorry I lied. I thought you wouldn't take me in."

"Lies break down communication between us; if the truth upsets me, dishonesty is worse."

"Yes, sir."

"Patricia, come here for a moment."

"Yes, sir."

"You don't need to fear me. May I hug you?"

She wrapped her arms around his waist. "Sir. I can hear your heartbeat. Chief Meyers?"

"Yes, Patricia."

"Your stomach is growling."

Horace hugged her tighter. "Go up to your room now."

"One more hug." She gave him another squeeze before heading for her room.

"What happened?" Andy asked.

"She lied about being seventeen, or eighteen, like she told Silas.

The advantage of her age is Dakota and I can file for custody. The best part is she wants to stay here."

"Sounds like the Lord answered prayers. She is receptive to adoption."

"Did she say something to you?"

"This much I can say: you need her as much as she needs you."

Tuesday, November 21, 2079

Patricia poured herself a glass of milk. "Mrs. Meyers, may I ride Salado? The stables are extra clean."

"Salado is the chief's horse. He is too spirited for you. Salado gives him trouble. We don't want you injured from falling off him. You can ride Peppermint, Danny, or Margo; I'll tell one of the stable hands to saddle one for you," Dakota said, flipping on the intercom. "Dylan, get Peppermint ready for Patricia; she wants to go riding."

"Peppermint? She saddles Salado herself and rides him. I told her she needed to ask you, but I kept yielding to her. She can handle him; Patricia is an excellent rider. We watch to make sure the stallion behaves himself."

"Thanks, Dylan. I will discuss the matter with her." Dakota leaned on her cane, pointing to a chair at the table. "Sit down; I need to talk to you."

A deep crimson color darkened her face. "Yes, ma'am. I'm sorry I rode Salado without your permission. He is fun to ride, and I love the way he goes over the jumps."

Dakota placed her hands over her face and looked between her fingers. "Tell me you go over the little jumps, the cross-rails, not the five- and six-foot ones."

"Salado steps over the cross-rails and the two-foot jumps. I took him over the six-foot-plus ones. Do you want to watch me? It would make me happy if you watched. Silas used to ride Peppermint with me, but he kept falling off."

"Fell off Peppermint? How?"

"She runs into the rails with him and bucks him off."

"Sounds like something Salado would do. How about him riding Lady?"

"His feet would drag—Oh, yeah. He wouldn't fall as far." She held the refrigerator door open and took out a carrot. "My bribes for Salado."

"What are we to do with you?" Dakota sat on the bench, resting her head in her hands, waiting for a response. "You are a remarkable young lady. What other talents are you hiding from us?"

"I don't mean to hide anything I can do; I thought you wouldn't be interested."

"Honey, we are. Andy claims you play the piano well—any other instruments?"

"See, I'm not lapping milk from a saucer." She shrugged and sat back on the bench and sipped from the glass. "I guess any instrument you put in front of me."

"With so much in common, you and Andy should give us a concert sometime."

"I'd love too." Patricia reached over and hugged Dakota and then pulled away. "I'm sorry. I didn't mean to. I'm not allowed to. Don't tell him I misbehaved."

"How is hugging me misbehaving? Did the chief tell you not to? I would talk to him if he did."

"No, but he scratched out the keeping pets in the house rule. When I see him and Justin talking, and Justin tells his dad about an accomplishment; pride beams from the chief's face. Once I thought I saw the same expression. He realized I saw him and is back to being Chief Meyers."

"My husband isn't the hard-core person he pretends to be."

"Otherwise I would be back at the farm, hanging upside-down in the food prep building with my bowels hanging to the ground."

"Don't say anything about him leaving you; nightmares keep him up at night."

"Mrs. Meyers, the thought gives me bad dreams. If he sent me back, it would hurt more," she said, toying with the carrot in her hand. "May I go riding?"

"Let me see you ride Salado, and Silas on Peppermint, if he wants."

"Andy took him up in the helicopter."

Dakota shuffled to the jump ring and sat on a wooden bench under a pine tree, wrapping her shawl around herself. Justin stood at the rail nearby. "Dylan said Patricia pleaded with him to clean the stalls. He thought she earned riding Salado. She doesn't want to ride Peppermint, Margo, or my horse."

Patricia led Salado to a bench, mounted and cantered him around the ring once. She moved to the first jump. Dakota placed her hands over her mouth as Salado made a nearly perfect jump. With each leap, Salado cleared the rail with ease.

"How did we do?"

"How much experience do you have riding?" Dakota asked, patting Salado's neck.

"Eight years. Until a year ago, Alexander got me away from Gifford. I didn't have time to ride and take college classes; my mom didn't give me enough credits. Salado is the finest horse I ever rode." Patricia slid off and pulled a piece of carrot out of her pocket.

"You enjoy being here, don't you?"

She laid her head on Salado's neck and fed him another carrot. "Yes, but I'm...here for punishment for what I did while at the camp. I'm not to be enjoying myself. I'll put Salado back in his stall and go to my room. Hi, Justin. Yeah, shouldn't be riding your dad's horse. I'm sorry."

"Dad won't be upset about her riding Salado. He never filed criminal charges against her, did he?"

"No, Sapros would force him to turn her over for execution on his next birthday. Your dad refuses to. He would rather cut out his own heart first. We plan to file papers against Renee DuPont to adopt Patricia. We want to hear your opinion before we talk to her."

"I like having her around; you and Dad love her."

"She needs to quit being frightened of him. Makes me want to cry for her, so starved for love."

"I told her, Dad treats her the same as he did Kassidy and me while we grew up. I told about times Dad sent us to our rooms with a glass of milk and a peanut butter sandwich for dinner. I despise peanut butter sandwiches to this day. She questioned if Dad hugged Kassidy and me. I said sure—he doesn't let a day go by without hugging us. He still hugs me although I'm grown and a Marine. She ran to her room. Grandpa Andy checked on her and found her asleep wearing Dad's sweatshirt and holding the teddy bear you gave her."

"Changes will come soon. The one issue: Renee is the biological mother. Our one claim is she is under our watch. God placed her here for a reason."

Wednesday, November 22, 2079

Horace stood, staring out the window of his office at Sapros Surveillance Spire, as storm clouds built to the south. Bluish-white strokes of lightning hit the top of a low mountain nearby. Observation drones zipped around buildings, searching for acts of crime. He took a sip of Colombian coffee, thinking about his conversation with his father. He had images of Patricia leaping into his arms, accepting the news of the offer to adopt her. An alternate scene showed her rejection, her hurling objects and yelling insults at him.

"Sir, did you hear anything I said? Distracted?"

"I'm sorry, Spence. What did you say?" He took the report tablet from Spence. "What is the weather report for today?"

"Warm, humid air moving up from the Gulf will cause severe thunderstorms with the likelihood of tornadoes late this morning; the front will bring cooler temperatures later."

"Any sightings of funnel clouds or twisters yet?"

"Radar indicates vortex signatures in Cullman County, but no confirmation. Tornado score is at six and may go higher."

"Are extra emergency staff on standby, including the base?"

He handed him an initial report from Commander Forthright. "Yes, sir. Sir, Huntsville authorities request our assistance at the Redstone Arsenal—three tactical weapons stolen."

"Three microburst pulse blasters, better known as the T-60. Does he have any leads?"

"At sixteen thirty hours yesterday, a guard checked and found the weapon's room secured. At eighteen thirty hours, the sensor gave a delayed alert: an unauthorized person gained access to the munitions room using an old passcode. The surveillance camera showed a subject wearing a military utility uniform with no insignia and a cap pulled down over his face entering the room and, two minutes later, leaving the area."

"How did the security system allow someone to come in with an outdated passcode?"

Horace stared at several balls clicking back and forth on a perpetual motion device. He turned to face Spence. "What happened?"

"A disturbance at the entrance distracted the guards. Picketers demonstrated against food hoarding at the arsenal. They continued until ordered to disperse. Enough time for the unknown person to enter and exit the weapons room. In my opinion, this points to an inside job. Security is top quality, or someone is an authority at hacking. Hate to say, Silas is the only data dink who can. He went to range practice last night, along with the instructor."

"Contact Huntsville; I need facts before talking to him. His work history shows he once worked as an intern while in high school. What passcode did the intruder use?"

"One, six, two, two, four, ampersand, nine. We can request Silas's old code."

Horace nodded. *Please don't let this be so.*

Spence connected the direct link to the Redstone Arsenal commander. "Security Chief Meyers, thank you for returning my call. I am Commander Forthright."

"Commander, have you uncovered any additional information since the initial report?"

"No, sir."

"We will assist you in any way we can. To whom did the outdated passcode belong?"

"The passcode is four years old, belonged to one of our high school interns, by the name of," he said, leafing through his report, "Silas Jenkins. We terminated him from here due to unauthorized access to classified information."

"Why did your system grant the use of the old code?"

"Sir, despite our best efforts, hackers bypass all security levels."

"What can you tell me about the person on the security video?"

"We believe this person is a male, at least six and a half feet tall. Medium build, not much else."

"What information do you have on this Jenkins person?"

"Last information on him: he attended a university in Birmingham; months ago, he dropped from our surveillance. He doesn't appear to have a home address. I tried to contact his parents last night; they insist he never contacts them. Until he comes to his senses, he should stay away. They claimed undesirable factions influenced him."

"Commander transmit the security video."

"Right away, sir. Appreciate your help. Video transmitting now."

Horace disconnected the feed and relayed the video to a nine-foot screen. A tall, masked male wearing a black utility uniform walked down the corridor. Reflections in the glass window revealed someone observing from the opposite direction. "Can you identify the person?"

"Stop video. Enlarge image 100 percent."

"I don't recognize the person. An accomplice? Witness? Statue? Someone used his old passcode, but the person going into the weapons room is too tall. Silas is more than capable of hacking into the system to activate his passcode again, but why not use a new one? Justin is tall enough to be the other person—like his build and the way he walks. The most prudent thing to do is to talk to them and hope we can rule them out."

Gifford's symbol of the Chimera rotated on the holopad.

"I am sure Sapros is about to brighten my day." He stood at attention. "Supreme Commander, I am honored to be of service to you today."

Gifford rolled his eyes at the two men. "What's this I hear about Redstone Arsenal? Three classified weapons are now somewhere unknown. I am sure you know full well what this means, Meyers. I'm holding you responsible for anything going amiss with those weapons. Am I making myself clear?"

"Yes, sir. Sir, we know of the situation and are working on the investigation. I am concerned about the ramifications if those weapons fall into opponents' hands."

"Whoever is involved, find them and give them the harshest penalty possible. Notify me upon conclusion of the task." Gifford's image disappeared from the holopad.

"Sir, what are your orders?"

"Rule out both from any connection with this; find out who did and let justice prevail." Garrison cover in hand, he motioned for Spence to follow. "Go back to the compound and ascertain who checked out last night. Exonerate my people."

"Aye, sir, if I find someone did leave during the crucial time line, I will update you."

"Approve."

An hour after arriving, Horace called on the address system. "Master Sergeant Meyers and Staff Sergeant Jenkins, report ASAP."

Minutes later, the two rushed in and saluted. He squeezed his whitened fingers together as he stared at the two. "Remain at attention. Do you need to tell me anything about what you two did last night?"

"Dad, I uh—" Justin said, "You will set off air attack alarms. We have a valid reason—"

"Address me as sir, not Dad. Go on," he said, pressing his thumb and index finger over his eyes for a moment.

He lowered his eyes as Silas remained looking straight ahead. "Aye, sir. I entered Redstone last night and retrieved something."

"Sapros is out for blood: yours. The miracle is he does not know the identities of those involved in the theft. Hand over the three T-60s; I can claim someone misplaced them."

"Three? Sir, I admit I went to Redstone last night and retrieved one of the T-60s. When I left, two remained."

"Staff Sergeant Jenkins, how are you involved? I find the incident as unbelievable. Would you be so careless as to use your old passcode?"

"Sir, we didn't. I found an active unused passcode. Afterward, I erased the code. Redstone's failure to upgrade permitted us to enter."

"While you were a high school intern, why did you hack into Redstone?"

"Sir, I found a possible data breach, I created a patch to block hacking. I tried to explain what happened. Top brass buried the report of espionage; embarrassed a sixteen-year-old student caught the intrusion."

Horace remained quiet, his eyes fixed on the two standing at attention across from his desk. "Now, what possessed you taking or retrieving government property? Those weapons are worth 965,000 credits each. Give me answers, now."

"Sir, we confiscated something belonging to our military unit. We needed to install the device in Elliott."

Horace slammed a book on his desk. "What in the hell does Elliott have to do with the two of you taking a weapon with extensive firepower?"

"The designers created Elliott as a sophisticated cyborg for tactical offensive and defensive purposes. While everyone went out to the farm, I deprogrammed most of his capabilities and initiated a complex operation reprogram for optimal function."

"So, explain the connection between the weapon and Elliott."

"Elliott's primary function is for battle." Justin shut his eyes. "He can be lethal without proper rebooting, hazardous if not controlled."

"You are not explaining why you took the weapon. Tell me. Now."

"We took the weapon to install in Elliott," Silas said. "Ambassador Stein provided the weapon. Somehow the weapon got diverted to Redstone. He is still in Canada and not expected to be available for another couple of weeks."

"Why didn't you inform me of this? I could have ordered Redstone to relinquish the weapon at once."

"Sapros would get involved and know you possess a weapon we do not want him knowing about."

"He knows the weapon is missing. Is anyone else involved? Did you involve someone else?"

"No, sir."

"Redstone sent me a video showing someone entered into the weapons room; a reflection of someone is visible in an office window." Horace held his hand out toward the monitor. "Tried to enhance to maximum but still cannot determine the identity of this person."

"Sir. If I may." Silas voiced commands into the projector. "Increase resolution 50 percent. Now enlarge another 50 percent."

"Alexander Sapros. Let's hope he did not recognize you. Gifford gave orders to execute whoever the guilty party or parties are."

"Dad tell us you're not—"

"Of course not. Silas, did you buy two minimal-functioning cyborgs from the Birmingham Police the other day to refurbish? How well do they perform?"

"They can walk and laugh."

"Can they withstand a laser blast set on the kill setting?"

"In their condition, not at all."

"Dress them in prison uniforms ready to go to the range the day after tomorrow at zero eight hundred hours. I'll notify Sapros of my success at finding the persons responsible and retrieved the weapons. Silas, can you duplicate the weapons?"

Silas nodded.

"I did not hear a response, Staff Sergeant Jenkins."

"Keep in mind the weapons may not function at proper levels."

Horace drummed his fingers on the desk, taking a long pause. "Both of you used an agency vehicle without authorization. You trespassed on another compound. Conspired to steal a piece of government property. Someone else stealing the other weapons is beside the point.

I ought to strip you both of your positions. Imprison you for three years and give you a dishonorable discharge. Staff Sergeant

Jenkins and Master Sergeant Meyers, I am waiving a page eleven of this incident. Report to Senior Drill Instructor Laurence tomorrow at zero four thirty on the obstacle course, which you will complete three times. After which, you'll go to the chow hall, have breakfast. Next, scrub the floors until they meet with my satisfaction. On-base liberty for one month. Am I clear?"

"Yes, sir."

"Should either of you fail to show up for the obstacle course, and I mean either of you, I will place you both in detention for three years, after which you will receive a dishonorable discharge. Have I made myself clear?"

"Yes, sir."

"Dismissed."

"Master Sergeant Meyers, I want to have a chat with you alone. Staff Sergeant Jenkins, you have your orders."

"Dad, what are you going to say?"

"Son, words fail me in expressing how disappointed I am with you. How did Silas talk you into a stupid idea as to take a weapon from the arsenal?"

"No, sir, it was my idea. We retrieved what belongs to our tactical unit. I'm sorry, Dad; not telling you made me irresponsible."

"Yes, you do know better. Son, if Alexander or the security federation had identified you and taken you into custody, I would be powerless to protect either of you. Not only are you irresponsible in your actions but your conduct is also unbecoming of a Marine, including your behavior with one of lower rank. I revoke your request for Officer Training School, demote you to the rank of sergeant, and complete the other disciplinary actions I mentioned. Now, get a hat."

"Aye, sir."

Thursday, November 23, 2079

Horace and Dakota tapped on the door to the tutorial room. "We want to talk to you, Patricia."

"Did I do something wrong?"

"Andy suggested we should come and talk to you about a matter we hope will make you happy."

"Time to leave? Must I go? I promise I will work harder to behave myself."

"Honey, we want you to stay here. Better still, if you agree, we want to adopt you as our daughter."

"My mother would never approve. I would love for you to be my parents; for now, I must pretend."

"We found plenty of evidence she is an unfit mother."

"But my mom is the only parent I know. Plus, the laws are on her side, not yours. Except you could use your position to force her to give me up."

"How did you learn so much regarding adoption regulations?"

"You tutored me how to research. I hunted to find a way too. I didn't know how to ask the two of you to adopt me. She is in prison for the rest of her life, so I can't go to her. I refuse to go back to the palace; I will run away. The remaining option would be for you to sentence me here for life, which would make me as happy as adopting me."

"We are both willing to take on Renee."

Silas and Justin sat at a table in the chow hall finishing their breakfast. "This is the severest punishment my dad ever gave me, making me eat breakfast in the hall, excluding recruit training. As a child, he would send me to my room with a throbbing bottom and a peanut butter sandwich for supper. The chow cooks don't make breakfast like Aunt Maddie. What kind of eggs do the cooks use? They don't taste like chicken eggs."

"They use powdered scrambled eggs, at least for the recruits. I don't taste grilled onions and cheese in them either."

"Explains the bland flavor. Sore muscles tomorrow."

"Yeah, your dad breathed fire last night. Still mad this morning at the obstacle course."

"Dad burned Laurence's ears for going easy on us. Laurence and Barber spat in our faces, screaming at ear-splitting levels. Both in a bad mood this morning."

"They are DIs; they do a job building Marines."

"I know. DIs breath gagged me; they must have eaten an early breakfast of raw onion, garlic, and Limburger cheese sandwiches."

"After you left the office last night, Dad gave me a permanent denial of my request for Officer Training School and ninja-punched me to sergeant."

"Ouch. I'm sorry. Guess being the son of a general of the Marines does not guarantee perks."

"Dad does not like to show partiality; be thankful he gave us a perk. At least the deck appears clean; we will have them sparkling in no time."

Silas nudged Justin as the senior officers marched into the hall. Horace opened a gallon container of expired maple syrup and dumped the contents on the floor. Spence tossed three dozen eggs to the sticky puddles along with the broken shells. Gabrielle flung bags of flour, mixing the ingredients with a rake. Mike contributed by squirting bottles of bacon grease, adding to the growing gooey mess, now resembling a piece of abstract art coating the floor.

"Lunch is at twelve hundred hours. I expect this floor to be spotless at eleven thirty hours."

"Yep, Dad is still upset with us. We better find pails of boiling water and scrub brooms, and I hope we find cleaner in the galley. Three hours to scour the mess off the deck."

"What about the floor-scrubber machine?"

"Great idea. We will have this place general-pleasing clean in no time." Inside the closet, Justin found a note on the scrubber. He came back to the dining room to read the memo: "Men, I took the power cord; you will find two pails and hand scrubbers located under the sink in the galley. The water heater is disconnected, so you must heat the water on the stove. Signed, General of the Marines Horace Wexler Meyers, Security Chief of the Southeast Quadrant."

"If we were not impressed before by how mad my dad is, this note uses his full title. We better straighten out the predicament we created."

Wednesday, December 13, 2079

Ariella sat in the cafeteria at the Ben Gurion International Airport in Tel Aviv, waiting for her father's flight to land. She dipped a pita chip into a small bowl of hummus and glanced up at the news monitors, noticing a reporter speaking to the prime minister of Israel. News scrolled across the bottom of the screen, stating an airliner from Toronto to Tel Aviv disappeared from radar and was presumed lost. Contact numbers for families of flight sixty-two ninety-eight appeared.

She activated her wrist phone. "Abba."

The voice mail said, "Ambassador Stein is not available for calls. At the tone, leave a message."

Moments later, two security personnel escorted Ariella into a private waiting room. "Ms. Stein, please come with us. We are sorry we failed to get with you before the news broke."

"Chief Meyers believes you learned from your error in judgment and allowed me to start your next level of training. I will familiarize you with the Sikorsky this morning."

"What is this thing?"

"A simulator of the exact model I fly for the general, not the Chinook. Sit in the pilot's spot. The cyclic is in front of you; it changes the pitch angle of the rotor blades cyclically. To your left is the collective; it changes the pitch of the rotors collectively and adds power to the blades. The collective gives you lift and makes the craft move faster. You may have a skill curve going from a cycle to the helicopter. On the collective is the throttle, which works the opposite of a cycle. The antitorque pedals are on the floor to turn the craft right or left."

"My head is spinning. Cyclically, collectively—both change the pitch."

"I'll go over this until you are comfortable. I won't have you out transporting the chief tomorrow. He would prefer I didn't."

"Might be years before the chief ever considers getting in the helo with me at the controls. Not sure if I would trust me at the controls."

"This helicopter flies itself but still requires an experienced pilot. Unexpected hazards can happen like weather changes, mindless drones, or other dangers in the way. Such as a knuckleheaded teenager flying around in a jetpack, playing dare. A pilot needs to know how to maneuver around them."

"What does the cyclic do?" Andy asked.

Silas hesitated a moment. "Changes the pitch of the helicopter cyclically? Whatever cyclically means."

"Intermittently."

Andy pointed to the pedals on the floor. "What are those things called?"

"Antitorch petals make the helicopter turn right or left."

"Antitorque pedals."

Andy pointed to different controls, explaining each of them. "Get the book from the pocket to your right. Here is your preflight checklist. In this simulation, you should find ten items which need addressing before we take off. Now is a time to ask, if you are having trouble."

"Captain Meyers, you need to walk me through this until I am familiar with this helo."

"Safety is vital on any flight. Most people charge up their vehicles before taking off. Not so with an aircraft. You don't want something falling off or have a total power failure, which is self-explanatory. Once you receive passing marks in the simulator, you will move to the Sikorsky. Built around 2017, it was once known as Marine One. Three presidents used this helo before the Pentagon decommissioned it. Chief Meyers decided to sit in the copilot seat instead, though his emblem is on the first seat. The president used this bird to go from the White House to Andrews Air Force Base and back, among other destinations.

"I can't believe this helo is so old. Looks brand-new." Silas ran a towel across the body of the aircraft, wiping fingerprints off the doors.

"The designers built them to last. Refitted for the chief. Still, an excellent piece of machinery."

Silas followed Andy, looking over the helicopter. "You sound gloomy, like you are relinquishing something."

"Age is inching up on me, Silas, I'm not getting any younger. He will need a new pilot one day." Andy went through the visual inspection and explained what complications Silas would need to find. "Now, if you come back with me to the hangar, I'll give you your books you need to study. Each section contains lectures and a quiz. So, don't rush through your reading. I expect you to study the material and will quiz you myself. Now, I suppose you might be hungry. Let's go find out what the cooks fixed for lunch."

Andy and Silas wandered into the family room as an Israeli reporter described the downing of an airliner from Toronto to Tel Aviv on a monitor. "Rumors are circulating Ambassador Stein is among those on board the doomed flight."

"What happened? Did the transfer reach the destination on time?"

"I don't know. Justin tried to contact Ariella, but she does not answer her phone. He is way past worried."

"I still can't contact Ariella, I called her house, and an assistant stated everyone is in mourning and cannot come to the phone and disconnected the call."

Silas rubbed the sides of his slacks with his hands. "I'm sure I got the transfer in time. Did they find any bodies yet?"

"Rescuers found wreckage but no bodies," Horace said, staring at the monitor. "They claim the area is infested with sharks, making a search difficult. I did not realize—Missy was my granddaughter until—too late. I could have taken her in and stopped her from boarding the flight. Now I have lost her; I pray Kassidy and Alexander can forgive me."

The telemonitor lit up with an incoming call from Sapros. "Lord, please give me the strength to cope with this enemy as you would want. I find myself unable to handle him on my own," Horace said. "Supreme Commander, I am honored to be of service to you today."

"Meyers, I'm sure someone informed you of the horrible loss of Ambassador Stein. Take charge investigating the plane crash and find out what happened and report straight to me."

"Sir, the Canadians and Israelis maintain authority over the accident, not the United States."

"The Israeli ambassador and citizens of our country boarded the flight; that is why you are to assume responsibility for the investigation."

"Would not the investigation fall under Federal Aviation Administration?"

"Not with a suspected terrorist from your quadrant."

"How so?"

"Information collected by my investigators uncovered a considerable number of declassified cyborgs stored at the Toronto airport awaiting transfer to board a trans-Atlantic flight."

"Explain why declassified cyborgs stored in Toronto involve a terrorist coming from my area. What would the connection be?"

"You are staffed with the top computer people in the country." Gifford's bald head blushed red; a vein protruded from his right temple.

"Are you requesting a trace on the cyborgs?"

"My experts attempted a trace. Someone wiped their record clean. Not so much as a yocto-byte of identifiable information. The Israelis are demanding a resolution. They tire me; figure out a way to have them thrown out of my country," Gifford said, pounding his fist on his desk.

"I'm sure they are insisting on answers. Israel will not accept this unfriendly gesture if you order all Israelis to leave the United States. As far as the crash goes, I assure you and the Israeli government my computer techs will do whatever they can to assist. My staff does not keep themselves apprised of flights to and from Toronto and Tel Aviv; we deal with situations concerning the security of the Southeast Quadrant."

"From the information given to me, the Red Mountain community boarded the flight, along with the ambassador."

"Sir, I'm requesting a list of all passengers on board and working my way through. I need to find any connections between who boarded the flight with enemies elsewhere."

"How did they obtain passage to Tel Aviv?"

"You ordered me to dispose of them; you did not specify how you wanted your goal accomplished. I gave the community passage to New Liberty; they are free to do as they wish. They did not make any trouble for you. Now, someone undermined my solution and caused an enormous pile of equine—"

"Not my difficulty at all. I am making you responsible for getting this fiasco corrected. Contact the Israelis and soothe their emotions. I don't give a rat's behind."

"I will do what I can."

"Meyers, you are the lone SC who has difficulty following my commands. I told you to deal with those people. I did not intend for you to give them to Israel. I expected them dead. You are in danger of committing treason. Official misconduct is the way you handle the affairs of the Southeast Quadrant." Gifford did not wait for a reply as his image vanished from the holopad.

He took the stack of reports and slammed them on his desk. "In times like these, the use of insulting metaphors to describe my sentiments about Sapros would be a temporary stress relief. No, I would wash my mouth out with a strong disinfectant, Greasy Creek Moonshine."

The emblem of the ambassador appeared. Ariella nodded; her voice broke as she spoke. "General Meyers, the prime minister requested me to take my father's place as the Israeli...to the Southeast Quadrant. After the funeral of my Abba and Hanukkah, I'll return to Birmingham. My return will be at the most a day or two after Hanukah. My mother will remain here with my grandparents. My assistants tell me Gifford assigned you to investigate the airliner going down. Is this correct?"

"First, let me offer my deepest sympathy to you, your family, and the people of Israel. Everyone loved Eliyahu. His death is a personal loss as I considered him a close friend," Horace said. "Yes, Sapros ordered me to investigate the incident. Anything I can do for you, Ambassador Stein?"

"My gratitude goes beyond a simple thanks. Israel does not want Sapros meddling in the Israeli-Canadian investigation. I'm counting on you to turn over everything you find to Israeli authorities. Is Justin available?"

Justin stepped into view of the monitor and patted himself on his heart. "Ariella, your Abba will always be here."

"I'm not behaving much like an ambassador."

"You are grieving; no one is expecting you to pretend nothing happened."

"I need to go; I am due at a briefing with the prime minister. I'm expected to be in mourning, but the prime minister declares the urgency of this matter requires my attention." Ariella gave a quick wave as the screen went black.

"Dad, please let me go to her, I won't be off base liberty until next week," he said, running his hand across his head.

"As security chief and a friend of the late...we will attend the funeral and pay our respects, along with my wife and devoted son," he said, signaling Andy to prepare the jet for departure. "You can finish your final week of base liberty when we come home."

Patricia's voice quivered as she stared at the monitor and shook her head. "Did Missy get on the plane? Say no."

"I do not know. Once the passenger list arrives—We will pray she did not board the plane."

"How will we tell Alexander and Kassidy?"

"Brokenhearted too. We will find a way, although it will not be easy. Do you need a hug?" Horace bent down, kissing her on the top of her head.

Maddie set a pitcher of apple cider on the dining table. "Lunch is ready. We are in shock. You should eat some lunch: tossed salad, cream of potato soup, and grilled cheese sandwiches."

"I'm not hungry." He pulled a chair from the table, awakening Leopold from his sleep, and brushed him off the chair. The cat jumped back in the seat, tail thrashed, and delivered a defiant meow. Horace placed the hissing feline on his lap.

"March upstairs and wash those hands, young man; quit playing with the cat."

Andy grinned. "Well, son, you better do as Maddie tells you to do before she takes the wooden spoon to you."

"Maddie never carried out her threat," he said, scratching Leopold's back.

"I might act on my promise, young man."

Sunny bounded into the room and leapt on Horace's lap. "Sunny will get me into trouble with Maddie."

"I am so sorry. I'll take those two off you," said Patricia.

Horace pulled Leopold closer to him, rubbing the cat's head with his chin. "No, let them stay; they adopted me and won my affection. Hey, the claws, Leopold. Maddie is about to give me trouble, my furry little friend. They are a delight."

He nodded at Maddie. "Gives me a new way to annoy my aunt. Please sit; lunch is now ready."

CHAPTER 16

Friday, December 15, 2079

Friends tiptoed into the house and offered their sympathies to Eliyahu's family. White sheets covered the mirrors. Men spoke in hushed voices, and women wiped their eyes with tissues. Several moved along a buffet table covered with a white tablecloth and silver candlesticks placing hard-boiled eggs, bagels, olives, and lentils on their plates.

A woman came up to Justin and Horace, introducing herself. "My name is Esther. I'm a friend of the family. Help yourself to the Seudat Havra'a table. The egg, bagel, and lentils are round as a symbol of the cycle of life."

Justin nodded. "Toda."

Some wore a torn black ribbon; others had small tears on their shirts. "May Adonai comfort you among the mourners of Zion and Jerusalem."

Avigail Katz stood behind her daughter. "Our Ariella speaks with admiration of you and Chief Meyers. Your coming means so much to us. Eliyahu was a wonderful husband and devoted father."

Horace took Avigail's hand. "Eliyahu's friendship meant something to me."

Another woman wiped her eyes with a tissue and sat on a low

chair close to the floor. "Are you friends of Ariella?"

"I will miss him, a dear friend of mine."

Ehud Stein touched a torn black ribbon on his lapel. "My son often spoke of you, General Meyers. Like Jonathan's friendship with David."

"A genuine compliment for friendship," Avigail said. "A friendship such as yours is rare these days. Even among government people."

Ariella leaned over on her stool. "I am sorry I did not introduce you. May I at least present you to my grandfather, Hayim Katz; Sav, this is Justin Meyers and his father, Horace."

Hayim gripped his hand, squeezing tight. "So, you are the one our Ariella is talking about. Tell me, young man, what are your intentions for my granddaughter?"

Justin's mouth dropped open. "Uh."

"Sav, Abba told me about how you interrogated him the first time he came to your house. Now you're doing the same to Justin."

Hayim wagged his finger at Ariella. "I told your Abba. Fathers, or in this case a grandfather, cannot be too careful."

Ariella smiled. "I'm sorry. Let's get something to eat. We will let my grandparents and your dad discuss a marriage arrangement."

He spun around as Ariella's grandparents and his father laughed. "What?"

Ariella took him by the arm and led him to the serving table. "My Abba would tell the story with a flourish and embellishment. Did Esther explain the different foods, why the hard-boiled eggs, bagels, and lintels?"

"Yes, this is intriguing, the cycle of life," Justin said, as a woman placed food on her plate. "The pregnant woman reinforces the idea of the cycle."

"The woman at the table is my cousin Miriam; she worked in Israeli intelligence and helped my father deal with Gifford." Ariella saw her grandparents speaking with Justin's parents. "Yes, I need to speak to your father alone. On the way back, if he wouldn't mind, to discuss Israeli matters."

Justin touched her shoulder. "All you need to do is tell my father you need to talk to him. Regardless, my dad will talk to you."

"Something I want to say about your father. While in the food prep room, your dad encouraged me to stay focused. The second those butchers came after me, telling me they are on the way. Heavy stun did not stop them; he ordered me to use the kill mode." Ariella said, taking the T-35 from her pocket for Justin.

"I thought you didn't know the 35 existed, yet you have more knowledge than I do." Justin held a plate of food. "What, no ham salad sandwiches?"

"Stop joking. Someone might misunderstand you. My grandparents are coordinating my future as a married woman."

Justin glanced back at Ariella's grandparents. "With a respectable Jewish man, I suppose. I guess they quit conspiring our marriage. They are talking to an older woman."

"Her name is Evelina, a yente."

"You mean like a *Fiddler on the Roof* yenta?" Justin said, eyes widening in panic.

"I am sure they're discussing the dowry and bride's price. I'm sorry, too funny. *Yente* means a gossipy woman, not a matchmaker. A busybody, yes; matchmaker, no. My aunt might delight in the idea, would not surprise me if she tried. Abba would be the first one to tell you about the inside joke, about him and his father-in-law. Sav Katz knew I would catch the joke."

Sunday, December 24, 2079

Ariella strapped herself into the seat. "Chief Meyers, my sincere thanks for all your help this past week in the investigation of the crash. Not for myself, but for the people of Israel. Did Justin tell you I needed to speak with you, in private?"

"Ambassador or not, I would talk to you once we are free to move about."

He swiped across his message pad. "Patricia and Silas are working on their studies. Patricia is having nightmares again and sleeping under Maddie's bed. Sunny ate another one of my dress covers, which means I need to buy more. Leopold brought a snake into—" he said, taking out a pad. "Note to self, remind Leopold, no pets allowed in the house."

Ariella stared out the window as the jet taxied down the runway. Israeli flags remained at half-staff in front of the buildings. She thought about her arrival in Israel as the daughter of the ambassador; now she found herself taking over her father's tasks. As the runway dropped lower, pressure built on her ears as the jet gained altitude. The Mediterranean Sea glistened in the sunlight below as ships became tiny dots.

"This is Captain Meyers. You can move about the cabin. Now, don't forget who is flying this thing. We will get hungry before too long."

Ariella reached down for her carry-on and pulled out a wrapped package with a note. "My mother packed enough for us. Says to make sure Justin eats the last knish."

"What does she mean?" he asked, selecting a toasted bagel and blackberry jam.

Ariella packed the note back into the bag. "Either a continuation of the inside joke furthered by my mother or she gave you a nod of approval."

"Well, what did her message say about me?"

"Only I am to make sure you get the last knish."

"Somehow I miss the humor."

"My Abba would fold up in laughter. I'm sure he is letting all the angels of heaven in on the joke now."

Horace selected a potato knish. "Would you like to speak now, Ariella? Maybe later?"

"Before we go back into the conference room, I need a word of prayer first. The Lord gave me new duties to perform, and I am so unprepared for what he wants me to do."

Ariella leafed through her Tanakh. "'Fear thou not, for I am with thee, be not dismayed, for I am thy God; I strengthened thee, yea, I help thee; Yea, I uphold thee with My victorious right hand.' Isaiah 41:10. Remarkable I happened on this verse. Abba would say God is speaking to me."

"He will lead you to do what is right in his sight."

"We need to talk now."

Horace waved to a chair across the table. "How may I be of help, Madame Ambassador?"

"Please, Ariella, at least for now. The empty chair at the end of the table where my father should be sitting…The Israeli intelligence contacted the prime minister with information concerning the supreme commander. Sir, if the Israeli government and I lacked confidence in you, I would not be speaking with you. Per intelligence gathering, Gifford Sapros intends on invading Jerusalem within the thirty-day morning for my father. The information doesn't mean he will; Israel will pursue a peaceful solution to this situation. Are you hosting Gifford's next birthday celebration at the compound?"

He got up and opened the refrigerator. "Well past the thirty-day time window. Would you like something to drink? I am getting a container of soda for myself."

"Water. Thank you."

"So, what does the Israeli government want to do?" He took a sip of the cola, allowing Ariella time to respond.

"The government wants me to give a gift to the supreme commander for his support in the investigation of the crash."

"I do not know how much Gifford contributed."

"Israel believes Sapros is involved with my father's death."

"Why the gift of gratitude? Your government is implicating a connection with Sapros's actions?" he asked, patting Ariella's hand. "Retaliation? I detect the expression in your eyes whenever a person mentions Gifford's name or when his face appears on a telemonitor. What information do you have about him?"

"Other than he killed my father?"

"Anyone touched my family. Yes, Sapros hurt my family. Assination is not the remedy. Ariella, God will give us a better way; revenge is not the answer. Deuteronomy 31:35 says, 'Vengeance is mine, and recompense, for the time when their foot shall slip; for the day of their calamity is at hand, and their doom comes swiftly.'"

"The Song of Moses. The passages are referring to those who cause Israel harm. Which Sapros intends. God uses human servants, often outpowered and outnumbered. God proves himself as Israel's protector. Think Gideon."

"He will. Ariella, discussing this with you is an act of treason on my part. Ever see what Sapros does with those who commit treason? He executed an SC from the Northwest Quadrant last year. Sapros imagined Richards plotted against him."

Ariella bowed her head. "Intelligence shows horrific accounts of what Gifford can do. This reason alone should give anyone a motive to stop him...I will inform Israeli intelligence to find another way to remove Gifford from office. We will need to act before April when he names Alexander as his successor. Remove Gifford, Alexander becomes Supreme Commander, and no guarantee he'll be an improvement over his father. Our option is to take out both."

"Alexander is my son-in-law. Patricia tells me he protected her and Kassidy from Gifford. I let them down not knowing Missy was their daughter."

Ariella remained silent for a moment. "We know of Alexander's capabilities. He can be as unpredictable and ruthless as his father. Based on reliable authority, Gifford will die the same way my Abba died. I do not know when or how. I told you all I know."

"Would you tell me, if you did?"

Ariella did not respond.

"I must warn the supreme commander. At my leisure. Make darn sure Kassidy is not on the jet."

"Yes, sir."

Perspiration beaded on his forehead. He prayed for a solution. *To arrest Ariella would mean her execution; however, allowing her to go on with her plan would propel the country into turmoil.* He listened to the hum of the jet engines and interlaced his fingers, rubbing them together. The knot in his stomach grew tighter. *If Gifford discovers Ariella's plot, I also stand accused. A risk I must take.*

Monday, December 25, 2079

Maddie greeted Horace and Dakota at the door. "Where are Justin and Andy?"

"They are bringing in the gear."

Maddie nodded to Patricia at a table with her Bible. "She wants to see you, Horace."

Patricia stood when they came into the room. "I need to talk to you, Chief Meyers."

"What is wrong? Don't cry, you can tell me."

"While you and Mrs. Meyers went to Israel, I went to the clinic about the missing child DNA location. Since I did not know if my father is Gifford or not, I wanted to find out if my biological father might be searching for me. The lab technician insisted you must sign the authorization papers to hand me over to—"

Horace sighed and laid his hand on her shoulder. "Do you want to find your father? I set those rules in place in case a parent should not assume custody. I agree Gifford would be one of them. Let's go down to the clinic to see what the results are."

"Chief Meyers, Mrs. Meyers needs to be in on the meeting."

"With both of us fighting to gain permanent custody of you, we filed court papers to adopt you to notify Renee."

She put her arms around Dakota. "I'm scared."

"Why are you scared?"

"Gifford is my father."

Dakota gave her a firm embrace. "Gifford will never touch you. We will keep you here and safe."

The doors slid open, military medical staff stood at attention. "Patricia told me she requested a parental DNA check. After receiving the results, a staff member informed her I needed to authorize papers."

"Let me get the supervisor."

"Supervisor? Why? Never had a supervisor informing me about parentage before. The tech gave me results. I signed the release or not."

"Chief Meyers, would you come to my office to discuss our findings?"

"Gifford is my father." Patricia fell to the floor and clung to Dakota. "Please, don't let him take me."

Horace lifted Patricia to her feet. "I promised you. We will not let Gifford get his hands on you."

The doctor reviewed the results. "Let me put your fears at ease. Your father is not Gifford Sapros. Your biological mother is not Renee DuPont."

"How can this be? She claimed she had me."

"She gave birth to you, but you are not her biological daughter."

"Who are my parents?"

Horace's voice broke. "They are looking for you? Their DNA would not be in the registry."

Patricia sat between them. "I won't go back to them; let me stay with you and Dakota."

"I promised I would return all missing children, provided the parents have clean records. Please don't cry. Kills me signing the papers."

"Sir, if you would sign these documents to release Patricia." He pushed the computer tablet across the desk.

"I am sorry. I have trouble reading," he said, choking as he attempted to read the document. "Dakota. This report states, Patricia Jezebel DuPont's biological parents are identified as Horace Wexler Meyers and his wife, Dakota Elizabeth Brown Meyers. Dakota, she is our daughter." He fell to his knees "Thank you, Father, for returning our daughter. I cannot express myself enough."

"I'm giving you privacy. On behalf of the DNA Child Find Program, locating your daughter is most rewarding."

Dakota wrapped her arms around Patricia. "My daughter."

"How? I am so confused."

"After the car crash, I became unable to have any more children. We tried and I suffered three miscarriages. Through a fertility clinic, we arranged for a surrogate to carry our baby. The treatment center implanted the embryo into a woman; she soon disappeared, along with you our unborn daughter. We searched for years with no luck."

Patricia held up both her hands, clenching them into tight fists.

Her face reddened, the voice grew louder. "Renee knows Gifford Sapros is not my father. She lied my entire life and led me to believe Gifford is my father. Why did she do this? Why did she keep me from you? The sexual acts my mother forced me to do...she wanted favors from—I hate her. I despise that—"

Horace stood and took her by the hand. "Come here, sweetie."

Patricia took a tissue from him, wiping her eyes. "Uh, calling you Chief Meyers doesn't sound right; neither does calling you Dad."

He hugged her. "Whatever is comfortable for you. Don't call me Pops."

"I thought of something,"

"What's wrong?"

"Well, it's embarrassing. Remember when you arrested me, and I tried to seduce you? You didn't excuse my poor behavior either. What about the felony charges you placed against me?"

"What charges? I never filed them. Gifford would have forced me to hand you over to the detention center for—" Horace bowed his head. "The thought of turning you over...I refused. Your terrified face told me you needed a father."

"What if I had refused mercy and requested to stay at the farm?"

"The thought of leaving you there gave me nightmares since you came here. Pleased to announce, since you have stolen our hearts, I sentenced you to life in this family. Am I clear?"

"Clear as a bottle of spring water. Um, if you get upset with me, will you"—she mimicked the way he emphasized each syllable—"Ms. Du Pont?"

"How about Patricia Meyers? I'm proud to claim you as my daughter."

"May I change my middle name to Lila?"

"Of course."

"Dakota, I know both of you love me. Harder to call you mom, since Renee is...well. She never acted like a mother."

Dakota smoothed Patricia's hair. "Things will be better now. I promise you."

"I expect you to obey the rules here; they will not change now we know you are our daughter. What do you expect from us?"

"My mind is spinning. One thing, I never heard my...say, I love you."

"Our hearts are bursting with love for you," Dakota said, hugging her. "Never believe we feel any less."

They entered the house as Justin's voice came from the back room. "Watch out, everybody, Sunny and Leopold are in stampede mode."

Sunny and Leopold ran into the living room and jumped between Horace and Dakota greeting them. "Blurty, you were right. Sunny is growing fast. How can anyone get mad with these two?"

CHAPTER 17

Tuesday, January 2, 2080

Ariella played back her holographic messages with Justin standing with his hands interlaced across his midsection. "Hey, Ariella, I have been trying to reach you since we got back from Israel. Tell me how you are doing. Phone me." Justin blew her a kiss as the message ended.

"Sorry, Justin. I'm so busy now." Ariella sat at a table opening the bottom of a chess piece. "I hate to do this to you, Moses; you must free the children of Israel once again," she said, pouring a substance into the hollow piece and replacing the seal. "Gifford won't realize what happened until he is standing before God."

The doorbell rang; one of her assistants opened the door. "Mr. Meyers, the ambassador isn't receiving callers today."

"Please, I need to talk to her."

"Is this personal or official?"

"Yes, an important issue needing her attention."

"Let him in; he will stand outside all night if you don't."

Justin handed Ariella a box. "This package came to our house, addressed to you."

"Yes, I am expecting this. Thanks. I wish I had free time to spend with you."

"You don't want to date me anymore? Contact me."

"Wait. Life changed my world into a life I never imagined. My new duties take up so much of my time. We can talk for a minute."

Justin nodded.

"What is wrong?"

"My dad is worried about you." Justin sat on the sofa.

"Did he send you over here to get information out of me? My assistant can make an appointment if he needs to discuss matters. Now, I am the ambassador; my schedule is full."

"He is worried your grief is getting to you and that you want to seek revenge on Gifford."

"Your gesture reminds me of your father."

"What are you meaning?"

"You lean forward and lift your chin. Your father did the same thing when we talked on the flight back."

"We both expect a straight answer."

"This is business between the Israeli government and Sapros. The security chief is not involved."

"Dad said you plan to give Gifford an extravagant chess set."

"A token of Israel's gratitude for the assistance in the investigation of the airline crash."

"Hmm. Did Sapros do anything positive? By laying roadblocks at every turn? My dad does what he can, but as soon as he makes an advance, Gifford tells him to stand down."

"Does he?"

"You should know my dad by now. He finds another way to conduct the investigation."

"Any reliable leads?"

"You mean any points that differ from Israeli intelligence? No. However, if he can prove the evidence, what is the benefit? Gifford is a tyrant and does not answer to anyone."

The holopad lit up with the symbol of the prime minister's office. "I must take this call. I will call you in the morning and have lunch at the Diplomat."

"I would like to date you, Ariella."

Tuesday, January 16, 2080

Patricia slouched on the loveseat with her legs propped on the chair across from her. She folded her arms and turned her head away from Dakota. "Nothing's wrong. You don't get it."

Dakota sat beside her. "Give me a chance. I remember being your age, believing no one understood or cared."

"My age? Like when televisions came with rabbit ears and received three stations, all the programs in black-and-white?"

"Use a respectful tone when speaking to me. Sit up straight. How many times must we have this discussion? Your behavior is unacceptable. You were so happy when we found out you are our daughter. Talk to me; what is going on? Andy said you won't say what's troubling you."

Patricia glared at Dakota in silence.

"I am trying my best to talk to you. Is your problem with Silas?"

Patricia rolled her eyes. "No, not Silas, Andy, Justin, or you. So, leave me alone."

"You didn't mention your father. Are you upset with him?"

"What about it?"

"Your father would move the world for you. Why are you mad at him?"

Patricia stood and opened the balcony doors to allow a cold breeze to blow the curtains. "A good father knows what to do. He doesn't give—Oh, forget it."

"You need to give him a chance. He is confused and getting impatient with your misbehavior. How is he not being a proper father to you?"

"No idea? Proof enough."

"I am warning you; your father will not put up with your behavior much longer. Mr. Ellis called for a meeting with your father and me regarding your grades. Can you shed any light on what is going on?"

She shrugged her shoulders and hummed a monotone tune.

"Stay in your room. You are grounded."

"So? I'll do what I want no matter what you say."

"You take one step out of this room, and if your father doesn't do anything, I promise you I will."

"Today, Patricia didn't show up," Jarrett Ellis said, turning an envelope over in his hand. "Chief Meyers, she failed to turn in her assignments and failed two tests on purpose. I tried to reason with her, telling her I'd be speaking with the two of you. All she gives me is a bunch of disrespectful backtalk. The chances of raising her grades to a minimal level are impossible. No other option but to fail her."

Horace sat back in his chair, his jaw muscles tightened. "One thing I promise you, I will adjust her behavior today. She will apologize to you for her bad conduct."

"I'm nerve-wracked beyond my ability to put up with her any longer. You are wasting your credits on Patricia's classes, including my time. I submit my resignation, effective as of now. Thank you for the opportunity." Jarrett took his satchel and hurried to the door. "I'm willing to teach the younger ones at the rescue, if you like. However, not Patricia."

He pressed his palms down on the desk. "Where. Is Patricia?"

"I restricted her to her room."

The outside security monitor showed Patricia in the jump ring with Peppermint. "I told her no horseback riding."

"She thought you meant Salado. She found a loophole in your orders."

"No...she didn't misunderstand either of us. I told her she could not ride the horses. Period. I come home after a delightful day at the office putting up with Gifford's latest outrage, and now this."

"Should I retire and work with your security team? More time with Patricia since she needs extra parental guidance."

"Blurty, you would become one of my subordinates. I'd treat you the same as any other member of my team. I don't want you a part of a verbal reprimand or worse if the squad fouls up."

"What about Justin?"

"Would you prefer I sent him to federal prison with a dishonorable discharge? Honey, you are my Alpha Unit, not my son who enlisted in the Marines. Wish to retire. Fine. Want more to do besides supervising Patricia, you can—"

"She's coming in now. I'm going shopping. We will continue this discussion after I return. I expect her to be alive."

"You're leaving for me to deal with her. We both should handle this situation together. She will be breathing when you return. I guarantee she will be more contrite."

Patricia slammed the doors, stomping her feet. "Well, what are you looking at?"

"In my study. Now."

Andy sat at one side of the table with Silas on the other. "Define gyroplane."

"The gyroplane is a rotorcraft whose rotors are usually engine-driven for takeoff, hovering, and landing."

"You defined gyrodyne. Let's try the next question. What is the main rotor?"

Silas grinned. "The rotor that supplies the principal lift to a helicopter or rotorcraft."

"True or false, the AOA is the angle between the chord line of a main or tail rotor blade and the rotational relative wind of the roto system?"

Silas smiled again. "False, the correct answer is the angle of incident. AOA, or angle of attack, is the angle between the airfoil chord line and the resultant relative wind."

"Excellent."

"Captain, I never thought flying a helicopter could be this complicated. Not like jumping on a cycle taking off down the road."

Doors slammed, followed by Patricia yelling, followed by the sound of breaking glass. "So, what? I'm failing my classes; it's my life, not yours."

Andy leaned his head back, closing his eyes. "Third time this week. What is today? Tuesday."

"Pat-ri-cia." Horace's voice grew louder as he reached the stairs. He paused at Andy's study door for a moment, looking inside. "Sorry, Dad, Silas."

"Patricia gave me enough clues she lied about her age. Chief Meyers said hands off until she is eighteen." Silas blew out a breath, glancing at the door. "He warned me before he found out Patricia is his daughter he'd turn me into a gelding. I told him I don't play with little girls." He drew circles on a piece of paper. "She sure acts fourteen."

"Does she ever talk to you?" Andy made marks on one of Silas's papers.

"Andy, I thought I fell in love with an eighteen-year-old woman… Found out she is a fourteen-year-old girl. Since her dad made her tell me the truth, we aren't speaking. I'm so frustrated because I can't make myself stop loving her." Silas slid a manual across the table leaning back in his chair. "Darn."

"When a person loves another, they will do the right thing. If God means for this to be or not, he will give you peace. Remember, Jacob worked seven years to marry Rachel. May not be easy, but he will give you peace. You are distracted; double check one of your answers."

"Patricia, you are wigging me out."

"Until I say otherwise, remain in your room. I'll be up soon."

"They do a lot of yelling, not much listening," Andy said, massaging his forehead with his hands. "My son is straight about turning you into a gelding."

Silas covered his hand over his mouth, turning to the sound of Patricia stomping up the stairs.

"I hate you." The slam of her bedroom door sent Sunny and Leopold running down the stairs to hide under a couch in the den.

"Silas. I need to speak with Andy."

"I'll be out in the simulator for a week or two or until Patricia settles down, whichever comes first." Silas put his hands into his pockets and went out the back door.

"What should I do, Dad? No matter what I say, Patricia grows angrier and rebels. I told her she could not ride any of the horses. Plus, restriction to her room for the rest of the day, and hand-write the house rules five hundred times."

"Before she found out you and Dakota are her parents, tilt your head down or lift an eyebrow, and she cried." Andy held up a hand. "She thought you would order her to leave, which she now knows you won't do."

"Why is she so hostile to us?"

The stairs creaked; she stopped at the door wearing riding apparel and Horace's sweatshirt and lifted her chin, standing with legs apart, hands on her hips.

"Patricia?"

"What?"

"What are you doing?" *Don't keep pushing me.*

"You can't tell by the way I am dressed? Like it or not, I'm riding Salado."

"No, you are not. Go back to your room, and—"

Patricia stomped up the stairs and slammed the door three times. Sunny and Leopold darted from under the couch and hid beneath Horace's desk.

He placed his hands on the desk and drummed his fingers. "I need to sit here...I'm too angry."

"Teenagers can be a handful. You were."

"I remember our rounds. Did I make a mistake giving her extra leniency because of abuse? Breaks my heart to get harsh with her. As much as I don't want to do this I—"

"Could I try to talk to her? How about Justin or Elliott?"

"Did Silas program Elliott off tours?"

"Soon."

Silas stood in the doorway of the study, glancing over his shoulder to the back door. "Excuse me, sir, Patricia took the back stairs and is heading to the stable; she intends to go riding."

"Time to stop talking. Stay with Andy, Silas." He stood, taking long strides to the back door. "Pat-ric-ia Li-la. You transfer your smart-alecky butt back in this house. Now."

His voice faded as he strode to the stables. "My hand and your bottom will have a discussion."

Silas sat twisting his Marine ring around his finger. He took a breath. "I tried to talk Patricia into coming back into the house, but, well I won't say what she did. I worry Patricia pushed her father too far. He didn't explode at Justin and me."

"My son's temper blows up on occasion; I hope she doesn't push any further and settles down while she can."

"The Chief won't hurt her…"

"Of course not. Patricia may find difficulty sitting down."

Ten minutes later she appeared at the door of the study her face pale, lower lip quivering. Horace stood behind her nudging her shoulder. "Silas, I–apologize for being so–vulgar to you." She ran up the stairs sobbing shutting the door with a soft click.

"Patricia gave Silas the middle finger salute when he tried to tell her to go in the house. Spence snatched her up putting her prone over his shoulder to hold her in place until I could take control. She called him, let us say a bunch of creative foul metaphors and kicked him. He put her down and stared down at the little wildcat until she got quiet. I ordered her to apologize to both Colonel Harris and Staff Sergeant Jenkins for her behavior." Horace settled himself at the table across from Silas.

"I tried to get her to come back in."

"Silas, can you excuse us again?"

"I'll be in the simulator, trying not to crash or make barrel rolls with the Sikorsky again."

"Silas put the simulator in practice mode. The computer won't flunk you. You should not be flying in your mood."

"Aye, sir. I'll sweep the deck in the classroom until she calms down."

"Dad, Patricia shattered the last ounce of my patience with her. I took her into the tack room to discipline her. I yelled at

Patricia like a drill instructor at a raw recruit. After I told her what I intended to do, she mocked my authority, using language I don't allow the drill instructors to use," he said, massaging the palm of his right hand. "After Spence came in, the expression on Patricia's face…I am going up to let her know how much I love her. I feel sick about—"

The stairs creaked as Patricia tiptoed into the room. "Daddy? I need to talk to you."

"I hope this is a positive sign and she is not up to more trouble making," Andy said.

"Go back to your room. I'll be up. We both need to talk."

"Yes, sir."

Patricia left her bedroom door open and sat on the sofa waiting. The back door banged shut as someone came up the back steps. Justin slipped into her room and settled himself beside her.

"Hey, sis. How are you doing? Dad and Colonel Harris are high and to the right with you."

"Don't understand."

"Means they are furious with you."

"Yeah, they are."

"I tried to warn you Dad had enough of your behavior."

"Nothing like being a total brat. Disobeyed Dakota by leaving my room after she grounded me. Did terrible things to Silas when he tried to talk me into coming back into the house. Cussed at Colonel Harris and kicked him. Dad came out of the house, dragged me into the tack room, and slammed the door." Patricia's voice broke. "He got in my face—and swore at me."

"Did you apologize?"

Patricia placed her hand on her backside. "No. Renee used profanity at me, and I returned the favor right back to her. Shouted at Dad—killed all the love in him."

"Patricia, Dad still loves you."

"Not after what I—"

"What did you say to him?"

"Can't repeat what...Terrible things."

"Oh, sis, he will forgive you. Yelled at Dad, wishing I kept my mouth shut."

"You?"

"Yes, your backside is as sore as mine then for mouthing off."

"Don't know if he can forgive me. What I said..."

"You are his daughter. Sis, he loves you. Talk to him." Justin took Patricia in his arms as she cried on his shoulder. "I am sure he is talking to Grandpa Andy, upset over what happened."

"Why?"

"He always does."

Horace coughed. "You wanted to talk with me. Justin, I would like to speak with Patricia alone."

"Sis, I'll be in my room studying, if you need me later."

Patricia nodded as Justin left the room.

"I am ready to listen."

"Yes, sir, I need to explain...my behavior. Ow," Patricia said, rubbing her bottom, and held her Bible out to Horace. "Here."

"Why didn't you show me this passage earlier? Had we talked about this together, we both would not be heartbroken for what we called each other."

She held her teddy bear close to her chest. "Because you would say I was stupid or give me a light swat to appease me."

"I would never call you stupid...No, you are right, I called you worse..."

"The names you called me. I...wanted to hurt you back. I hate what I shouted at you. Don't look at me with so much hurt in your eyes. Next time I will keep my mouth shut. Can you forgive me?"

"Yes, I forgive you. Your mother and I should give you a lot more hugs. Before DNA Child Find, we loved you as a daughter. Forgive me?"

"For the spanking? Thought I needed a good one. Would you stay and hold me until I fall asleep, so tired from crying?"

Patricia shut her eyes, listening to him sing. "Jesus loves you this I know, for the Bible tells me so."

Dakota placed a blue canvas shopping bag filled with packages of balloons and ribbons on the desk. "Silas informed me Five-Star stopped Patricia's out-of-control behavior."

"He is sick over losing his temper." Andy helped Dakota with the additional bags. "He didn't want to use corporal punishment."

"Dinner will be ready in about forty-five minutes. Should the staff make a peanut butter sandwich to take to her?" Maddie shook her head. "Broke his heart to—Do you think she will come down?"

"Depends on what Horace decides after he finishes talking to her." Dakota raised her brows. "I told him; he needed to do something before she pushed him past his breaking point. We didn't know what we should do to curb her rebellious behavior." Dakota shut her eyes and opened them again. "Got quiet up there. I thought I heard him singing. He is coming down now."

Horace glanced back up the stairs. "She acted like a brat, her words. Patricia showed me a verse in the Bible, Proverbs 13:24 from the God's Word translation. What did she do with the Bible I gave her? This version reads, 'Whoever refuses to spank his son hates him, but whoever loves his son disciplines him from early on.' Plus, another verse," he said, puffing out his cheeks. "She baited me. I did not keep myself under control. Her words pierced my heart. It scares me how angry I got with her. Used foul language, shouting at my baby girl." He spread out his hands. "Never lost my temper in front of my Marines. Chewed shirkers out a few times sure. Today, however..." He covered his hands over his face. "Patricia wore my sweatshirt. She cried out to me, too blind with anger."

"Not trying to judge you...I would have reacted the same, son."

"Yes. You would have. Patricia doesn't need to believe this is how a parent, or how a father, proves his love to his daughter. Nor how a man should treat a woman." Horace sat at the table and rubbed his right hand.

"How is she doing?" Dakota sat next to him.

"Cried herself to exhaustion, falling asleep in my arms. I will never allow myself to lose control again. She will eat with us when supper is ready. No horseback riding for a week. You are not to go soft on her, Blurty. We must enforce the rules as we did with Kassidy and Justin.

"I'll remind you too, Mr. No Pets in the House. I will retire to supervise her and monitor the security zones freeing a resource for you."

"Blurty, we argued earlier."

"Five-Star, you are at the office, running security checks or at tactical. I am at the university, and Andy is training pilots. Mr. Ellis won't tutor her now, so what are we to do? We can't expect Maddie to control Patricia or allow her to run wild."

"I told you, retiring is fine. However, you cannot be under my supervision. How would my officers act if I placed you, the general's wife, under their supervision? Either they will think they are to give you a soft job or you are spying on them."

"I'm leaving to let you two talk this out." Andy closed the door behind him.

"Your father, Justin, and my cousin all work for you. What difference does me being your wife make?"

"Blurty, no more discussion on the matter."

"You are unfair. You are the general. Remember when you told me the Lord assigned me to your unit. What happened?"

"Dakota, you are ridiculous. Nepotism is in all four quadrants. Unlike other SCs allowing the family to pull rank."

Her jawline tightened as she steadied herself with a chair. "I wouldn't."

"Neither do Justin or my dad. Mike, he earned his rank. However, we are to abstain from all appearance of evil. I am trying hard to change the mindset in this quadrant. To change the attitude of the other chiefs is difficult if not dangerous. If I placed you in a Marine controlled position, they would claim I am no different from them."

"Must they know?"

"Have any ideas on how to keep them from finding out, considering everyone knows you?"

"Five-Star. Let me help."

"Blurty after Gifford took his father's place, this became a changed country."

"You can use my expertise, free up Silas for better use of his abilities."

"No."

"Don't cut me off. Allow me to do something."

"Maddie, ask the staff to prepare two plates of peanut butter sandwiches and glasses of milk, you may sneak a dessert up with my permission. I will have supper with Patricia; she should not be alone. We broke each other's heart."

Monday, January 22, 2080

The stall gate made a long, loud squeak; Patricia led Salado out into the corral by the halter and patted his neck. "Atta boy, here is a carrot; I can ride you tomorrow fella." She took a rake into the stall, replacing the horsey smelling hay, and put fresh water and feed into the troughs.

Silas leaned on the railing with his arms folded. "Morning, Patricia."

"Hi. Is Grandpa Andy taking you up in the helo?"

"We need to talk when you finish. Meet me at the bench by the jump ring when you're through."

"I am ashamed Silas; I rather not talk about the other day." She bent down picking up the rake. "Is it your turn to tell me how rotten I behaved? Everybody else did. I guess Sunny and Leopold would too if they could talk."

"Andy called you rotten?"

"No, he won't accompany me, until my punishment is over, which is tomorrow. We planned on surprising everybody with a concert this evening Grandpa Andy on the piano and me on the violin, playing *Ode to Joy* and others. Now, I ruined everything."

"Your Grandfather still wants to play music with you—Oh come on. The restrictions end tomorrow."

Patricia tilted her head to Dylan and Colonel Harris. "They watch me now, I guess they are to report to my Dad if they catch me bratting up again."

"Did you speak to Mr. Ellis yesterday?"

"Dad made me apologize for my behavior. I promised him my conduct would improve and begged him to be my instructor again."

"Will he?"

She unbolted the stall gate. "Need to put Salado back into his stall. It's too cold outside for him without his blanket. Mr. Ellis is making me start the class over. Late to class or fail to turn in my assignments once, I will explain myself to my Dad."

Silas stepped back from the railing. "I still want to talk to you."

"Come on, back in the stall." She held out an apple to Salado and closed the stall door.

He followed her to the bench; she wiped her boots on the dead grass removing horse manure from the soles. "I keep finding new ways to step into poop. Must be one of my talents. I'm ready. Silas, rip into me."

"I don't plan to yell at you. I won't be riding with you. You lied about your age."

"Now you tell me this. You haven't spoken to me since I told you my age. Silas, let me apologize again for the way I treated you. A Christian should never behave as I did. May I ask you a question?"

"What do you want to ask?"

"Why didn't you drag me back into the house, as you threatened?"

"I didn't want to use force on you. Colonel Harris nor I wanted to risk injuring you. I told your Dad for him to handle you."

"Can you forgive me?"

"I forgave you. At first, I felt you got what you deserved. Andy explained why you acted like a brat. I couldn't stay mad, and well, hearing you cry—" He pulled a Bible from his pocket. "Read this."

"Exodus 20:12. 'Honor your father and mother, and your days may be long upon the land which the Lord your God is giving you.'"

"The fifth commandment. When you dishonored your parents, you dishonored God. I'm not trying to be mean to you; you love the Lord and want to please him. Don't harm the relationship with your parents or God. You asked your parents to forgive you. Did you forgive your Dad?"

Patricia shuddered as she wiped away a tear. "My father doesn't need my forgiveness; I told him he gave me what I begged him for, proving to myself Dad loved me. My mistake, not considering how much love Dad might apply to my seat."

"You need to tell him you forgive him; he is beating himself because... harder than he intended. Your father loves you. Did you ask for God's forgiveness? You need to forgive yourself. Go talk to the Lord."

She nodded.

Horace called from the study. "Come here for a moment."

"Yes, sir."

"Why are you going to your room? You're not restricted."

"I need to talk to Jesus about my behavior last week."

"Did Grandpa Andy talk to you?"

"No, Silas showed me in the Bible I dishonored God by disobeying you and Dakota. I need to pray."

"Come in. We should pray together."

Silas stood at the corral feeding Peppermint a carrot. The horse nickered as he patted her neck. "Promise not to throw me anymore, will give you more treats. You like these, here is another. No bucking. Don't do rodeo. Next time you get horse cookies."

"A word with you. Have a seat over here."

"I'm sorry sir, I overstepped my bounds. Patricia kept hammering herself. Either she told you, or I opened my mouth for nothing."

"As a father, I am supposed to know what to do. I beat myself to a point I didn't pray to God for guidance. You did," he said, interlacing his fingers together and resting his chin on his knuckles. "My father informed me you are in love with Patricia."

"Sir, she is fourteen, and I understand your feelings. I'm trying so hard not to love her, but the harder I struggle with my emotions… Should you think it's best for your daughter, I will leave. May I request you transfer me elsewhere?"

"I can't afford to lose one of my valued Marines. The two of you talked about Jacob and Rachel. I believe you do love her and will wait until she is ready for a dating relationship. In time, I will allow her to stretch her wings and consent for you to call on my daughter chaperoned. For now, you may join us for family Bible studies and devotions, each morning after breakfast and every evening after supper."

"Yes, sir. I would be happy to join in for devotions. Relationships take time. She took my arm at the Birthday Ball but objected to my arm around her shoulder at the picnic. Justin explained how Patricia grew up. We may not know the full story."

"One more thing before you go back to your cottage."

"Sir."

"About me turning you into a gelding."

"I promise I will not—"

"Silas, you are a man of integrity."

CHAPTER 18

Thursday, January 25, 2080

A sergeant called out, "Sir, the Chimera Two is approaching southeast airspace, requesting clearance to land. What should I tell them?"

"What do they want?"

"The Legatee wishes a meeting with you."

"His reason?"

"Concerns the Red Mountain community."

"Request denied."

"He's pleading. He wishes to see you in person. Chimera Two, time of arrival is forty-five minutes."

"Call the Honor Guard; we will reverence the Legatee on the tarmac."

"Aye, sir."

Horace stood at the end of the red carpet, waiting for the doors of the Gulfstream to open. His heart jumped as Alexander extended his hand to Kassidy; together they walked down the stairs of the plane.

"Dad?"

"God answered our prayers." Horace's voice broke as he took Kassidy into his arms to hug and kiss her.

"Let us go to the house; everyone is praying for you."

"Dad, we need to talk to you and need your help."

"Yes."

"Let me apologize for our last conversation. My father came into the room, prohibiting me from speaking as I wished. I hoped you would understand my message."

"Someone is here who wants to see you. Thank you for protecting my daughter."

"My father made life difficult when the two of us married. However, I did my best to protect Kassidy."

"Let me restate my meaning. You protected both of my daughters. Patricia DuPont is my daughter taken from us by Renee and Gifford. Alexander, Patricia told me you sheltered her from Gifford the best you could. I am forever grateful to you. Come into the house; we have news that will not be easy for you to hear."

"You knew about the raid at Red Mountain. Missy had a Chimera tattoo on her wrist. As far as I know, she boarded the plane to Israel."

Kassidy slumped to the ground; deep sobs vibrated from her chest. "My baby."

Alexander lifted Kassidy to her feet, and Horace carried her to the house as she cried.

"Responsible for the death of our daughter..." Alexander held Kassidy's hand. "He must be demon possessed. Did a gold lion come back with you from Israel?"

"Yes."

Alexander buried his face in his hands. "My informants tell me of a conspiracy to assassinate my father and me. Should anything happen...I know it's unnecessary to ask this, but please protect Kassidy. I made an excuse to keep Kassidy away from the palace until after Gifford's birthday. I'm leaving her with you. Make sure the lion is in the cargo hold when Gifford boards the jet to Philadelphia, whether or not I'm on the plane. The nightmare will end; the nation can heal. I trust you made the arrangements, so this plan will follow out."

"Let us discuss alternatives to your strategy in the event the plan fails."

Monday, February 5, 2080

Horace stood at the podium as officers gathered for the morning briefing. "Most of you are aware Sapros gave us the honor requesting we celebrate his birthday here. Short notice, I understand." He held his hand up as the crowd of military personnel groaned. "I understand how you feel. Remember to continue the way we are; it requires us to put up with many inconveniences. I could not provide you with the protection I do without indulging the man's greed for the opulent. We have a mere two months before his birthday."

Andy took the microphone. "I will give you your assignments. Colonel Harris will oversee security in the general's residence. Staff Sergeant Jenkins, with Lieutenant Colonel Billings, in the helicopter—a worthwhile experience for you. Major Rios, in charge of security in the parking area. Dakota Meyers, your assignment will be by your husband's side as part of his security squad. Ms. Meyers will plan the horse show; riders will wear ceremonial dress uniforms," Andy said, winking at her. "Sergeant Meyers supervise Ambassador Stein's security detail. You won't mind the assignment."

After the crowd dispersed, Patricia bent down to pick a flower. "I miss the puppies; I'm glad they all found homes. Too quiet around here. Those puppies filled my time. Now Sunny and Leopold, but they love you better, Dad. The moment they hear your vehicle coming, they rush off, doing double time to greet you."

"Did you clean the stables today?" Horace asked, smiling at Dakota.

Dakota hid her mouth. "The stalls are a mess."

"Two hours ago. Well, sure, but I can't go in there to clean the stalls whenever a horse takes a poop. I would be there all day doing nothing else."

"You need to recheck them. Stall eight needs your attention." He hid a smile with a folder.

"Impossible for anything to make a mess. Oh, oh. Don't tell me." Visions of the dog asleep on top of torn horse blankets followed her. Sunny bounded up behind her and bumped her leg. "You aren't in the stables making a mess what—" She slid black the latch to the stables and stepped inside. A gray Andalusian mare with long mane nickered at her. Pink and white balloons lined the stall, with *happy birthday* in bright colors printed on them.

"Daddy. What is her name?"

Dakota smiled. "Euprepeia. The name is Greek, meaning "beauty, gracefulness." Like Salado, she is feisty. Salado likes her, perked his ears up when he saw us sneaking her to the barn."

"Eupre—uh, I will need the practice to pronounce her name. I will need a saddle. Guess I need to earn credits to buy a jump saddle."

"Go in for the rest of your birthday surprise." Dakota slid her arm around Horace.

Patricia stopped as she reached to unfasten the door, taking several steps backward. "I can't go in there. It reminds me of—I am so embarrassed by my bratty behavior."

"All is forgiven."

"I will think before testing you and Mom on a passage I find in the Bible." Patricia held her hand out to Dakota. "I'm sorry for being so rotten to you."

"Honey, these are happy tears; you called me mom."

"I prayed I would feel you are my parents and not pretend parents. Mom felt natural."

"The three of us walk in together for a happy reason," Horace said.

"My gift includes a thick, soft, cushioned saddle?"

"Saddle, yes; soft and cushioned, no."

Horace put his arm around Dakota's shoulders as they leaned on the rail. Patricia cantered her horse to the first jump. Euprepeia skidded to a stop as Patricia sailed over, tumbling to the ground on the other side.

"Patricia." He cleared the rail and knelt beside her.

"Well, this isn't the first time I went over a jump without the horse. Guess I wasn't graceful bouncing on my backside." She stood, brushing the dirt from her jeans.

"You inherited your mother's gracefulness." He held the reins of

Euprepeia as they walked to the gate of the ring. "I am taking you down to the center to make sure you are uninjured."

"Dad, I have fallen off horses from the size of Lady to Salado. I am fine."

"Are you telling me you fell off Salado?"

"Well, I did, but after you permitted me to ride him."

"How does allowing or denying permission affect falling off Salado?"

"Salado threw your father off a time or two."

"Hey, he was younger and more spirited the last time he bucked me off."

"Sure. Like three months ago before Salado was saddle-broke. Come on, fess up—Patricia can handle the horse better than you."

"She cheats. She gives Salado carrots and kisses. Of course, he will let her ride him. The way to a horse's heart…"

"Try doing the same thing."

"Now, what would my Marines say if they saw me kissing a horse?"

"I don't know. Maybe call you…weird," Patricia said, saluting with her riding crop.

"Been called worse. I cannot imagine our lives without her."

Patricia mounted her horse again, circling the ring as she headed to the jumps, clearing each one with ease. She trotted the horse to the railing. "Grand champion winner?"

"We should compete next time, you with Euprepeia and Salado with me."

"What is the grand prize for winning?"

"A bear hug from the loser."

"Either way, both of us win." She walked up and wrapped her arms around him. "There, I gave you the winner's hug. Now I will earn mine from you." She held the horse's reins, returning to the barn, as her parents stood with their arms around each other's waists.

"Are you pacifying me, Five-Star? I am a member of the security team?"

"Anyone tries something, the last person they would suspect on my security team would be you—That isn't what I meant to say."

"You better be glad I love you, Five-Star." She took her cane and tapped him on the leg.

"From the time I heard those words come out of your mouth."

Maddie met them at the back door of the house. "Horace, Chief Chatterjee, and another woman came to discuss Patricia."

"Who is the other woman? What do they want with our daughter?"

"They would not tell me; they insisted on speaking to you."

"Patricia, sweetie, go upstairs and clean up for dinner. I'll check what is going on."

"Dad, I'm scared."

"I will handle this. Do you want your mom to stay with you?"

"With me—and you, for whatever they want."

"Dad, Kassidy and I will sit with her. You and Mom handle this. We will be in the music room, with Grandpa."

"I will give you any help to protect Patricia."

"Alexander, I am sure I can handle this. Should I need your help, pay attention to the monitor if I scratch my ear."

Chief Chatterjee and a petite woman with bright-red hair, her lavender eyes outlined with a thick red eyeliner, waited in the foyer. The woman rose from the couch; her translucent red tunic with silver glitter left her buttocks exposed. She extended a hand of greeting. Her long manicured fingernails shaped like bayonets did not distract from the tattoo of a purple Chimera surrounded by yellow stars.

"In my opinion, the weather is too cold to be wearing a dress like yours, also inappropriate. Chief Chatterjee, would you introduce your guest." The pungent scent of gardenia blossom cologne filled the room; his throat scratched, and his eyes watered as he tried to keep from coughing.

"Chief Meyers, this is Renee DuPont, a detainee in my custody. She claims her daughter, Kitty DuPont, is under arrest on your compound. We hold court orders for you to transfer her daughter to my detention facility, so they may spend their prison sentences together."

Horace read the papers. "You are mistaken. No one by the name of Kitty DuPont is on my compound. You did not follow proper court procedure in filing your petition; anyone could request a stay."

"This is absurd. I have all the paperwork right here." Renee held the birth certificate above her head.

"As in cases of two non-transgender same-sex couples, one may be a biological parent; the other cannot, though both names appear on the birth certificate. Your name on the document does not mean you are the biological mother of Kitty DuPont. My lab is available and can confirm the results in a matter of minutes. We want positive proof the person named in the court document is your daughter; I am sure you will not mind the simple test."

"Gifford Sapros, he wants his daughter returned to him." Renee's eyes traced the outline of the high ceiling.

"Explain why you are concerned with her? How many months have passed before you made this claim? Why now?"

"Gifford is interested in placing Kitty in a high position at the palace. Chances like the one he is offering do not come by luck. I want only the best opportunities for my daughter. Where is Kitty?"

"Like I told you, no one by the name of Kitty DuPont is under arrest in my facility."

"Here is a warrant to search your entire compound; should we find Patricia DuPont, we will take her from this place to the facility where I have Renee incarcerated." Chatterjee thrust the paperwork at him.

"You have much time to waste. Camp Sumiton is over fourteen hundred square miles. Chief Chatterjee, you offer no proof this woman is the biological mother. Again, I offer the DNA test. Should they match, as you claim, I will allow you to take her. Provided she will go with you."

She twisted the paperwork in her hands and her faced reddened. "You are stalling. Give me Kitty. Now."

"I never filed criminal charges against Kitty. For you to transfer her to the same facility as Ms. Dupont would require paperwork go with her. I did not file any affidavits against her. Now, your one claim to Patricia is she is Renee's daughter. Chatterjee, you cannot place a person in prison without criminal charges; am I correct or not?"

"I could file false accusations," Chatterjee said, scratching her eyebrow. "As long as nothing reflects on Gifford, I can heap on the bilge."

"Which would force me to file a counterclaim based on fact, not fiction. In my entire career, I have never filed false documents. Nor do I intend to do so now. Either produce proof or back off."

"I demand to search your property and take my daughter with me," she said, poking him in the chest with her fingernails.

"Madam." He held her hands tight away from him.

"Uh, sir."

Andy grabbed Patricia and held her in his arms. "Quiet. Your dad is getting ready for the kill, to use a cliché."

"Renee will regret taking on Chief Meyers. I will execute the Queen of the Dogs myself."

"Alexander, my dad is a caring man. He took me in and brought me to his home before knowing I am his daughter. As much as I hate Renee, please don't execute her."

"You became quite a young woman. I will always think of you as my sister."

Andy pointed to the monitor. "He is ready to take Renee down."

"Let us make this easy. You are here and can submit a DNA sample; Gifford is not. I will take his place. You say, assuming you are telling the truth, this test would rule me out as the father of Patricia, correct?"

"Correct," Chatterjee said, making eye contact with Renee.

"Patricia submitted her DNA when I brought her here. A quick and uncomplicated way to prove your paternity." The three women follow him as he gazed into the monitor and gave a slight smile. "Love you."

They stepped out of the elevator and walked up to the desk,

requesting Patricia DuPont's DNA string. "Now, give this woman a swab, so she can give a sample of her DNA. One to me, so the test rules me out as Patricia's father."

The technician lifted her eyebrows. "Sir? Aye, sir." She held out a sterile swab to each of them. Fifteen minutes went by before the report results returned. The assistant put them on the monitor screen. "Here are the results. Renee DuPont, you are not the mother of Patricia DuPont. Chief Meyers, you are the father."

She dropped to her knees and screamed, "All lies."

"DNA does not lie."

"This is illuminating since a woman contracted to carry our baby as a surrogate ran away over fifteen years ago. We searched for her for years; we prayed for our daughter's happiness. The truth came out; you made Patricia miserable. Now, for the sake of making sure, Alpha Unit, would you submit a sample of your DNA?"

"Happy to do so. I know the results. Do you wish to push the issue? Will you back off and leave our daughter and us alone?"

"Before we go further, a word of warning. I could charge you with genetic fraud, kidnapping, extortion, child abuse, child endangerment, involvement in sexual abuse of a minor child and negligence leading to the death of children. Do you wish to add any further felony charges upon yourself?"

"Kitty lived with me for fourteen years. She loves me. I am the only mother she knows. By law, she may choose whom she wishes to live with."

He kissed Dakota's hand. "You are correct; the choice is Patricia's. We'll go into the house and call her."

"Kitty never allows anyone to call her by her birth name. You think so little about her. What kind of parents are you?"

Patricia stormed into the living room, her face flushed, eyes narrowed. "Renee, you dare to judge any parent. I will never refer to you again as my mother. What was I to you? A ticket for whatever you wanted from Sapros?"

"Kitty, you're mesmerized by this luxury around you. His spoiling you doesn't equate to proper parenting."

"My name is Patricia Lila Meyers."

"Lila is not your second name; it's Jezebel. Once, you wanted to be called Jez."

"Another example of your pathetic parenting skills. My real parents changed my last name, and I selected my grandmother Meyers's name as my middle name."

"No one can question my abilities as a mother to you."

"Question your skills? Do you remember what today is?"

"Why is this day special?"

"I guess not, at least not to you."

"I am a fantastic mother."

"What you did doesn't qualify for the bottom level of rotten. I received no concept of right and wrong. You forced me to…Since I came here, my parents taught me how to become a responsible adult. In the few months since I came here, my real mom and dad have shown me more love between a parent and child than you did my entire life. You took me to the palace, servants everywhere. Surrounded by luxury, one enormous difference, no love. Call what you put me through as love—" Patricia walked up to Dakota and placed her arms around her. "Under no circumstances do I wish to gaze upon your face. And I mean never. For the way you smell, you are nothing but a cheap, cut-rate whore."

"Apologize. Now."

"I'm sorry."

"Not to me. To Renee. Apologize."

"The correct term…" Patricia spat on her. "A bargain-basement street slut."

"Go up to your room, we will talk later."

"Yes, sir."

"The correct response is aye, sir, young lady."

"Aye, sir. Excuse me."

Renee wiped the saliva from her face, pointing to the stairs. "You call what she spewed out an apology? I thought you would have instructed her better."

"Indeed. Patricia gave you more than you deserve. You should be the one to apologize. My recommendation is you leave this property before I file charges against you. You are not to set foot on my compound again or contact our daughter."

"Come on. We better go. Court orders will not help. You are not Patricia's biological mother, nor does she want to live with you. She is happy here; if you hold any love for her, leave her alone."

"I'll take this up with the supreme commander. He will side with me. He wants the little strumpet for himself. She will become one of his prize mares. My daughter owes me. Kitty will be back with me," she said, accenting her words by poking him in the chest with her fingernails. "I'll get the little brat back. No matter what."

"Stop."

"You are giving me Kitty?"

Horace hit the intercom and grabbed her by the arm. "Security come to the living room area; I am making an arrest. You should have kept your mouth shut. I will make sure your miserable claws never touch my daughter."

Five security personnel filed into the room. "Sir."

"Take this person and place her in one of the holding cells until I decide what will become of her."

Renee spat on him. "No apologies about how I raised Kitty. Kitty is mine; I carried her for nine months. She had constant needs and cried too much. I only suggested she do small favors, so I wouldn't put her in a facility while working. No, Kitty is too selfish."

"You will rue those words, madam. Security escort this person from my sight," Horace said, turning his attention to Chatterjee. "You better not be part of this plot."

"I thought—she told me the truth about being Patricia's mother. I am sorry, Chief Meyers; she did not tell me the truth. I will transfer her paperwork to you, and whatever sentence you want to give her is up to you. Northeast Quadrant SC sentenced her to my facility for eighty years. My opinion on the matter is you should shorten her imprisonment time via means of termination. Again, I apologize for my part in causing you and your family so much pain." She held the door open to hurry down the walkway.

"Patricia, come here."

"Am I in trouble?"

"How you pull on my heartstrings." Horace held her in his arms. "No, I am not punishing you. I want to talk to you about Renee. What are your feelings for her sentencing?"

"Her getting a chance to come near any of us again frightens me. What is this Mars prison you talked about?"

"A high-security prison. Inmates maintain the right to appeal once booked in, waiting for transport to Mars. Gifford can concur with the sentence or commute sentence to time served."

"Provided he agrees to Mars, will he find out where I am?"

Dakota placed her arms around Patricia. "We will keep you safe."

"She will no longer be a problem."

"Will you execute her? Please give her a chance to accept the Lord as you did with me."

"I always give people a chance."

"She may need a lot of time. All she ever taught me is how delusional people who believe in God are. Witness to her, and she refuses. What will you do?"

"Up to the last moment, she will know her time expired."

"What if she accepts Christ?"

"Provided she receives the Lord, Renee will want to ask for forgiveness from you. Regardless of her decision, you need to forgive her."

"All I can remember is the pain she caused me."

"Dakota and I will need to forgive her for stealing you from us. Jesus forgave those who crucified him, meaning we are all responsible for his death on the cross. We must forgive others; the same way Christ forgave us."

"How can I forgive her for what she did?"

"Honey, the three of us will pray together for the ability to forgive. We will pray we can forgive Renee and heal from our wounds, and she will accept the Lord as her Savior. The Lord sent her here for this purpose, though she does not believe. We must present the gospel to her."

"How can you make sure Sapros won't take me? I am terrified of him. He is mean and nasty."

"Sapros will not take you from us. I will make sure he does not."

Patricia gave him a tight hug. "Gifford is so evil. He could cause a lot of headaches for you and take you away. I can't lose you, Daddy."

"You are not losing me. My security team is on full alert. Sapros or any of his minions cannot come within a thousand miles of here without me knowing about their approach. I equipped the compound with bunkers to keep everyone safe."

"Don't you mean us, instead of everyone?"

"Listen. I would give up everything to protect you and everyone in my compound. Now, remember, we must plan for a birthday bash. He expects me to dazzle him with pomp and profligate spending. He will receive what he desires, dazzled right into orbit."

"I promise you. My father expects extravagance; a gold lion should satisfy his lust for all eternity." Alexander took Kassidy by the hand. "We must fly back to the palace before he becomes suspicious of our whereabouts. I tried to make excuses, but he threatened to dispatch a search."

CHAPTER 19

TUESDAY, FEBRUARY 6, 2080

Horace walked into the detention center and took a chair at a wooden table. "Bring in prisoner DuPont."

Two guards escorted a woman; her face appeared pale, her fingernails trimmed and without polish. She wore an orange prison uniform. Her thin, dingy, graying brown hair, instead of her vibrant red wig, lay entangled to her shoulders.

"Have a seat. You could be a decent human, provided you so choose."

"Are you sentencing me to the Mars penitentiary?"

"Do you wish to make a statement before I announce your penalty?"

"Martian prison colony?"

"No."

"Back to Chatterjee's penitentiary? Four-score times left on my sentence."

"On the contrary, I'm reducing your sentence, ending in two weeks."

"What do you mean?

"Chatterjee recommended I reduce your sentence by seventy-nine years, but you still will be spending the rest of your life in prison." He held his Bible, leafing through the pages.

"Sentence ends in two weeks. How is...Oh no. Please. Don't."

"Your execution is set in two weeks. How do you plan to spend eternity?"

"I'll be dead. A state of nothing. I will no longer exist. The term is meaningless."

"Are you sure?"

"ADRS, you are in the later stages," she said, hitting the handcuffs on the table.

"I am not delusional, insane, or suffer from acute deteriorating religious schizophrenia."

"Did you poison Kitty's mind with your illness?"

"Renee, I forgive you for stealing Patricia from Dakota and me."

"Give Kitty back and let us go."

"A release from prison is not what I meant. Do you have any guilt for kidnapping Patricia?"

"I bore her for nine months."

"You stole her from us. Do you harbor any remorse for the way you treated Patricia?"

"No. I raised Kitty as I saw fit."

"How you...?"

Horace closed his eyes and took breaths and exhaled. He kept his hands on his thighs as he thought about what he would say next. "I still forgive you. Tomorrow, I will talk to you again, and every day until the last day of your final two weeks," he said. "On the appointed day, the guards will escort you to the target range. They will use their pulse blasters. Not a pleasant death; think about your future."

"May I visit with Kitty one last time?"

"Provided she agrees. Guards take her back to her cell."

"Aye, sir."

Horace sat at his desk reading his Bible as Patricia peered into the room. "Come on in."

"Did you make any progress with her?"

"She wishes for you to visit her."

"Are you telling me to visit her?"

"No. Did you forgive Renee?"

"I'm still struggling and worried about seeing her again. Will I behave as a Christian? What if I displeased the Lord?"

"I admit I am having difficulty also. Let's pray together and ask the Lord to give us an extra dose of his Spirit, so we will be able to have forgiveness."

Friday, February 9, 2080

Patricia sat on a bench next to the jump ring, tossing sunflower seeds to a flock of mourning doves. The sounds of horses plodding to the jump ring caught her attention. Silas led them with carrots as he coaxed them to follow.

Silas called out. "Do you want to go riding and talk?"

"I do."

Saturday, February 10, 2080

"I thought you and Silas planned to go riding this morning? Are you teaching him to ride Peppermint?"

"We went riding yesterday. Silas and Peppermint entered an agreement. Silas and I came to one too. Wish he didn't think of me as a dumb little girl."

"He calls you dumb?"

"No, we can be friends but nothing else. I am nothing but a silly kid, Justin's little sister. We talked about Renee—how I could recover from my resentment and forgive her. Did she show any shame for the things she did? Daddy, when I told Silas you set her execution for next week, his mood changed. He didn't want to talk about her. Did Silas draw one of the lots?"

"Those chosen for the execution squad will draw lots the day before. Most Marines become apprehensive when they know they might draw the lot. Right after team selection, the squad will practice on a test dummy. The next day, the guards will escort her to the range and secure her to a post. I will offer a blindfold if she wants one. The unit will come out in a single file line about twelve feet away. I'll be standing to their right and give the order to fire."

"After three days, did she show the slightest trace of regret or ask for mercy, as I did?

"No, Renee claims I am delusional and accused me of poisoning your mind. I will try again tomorrow, and every day, until—"

"Let me go with you tomorrow and try."

"Are you sure?"

"I need to tell her I forgive her."

"Have you?"

"Enough. I don't wish her to die without the Lord."

"Agreed, right after morning devotions."

Sunday, February 11, 2080

Horace descended the stairs in his Alpha uniform, holding his cover in his hand.

Patricia met him at the base of the stairs, her voice hoarse. "What if she won't accept Jesus?"

"We do what we can to tell her about the Lord, and if she rejects him, the full responsibility is on her."

"A part of me still loves her. I—" Patricia wrapped her arms around him. "I'm scared for her."

"We better move. Mr. Ellis will be here soon, and you do not want to be late for class. I will explain your tardiness if we are late. Silas will drive us over to the detention center and back."

A buzzer startled Patricia as the laser doors shut off.

"Attention."

"Escort prisoner DuPont here."

"Aye, sir."

"Who is she?"

"Kitty, don't you recognize me?"

"Renee? My father told me you wanted to see me."

"Are you aware your father will murder me next week?"

"You mean execute you for the crimes you committed. So, why do you want me to come here?"

"You have grown up, Kitty."

"I am Patricia, not Kitty. Again, why did you ask for me?"

"I thought you could talk your father into reconsidering my execution."

"The decision is mine. Don't make Patricia suffer guilt for your actions."

"The reason I agreed to come to see you is to tell you I forgive you for what you did. For allowing Gifford to abuse me, the beatings I endured from the two of you. You took me from my parents and kept me from them for fifteen years."

"Why?"

"Because of Jesus."

"Your father poisoned your mind."

"Don't give me all your psychobabble bull—" Patricia peered at Horace. "I'm sorry, Daddy. I almost slipped."

"Try again, sweetie. Remember, focus on what you told me."

Renee narrowed her eyebrows and clenched her fists. "Kitty, your father terrifies you. Tell me the truth."

"I plead with you; don't die without Jesus."

"You want me to live?"

"Give your life to Jesus, so he will forgive you. I need to feel sure you will go to heaven when you…next week. The thought of you spending eternity in hell is unbearable." She put her hands over her face. "Let us talk to you about Jesus."

"Take me back to my cell now." Renee stood and pushed her chair forward. "Patricia, you and your father come back tomorrow and talk."

"The Holy Spirit is working on her."

"She called me Patricia and didn't go into one of her dramatics about mentioning Jesus."

"Reality of one's quickly impending death makes people evaluate their lives. Let's pray she is one of them."

"Do you think she will accept Christ?"

"Honey, people come so close to inviting Jesus to save them and reject him. Most of them are not facing execution but health issues or another matter."

"Will you give her mercy if she asks?"

"No promises; sinners must decide on their own. She needs to accept Christ because she wants grace from God. Not from me. Don't give her the idea I will reduce her sentence if she receives Christ."

"Why not?"

"She could pretend to accept Christ to get a lesser sentence. Her acceptance must be genuine. You're not the same person, nothing like Kitty. Renee sees the change in you. Galatians 6:6–8 says, 'One who is taught the word must share all good things with the one who teaches. Do not be deceived; God is not mocked, for whatever one sows, that will he also reap. For the one who sows to his own flesh will from the flesh reap corruption. But the one who sows to the Spirit will from the Spirit reap eternal life.' God will know if her confession is genuine if we do not."

Monday, February 19, 2080

A corporal sat in the Jeep as Horace and Patricia climbed in. "Renee's execution is tomorrow morning. I ache because she won't accept Christ."

"Never is easy. I will say this is the last full day, and I will not allow another visit. Remain in the house until everything is over; you are not to come to the field to witness the execution. Patricia, you are to obey my orders; do you understand?"

"Yes, sir, I'd rather not watch. Did the team draw lots?"

"Before breakfast."

"The reason Silas missed breakfast and devotions this morning?"

"Silas went to practice."

"I wish he hadn't drawn one of the lots. He worried about what...after he—Daddy, why does Silas concern himself with how I feel about him if he considers me a dumb...little girl?"

"Silas doesn't want you stung. How do you feel about him?"

"I am comfortable around Silas. He understands all my terrible secrets. I'm scared, not of Silas, but if a guy charms me and says all the right things, that I will make a dreadful mistake."

"You are a brilliant young lady; pray God will protect you from anyone who harbors bad intentions for you. We are almost at the detention center. We will discuss this later."

They sat at the table in the interview room waiting for Renee, now wearing a shapeless black dress resembling flour sackcloth, with the hemline touching her knees. Her hair, clean and combed and pulled back into a bun, emphasized the wrinkles around her eyes.

"This is my last visit with Patricia?"

Horace shoved a paper across the table. "Yes. This is your last-meal request form. Select items you would like served to you before noon today. Otherwise, your usual supper."

She placed her hand over her mouth. "My time is over. Tomorrow morning, I die."

"At zero seven forty-five hours, the guards will secure you to the place of execution where you give your final statement. The last word you hear is *fire*. What takes place next will not matter. You will stand before God for judgment of your life. We are making one last appeal; are you prepared to face God?"

"Ask God to save you. The Lord has not given up on you, except once my dad gives the order."

"Kitty, I do not fear what lies after death. No gods; nothing out there. Be with me, so I may see you one last time."

"Request denied. Your opportunities to ask for mercy are soon ending."

"What do I need compassion for?"

Patricia turned her back and placed her hand on the door. "I tried; I can do nothing more. You have the option to go to heaven or hell; you decide your destination."

"Hell does not exist!"

"At zero eight hundred hours tomorrow morning, you will meet the truth, and remember all the times we came out here trying to point the way to salvation and you refused. Eternity is a long time for regrets."

"Tell you what—I'll accept Jesus if you let me live another week."

"Second Corinthians 6:2: 'At an acceptable time I hearkened unto thee, and in a day of salvation did I succor thee: behold, now is the acceptable time; behold, now is the day of salvation.' No delay in the execution. God knew before creation if you would accept him or not. He loves you, and he does not want you in hell, but so far you continue to choose hell as your designation."

"Take me to my cell."

Tuesday, February 20, 2080

The intercom next to the bed buzzed. "General Meyers."

"Sir, prisoner DuPont requests to speak with you. She claims her request is urgent before the appointment this morning."

"About?"

"Her soul."

"I'll be down." He got up as Dakota sat up in the bed.

"Do you think she is trying to buy time. Or—"

"Pray the Holy Spirit got through to her. I'll let you know what happened."

He walked into the interview room. Renee, shackled and in a gray jumpsuit, stood with her hair combed back in a ponytail, eyes red and watery. She spoke in a hoarse voice.

"Chief Meyers. I appreciate you coming to see me at this hour when you didn't have to."

"You wished to speak to me about your soul, correct?"

"I thought about what will happen after...these past several days. Before I go, you should know I got down on my knees and prayed. I asked God to forgive me, but I don't know if I am saved."

"Do you want to accept God's gift of salvation?"

"Please. Help me with this."

"Of course. Renee, we will pray together. You must mean every word you say."

She nodded, bowed her head, and repeated the sinner's prayer.

"Forgive me; I must tell you what I have done. My name is Millicent Knupp. After I gave Dakota information when she investigated Ian all those years ago, Ian promised he would get revenge on Dakota and me. For a small favor, Gifford promised to protect me. Favors costing a great deal of pain and anguish, more than I ever thought. Gifford found out you and Dakota commissioned a surrogate; he coerced doctors to implant the embryo in me."

"Yes, we know about you fleeing when Gifford ordered you to have an abortion."

"I hid her as long as I could until Patricia grew enough Gifford wouldn't bend so low to order her killed without reason." She took a tissue from him and continued. "Everyone is right—I was a horrible mother. I could have returned her home to you, but Gifford frightened me. All the lies I told to keep us alive, and what I allowed Gifford..." Renee laid her head back and shut her eyes. "She is accurate about me using her to gain favors. Selfish, inexcusable reasons, when at any time I could have contacted you. Oh, please, Lord, forgive me."

"Go on."

"My submission ensured a way for us to survive. Later, Alexander protected her the best he could. Gave money for her education. Her musical talent amazed me. She can do what she sets her mind to. Women who get involved with Gifford pay a heavy cost to gain a high position...Gifford disapproves of females having too much talent and boldness. Patricia...has both."

"Why did you come here looking for her?"

"Convinced Chief Chatterjee I had a claim to her. Gifford knows Patricia is here. He doesn't want her for a stable mare; he wants her dead. All he needs is an excuse, any excuse."

"I would have protected both of you had you told me."

"Didn't know you. All the security chiefs I know are no different from Sapros; they are as ruthless and corrupt. The two of you came to the palace, and I could see how much Patricia resembled your wife, so had her skin bleached. Yes, I used to beat her. The same beatings Ian and I got growing up."

"Why did you play up to Patricia's fantasy of being a cat?"

"She could bite him with the teeth. Make sure I was with her to snatch her away from him. He forced me to thrash her, so he would permit me to remove her from the palace. It's no excuse."

"Are you looking for sympathy from me?"

Renee folded and unfolded a piece of paper. "My goal was to make you angry enough to arrest me. I thought whatever you did would be kinder than Gifford or Alexander capturing me. Patricia needs to heal. She won't be able to with me around. Here is a letter; would you give her this after everything is...over? Alexander will execute me as soon as he assumes authority. One more courtesy, please, Chief Meyers. Would you baptize me?"

"Of course."

Patricia sat in the living room with Dakota, Justin, Andy, and Maddie. The antique clock on the fireplace mantle ticked the seconds away. "The ticking sounds extra loud this morning. Seven fifty-eight...Renee... Mom, why do I feel so bad?"

"Honey, you care about her soul. You are so much like your father, an intense sense of compassion for people." Dakota put her arm around Patricia's shoulder.

Andy took Patricia's hand. "Sweetheart, she chose her path. You and your father did all you could to change her mind. Don't condemn yourself for what she did."

"What time did Dad leave this morning? I heard the door open and your voices."

Dakota twisted her wedding band around her finger. "Around

three. Takes time to prepare."

She wiped her eyes. "Four minutes past eight. Renee is dead. I feel stupid for crying over her. How long before they come in?"

"I don't know, honey; this is the first execution on the base."

"I need to keep busy; better clean the stables."

"Dylan cleaned the stables earlier this morning. I called Mr. Ellis and reset your class for next week."

"I'll keep going. I am not a delicate glass ornament."

"Sis, you are strong; you show your strength every day."

The sound of the back door opened, and the low voices of Horace and Silas drifted into the room. Andy got up and moved to the chair across from the sofa. Horace sat beside Patricia, hugging her. "Renee wanted me to give you a letter she wrote this morning and this box."

Patricia took the letter; her hand shook. "I can't read this. Here."

"This may help you. It reads:

My Dear Patricia,

I know you love your parents, and I'm happy for you. I want you to know after talking to you and Chief Meyers yesterday, I thought about where I would spend eternity; I prayed to God to forgive my sinful soul. I believe God has pardoned me, and one day, we'll see each other again in heaven, with genuine heavenly love between us. I know you told me you forgave me, and I pray God in time will heal you from all the pain I caused you.

I also pray your family will forgive me for the agony I caused them. I did not ask Chief Meyers for mercy as I knew my being alive would only delay your healing. Your father executing me was the most merciful thing he could have done. I cannot undo the stuff I did, but in the box contains something belonging to you.

Renee"

Patricia opened the box; she lifted an envelope with a blank tablet. A handwritten note lying on the bottom of the box read: *I should have given this to you a long time ago. The credits Alexander sent to you for expensive schools, music lessons, and horse-riding lessons. Which I did on the cheap. Here is the remainder of the credits belonging to you.*

Patricia pressed the button on the tablet. "Balance of 150,000. I will send this to Alexander."

Silas knelt beside Patricia. "She faced her death without cowardice. Her last words: 'Tell Patricia I now understand what real love is.'"

"Thank you, Silas, for telling me."

"A detention guard called through the chain of command early this morning. Renee requested to meet with me. After she asked Jesus to forgive her; she wanted me to baptize her. We drove her down to the recreational indoor pool where I baptized her and placed her back in her cell. Patricia, she told me she never felt more peaceful and thankful I gave her the time to accept the Lord. A difficult command to fire."

Silas sat in the study highlighting essential points to pass the written test to become a pilot. Someone tapped on the door. "Why are you knocking on the hatch? Come in," he said. "Sir, I thought you were Captain Meyers."

"Let's have an open conversation. You may not mean to, but you are confusing Patricia with mixed messages. She claims you act like you have feelings for her; afterward—I am using her words—she is a dumb little kid."

"I didn't intend to make her feel I thought of her as a dumb kid. She is a brilliant Christian teenager who will be a woman one day."

"Did Patricia say something to you?"

"No, why do you ask?"

"Something Patricia and I discussed earlier. She should not be afraid; neither do I wish to be an overprotective father. Patricia needs to learn to handle life's hurts. You understand, when you believe you found the right person, one day without warning that person packs up and leaves with no explanation."

"Happened to me more than once. One day she may grow away

from me; genuine feelings, not an infatuation to turn off when a new guy comes her way. The reason I'm keeping my distance...I guess I am taking the risk of losing her to another man."

"Patricia says she is comfortable around you. She worries about guys coming on to her, the lines they use and making a terrible mistake. Do the others talk about her past? She made an odd comment; you didn't make her feel like trash."

"A lot of the guys talk about Patricia being a rescue and a few details everybody knows. Medical information is a matter of public record and what happened at Camp Chickamauga. Most of the guys are respectful to her. She told me she overheard a stable hand telling Dylan she is nothing but a piece of ghetto trash."

"Tell me who called her—"

"The new guy, Reggie. Dylan fired him."

"Dylan's decision on hiring and firing of stable hands belongs to him."

"Sir, you have a point about this conversation. I promised not to upset your daughter."

"Do you want to date Patricia?"

"What decent place can I take her that's not contaminated by Sapros?"

"All dating will be here. This base offers many activities to choose from."

"A candlelight dinner at the chow hall?"

"Be careful not to push her. Silas, the chow hall?" He sat back in the chair. "I would hope you would want to impress my daughter more than the chow hall."

"Pizza and a movie night."

"Right, they put little candles on tables for movie night. Next movie night will be an old classic, *No Time for Sergeants*. A comedy that makes you proud to be a Marine."

"A movie about Marines?"

"No, but hilarious. Makes you proud we are not like Hollywood's portrayal of the Air Force."

Silas shut his book. "Justin and I have patrol duty this afternoon.

May I request permission to ask Patricia after this evening's devotions?"

"Justin and Ariella will dine with you."

"Aye, sir."

Justin tossed the security fob to Silas and climbed into the Jeep to drive throughout the base. "This is the third time this month I drew snoopin' and poopin' duty. I don't mind, kinda boring. Unless I catch a speeder, or a dim-bulb running a stop sign, most the time a recruit getting first liberty. I assisted Lieutenant Musgrove's wife heaving their bulldog into a vehicle for her to take him to the vet. Grumpy pup did not want to go. Her husband came up, one word to the dog, and Snuffy hopped right in."

"Kinda like after your dad gives a command."

"Where do you want to go? We could drive and check the barracks area, the driving course, down to the movie theater, the commissary, or up to the turbines and hunt for poachers."

"Anywhere is fine with me; since I'm driving, I choose. I don't want to go to the...range. The memory still lingers."

"I understand."

Silas drove on the bumpy road; he pointed to a burgundy SUV approaching, creating a billowing dust cloud behind. "Hey, your dad's security vehicle."

"What is Dad doing?"

"Well, he shot through the stop sign."

"Meyers to Security One Actual."

"Security One."

"What is your position?"

"My office."

"Did you loan your vehicle to anyone?"

"Negative."

"An unknown person is speeding in your vehicle. Whomever the person is ran a stop sign...no, two stop signs now. The subject is not stopping. We are in pursuit and deploying the engine kill."

"Drag the culprit here in handcuffs."

"Aye, sir."

The vehicle decelerated to a stop, and the door eased open.

Silas spoke into the public address system. "Put both your hands up where I can see them. Female. The chief demands you meet with him for an appropriate little chat."

He flung open the door and grabbed her by the upper left arm. "Patricia. What are you trying to do? Kill yourself?"

"Silas, I had so much fun...getting you to chase me."

He shoved her prone over the hood. "Give me your right hand, now your left. What got into you? You scared the life out of me pulling this stupid stunt. What if you had crashed?"

She stumbled as she tried to kiss his ear. "Whoops, I must be a bit tipsy. Silas, why are you so mad at me?"

"I will talk with you when you are sober."

"Why are you yelling at me? I went out to have a little fun. What is your stew?"

"You are clueless on your little game. If you got injured or, God forbid, worse..."

"You didn't tell me why you are yelling," she said, snickering. "I can hear you fine. I'm not deaf."

"Because I am in love with you, Patricia. I don't want you hurt."

"You love me? Want to know a secret? Silas, I hate Renee. I do. She ignored me when I got drunk the first time—she went to a party. At twelve—we got drunk together." She beat her fists on the ground. "I hate you, Renee."

"You are intoxicated, sis."

"Bro wins the security agent's observation spill pies—uh, skill prize—of the day. Heck right. Wasted, plastered, sloshed, and... soused."

"You are in double-barreled trouble with Dad." Justin and Silas dragged Patricia to the back seat of the patrol unit.

"Yep, Daddy will blow steam. I forgot to do something. Will Daddy remember what he told me to do this afternoon?"

"Your homework?"

"Oh yeah...I'm in a bunch of horse—Justin. Know what? It doesn't matter. Nope, cuz—I don't know why." Patricia shook her head. "Whoa, everything is spinning."

"Give me the name of the person," he said, pulling the seat belt tighter, "who gave you alcoholic beverages."

"Hey, Silas, not so rough."

"Blow into this thing until I tell you to stop." Silas held out a small breathalyzer. "Now blow, blow, blow, stop. She blew a zero point one two five. Well past the legal limit."

"Ouch—You are in trouble now...She bit me; I'm adding battery to the report."

"Silas, you're cute when you're mad. Call me Kitty."

"She's back to being Kitty." Silas gave another tug on the security belt.

"Tell me who gave you alcohol, Patricia? Or Kitty? Whatever name you want to call yourself."

"No need for you to get all huffy-stuffy, Justin, over my taking a drink or two."

"One more time: who gave you the alcohol? You are a minor." Justin's face reddened as he dropped Patricia's riding helmet into the back seat.

"A recruit gave me brandy. Wanted to celebrate his grad-u-ation." Patricia snickered again. "So, I celebrated—with him. He passed out and is snoring away—under a crabapple tree. I hope one of those apples don't fall on his head."

"Did he do anything besides give you alcohol?"

"Nope. Too much of a gentle-mum—a drunk one—but a gentle-mum.

"How did you get the chief's vehicle?"

"I took it. Silly question. Silas should know."

The radio crackled. "Security One Actual to Meyers."

"Here we go. Dad wants answers," said Justin. "Sir."

"How soon will the subject be in my office?"

"About five minutes."

"What is the condition of the suspect?"
"Rather intoxicated."
"Silas, everything is spinning again."
"Patricia puked all over the Jeep."
"Careful, Silas, I don't want what you are saying transmitted."
"Too late. Get Patricia in here. Now."
"Aye, sir."
"You kept the mike open, making sure your dad heard Patricia."
"He will find out when we bring her to the office. This way I gave him time to cool off."
"Daddy? Daddy—he sounds furious. Who is he mad at?"
"You."

Silas pulled to the front of the tactical office and parked. Justin drove behind in Horace's car. "Time to explain your antics to your father."

Spence came to assist Silas. "Patricia? Did you go on the wild ride? Take my advice and don't provoke your dad any further."

Silas knocked on the office door.

"Enter."

He sat at his desk, shaking his head, as Patricia tried to keep her balance. She pulled her hair over mouth to muffle her giggles.

"Hi, Daddy. Sorry, I can't stand—too good. Silas here," she said, patting Justin on the arm, "this gallant Marine, Silas, needs to hold me up or I will fall and bust my keister."

"Take her to the drunk tank until she sobers up. Give her an orange inmate jumpsuit. Her hearing will be in the morning. Staff Sergeant Jenkins, you and Sergeant Meyers be here to testify. Patricia's ability to recall what happened may be limited."

"A drill instructor found a recruit inebriated and wants to place him in the brig," said Colonel Harris.

"Number two tank. I will set the recruit's hearing for zero eight thirty hours."

"Patricia told me a recruit gave her alcohol to celebrate his upcoming graduation; he passed out under a crabapple tree. Colonel Harris might be referring to the same person."

"I trust you recorded the event."

"Yes, sir. We recorded everything."

"Be here at zero eight hundred hours tomorrow."

"Aye, sir."

Wednesday, February 21, 2080

Patricia sat on a concrete bench inside her cell. She rubbed her temples and supported her back against the cold wall. "My head is throbbing." A stomach-churning scent floated from the breakfast plate. The sight of runny scrambled eggs, dry toast, and over-crisp, greasy bacon lessened her desire for food. "I'm sick; my head is exploding."

"You have a hangover," said Major Rios, disarming the security door. "I'm escorting you to your father's office for your hearing."

"My hearing? Why?"

"For starters, you drove your father's staff vehicle while intoxicated, count one. You ran from Silas and Justin when they tried to pull you over, so count two, fleeing to elude. Also, count three, battery on a Marine. Do you remember anything?"

"I remember driving around in my dad's utility vehicle. A hearing? He is way past mad at me, isn't he? Silas must be—I don't want to think."

"I would say nothing to agitate him anymore, Patricia."

"What will he do? I'm scared."

"Staff Sergeant Jenkins?"

"No. Dad must be fuming. Is this a legal proceeding or an informal one?"

"Lucky for you, unofficial."

"The recruit who gave you alcohol is in bigger trouble. Ben Masters is facing a hearing for getting intoxicated on-base and providing alcoholic beverages to a minor."

Patricia placed her hand on her stomach and leaned against the wall. "I made a mess this time. What do I say to my dad or Silas?"

"The chief is waiting. Your stalling will drop you into deeper bovine patties."

She crept into the office and stood next to the desk. Horace sat back in his chair. "Well, young lady, what do you wish to say for yourself?"

"Daddy, I—I am sorry. I don't know what to say, except I'm sorry."

"You will watch how you behaved yesterday. Staff Sergeant Jenkins run the entire recording."

"About the video. You need to know what—"

"Play the video."

"Aye, sir."

She viewed herself staggering, falling, slurring her words, screaming about Renee asking why Silas yelled at her. She gasped, looking over to where Silas stood.

"Sir."

"Ms. Meyers, I am revoking your driver's license until you are eighteen, nonnegotiable. I am giving you two alternatives. Ten days in the brig, after which attend intoxication diversion school. Also, ride with the Birmingham Police for one month and respond to all traffic crashes involving fatalities. Your other option is to remove your name from consideration for the cadet program, and you may not enter the corps."

"I hope to make you proud of me again. I will take the ten days in jail plus the other stuff...Daddy?"

"Yes, Ms. Meyers."

"Daddy don't act like you never met me before."

"I do not recognize who you are. The person in the video is not my daughter. You better figure out how to return her."

"Daddy?"

"Address me as Chief Meyers, am I clear, Ms. Meyers?"

"Yes, sir, Chief Meyers."

"Major Rios, haul prisoner Meyers back to her cell."

Thursday, February 29, 2080

Eight days passed by at a slow, agonizing pace, as the buzzer sounded to allow someone to enter the detention area. Patricia pressed her face close to the laser beams, craning her neck to see if a family member came to visit. Each time brought disappointment. "Daddy. I'm sorry." She lay down on the slab, stuffing a small pillow under her head, turning back and forth.

"Ahem."

"Daddy?"

"Silas. Your dad allowed me to visit you."

"I don't know what to say to you about many things. I don't remember biting you."

"You were intoxicated, and I am heartbroken disappointed in you. I thought you changed, but you are still Kitty."

"Why are you calling me...?" she asked. "I'm not the same person anymore. Not since I became a Christian."

"You didn't act like one last week."

"I prayed to Jesus to pardon me, Silas. Will you forgive me also?"

"Yes, of course I do. A few things I said to you, forget them."

"You mean calling me Kitty or when you told me you loved me."

"Both."

"You're not saying much. You're still mad at me like everyone else. What did my dad want you to tell me?"

"Say how I felt about what happened."

"Is what you said in the arrest video a clue?"

"You scared me. Didn't expect to pull you out—a brainless recruit maybe."

"Too drunk to notice."

"Too intoxicated to realize you called Justin by my name."

"Why hasn't anyone come to see me?"

"Your dad will come in later to talk to you. Chief Meyers came in during the night while you slept to check on you. You broke his heart again. He hated putting you in this cell." Silas put his hand on the back of his neck. "Shouldn't tell you this, but every night your dad slept on a cot in the corner out of your sight in case you had nightmares. He heard you crying yourself to sleep."

A loud buzzer and the sound of the electronic security shutting off. Patricia recognized the sound of her father's footsteps as he walked down the corridor.

"Disengage cell three."

Patricia stepped away from the opening, expecting Horace to enter. "Come out—your mother talked me into bringing you home early. I received excellent reports on you these eight mornings."

"Yes, sir, Chief Meyers."

"I wish you would call me Dad or better yet, Daddy."

She put her arms around his waist crying. "I'm sorry."

"Sir, I am returning to duty."

"I expect you at devotions this morning, Silas."

"Aye, sir. Thank you."

"You, young lady, shower, put on fresh clothing, eat breakfast, and attend devotions."

"Yes, sir."

"After devotions, Silas and I will hold an extended discussion with you."

"I'm ready for my scolding. Why Silas?"

"We need to resolve a situation between the two of you."

Patricia sat at the table folding and unfolding a napkin as family members departed from the dining room. She peered up at him and Silas sitting across from her. "I'm ready."

Horace handed her ten photographs of a vehicle split in two. "Examine these."

A man and a woman sat in the front seat, their bodies mangled. "A drunk driver struck my father-in-law's vehicle, killing my in-laws and leaving your mother with disabilities."

Patricia gasped as she leafed through the photographs of the grandparents she never met.

"If you got involved in a crash like this, would venting your anger by getting drunk be worth the lives lost?"

"Daddy, I—"

Horace handed a paper to Patricia. "I am assigning you to write a paper. You are to write a ten-page paper regarding the following verses, Proverbs 20:1 and Ephesians 5:18. You may use any of my commentaries and must include at least nine sources. The paper must be in proper formatting, plus a title page, footnotes, and a bibliography. No freedoms until your assignments are complete with a minimum score of ninety-five. Room liberty until you finish your task other than coming down for meals and devotions. Afterward, start the diversion class and ride with the Birmingham Police. Do you understand?"

"Yes, sir."

"Once I am satisfied with your paper, I will restore some of your privileges and discuss new ones. I hope this is an incentive for you to work hard on your assignment."

"Yes, sir."

"I hate having to do this, you need to think before you act."

"This is twice I humiliated you, Daddy. Silas, I wouldn't blame you if you hate me for the way I treated you. In the video you called me Kitty. I rather you had...never mind."

"I don't hate you, Patricia. Sir, I am assigned to air patrol with Lieutenant Colonel Billings this morning." Silas pulled his garrison from his belt and exited.

"Daddy, would you come up and speak with me?"

"About your assignment?"

"No, I need to talk to you."

"Up soon."

They sat on her sofa. "Talk. What is bothering you?"

"I saw the video...I lashed out at Renee. I don't understand why. I told her I forgave her, but the video made—well, you know."

"Tell me your feelings."

"I'm angry at Rene because she is dead. What she put me through."

"Is part of your anger because I ordered her execution?"

"I guess. Now I can't say how I feel. I don't know."

"She let her life end the way she wanted. Allow the Lord to heal you."

Patricia laid her head on Horace's chest. "On the video when Silas arrested me...I am so ashamed of myself. Do you think he will ever...? Needed to ask for his understanding so many times."

"You took risks of injuring someone, including yourself. I met him at the scene of a fatal involving his fiancée. He is sensitive to the sorrow involved when a loved one dies in a collision."

"If Silas didn't think of me as a dumb kid before, he knows I am now. I wasn't aware of anything going on. I remember seeing you and telling you I couldn't stand.

"I made the wrong choice sending you to the brig. You frightened me so much. I had more reason to place Justin and Silas in prison than you."

"No, you sent me where I needed to go. I never want to drive drunk again. The expression of disappointment you gave me..."

"What did you learn?"

"I remembered being upset and wanted a distraction, so I went for a ride and—Daddy, my horse; I left Euprepeia tied up at the recruit barracks area."

"One of the drill instructors rode her back to the stables; the other drove Recruit Masters to the brig."

"What did you do to Masters?"

"Recruit Masters will receive a formal hearing next month. The panel often recommends a dishonorable discharge."

"I feel like it's my fault."

"Ben Masters caused this on his own. To give alcohol to a minor would be enough for a six, six, and a kick."

"I have caused you so much pain since you brought me here. I'm sorry."

"You gave me more joy than trouble. Now you need to work on your paper. I expect you to do an excellent job. I can tell if you are bluffing your way through the paper."

"Yes, I know you can."

"Use your Bible and access my computer library; I will check on your progress this evening before devotions. You should have selected at least four sources to use in your paper and an outline."

Friday, March 1, 2080

"Your dad gave me permission to ask you out on double dates with Justin and Ariella."

"This is hard to discuss with Daddy sitting here. Silas, in the video—"

"Yes, I meant every word. Your dad understands; if he did not approve, I would leave for your sake."

"Silas, I'm fifteen; the thought thrills and scares me."

"What scares you, Patricia?"

"Almost everything."

"Justin and Ariella can tie me in a knot if I so much as make a wrong move. I won't hold your hand."

"I don't want to be squeamish after dark. If I think someone is about to touch me, I get scared."

"Do you want me to announce, Patricia, that I am going to reach my arm around you?"

"Should I slap you for teasing me or laugh?"

"Please, I'm hoping you will."

"Slap you?"

"Friday's movie, the animated film *Jungle Book*. Bunch of the guys sing, dance along, and act silly."

"Daddy, may I go?"

"Would I be sitting here allowing Silas to ask you out if I disapproved?"

CHAPTER 20

Monday, March 18, 2080

Horace slapped his hands together and smiled at Patricia. "I need to go on security checks. Want to come with me?"

"May I?"

"Keep the log on the businesses we check on."

"Yes, we studied conducting business inspections in class."

He gestured to the stairs. "Get dressed; your Charlie Cadet uniform is on your bed."

"You mean, I passed my test?"

"You earned the high scores. Now, scoot."

"You are so proud of her." Dakota laid her head on his arm.

"I couldn't be any prouder of her." He spread out his hands. "If possible, I would burst." Fifteen minutes later, he hurried down the steps in his Alpha uniform and glanced about for Patricia.

"She wants to make an entrance to see our expressions when she comes down."

"Yes, the special moment all cadets and Marines dream about. I remember coming down in my dress blues."

She walked down the steps and smiled. "Am I ready for duty?"

"Where is your cover? When we are both in uniform, you are to address me as Chief Meyers."

"Yes, Daddy, Chief. I'll get it right."

"When I order you to do something, respond, 'Aye, sir.' When I ask you a question say, 'Yes, sir,' or, 'No, sir.'"

Patricia ran upstairs. "Aye, sir."

"Now am I in proper uniform, Chief Meyers?"

"Beautiful. A Marine does not wear a cover indoors unless they are under arms."

She removed her cover, standing at attention. "We are both in uniform—you are to address me as"—she paused, looking at her name tag— "Cadet P. Meyers...Daddy."

"Must be more serious-minded. You are allowing me too much fun, Cadet P. Meyers."

"Straighten up, Chief Meyers; now, let's move."

He clicked his heels together to stand at attention and saluted. "Aye, ma'am."

Patricia giggled and returned the salute.

"I am exploding with pride." Horace reached over and kissed Dakota.

Horace eased the vehicle through the crowded streets; people stopped along the side of the road, making obscene hand gestures. Masked individuals stormed forward, banging on the windows. "Ignore them. They want a negative reaction out of us. We will give them a small static-electric shock, which should make them back off."

"Chief Meyers, those men by Gifford's poster?"

A group of traffickers chased a small girl through the crowded sidewalk. People stepped in front of them to block the trailing men, allowing her to flee. "Let her alone."

"Keep your snout to yourself. Fresh toys bring us thousands of credits on the exchange."

"You little rug rat, you come back here. Wait 'til we get—"

"Mommy."

Horace keyed his microphone. "Security One Actual, dispatch protection drones to my coordinates corner of Sapros Boulevard, cross street Sixty-Fourth Avenue. Five males are chasing a three-year-old female."

"En route."

He shoved the door open, jumped out, and aimed his weapon at the men. "Freeze. Slam your freaking ugly faces on the sidewalk—now."

Within seconds, the drones encased the men in a capture net. Moments later, three cyborg officers interrogated the males. A woman with waist-length medium-brown hair ran to pick up the crying child. She recognized the vehicle and approached.

"The police told me you called for security drones."

"Yes."

"I am from the Northeast Quadrant. Our SC would never interfere with the trafficking of children. You saved my little girl."

"My pleasure. Years ago, a woman stole my daughter from my wife and me, took fifteen years to find her. To stop those men from breaking a mother's heart is the least I could do."

She opened and closed her purse. "Many security chiefs make unreasonable demands for favors, regardless if the person possesses what they want or not. I possess nothing of value to give you to show my gratitude."

"Yes, you do. I demand you hug your daughter and smile at me. By law, you must honor my request."

Tears streamed down the woman's cheeks as she gave her daughter a tight embrace. With deliberate steps, she strode up to Horace and hugged him. "Thank you. I am so grateful to you and the Lord Jesus—"

"Yes, he deserves all the credit. He made sure I arrived at the right time. I did what the Lord wanted me to do."

"You're not like the others; are you a Christian?"

"Yes, honored to say so."

"I will pray for your safety, Chief Meyers. You took a risk telling me you are a Christian."

"May I ask your name?"

"Londyn Downing and this is my daughter Destiny. Can you say hello to our hero, Destiny?" The child hid her head on Londyn's shoulder, turning to smile at Horace. "Guess she is playing shy today. I must go."

"Lord, keep them safe."

He got back in. "How are you doing?"

"I hoped for excitement—nothing like this. Can you find another incident for us?"

"We happened up on this one; most of the time, we clean up the mess afterward instead of prevention. A part of the duty we perform."

Horace drove to the old theater district, turning in to an empty strip mall. "Your brother once worked here, not long before we found you." He went around the parking lot of Ollie's Little Norway. The sign hanging by one hinge made loud squawking-hen-like noises as the wind blew.

"The place deteriorated since Ollie closed Little Norway."

"Daddy, I mean, Chief Meyers, I saw a little girl peeking out one of those windows."

Horace pulled around to the back of the restaurant and parked. He opened the door. "Stay with me, Cadet Meyers." He took a silver object from his belt. "Remain right behind me."

"Aye, sir."

Drops of fresh blood stained the east windowsill near the corner of the rear door. The delivery entrance sat ajar, splintered wood around the frame denoting a person gained entry in the recent past. He walked next to the wall facing the door, his weapon drawn and ready. He leaned his body to the left, holding his palm up behind him, signaling Patricia to stop.

The door flew open, taking him by surprise. Five males, wearing black ninja-like apparel, hurtled heavy boxes and shouted obscenities. He aimed the T-35 at the group. "Freeze. Hands above your heads. On your knees."

A female lunged in front of him and crescent-kicked the weapon out of Horace's hand. Another grabbed the laser blaster off the ground and aimed at Horace's head. "Get ready to die."

An energy burst jolted the black-clad team to collapse to the ground, and Horace toppled to the right. He regained his balance. Patricia stood behind him with both arms extended and a slight bend to her knees, holding a T-35 set on heavy stun.

"Quick. Your flex cuffs." He grabbed one man, forcing him to lie prone. "Cuff the one in front of you, Patricia." Horace took flex cuffs from his pouch and handcuffed a third person. "I need transportation at my location."

Security vehicles slid to a stop; guards jumped out of the trucks. Investigators entered the building, aiming their weapons in defense. "Sir, securing the premises now, looking for additional."

Horace nodded.

"I told your mom, if I got any prouder, I would burst. Now, I cannot express how grateful I am. My amazing, sweet daughter. Where did you get a T-35? I am beyond thankful; who taught you to use the weapon?"

"Ariella trained me; she thought I might need this thing. Heavy stun, narrow beam."

"If you set the beam any wider, you would have knocked me out. Enough breezed to knock me off balance. I knew you fired a weapon. I could have lost you."

Patricia hugged him. "Daddy, they wanted to kill you. I mean, Chief Meyers."

Investigators came out of the building. "Sir, we secured the building. We found two additional subjects, an older man and a little girl."

He wiped his lips. "Bring them out."

"Sir, he says his name is Ollie Johansen; the little girl is Melissa Sapros. Should we call Supreme Commander, advising about the little girl? She wears his mark."

"No. Bring both here."

Ollie walked out the door, thinner since he left for New Liberty. Missy dragged the now raggedy Princess Lisa doll behind her. She dropped her toy and ran squealing to Patricia. "Aunt Tisa. I mist you."

Patricia lifted Missy, hugging her. "I missed you too. You are going to make somebody happy to see you. Missy, this is your grandpa Chief Meyers."

Horace held out his hands to take Missy. "Patricia, let me hold my granddaughter." He took Missy, kissing her cheek.

"Chef. Princess Lisa got dirty." Missy laid her head on his shoulder.

"It's all right, sweetheart."

"Your mouse-tash tickles."

"My mouse-tash tickles. Okay, sweetheart." Horace went to his knees, looking up at the sky. "Thank you, Lord, for your blessings today. You saved my life, transformed my amazing daughter into a magnificent woman. Returned my granddaughter whom we thought was dead. I can never give you thanks enough, Lord, for all the blessings you have given me today."

He stood and kissed Missy on her cheek. "Ollie, what happened? I thought everybody boarded the plane?"

"Little Missy got scared an' ran off. An' I went to catch her. Right after I found her, she needed to use the restroom. When we got back, the plane backed out, preparing to take off."

"You walked all the way?"

"No, kind people gave us rides, as far as a hundred miles or more."

"Did Ambassador Stein board the plane?" He hoped for the slightest possibility of another miracle.

Ollie furrowed his brow. "Yes, did he ever contact ya? What happened?"

"The plane went down over the Atlantic, no survivors. You never heard any news?"

Ollie closed his eyes, placing his hands over his mouth. "I tried so hard to protect those people. I hid the entire time, travel by night an' hidin' durin' the day."

Horace held his hand out. "Ollie, I would like to introduce my daughter, Patricia. I'm so proud of her today. She saved my life."

Ollie took Patricia's hand. "You rescued more than one, the life of this ol' codger and Lil Missy. Those men wanted to kill us. They claimed they came from the…Think they called themselves Alpha Squad Nine."

His face paled, stiffening his body. "Quick, into the vehicle." He slid the side doors shut, glancing over his shoulder, and spoke a voice command. "Home, fastest route."

"What about the prisoners?"

"Leave them for Sapros. We need to get back. Gifford and company are on the way."

"Daddy?"

"We will be fine." Inside the SpeedTube, the SUV speed rose to 150 miles an hour and slowed to a stop at the rear gate. He called out his security clearance code to unlock the doors and punched the intercom. "Full alert. Expect advancing teams from Alpha Squad Nine. Do not allow them to enter our airspace. All report for duty."

"Hostiles advancing from the east. Fighter jets are advancing on Georgia's airspace in about ten minutes."

Multiple monitors displayed Lieutenant Colonel Billings, Andy, and others running to the helicopters and fighter jets.

She nibbled her fingernail as additional uniformed people dashed into the control room taking their post. "Did I cause this?"

Voices called out. "Sector team one?"

"Sector team two?"

"Here."

"Squad one."

"Here."

"Air one."

Andy's voice: "Here."

"Air two."

Lieutenant Colonel Billings' voice: "Here."

The roll call continued. Horace positioned himself on the observation platform. "Cadet Meyers come with me. Proud of you, took a lot of courage to do what you did today. Now, show your courage again. Take a post at the monitor. Works similar to the T-35. See this ring?"

Patricia nodded. "What do I do?"

"Line up any black helicopters with a red Chimera in the center of this ring; when they are in range, the scope will flash blue. Push the trigger. An electro-pulse will knock out the guidance system on the craft, forcing them to land. Do you think you can handle this weapon?"

"Yes, sir."

"Stay focused, concentrate, do not move from your position until I come to get you. Understand?"

"Yes, sir."

Fighter jets and helicopters circled the airspace. A male voice called out. "Chief Meyers, radar indicates twenty helicopters are approaching our airspace from the northeast, twenty fighter jets from the northwest. Ten minutes to intercept. One private jet identified as the Chimera One. Sir, the supreme commander is on board."

"Coast Guard Admiral Thornburg is dispatching support. They will intercept, diverting hostiles. Maxwell Air Force Base is sending fifty fighter jets, and the Army ordered fifty Black Hawk helos from Fort Rucker. Southwest Quadrant is offering their assistance."

"Get ready, people. Gifford is not coming to throw us a party." He called out, "Move the children to the bunkers until I give the all clear."

Justin ran in and took a seat beside Patricia. "Are you ready, sis?"

Patricia nodded, resting her hand on her stomach. "My stomach is in knots."

"Breathe in deep and be ready to let your adrenaline flow."

The monitor announced an incoming call from the supreme commander. The tactical room became silent, expecting an explosive outburst from Gifford. "Supreme Commander, I am honored to be of service to you today."

Gifford slung his red cape over his white toga. "Cut the crap,

Meyers; I demand you surrender the person who shot my men this afternoon. Anyone who assaults the supreme commander's security agents attacks me and will face execution. Give me the individual, and I will overlook your transgression of treason."

"Why do you think a person from my compound is responsible?"

"Witnesses in the area claim your government vehicle was behind the closed-down strip mall during the time of the shooting. In my mind, an accusation is proof."

"Are you accusing a Marine of firing on your agents? I wore a body camera, they attacked me, they did not wear identification, nor did they identify themselves before the confrontation. A clear case of self-defense."

Justin spoke into his microphone. "Silas, in here, quick. Ariella, are you listening?"

"Sapros is in my sights. Ready to fire when ordered."

"Meyers, I am aware your fighters locked their weapons on this jet. To make this bad situation go away, I will make an exchange."

"I don't cut deals, Supreme Commander."

"Multiple squads are responding from other quadrants; you are outnumbered and out-gunned. Fighter jet one, what is your status?"

"Within the range in two minutes from the northeast, wings level."

"Stand by."

Justin whispered into his mike, "The enemy locked their weapons. Southwest is sending support; fighters' arrival in twenty minutes. Staff Sergeant Jenkins can knock out Sapros defense communication systems. Squads will need to be less than fifteen yards apart to communicate."

"What about their weapons?"

"They would be useless."

"Now."

Patricia aimed her weapon and fired energy bursts at the aircraft as Justin gave the coordinates of the combatants. "Do they know I am firing upon them, Justin?"

"Not yet. Not until Gifford orders them to fire."

"Supreme Commander, my forces surrounded you; your weapons are useless. Surrender, or your entire fleet will come down in flames."

"Cleared hot, take out Meyers's house."

"It's a no-go. Our systems are overloaded. Cannot deploy."

"Cadet Meyers fire a warning shot in front of the fighter jet."

Justin whispered, "Keep the crosshair aimed before the nose of the jet."

"This is Squad Leader One to Supreme Commander; a pulse blast missed my aircraft."

Sapros swiveled in his seat, pounding on his desk. "All fighter jets cleared hot, fire upon the compound."

"Negative, cannot deploy. I show multiple aircraft malfunctions. No-go. All fighters report back to the base."

"Supreme Commander, you must surrender."

"Give me the person who killed my agents."

"You cannot bargain with me."

"How so, Meyers? I hold no qualms if you witness me shooting Kassidy."

"Any harm comes to my daughter; your plane will come down. I promise you."

"Meyers, you are risking your daughter's life, including your unborn grandchild. Oh yes, your daughter is pregnant, by my fabricated son. I may not kill your daughter, but I will destroy the baby boy she carries. If she survives. So much better for her."

Silas sent a message to Horace. "Gifford's pulse weapons are useless. Though I can't control objects like knives or other instruments."

"Let me speak to Kassidy."

"Denied. Can you bear Kassidy's screams when I cut the fetus out of her body? Meyers, what is your reply?"

"My honor guard and I will greet you on the tarmac to surrender the individual responsible for killing your men."

Justin's face paled. "Don't worry, sis."

"Daddy?"

"Dad will not hand you over."

Justin put his arms around Patricia.

"We will meet you in thirty minutes."

The monitor went blank. Horace gripped the control panel and bowed his head. He remained motionless, taking a deep breath, signaling for the guards to ready themselves. "Delta Squad, in your positions. I must prepare to meet the supreme commander. My dress blue uniform ready. Where is Silas?"

"Coming."

"Support is still on their way."

"Understood."

Patricia trembled, holding Justin's hand. "What did I do?"

Minutes later, Horace came out in his dress blues and walked to the door. "Honor Guard, escort me to the supreme commander. Follow me—we will give Sapros his due. Colonel Harris, Major Rios, keep my family in the pavilion until this is over, from my experience as long as Gifford gets what he wants...a quick execution."

"Will I die? Justin, I'm scared."

He put his arms around Patricia. "Dad has a plan; he must."

"A moment of your time, Staff Sergeant Jenkins. If this plan fails...Patricia," Horace said, whispering.

"Aye, sir. The plan will not fail."

He patted Silas on the left arm, signaled to the guards to exit the building. "This means so much, Silas. You are an honorable man."

Two rows of seven Marines, with Horace between them, marched to the jet. The group stood at the edge of the carpet as two sergeants placed stairs in front of the plane. Silence descended on the group; the handle on the door turned. First, Alexander came down the steps with Kassidy following. Gifford next, holding up his arms, waving them about for the polite applause from the small crowd of people. "Ode to Gifford" played while Sapros descended the steps and stopped when Gifford snapped his fingers together, bringing the music to an end.

Horace faced Gifford, waiting for him to return his salute.

"Where is the prisoner?" Gifford swept his cape over his shoulder. "Meyers, where is the killer?"

"I will give you the prisoner once you release Kassidy and let her go to her mother."

Gifford snorted, waving for Kassidy to approach. A first sergeant took her by the arm to lead her to the pavilion. Kassidy paused; she buried her face in Horace's chest, embracing him.

"I love you, Dad."

"I love you, honey."

A Marine led Kassidy to the pavilion, placing her next to her mother. "Mom, I am so scared."

Dakota whispered. "No matter what happens, God is in control."

"Your daughter is back with her mother. Now, Meyers, where is this criminal?"

"You are looking at him, Supreme Commander. I shot those agents."

"Daddy. No."

"A word with my daughter, please."

"Be quick; let's finish this so I can be on my way to Philadelphia."

"Cadet Meyers, go to the pavilion. I am giving you a direct order. Listen, sweetie. When this is over, how about a tour of the puppy kennel."

Patricia pivoted to face Gifford, standing at attention. "Chief Meyers did not shoot your agents. I did. Your goons attacked my father. He did nothing to provoke their assault."

"Patricia, no. Come back here," Dakota called out with heaving sobs, collapsing into Justin's arms. "I can't lose both of you."

The family stood in dazed silence, unable to prevent the events about to happen. A tear slid down Major Rios's cheek; Colonel Harris whispered a silent prayer.

He knelt beside Patricia. "You must be brave, Cadet Meyers.

Cadet Meyers is under my direct supervision. I take full responsibility for her actions. All I ask is for you to let her go. She is inexperienced, started working today."

"Well, well, Ms. Kitty DuPont. I searched for you, you little demon." Gifford pulled back his cape, displaying his arm with deep scars that resembled cat bites. "You little brat. I'm giving you my justice, one of which you deserve. To make an example to others, Meyers, your daughter dies a painful death before I execute you."

"I'm sorry, Daddy."

"Stand at attention, Patricia."

Gifford jerked his head for a guard to take Patricia and place her in front of him. "Alexander, give me the T-60, the one with the slow, agonizing death beam."

Alexander stepped forward, opening a wooden box. Horace recognized the humidor he gave Gifford. "Point the blue end at the prisoner. Next, press the button," he said, stepping back as screams came from the pavilion.

"I'll be waiting for you in heaven, Daddy." Patricia stood swaying as she held her breath, staring at Gifford.

"Let this be a warning to all, not to go against me." Gifford raised his hand and aimed the weapon. "Fire malfunction." His face burned red as he glared at Alexander. Delta Squad surrounded Gifford with their weapons drawn. Alexander strode to Gifford and snatched the T-60 out of his hand. "I will not allow you to murder any more innocent people."

"Take him into custody," Horace said.

Alexander signaled off Gifford's armed bodyguards. "Stand down. Are you all unable to hear? I said, stand down. This is Supreme Commander Alexander Sapros, all advancing quadrant support return to base. I am terminating the mission; repeat, the operation has been canceled. All units acknowledge."

Gifford snatched a T-35 from one of his guards and aimed at Patricia. Horace fired into Gifford's midsection. His knees buckled as he dropped to the tarmac, rasping out his final breath.

One of Sapros's guards raised his rifle to slam the butt in Horace's face.

"Brad!"

The guard spun around, facing Patricia as he aimed his weapon at her.

Screams came from the pavilion as Patricia directed her T-35. "Full power set on kill. Fire." He fell to the ground, staring up at Patricia until his eyes glazed over.

"Daddy."

Frozen, not speaking or moving, Horace appeared to stare at Brad lying on the ground.

"Daddy, what is wrong? Talk to me."

"Elliott is not functional, Patricia."

"What? But Daddy?"

Patricia pivoted as excited voices came from the pavilion.

"Dad."

"Horace."

"Sir."

Horace's voice called above the happy greetings. "Patricia!"

"Daddy?" She ran to the voice jumping into his arms. "How? How?"

Silas caught up with her. "We thought Elliott would make a body double for the general. Although he still required some computer upgrades," Silas said, imitating Elliott's quirky movements. "General Meyers controlled him from the tactical room. I attached electrodes to him, feeding into Elliott's system. Every blink of the eye, the android did the same."

"I guess if you two hadn't committed the ridiculous stunt, the plan, the outcome might not have been a happy one." He gave Patricia another hug.

"How did Elliott resemble you? Down to your expressions. Elliott looked nothing like you. I put my head on his chest; I could hear your heart beat and your stomach make those funny noises. The expression you gave me when...I could not think. I thought Gifford would kill you because of me, and I wanted to go with you. Daddy, being responsible for your death—I would not be able to handle..."

"How would your mother, sister, and brother feel, losing both of us?"

Patricia stood still, unsure of what to say.

"Cadet Meyers, I did not hear a response."

"I did not think...at all."

"You disobeyed a direct order, Cadet Meyers. You endangered your life, including everyone on this compound."

"I'm sorry, Daddy, I mean, Security Chief Meyers." Patricia kept her head straight, pressing her teeth on her lower lip, resisting the urge to glance at the ground.

"In the morning, we will discuss what disciplinary action I will mete out to you. Until morning, give me a big hug."

"If I may, sir, speak with you before the briefing. I need to advise you what I intend to tell the people."

"I am honored to be of service to you today, Supreme Commander."

"I hope you are sincere. We don't want to go by the last name of Sapros; I'm changing our last name back to Christiansen. Now, we must talk in your office. The Sapros News will broadcast right away. Let's go before I lose what courage I possess. The Sapros name infected everything everywhere, I will start by removing his name from everything named after him."

"How can I be of service to you, Supreme Commander?" Horace asked, closing the door.

"We need to discuss my position in the new government, sir."

"Why do you address me as sir? Supreme Commander is higher than a general?"

"I respect you, as General of the Marine Corps and as my father-in-law. I'm requesting you become my successor when I resign, effective January of next year."

"I need to pray about this, Alexander. Antipolitical groups may argue this is an example of government corruption."

"Security chiefs earned bad reputations. You have more honor than anyone I have ever met."

"Last time this country elected a president, my father was eleven years old. People should expect better from officials. How long since a United States president displayed ethical morals? Leaders have failures: Moses, King David, Solomon."

"No one is perfect," Alexander said. "None of us."

He paused and rubbed his temples. "Although acting within my power, I made myself no better than the others. I have no feeling of remorse for ordering one of my veterinarians to geld a man, walking away, while he screamed in pain. Given a chance to do over, he would not be breathing. I ordered Renee DuPont's execution, for selfish reasons, keeping Patricia safe, when putting her in prison on Mars would suffice. My motive, revenge for her stealing Patricia and subjecting her to those years of misery."

"Renee led me to think of Patricia as my half-sister, and I protected her as much as I could. I wanted to send her to you, for protection. I couldn't believe what the fiend inflicted on his daughter, much less what her mother allowed. My father never had any love for his children. The one positive aspect I can say about DuPont is she hid Patricia, although the reasons are less than honorable and temporary. If you hadn't executed her, I would have."

"Alexander, I owe you for keeping my daughters safe. Is my taking your position the solution?"

"I wish to restore this country as much as possible to her former glory. Together, we can accomplish turning this country around."

"Only God can put this country in order again. I am willing to accept a position as a coregent but nothing more. Come, the Lord answered a prayer. Find Kassidy; prepare yourself for wonderful news."

Kassidy pushed the door open, carrying Missy. "Daddy." Alexander took Missy in his arms and held her close.

Horace bowed his head for a brief prayer, thanking God for restoring his family.

Thirty minutes later, the tactical office door opened, Alexander first carrying Missy, Kassidy next, followed by Horace.

"Daddy?"

He knelt beside Patricia. "You have nothing to worry about, my sweet daughter. God will see us through. Alexander will do the right thing. Watch and see."

Patricia gulped as he approached the podium and stood behind Alexander. She glimpsed at Justin and back at her father again.

"Odd, the supreme commander always follows the person of lesser rank. Alexander knows proper protocol. Why is Dad walking behind Alexander?"

"Live in five, four." A female behind a camera held up her fingers for the countdown.

Alexander took a breath. "Citizens. Today, I come to inform you of the sudden death of my father, Gifford Sapros. He named me as his successor while in route to Security Chief Meyers's compound for the formal announcement. The position of supreme commander of the United States is now my responsibility. General Meyers agreed to become my coregent supreme commander until elections are restored."

Alexander paused again, bowing his head. "Many of you are aware my father was an evil man; others believe otherwise. I could not stand by, permitting him to execute two innocent people for a crime neither of them committed. A crime perpetrated by the late supreme commander. Security Chief Meyers, along with his courageous team, overthrew the supreme commander's plot, enticing him to land his plane. At this point, his Marines apprehended Gifford Sapros. My father grabbed a weapon and attempted to execute Chief Meyers's fifteen-year-old daughter. What appeared to many as Security Chief Meyers's instant response to protect his daughter was, in fact, an android body double programmed to defend Cadet Meyers.

I will remain supreme commander until citizens can elect a new commander-in-chief. May I introduce to you Co-Regent Supreme Commander Horace Wexler Meyers."

He stepped up to the podium. "Thank you, Alexander Christiansen, for having confidence in me to take the humbling responsibility. We hope to correct the errors the former commanders made and regret being unable to bring back the innocent who perished under their regimes. We plan to restore many of the freedoms and rights enjoyed by those old enough to remember them. To those who don't, for the first time, there will be freedom to speak without fear of reprisals regarding political and religious issues. By executive order, we will repeal the title of supreme commander and reinstate the title President of the United States. In coming months, we intend to contact President Adeline Forrester of New Liberty with the goal of restoring the divided United States. No doubt a difficult decision for New Liberty.

Until we resolve issues between our two countries, we will use "God Bless America" as the national anthem. We will seek justices familiar with constitutional law so the courts will render rulings based on the US Constitution and not the dictates of the person sitting in the executive office. We will urge Congress to begin a plan for a free election for a new president once our nation becomes stabilized. After which, elections will occur every four years on the first Tuesday in November, with the inauguration on January 20 the following year. We are ordering an oversight committee for management of the election committees, so citizens can feel the elections are free of corruption. This philosophy must reflect the dignity of this high office. Psalms 33:12 says, 'Blessed is the nation whose God is the Lord.' I will speak to you again soon, and may God bless you all."

CHAPTER 21

Tuesday, March 19, 2080

Justin stood at attention and saluted. Sunny's wagging tail hit the side of Horace's desk, sounding like a grandfather clock.

"At ease. Why the formality?"

"About yesterday. I'm ashamed because I did not confront Gifford. My kid sister showed more bravery than I did. I do not deserve to wear the uniform."

"I gave orders for you and the rest of the family to remain at the pavilion. Patricia disobeyed my order."

"I am a coward; you cannot depend on me."

"Not true. Yes, you and Silas messed up. He is working hard to prove himself worthy of being a Marine. You have the same chance, if you wish."

"Dad, something happened when you told me how disappointed you were with me."

He pulled out a chair to have a seat next to Justin. "A Marine never gives up. Tell me, why did you join?"

"To please you."

"Son, a person commits to serve their country with honor, not to delight a parent. Did you enlist for the wrong reasons?"

"Maybe I did."

"If you had another chance to either enlist or not, which would you choose?"

"I grew up; I would be like you."

"I think this talk is a father-son heart-to-heart more than a general to sergeant. Justin, you have been on this base working security. What do you want to do? As coregent of the United States, I know we need a military advisor who can speak Hebrew."

"Military advisor is a commissioned officer or at least a warrant. You denied my application to OTS."

"I will rescind the order if you wish to take the offer. The job requires a lot of traveling. Or I could recommend sentry, standing at the door of the executive when Alexander and I are conducting business."

"I would like the military advisor, sir. I know the other is a great honor, but if a bee landed on my nose, I might—"

"Start training on Monday."

"Aye, sir. Thank you."

"I am proud of you."

Colonel Harris leaned into the doorway. "You requested to see me, sir."

"Spence, yes. Grab a chair."

"Daddy?"

"You may enter, Cadet Meyers."

Spence stepped back from the door and acknowledged Patricia.

"Colonel Harris, remain here. Cadet Meyers, do you wish to say anything regarding defying my direct order yesterday?"

"I'm in a lot of trouble."

"What do you believe I should do?"

"Give me another chance."

"In the past, I demoted Marines for disobeying an order. Since demotion to a lower position is impossible, Cadet Meyers, my only option is dismissal."

"I'll take the obstacle course, scrub the chow hall deck. Don't let me ride the horses for a month."

"Breaks my heart to do this. Tried to tell you; you were talking to Elliott, not me. You disregarded my order. I understand you disobeyed me because you love me. Delta Squad had weapons aimed at Gifford. Sweetie, I couldn't risk the chance of you getting in the line of fire. One way or another, Gifford was going to die yesterday, regardless. Praise God; Alexander kept his men under control."

"I was too scared and angry at Sapros."

"Colonel Harris, what disciplinary action should I take against Cadet Meyers?"

"Sir, she did not defy my orders. She disobeyed you. Technically, she refused to comply with Elliott. Patricia did not back down from Gifford. She also took out Brad when he tried to kill you. Had I been in Patricia's place, I would have disobeyed your order, and for the same reason. Or if you covered for me, still would have disobeyed your order. You brought us here under your protection; any of us would have refused to obey your order. I can speak for the entire team: time for us to protect you. I worked under different chiefs, and you are the most honorable and the only one I considered an honor to work under. I would be happy to have Patricia on my team."

"So, you are not letting me off easy. Cadet Meyers is my responsibility as the general and as her father."

"Whatever you plan to do, Daddy, do it."

"Patricia, go upstairs to remove your uniform; bring all of your uniforms down to hand over to Colonel Harris."

"Daddy, no."

"Patricia. You heard me." He stood and guided Patricia out the door, pointing to the stairs.

"From her expression, removing her from being a cadet bruised her worse than if you struck her. To remind you, I am one of your Marines; never once have you called me sweetie. You are showing favoritism."

Horace twisted his mouth, smacking his lips. "I'm not making any comment. Spence, Patricia lacks discipline; my sending her to recruit training will solve the problem."

"If I learned anything about Patricia, she will do anything to please you."

"Prove to herself, not me. Something you stated, Spence, about Patricia taking out Brad. She does not show the slightest trace of emotion she took a person's life."

"She may think showing any sign of regret about taking a life is a sign of weakness. Have one of the chaplains she feels she can trust talk to her. Better yet, Silas or your dad."

He nodded. "I'll be traveling to and from Philadelphia over the next few months. Alexander warned me too many in the civil service are Gifford loyalists; they will not be welcoming my efforts with leadership," Horace said, flipping through the morning security briefings from the quadrants. "He suggested merging the security chiefs into one. Few people trust SCs due to massive corruption and abuse of power. I plan to remove those generals from their office. What about Lieutenant Colonel Billings as commander here?"

"Five-Star? I need to speak to you."

"Blurty. What brings you to my humble office?"

"Patricia tells me you relieved her of duties. She wants to stop crying first, before bringing her uniforms down and act like a Marine you can be proud of."

He leaned forward, placing his elbows on the desk. "I am proud of Patricia. More than I thought possible. I am taking her uniforms because she will get new ones."

"Why new ones?"

"Recruit uniforms. I plan to send Patricia to recruit training for her to learn proper discipline."

"She's fifteen. Two years too young."

"I signed a waiver; the induction center will expect her within the hour."

Patricia slipped into the room. "Colonel Harris, my uniforms." She laid them on the desk and then stood at attention and saluted.

"As a civilian, regulations do not require you to salute. You're free to speak, if you wish."

"I must hold the world's record for the shortest stint as a cadet in the Southeast Quadrant or the world. I am a failure."

"Are you giving up?" he asked, holding out his hand.

"No. You made me quit; I wanted to stay in to serve—"

"Since you say you don't want to give up, I offer this challenge to you. Go through recruit training, twice."

"Why?"

"To learn to follow orders and see if you have the will to be a real Marine."

"When do I start?"

Spence stood, placing his hands on his hips. "Now. You are to report to the induction center and get your gear and receive your next instructions from your drill instructors. Now go—you have ten seconds to get there, and you wasted four standing here."

"Aye, sir." Patricia, bolting to the door, said, "Woo-rah."

"The first thing the DIs will teach her is to say ooh-rah. She will return for directions to the induction center. Spence, tell those DIs if she plays the Daddy card to let me know."

"Aye, sir. Should I give Bell, Lister, and Valles any special instructions?"

"Tell them to treat her the same as any other recruit…, sweetie."

"Aye, okay. You got me."

"Somehow, I have this inexplicable feeling you will get me back."

"At my leisure."

Horace flipped on the security monitor outside and pointed at the screen. "Silas is taking her to the induction center."

"Want me to speak to Staff Sergeant Jenkins regarding giving Recruit Meyers too much help?"

"No need to; I'm keeping him busy while she is in training."

"Such as?"

"OTS."

CHAPTER 22

Tuesday, June 11, 2080

News monitors flashed scenes of smoke billowing from burning vehicles; gangs clubbed cyborg police officers as others waved the Chimera flag and shook their fists at the cameras. Mobs of college-aged students wore Halloween masks smashed windows with rocks and slung Molotov cocktails into the palace. Protestors held signs and chanted on bullhorns. "Justice for Gifford. Kill Alexander, the traitor. Hang Meyers, the murderer." Others beat on drums, garbage cans, used bats to pound a vehicle, lit firecrackers and tossed them at approaching armored military vehicles.

Disguised mobs kicked and punched bystanders who fell to the ground. His knuckles turned white as he gripped the sides of his desk. "Spence, what is going on at the palace? Arrest all those involved. Those arrested will clean up the mess they made."

"Aye, sir. Brigadier General Billings is sending additional units to assist."

Hannah Atwood posed as a reporter and touched the shoulder of an adolescent. "Excuse me for a moment. Would you explain why you are protesting here?"

He rubbed his lip and wondered. *Lieutenant Atwood. What is she doing at the palace? She is supposed to be supervising the*

Crucible. Why is she in Philadelphia?

"Brigadier General Billings. Report to my office."

She curled her fingers around her thumb into a tight fist and struck the reporter on her left cheek. "This is why I am here. To show we're not taking any more—Hey."

Hannah clutched the teenager's arm and shoved her face to the ground. She placed her knee on the curve of the activist's back and handcuffed her. A recruit pulled the kicking and spitting demonstrator to her feet and pushed her ahead to a laser holding cage awaiting transportation to a detention center.

"I think I broke my thumb."

"Learn how to fight before throwing punches."

Additional uniformed personnel surrounded the crowd, beating batons against riot screens. Recruits marched forward; pulses of electric charges crackled and snapped from their shields. Protestors fell to their knees, raising their hands above their heads, surrendering to arrest.

Cameras scanned as they continued their advance. *Oh no, Patricia. Please, Lord, let nothing happen to my daughter.* He grimaced as a man knelt with his hands hidden behind his back. He removed a club from his backpack and struck Patricia's padded shins. The electric pulses stunned the man until he withered on the ground. Two cyborg police dragged the man away as Patricia moved forward in a tight line, pushing the protestors closer in a circle.

"Sir."

"Mike why are the recruits in Philadelphia and not taking the Crucible?"

"You promoted me, Horace. Thus, my duties include the deployment and preparation of Marines. Alexander requested our assistance. Lieutenant Atwood suggested we put the recruits to a duty test. We would not send them off by themselves. Israeli and New Liberty forces joined operations to help quell the disturbances. As soon as we have the situation under control, evacuation of Alexander and his family will begin."

"At fifteen, Patricia shouldn't be in combat duty in any event."

"She can handle confrontational situations. You ordered no special treatment. She and Justin are deployed. Remember, they are my cousins. I love them as much as my nieces and nephews."

"A thug hit my daughter with a club," Horace said, raising from his seat to pace. "She better not be injured."

"Everyone knew the risks when they enlisted. We equipped them with protective riot gear. Injuries minimal."

"The greatest risk Patricia will feel is the possibility of disappointing me."

"May I suggest making sure she—"

"Five-Star. Our daughter is on the news. Why is she in a war zone?"

"Mike deploys personnel as needed. I'm getting ready to take my position as..."

"So, you allowed Mike to send Patricia? What about Spence?"

"I will not micromanage my military leaders."

Mike cupped his hand to his ear and nodded. "Lieutenants Jenkins and Meyers landed at the palace with Lieutenant Colonel Rios. Ready to transport everyone out. They should be in the air in less than ten minutes."

News monitors followed the helicopter flying toward New Liberty airspace. Spokesperson Daniel Guerin said, "President Forrester is in full support of Coregent Meyers in the evacuation of Alexander Christensen's family and staff. The Northeast Quadrant's stability deteriorated to the point we must avoid getting ourselves into a war. Legatee Meyers and Supreme Commander Christensen have promised to protect New Liberty and bring an end to the unrest."

"Is Silas flying one of the helos? Who is flying the other since you are not?"

"Anderson. He volunteered to transport support troops where they are needed the most."

"One helo. Where is the other? Can we see what is going on?"

"Connected to Justin's helmet cam."

Silas dispatched a drone to get a view beyond the stone fence as pro-Sapros military units fired laser weapons toward them. Justin's stretched out his arm and released another small drone to distract the advancing forces. Gabrielle peered over the barricade, hesitated for a moment, and rushed toward the northeast corner of the palace. A man in a uniform bearing the New Liberty flag on his shoulder stood with his back against the northwest wall. Shadowy movement from the east side of the building...a woman in uniform with the Star of David slid next to Gabrielle and moved in ahead of her. The Israeli pointed a weapon several degrees into the air; she braced herself for the recoil as a plastic netting dropped on top of the gang, disabling any movement. Horace sighed with relief as the anti-Meyers troops filed in line as the military officers took them into custody.

"We cleared the palace, family en route to Southeast," Justin said, placing his weapon over his shoulder.

"Do you have a visual on Patricia, Justin?"

"Negative, sir."

Protestors knelt on the grass as Patricia walked along the lines of arrestees and recognized a female Sapros supporter from Camp Chickamauga. A woman with gray eyes and dark-brown hair sat on the sidewalk with her hands cuffed behind her. She tilted her head back and spat on the ground.

"Scum."

Patricia strained to control herself as the woman shouted obscenities at her. "What is your name?"

"Sage Moss." The woman's eyes shifted to the left.

Footsteps approached Patricia from behind. She stepped back to keep the arrestees in view and tucked her chin toward her chest and spun around, leveling her weapon toward the advancing man.

"Whoa, Patricia. Dad sent me to find you."

"You should have called."

"Dad's stress factor maxed past safe zone and directed me to find you."

"My squad is here, along with the DIs. You are not to help me, so..."

"Orders from General Dad..."

"No help from anyone. Period. Regardless, no assistance from Dad or my brother, and...you are now a...lieutenant...I didn't salute."

"Feels weird, my kid sister saluting me."

"Need to usher these prisoners to the loading area. Sir."

Justin shook his head as Patricia pulled up the female to lead her away. She turned around and signaled her team to bring the additional prisoners to follow.

"Hey, Justin, don't shake your head. You gave us all vertigo."

"Sorry, Dad."

Prisoners boarded a transport helo. *Must be around one hundred arrests today.* Justin jogged to catch up with the recruits. "Master Sergeant Lister, may I have a word with you?"

"Yes, sir. What may we do for you?"

"I'd like to speak to the boots if I may. I want to compliment them for a job well done."

"Of course."

"Good work this afternoon," Justin said. "You are well on your way to becoming proud Marines."

"Thank you, sir."

Justin stepped off the aircraft as Patricia rushed toward a café across from the palace and took a defensive position. *Now what is she doing*? She held up her hand and waved for someone to approach. The woman with the Star of David flag on her sleeve knelt beside her.

"Justin, keep your camera aimed toward Patricia, in case we need to send in more support."

"Mom is in panic attack mode?"

"No, I am not—Your father is near frantic."

"Blood pressures spiking?"

"Never mind. Keep your helmet on Patricia."

"Aye, sir."

"Ariella?" *Why is the ambassador getting involved?*

"IDF sent Ariella to maintain her credentials for field instruction."

Patricia pointed to a café as Ariella followed. Behind her, four recruits, a soldier from New Liberty behind them. Lieutenant Atwood crept toward the door. They raided the building minutes later and exited with a man, hands bound behind him as Patricia and Ariella dragged him by the feet toward the transport.

"Captain Meyers, sir. Ready to return to base," Patricia said, climbing into the helicopter and stowing her gear.

Andy smiled and returned the salute. The remainder of the squad entered and strapped themselves inside. The beating of the blades grew louder until the craft lifted off the ground.

"Recruit Meyers. I have a message for you. Good job. Wave to Mom and Dad. Now, everybody. All accounted for, sir. We are heading home."

Wednesday, June 12, 2080

Horace paced the office, listening to Lieutenant Atwood's report on completion of recruit training. *A high-quality group of recruits this time.* "Fail Recruit Meyers."

"Senior Drill Instructor Elysse Bell asked me to speak to you about your daughter. We do not want to send her through the second time. Squad 1640 knows she deserves the recognition," Lieutenant Atwood said. "The Marine Corps Association and Foundation is honoring her with the 'Chesty' Puller Recruit Company Honor Graduate Award. We did not go easy on her. In fact, we worked her harder. Required her scores equal the minimum of the men, and she did."

"To send her through the second time would break her heart. My Alpha Unit would crack my head if I kept our daughter back. Does Recruit Meyers know about the award?"

"No, sir, she is aware of her top scores and will receive acknowledgments. Lieutenant General Harris requested you do the honors."

"More?"

"Yes, sir. She will receive two."

"The other?"

"You will find out when she does, with your approval."

He nodded. "May I ask if this second award would cause an outburst?"

"Depends on how easy you become emotional. One little clue. You have been looking forward to presenting a new Marine with this award. Everyone expects emotion."

Saturday, June 15, 2080

The band played in the warm morning sun. Graduates paraded on the field. Squad leaders in their dress blues marched forward and stood at attention in front of the presentation platform. Horace said, "Congratulations, you are now Marines. I have a few awards to hand out. First is to Private...excuse me, Lance Corporal Patricia Meyers. Somebody failed to inform me again...Ahem...I am privileged to present Lance Corporal Meyers with the 'Chesty' Puller Recruit Company Honor Graduate Award. I promised myself I wouldn't do this."

Soft laughter rose from the crowd as Horace wiped his eyes. "Now, in this envelope is a surprise. Certain DIs kept more than one secret from me," he said, pulling out the black padded folder. "Pardon me while I control my parental pride. Lance Corporal Meyers broke the recruit qualifying record by two points. She earned the Marksmanship Award and the General Meyers Recognition certificate."

"Thank you, sir. Tried for a perfect score."

After the last of the awards and recognitions, the DIs gave their final official command to the Marines to dismiss. Horace said, "Senior Drill Instructor Bell, you turned my little girl into a Marine. Dreamed of her jumping into my arms calling me Daddy. Although she is about to break, tears are forming in her eyes."

"Lance Corporal Meyers stop torturing the General and give

him a hug," Spence said, "That's an order."

"Aye, sir."

Before she could reach out, Horace hugged Patricia, removed her cover and kissed the top of her head. "We are so proud of you, Sweetie."

"I love you, Dad. Oh, Mom." She turned and saluted her brother. "Sir."

Justin bowed his head his shoulders started to shake. "Oh, Sis. This is too funny. Don't forget you must salute Silas and address him by his title."

"Where is Master Sergeant Jenkins? You tried to trick me into calling him by his first name."

"Lieutenant Jenkins will be here soon, had something to do first."

"He missed my graduation?"

"He attended, he'll be back."

"Before I forget, your duty assignment is with the President's Own. Since you are only fifteen, the only place I could assign you is the band. Emergencies may arise where you might be assigned to support staff in security."

"I love to play music for people."

"You have ten-days leave coming. What would you like to do?" Horace asked, waving his hand in the air as a vehicle approached.

"Ride my horse. Sleep as late as I want in my bed. Take a long hot shower. Eat a meal without having to gulp and barf. Most important, spend a lot of time with my family."

"What about me? Salute me, Lance Corporal."

"Aye, sir. I'm sorry Lieutenant Jenkins, won't happen again."

Silas drove the two miles as the group sang the Marine's Hymn. As the house grew larger, Patricia grabbed the hands of her parents. First out, she ran to the house and opened the back-door. Sunny greeted her by licking her face as Leopold jumped in her arms and climbed to her shoulder.

"It is good to be home again."

CPSIA information can be obtained
at www.ICGtesting.com
Printed in the USA
FSHW020010220219
55849FS